ELIZABETH McKENNew Yorker,
the *Atlantic Monthly*, ... *ing* and the
Pushcart Prize antholo... ...lifornia.

Praise for *The Portable Veblen*:

'This unforgettable novel offers a heartfelt and sincere investigation into the paradoxical nature of love, familial as well as romantic. A wild ride that you will not want to miss'   *San Francisco Chronicle*

'Tackles with a refreshing lightness everything from marriage to evil pharma companies, war veterans to neuroscience'   *Irish Times*

'Accurately and funnily capture[s] the complexities of modern families ... *The Corrections* meets *The Wallcreeper*'   *Huffington Post*

'The squirreliest novel I ever read. I enjoyed it completely'

URSULA K. LE GUIN

'One of the great pleasures of reading Elizabeth McKenzie is that she hears the musical potential in language that others do not ... Her dialogue has fizz and snappity-pop. It leaves a bubbled contrail'   *New York Times*

'McKenzie is a surprising and wryly funny writer, as sharp-eyed about destructive relationships as she is about plants and animals'   *New Statesman*

'Offbeat, thoughtful, mischievous … McKenzie [has] a pin-sharp eye for the tragic-comic, and for dialogue'   *Herald* (Scotland)

'Modern romance, Big Pharma, and one very intuitive squirrel collide in McKenzie's clever, winningly surreal novel'
Entertainment Weekly

'Full of vibrant passages that practically leap off the page and twirl around the room'   *Dallas Morning News*

'Riotous … A delightfully knotty synthesis of psychological study, philosophical inquiry, romantic page-turner, and economic critique'   *Electric Literature*

'A funny, deeply critical book with the heart of a cynic and the texture of a soufflé. If *The Portable Veblen* has a flaw, it is that its caricatures are so on the nose as to make the reader hope to flee the human race'   *Boston Globe*

'Totally endearing. As wise as it is squirrely'   *NPR*

'Oddball characters and plot turns abound, including talking squirrels and bureaucratic ironies worthy of *Catch-22*. But a sober question occupies its core: Do our parents' best intentions do us harm?'   *Minneapolis Star Tribune*

'No matter how many novels you've read, it's safe to say you've never read a novel like *The Portable Veblen*'   *Slate*

ALSO BY ELIZABETH MCKENZIE

Stop That Girl

MacGregor Tells the World

My Postwar Life (editor)

THE
PORTABLE
VEBLEN

Elizabeth McKenzie

FOURTH ESTATE • London

Fourth Estate
An imprint of HarperCollins*Publishers*
1 London Bridge Street
London SE1 9GF
www.4thestate.co.uk

First published in Great Britain by Fourth Estate in 2016

First published in the United States by Penguin Press,
an imprint of Penguin Random House LLC in 2016

7 9 8

A portion of this book appeared in *The Atlantic*.

A catalogue record for this book is
available from the British Library.

ISBN 978-0-00-816038-8 (Hardback)
ISBN 978-0-00-816063-0 (Trade Paperback)

Designed by Meighan Cavanaugh

Printed and bound in Great Britain by
Clays Ltd, St Ives plc

MIX
Paper from
responsible sources

FSC® C007454

FSC™ is a non-profit international organisation established to promote
the responsible management of the world's forests. Products carrying the
FSC label are independently certified to assure consumers that they come
from forests that are managed to meet the social, economic and
ecological needs of present and future generations,
and other controlled sources.

Find out more about HarperCollins and the environment at
www.harpercollins.co.uk/green

For James Ross Cox

Contents

"If you love it enough, anything will talk with you."

—G. W. CARVER

THE
PORTABLE
VEBLEN

1

END THE ATTACHMENT!

Huddled together on the last block of Tasso Street, in a California town known as Palo Alto, was a pair of humble bungalows, each one aplot in lilies. And in one lived a woman in the slim green spring of her life, and her name was Veblen Amundsen-Hovda.

It was a rainy day in winter, shortly after the New Year. At the end of the street a squirrel raked leaves on the banks of the San Francisquito Creek, looking for pale, aged oak nuts, from which the tannins had been leeched by rain and dew. In muddy rain boots, a boy and a girl ran in circles, collecting acorns, throwing them, screaming with delight in the rain. Children did this every day, Veblen knew, scream in delight.

The skin of the old year was crackling, coming apart, the sewers sweeping it away beneath the roads. Soon would come a change in the light, the brief, benign winter of northern California tilting to warmth and flowers. All signs that were usually cause for relief, yet Veblen felt troubled, as if rushing toward a disaster. But was it of a personal nature, or worldwide? She wanted to stop time.

The waterway roared, as frothy as a cauldron, a heaving jam of the year's broken brambles and debris. She watched the wind jerk the trees, quivering, scattering their litter. The creek roared, you see. Did water fret about madness? Did trees?

With her walked a thirty-four-year-old man named Paul Vreeland, tall and solid of build, branded head to toe in a forge-gray Patagonia jacket, indigo cords from J. Crew, and brown leather Vans that were showing flecks of mud. Under her raincoat, Veblen wore items of indeterminate make, possibly hand-cobbled, with black rubber boots. She was plain and mild in appearance, with hair the color of redwood bark, and eyes speckled like September leaves.

They stopped at a mossy escarpment in a ring of eucalyptus, redwood, and oak, and a squirrel crept forward to spy.

"Veb," the man said.

"Yes?"

"I've been insanely happy lately," he said, looking down.

"Really?" She loved the idea of spending time with someone that happy, particularly if insanely. "Me too."

"Tacos Tambien tonight?"

"Sure!"

"I knew you'd say sure."

"I always say sure to Tacos Tambien."

"That's good," he said, squeezing her hands. "To be in the habit of saying *sure*."

She drew closer, sensing his touching nervousness.

"You know that thing you do, when you run out of a room after you've turned off the light?" he said.

"You've seen me?"

"It's very cute."

"Oh!" To be cute when one hasn't tried is nice.

"Remember when you showed me the shadow of the humming-bird on the curtain?"

"Yes."

"I loved that."

"I know, it was right in the middle, like it was framing itself."

"And you know that thing you do, when telemarketers call and you sort of retch like you're being strangled and hang up?"

"You like *that*?"

"I love it." He cleared his throat, looked down at the ground, not so much at the earth but at his footing on it. "I am very much in love with you. Will you marry me?"

A velveteen shell came up from his pocket, opening with a crack like a walnut. In it gleamed a diamond so large it would be a pill to avoid for those who easily gag.

"Oh, Paul. Look, a squirrel's watching."

But Paul wouldn't even turn, as if being watched by a squirrel meant nothing to him.

"Oh my gosh," she said, examining the alien stone, for which she'd never yearned. "It's so big. Won't I smash it into things, won't I wreck it?"

"Diamonds can't be smashed."

"I can't wreck it?" she asked, incredulously.

"You can't wreck anything. You only make things great."

Her body quickened, like a tree in the wind. Later, she would remember a filament that passed through her, of being glad she had provided him happiness, but not really sure how she felt herself.

"Yes?" the man said.

The squirrel emitted a screech.

"Is that a yes?" Paul asked.

She managed to say it. Yes. Two human forms became as one, as they advanced to the sidewalk, the route to the cottage on Tasso Street.

Behind them, the squirrel made a few sharp sounds, as if to say he had significant doubts. As if to say, and she couldn't help translating it this way: *There is a terrible alchemy coming.*

SUCH WAS THE engagement of Veblen Amundsen-Hovda, independent behaviorist, experienced cheerer-upper, and freelance self, who was having a delayed love affair with the world due to an isolated childhood and various interferences since. At thirty she still favored baggy oversized boy's clothes, a habit as hard to grow out of as imaginary friends.

That night in her cottage the squirrel paced the attic floor. Rain pelted the rooftop and a low-pressure system whipped the tall trees the town was named for. When his acorn lost its flavor, the squirrel hurled it in a fit of pique, and Paul banged on the wall from below.

You want a piece of me? Only bottled-up jerks bang on walls from below.

The squirrel had his resources. All he had to say was *End the attachment* and the leaves would fall. It was an important job in autumn to visit all the ones he'd planted and stare down their boughs. *End the attachment.* The trees went bare. The days grew short and cold.

That night in bed, she fell upon Paul with odd ferocity, as if to transform or disguise the strange mood that had seized her. It worked. Later, holding her close, Paul whispered, "You know what I'll remember forever?"

"What?"

"You didn't say 'I'll think about it' when I asked you. You just said *yes*."

She felt the joy of doing something right.

Overhead came a Virginia reel of scrapes and thumps, embarrassing at this juncture, as would be a growling intestine under the sheets.

"Do you think it's rats?" Paul asked.

"I'm hoping it's squirrels."

"This town is infested with squirrels, have you noticed?"

"I'd rather say it's *rich* with squirrels."

"The rain's driving them in," Paul said, kissing her.

"Or they're celebrating for us, prancing with joy."

He butted her gently. "My parents are going to be blown away. They'll say I don't deserve you."

"Really? No way."

"What'll your mother say?" Paul wanted to know.

"Well, that it happened fast, and that she'll have to meet you, immediately if not sooner."

"Should we call and tell them?"

"Tomorrow."

She had an internal clock set to her mother's hunger for news, but sometimes it felt good to ignore it.

"What about your father?" Paul asked.

"Hmm. He'll just say we'll never be the same."

"We're old enough not to care what our parents think, but somehow we do," Paul admitted, philosophically.

"That's for sure."

"Because they allowed us to exist."

She had once concluded everyone on earth was a servant to the previous generation—born from the body's factory for entertainment and use. A life could be spent like an apology—to prove you had been worth it.

Pressed against him, aware of the conspicuous new ring on her hand catching on the sheets, she jolted when he uttered in his day voice: "Veb, those noises don't bother you?"

Not wanting to be mistaken for a person who resides obliviously in a pesthole, she explained, "I have this strange thing. If someone around me is bothered by something, I feel like I'm not allowed to be bothered."

"Not *allowed*?"

"It's like I'm under pressure from some higher source to remain calm or neutral, to prevent something terrible from happening."

"That's kinda twisted. Do you spend a lot of time doing that?"

She reflected that leveraging herself had become a major pastime. Was it fear of the domino, snowball, or butterfly effect? Or

maybe just a vague awareness of behavioral cusps, cascading fail-
ures, chain reactions, and quantum chaos?

"It's instinctive, so I don't even notice."

"So we'll never be able to share a grievance?"

"Oh! I'll work on it, if sharing grievances means a lot to you."

He sniffed. "I don't think it's unreasonable to dislike the sound
of gnawing rodents near our bed."

"True." She laughed, and kissed his head.

IN THE NIGHT she reflected that the squirrel was not *gnawing*—
in fact, maybe it was orchestrating a master plan.

And Paul, she would discover, had many reasons to object to
any kind of wild rumpus heard through walls, but had yet to understand the connection.

And she herself could withstand more than her share of tres-
passes by willful beings.

These embedded differences were enough to wreck everything,
but what eager young couple would ever believe it?

IN THE MORNING, moments after Paul went out to buy pastries,
a fluffy *Sciurus griseus* appeared on her bedroom sill. Its topcoat
was charcoal, its chest as white as an oxford shirt, its tail as rakish
as the feather in a conquistador's cap. The western gray sat with
quiet dignity, head high, shoulders back, casting a forthright glance
through the window with its large brown eyes. What a vision!

She sat up in bed and it seemed quite natural to speak to the
animal through the windowpane, though it had been a long while

since she had known any squirrels. "Well, then! You're a very handsome squirrel. Very dignified." To her amusement, the squirrel lowered its head slightly, as if it understood her and appreciated the compliment. "Are you living upstairs? You're a noisy neighbor, and you kept Paul up all night long!" This time, the squirrel picked up its head and seemed to shrug. A coincidence, surely, but Veblen hiccuped with surprise. And then the squirrel reached out and placed one of its hands onto the glass, as if to touch the side of her face.

"Oh! You're really telling me something!" She extended her hand, but the new ring seemed to interfere, flashing and cold on her finger. She pulled it off and set it on the nightstand. With her hand unadorned, she felt free to place the tips of her fingers on the glass where the squirrel's hand was pressed. The squirrel studied her with warm brown eyes, as if to ask: *How well do you know yourself, and all the choices you could make?* As if to tell her, *I was cut loose from a hellish marriage, and I want to meet muckrakers, carousers, the sweet-toothed, and the lion-hearted, and you don't know it yet, but you are all of these.*

"I—what?" Veblen said, mesmerized.

Then, with a flick of its tail, it dashed away.

She jumped out of bed and threw on her robe and hurried out the back to see where it went, spying nothing but the soft winter grass and the growing wands of the lilies, the wet brown bed of needles beneath the Aleppo pine, the weathered fence line filigreed by termites, the mossy stones by the garage, the lichened roof. She was proud of her humble cottage on Tasso Street.

Then she went back inside and grabbed her phone to spring the news on her mother. Nothing being fully real until such springing.

And nothing with her mother ever simple and straightforward either, and that was the thrill of it. A perverse infantile thrill necessary to life.

Linus, her stepfather, answered. "Hello?"

"Oh, hi, Linus, morning! Can I talk to Mom?"

"She's asleep, dear. I'd say try in another few hours."

"Just wake her up!"

"Well, she had a hard night. Had a reaction to the dye on a new set of towels we brought home. She's been flat out since yesterday afternoon."

"That's sad. But I need to talk to her," Veblen said, grinding some coffee.

"I'm afraid to go in there, you know how she gets. I'll open the door a crack and whisper."

Veblen heard the phone moving through space, then her mother's cramped voice issuing from her big, despotic head obviously at an angle on a bolster. She was never at her best in the morning.

"Veblen, is something wrong?"

"No, not at all."

Out the window, young moths flitted from the tips of the juniper. A large black beetle gnawed the side of the organ pipe cactus, carving a dwelling of just the right size in the winter shade.

"What is it?" asked her mother.

"A squirrel just came to the window and looked in at me."

"Why is that so exciting?"

"It held out its paw. It made direct contact with me."

"I thought you were over that. Dear god. Do Linus and I need to come down and intervene?"

ELIZABETH MCKENZIE

Melanie C. Duffy, Veblen's mother, was avid at intervening, and had intervened with resolve in Veblen's life at all points, and was especially prone to anxiety about Veblen's physical and mental health and apt to intervene over that on a daily basis.

"Oh, forget it. Maybe it was trying to see my ring."

"What ring? I'm trembling."

Veblen blurted: "Paul asked me to marry him."

Silence.

"Mom?"

"Why did you tell me about the squirrel first?"

She found herself in earnest search of an answer, before snapping out of her childhood habit of full accountability.

"Because you like to know *everything*." She pulled her favorite mugs from the cupboard, wondering when Paul would get back.

"It's very odd you told me about the squirrel first. I haven't even met this man."

"I know, that's why I'm calling. When can we come up?"

"You said at Christmas it was nothing special."

"No, I didn't. I just didn't want to talk about it yet."

"Didn't you have any sense of wanting my input?" And such an ironic question it was, for there had already been so much input, so much.

"Of course. That's the point." She held the phone tenderly, as if it were an actual part of her mother.

"I feel excluded from the most important decision of your life."

"No, Mom, I'm calling you first thing because you're the most important person to me."

There followed a silence, for her mother tended to freeze up and ignore compliments and love, and court instead all the miffs and tiffs she could gather round, in a perpetual powwow of pity.

"Well. Did you say yes for all the right reasons?"

The coffeemaker gurgled and hissed, a tired old friend doing its best. "I think so."

"Marriage is *not* the point of a woman's life. Do you understand that?"

"By now."

"Do you love him?"

"I do, actually."

"Is everything between you, good, sexually?"

"Mom, please! Boundaries or whatever."

"Don't say *boundaries* like every teenage twerp on TV."

It bothered Veblen's mother that most people were lazy and had given up original thought a long time ago, stealing stale phrases from the media like magpies. Fair enough. The problem was that her mother always overstated her points, ruining her credibility. Veblen had learned to seek out supporting evidence to give her mother's unique worldview some muscle, and in this case she'd found it in the writings of the wonderful William James: "We must make search rather for the original experiences which were the pattern-setters to all this mass of suggested feeling and imitated conduct."

"Okay, Mom. *That's private.* Better?"

"Yes. It's very important, and it's also important to avoid hackneyed phrases, especially snide ones, which sound very déclassé."

Veblen pressed on. "We have things in common with his family and they seem really nice."

"A nice family counts for a lot, but it's not the be-all and end-all. What do you tell him about me?"

She could hear her mother scratch her scalp, raking dead skin under her nails. "Good stuff. You're hard to sum up. That's why we have to meet."

"I don't know, Veblen. Nobody likes me when they meet me."

Veblen replied faithfully, "No, not true."

"Historically it's quite true. Especially doctors. Doctors abhor me because I don't kowtow to them."

"He won't be your doctor, he'll be your son-in-law."

"I've never met a doctor who didn't wear the mantle of the doctor everywhere."

Veblen shook her head. "But he's in research, it's different."

From bracing them in defense since girlhood, her guts were robust, her tolerance for adversity high. By clearly emphasizing all that was lacking in others, by mapping and raising to an art form the catalog of their flaws, Veblen's mother had inversely punched out a template for an ideal human being, and it was the unspoken assumption that Veblen would aspire to this template with all her might.

"It's very interesting that you've chosen to marry a physician," her mother noted, with the overly crisp diction she employed when feeling cornered.

"There are a lot of physicians in the world," Veblen said.

"We're not paying for a big wedding. It's a complete waste."

"Of course I know that."

"He'll expect one if he's a doctor. They're ambitious and full of themselves!"

"There's only one answer to this—to come visit right away," Veblen pressed.

"He'll have a field day, spinning all kinds of theories about me."

"This is happy news, Mom! Would you please cool it?"

"What does Albertine think of all this? I suppose you've told Albertine all about it?"

"No, I haven't told anybody, I already said that."

In the background she could hear Linus consoling.

"Linus is asking me to calm down," Melanie said. "He wants to check my blood pressure. Who will you invite?"

"To the wedding? We haven't thought about it yet!"

"We have no friends, which is humiliating."

Why was it suddenly humiliating, after years of hiding away from everybody? Veblen watched a single hawk circling just below the clouds.

Linus's voice came on the line. "Your mother's face is flushed and her heart is racing."

"A little excitement won't hurt."

"I need both hands now, I'm going to say good-bye. You'll come see us soon?"

"We'll come soon," said Veblen.

SHE WASHED DOWN tabs of Vivactil and citalopram. The coffee was piping hot. She twisted a clump of her hair. What was that list again? *Muckrakers, carousers, the sweet-toothed, the lion-hearted?*

Sometimes when Veblen had a deadline for a translation she couldn't tell anyone she had a deadline because it was work she wasn't paid for, and furthermore, it wasn't a real deadline, it was a self-imposed deadline. What kind of deadline was that? Could Paul appreciate her deadlines? It would mean a lot to her if he could.

Paul didn't know she took antidepressants, but she also didn't talk about what toothpaste or deodorant she used (Colgate and Tom's).

And he didn't realize she hadn't graduated from college either. That embarrassed her, and was probably something he should find out soon. It simply hadn't come up. Since when you marry you are offering yourself as a commodity, maybe it was time to clear up details of her *product description.* Healthy thirty-year-old woman with no college degree. Caveat emptor.

In spite of her cheerfulness in the presence of others, one could see this woman had gone through something that had left its mark. Sometimes her reactions seemed to happen in slow motion, like old, calloused manatees moving through murky water. At least, that's how she'd once tried to explain it to the psychiatrist who dispensed her medications. Sometimes she wondered if she had some kind of processing disorder. Or maybe it was just a defense mechanism. One could see she was bruised by all the dodging that comes of the furtive meeting of one's needs.

FOR SEVERAL YEARS before meeting Paul, Veblen had steered clear of romantic entanglements, haunted by runaway emotions and a few sad breakups in the past. "No one will ever understand me!" she often cried when feeling sorry for herself. Sometimes it was all she could do not to bite her arm until her jaw ached, and take note of how long the teeth marks showed. She had made false assumptions in those early experiences, such as that love meant becoming inseparable, and a few suitors came and went, none of them ready for all-out fusion. She began to realize she hadn't been looking for a love affair, but rather a human safe house from her mother. A legitimate excuse to be busy with someone else. An all-loving being who would ever after uphold her as did the earth beneath her feet.

She came to recognize her weaknesses through these trial-and-error relationships, and lament that she had them. In a tug-of-war of want and postponement she continued with her deeply romantic beliefs, living in a state of wistful anticipation for life to become as wonderful as she was sure, someday, it would.

Veblen's best friend since sixth grade, Albertine Brooks, smart and training as a Jungian analyst in San Francisco, had been alarmed by the sudden onslaught of Paul: Veblen, she felt, had unprocessed shadows, splitting issues, and would be prone to animus projections and primordial fantasies with destructive consequences. But Veblen only laughed.

Over the years, they had discussed, almost scientifically, the intimate details of their romances—for Veblen starting with Luke Hartley in the back of the school bus returning from a field trip to the state capitol. Sure, he'd paid heaps of attention as they marched through the legislative chambers, standing close and gazing raptly at her hair, even plucking out a leaf. Sure, he asked her to sit with him on the bus. Yet it wasn't until the last second, when he touched her, that she believed he might have feelings for her. She told Albertine about his milky-tasting tongue and roaming, hamster-like hands, and then Albertine prepared her for the next step, of unzipping his pants. And with Albertine's pragmatic voice in her ear, that's what she attempted next time she and Luke were making out on the athletic field after school. A difficult grab under his weight, shearing her skin on the metal teeth—as she grasped his zipper he pushed her away and groaned, "Too late."

Too late? Wow. You had to do it really fast or a guy didn't want anything to do with you. She pulled away, staring dismally over the grass, a failure at love already.

But Albertine said later, "No, you dummy. He meant he'd already ejaculated!"

"Huh?"

"What were you doing right before?"

"Just rolling on the lawn, kissing."

"Okay, exactly."

"You mean—"

"Yes, I mean."

"Oh! So that's good?"

"Good enough. It could have been better."

In that instance, Albertine helped Veblen overcome her habit of assuming fault when someone said something cryptic to her.

"So you think he's still attracted to me?" she asked.

"Yes, Veblen."

"Wow. I thought it meant I blew it."

"He *wished* you blew it."

Veblen wrinkled her nose. "But you don't actually *blow* on anything, do you?"

"No," said Albertine, pityingly.

Albertine had, for her part over the years, partaken of a number of gritty encounters that had led to a surprising lack of heartbreak. Veblen could never dive in with someone like that and not feel anything. She'd always admired Albertine, who put her ambitions before her family or guys, and didn't cling to anybody but Carl Jung.

She frequently lent Veblen books to help with her psychological development, but none of them seemed to address the central issue: Veblen's instinctive certainty that the men who asked her out would not understand her if they got to know her better.

Then along came Paul. Little more than three months ago they had been strangers at the Stanford University School of Medicine, Veblen a new office assistant in Neurology. There, every morning, she took to her desk wedged between the printer and the file cabinet, threw her bag into a drawer, pulled out her chair, logged in. Horizontal ribs of light flickered across her desk, signaling her last allotment of morning. Later the sun would hit the handsome oak in the courtyard and make its sharp leaves shimmer. In between, she'd harness her fingers and drift away, typing up the minutes from the Tumor Board or a draft of one of the doctors' professional papers or case notes. She was amazingly good at *dissociating,* alleged to be unhealthy, but which she had found vital to her survival over the years.

Across the office sat Laurie Tietz, a competent, muscular woman of forty with a pursed mouth that looked disapproving at first, but really wasn't. Veblen felt uncomfortably watched the first time Paul stopped by to see her, but no, it was only the set of Laurie's lips. Veblen liked her, despite being captive to her daily conversations with her husband about their home improvements and shopping lists. "Pick up some cheese and light bulbs today, don't forget. Love you."

That was the part she hated—when Laurie said "Love you."

Dr. Chaudhry would arrive carrying his briefcase and a Tupperware tub filled with snacks made by his wife. He was a small, quiet man with large round eyes, a shaggy mustache covering his lips, slightly bent aviator glasses, and broken embroidery sticking up like ganglia from the fabric of his white coat. *Lewis Chaudhry, MD.*

From her desk on any given day, she could see squirrels hurling themselves through the canopy of the trees, causing limbs to buckle and sweep. She started to realize that squirrels were the only mammals who lived right out in the open near humankind. Despite this aura of neighborliness, recipes for squirrels were included in the *Joy of Cooking.* Was this a curious case of misplaced trust?

That was the day Chaudhry approached her with a manila envelope—the "envelope of destiny" she and Paul came to call it.

"Do you know where to find the research labs?" Chaudhry asked her.

"Sure."

"Find Paul Vreeland. Then tell him the road to hell is paved with good intentions."

Veblen raised her eyebrows. "Wouldn't that be kind of—awkward?"

"Tell him it's coming from me."

She still wasn't crazy about the idea. "Why? What did he do?"

"He had a great opportunity here and he's throwing it away."

"Gee, that's too bad."

"He is not the first," Chaudhry said.

That hall, with its sharp smells and vibrations and a high number of bins for hazardous waste, was unknown territory for her. At last someone directed her to Vreeland's lab, and she entered after knocking a few times without response. Curled over a buzzing table saw, with his dark hair hanging over his safety goggles, he looked every bit a mad scientist absorbed by his master plan.

"Dr. Vreeland?" She cleared her throat. "Hello? Excuse me!"

Her nostrils contracted from the stench of singed flesh. Maybe she tottered or blanched. He glanced up and ripped off his goggles, his elbow sending a row of beakers off the table while the saw screeched on, spraying a curtain of red mist onto his lab coat and the wall.

"Oh shit!" Glass snapped and crackled under his soles as he threw the switch on the saw and covered the gory mess with a blue apron. An ominously empty cage sat atop the stainless steel slab. "Sorry, I didn't hear you come in. God."

"Yeah, sorry, I knocked, I wasn't sure—"

He insisted it was his fault, not hers, he didn't mind that she came in, hours would go by when no one came in, he'd get wrapped up and forget the time, and when she asked what he was doing he began to explain his work, mentioning apologetically that small mammals were suited to neurological research because one could easily expose the cortex, apply special dyes or probes or electrodes directly, to observe the activities of neurons and test for humans, and in his case, for the men and women of the armed forces, who needed breakthroughs fast.

"Basically I'm moving toward a breakthrough for brain injury treatment," he concluded, smoothing down his hair, and it was at that moment she realized how adorable he was. "I'm a little obsessed right now. I dream about it at night."

"Is that all you dream about?" she asked.

He might have blushed. "Well, maybe I need a new dream," he said, with an endearing look on his face.

"Oh, well. Sorry to cause such a ruckus," she said, wondering why she had to sound so weird. Who said *ruckus* these days? "It was for this," she said, handing him the envelope.

"Oh, from Chaudhry. Finally."

As he glanced into the envelope, she picked up the product literature for the Voltar bone band saw.

"Wow, are these features really great or something?"

"What features?"

She read them off: *"Diamond-coated blade has no teeth and will not cut fingers! Cleans up quick and easy! Wet blade eliminates bone dust! Splash guards and bone screens included!"*

"It's always a little shocking to see the commercial underbelly of research," he agreed. He had dimples, and friendly eyes. "There's this whole parallel consumer reality in the medical and defense industries; it takes some getting used to."

And right there, Veblen had been lobbed one of her favorite topics: the gargoyle of marketing and advertising. "I believe it. But what's weird about this—marketing is supposed to kindle the *anticipatory daydream,* supposedly the most exciting phase of acquisition. But here, what would be the daydream?"

"Freedom from bone dust, of course—which is very exciting. Look at this thing," he added, springing over to open a drawer from which he removed a two-and-a-half-inch disk that resembled the strainer for a shower drain. "This is the titanium plate we screw on after a craniotomy."

"Oh, really?" From the sleeve she read: *"Reconstruct large, vulnerable openings (LVOs) in the cranium! Fully inert in the human body, immune to attack from bodily fluids! Cosmetic deformity correction to acceptable levels!"*

They both laughed nervously.

"Weird. Are 'large, vulnerable openings' so common they need an acronym?" she asked, suddenly blushing.

"Um, yes, as a matter of fact, they are."

"Oh."

"And it's good," he added.

"Why?"

"Well, I mean, if the LVO is the result of a procedure to improve the condition, then it's good." He tossed the plate back into the drawer, and went to the sink to wash his hands.

"I've seen those at the hardware store for about ninety-five cents," Veblen said.

"Try between two and three thousand for us."

"That's crazy!"

"Yeah. So. I was about to take a break. Want to get something in the café?" he asked, looking away.

"Oh? Sure, why not."

They had coffee and oatmeal raisin cookies together, on the palm-potted atrium where the staff went for air. This was early October, warm and bright. Veblen wore a thin sweater inside the hospital, but peeled it off, conscious of her freckly arms, wondering if the invitation to the café meant he liked her. She was still afraid to assume such things.

"What do you do here?" he asked.

"Administrative-type stuff," said Veblen. "I move around. I was in Neonatology for a year and a half, Otolaryngology almost three years, and this is my third week in Neurology."

"Are you—going into hospital administration?"

"No, this is just for now. I do other stuff, like I'm pretty much fluent in Norwegian so I do translations for this thing called the Norwegian Diaspora Project in Oslo."

"Wow, that's interesting. Are you Norwegian?"

She was Norwegian on her father's side, and further, she'd been named after Thorstein Bunde Veblen, the Norwegian American economist who espoused antimaterialistic beliefs and led an uncommon and misunderstood life. (A noble nonconformist. A valiant foe of institutions and their ossified habits of mind.) The Diaspora Project had a big file on Thorstein Veblen, and thanks to her, it was getting bigger all the time.

"And I'm a major typer," she added. "Like, I'll type the lyrics of a song while I'm listening to it." Why had she said this? It was only a side pocket of her whole entity.

"So you're—the typing type."

"I see myself more as a publisher." Then it was a matter of explaining how as a somewhat obsessive child she'd carry her portable typewriter around in its case, was never without it really, paying visits to neighbors down the road, teachers and friends, to type up poems, recipes, memories, anecdotes, whatever the person had to share, in order to present them with the supporting documents of their consciousness. A traveling scribe.

"One of those old manuals in a case?" He looked at her, intrigued. "Wasn't it heavy?"

"I didn't notice. It was covered with stickers."

"Like a hippie guitar case."

"Yeah, but inside it smelled like a hundred years old. Every time I'd open it I'd feel like I was in another world."

This was a sure badge of her youthful dorkdom. But she felt what she said meant something to him, or could. He asked the usuals, but without the pat cleverness so detestable in flirts. He was no flirt. She learned he'd done his residency at UCSF, gotten the fellowship at Stanford, all the markers of success, and now Hutmacher Pharmaceuticals, one of the giants, had picked up the rights to his research and his device, had flown him to Washington, and the Department of Defense was involved. After the New Year, he would be heading a clinical trial at the veterans' hospital in Menlo Park.

"Wow, that's great. Is Dr. Chaudhry sad you're leaving?" She led him on.

"Basically. He's a good guy. A little play-by-the-rules, but for him it works."

She thought she understood, had context for Chaudhry's earlier remarks. Paul was up and coming. Chaudhry was holding on.

He was handsome in a rumpled way, with a great smile. He had the air of an underdog, despite his accomplishments. He seemed sad and sober and boyishly hopeful, all at once. A sparrow swooped at crumbs.

"Need to get back?" he asked.

"Probably."

"I take hikes in the hills," he said. "Um, would you like to come along, sometime?"

"Yes, sure."

Paul had a funny look on his face, and smoothed back his hair again. "How about Saturday?"

They met on Saturday. The stakes were greater. Glimpses of untold vistas lay ahead as they walked with put-on carelessness, kicking rocks and plunging hands in pockets, bumping into each other every now and then. With every step, options jettisoned. Both recognized an affinity, one without an easy name. Maybe the rural surroundings where they had been raised, and hints of great backlogs of family folly. She thought he was more adorable by the moment.

They had dinner together that night.

The first kiss came not unforeseen outside his car, in the moonlight; great long kisses outside her house, the slight rub of his whiskers chafing her face in a kind of rough ecstasy, the cool tip of his nose that brushed her cheeks. He smelled like juniper berries and warm laundry.

"The look on your face when you came into the lab—"

She laughed. "What did I look like?"

"You have a very expressive face, a beautiful face."

Something was worrying her: "You know, I know it's important to help the men and women of the armed forces, but you're not torturing animals, are you?"

"Yes, we're secretly waterboarding our rodents. It's hard to pour the water down their little snouts, but as the saying goes, *Ve have our vays.*"

She pushed him. "They have feelings, just like we do. If only they had a translator."

He looked at her closely. "Thank you for pointing that out. So what do you think?" he said, stroking her hair. "Should I come in?"

Was it too fast, or should one simply act? "We just met— yesterday."

"We could play cards."

"Right."

"Or not."

"True."

He kissed her face, her eyes. "But I'll leave."

It seemed he was already there, under her skin. She didn't know when she'd wanted to kiss someone this much. "It's okay if you don't."

"Oh, if I don't?"

"Right."

"Leave?"

"Yes."

"You mean stay."

"Stay."

"Ah."

"Come on, then."

"I will. I will come on."

It was a night of wonders. She was so attracted to him it was scary, and would require management. For the first time, she didn't tell Albertine everything, or her mother. She kept it all to herself, a milestone of significance.

All along she basked in the big-picture assumptions he made, the lack of ambivalence over whether or not they'd proceed. In three months, they'd become nearly inseparable. His certainty relaxed her, gave her the room to reflect on her own hidden restlessness. When he said things like *We're made for each other. You're perfect for me,* she felt embraced like never before, at last taking the chance to examine the perplexing knot it all produced, without the added fear of losing him.

2

SAUERKRAUT AND MACE

As it turned out, Paul had gone shopping for more than breakfast.

She watched from the window as he wrestled something from the trunk of his car. Under a clearing sky, a newly minted object threw its shadow onto the walkway, coffin-shaped, about two feet long.

"Oh my god, a trap?" she said, at the door.

"It's my stated goal to keep pests out of our lives," he announced, and she thought nervously of her mother.

"What if we don't agree on what's a pest?"

"Veb, I got no sleep last night. You should be glad I didn't get the guillotine kind."

The packaging boldly proclaimed:

> ## Humanely TRAPS, not KILLS:
> Squirrels
> Chipmunks
> Shrews
> Voles
> and other Nuisance Critters!

"I hate the word *critters!*" Veblen said, displacing her negative feelings onto an innocent noun.

He persisted, pointing to the fine print. "Look at this."

Squirrels can cause extensive damage to attic insulation or walls and gnaw on electrical wires in homes and vehicles, creating a fire hazard.

"Paul, don't you see, that's propaganda to motivate you to buy the thing."

"But it's true."

"This morning it came to the window—I think it wants to befriend me," Veblen said, quite naturally.

"You can make other friends. This squirrel isn't a character in a storybook. Real animals don't wear shawls and top hats and write poetry. They rape each other and eat their own young."

"Paul, that's an excessively negative view of wildlife."

Nevertheless, he seized the wooden chair from beside her desk, took it through the bathroom door, and dumped it in the bathtub, to stand on it and shove aside the square of white, enameled plywood covering the opening to the attic. She provided him with the flashlight from her bedside drawer. His thighs flexed like a warrior's. A strange little riddle began in her head:

The man pops squirrels, the man pops mice—
(What man? Not Paul?)

With a riddle-me-ree he pops them twice;
(Twice? Isn't once enough?)

He pops his rats with a riddle-me-ree
(Oh no, it *is* Paul!)

He popped my father and he might pop me.
(How terrible! Was Paul experimenting with squirrels?)

"Nesting materials in the corner," he yelled. "God. Looks like fur on the beams!"

Was this the stuff married life would be made of, two people making way for the confounding spectacle of the other, bewildered and slightly afraid?

"Paul, did you know, the year Thoreau spent at Walden Pond, he spent a lot of time totally enchanted by squirrels?" If squirrels were good enough for Thoreau, after all, what was Paul's problem?

"No, I didn't."

"Have I told you about the great squirrel migrations of the past?" She steadied the chair.

"You must have been saving it up."

"Yeah. Squirrels are actually one of the oldest mammals on earth!" she told him, with curious pride. "They've been in North America at least fifty million years. That's a long time, don't you think? I mean, people brag about their relatives coming over on the *Mayflower* in 1620, so I think squirrels deserve a little respect, don't you?"

She could see him scanning the corners of the attic for entry holes, and he didn't reply.

"Anyway, settlers and townspeople across North America wrote in their diaries about oceans of squirrels that would flood through the fields and over the mountains, as far as their eyes could see! Can you imagine it? It was like an infinite gray blanket. At times, whole tides of them were seen swimming across rivers, like the Hudson, and the Missouri, and the Ohio. Even Lewis and Clark witnessed a migration! In 1803. In southern Illinois in the 1880s, it was reported that four hundred fifty *million* squirrels ran through this one area, almost half a billion!"

"This is true?"

"Yes! It's very well documented."

"Sounds like a Hitchcock movie."

For the record, she wished he'd said "Wow!" or "Amazing!" or something flavored with a little more curiosity and awe, because those mass migrations had always represented something phenomenal to her.

"The solidarity is what I love about it, all of them deciding it was time to go and then setting out together," she tried, for she loved Richard Rorty's writings on solidarity and had no trouble applying it to squirrels.

"Probably in a blind panic, burning with mange."

"Paul!"

"I don't have the same feeling about squirrels, Veb."

ELIZABETH MCKENZIE

This was upsetting for some reason. Although Paul wasn't the only person who thought squirrels were nasty, furry bastards with talons like birds and the cold hearts of reptiles.

Even Beatrix Potter's *The Tale of Squirrel Nutkin,* a classic of children's literature, by an introverted woman who generally adored small animals, offered up a pesky idiot-squirrel who riddles a landed authority figure into a fury. But was Nutkin as frivolous as he was made out to be? She had a few theories about that.

"Thorstein Veblen would say people hate squirrels," she called up to him, "because that's the only way to motivate expenditures on them—such as buying traps or guns. It's the same with stirring up *patriotic emotionalism,* because it justifies expenditures for defense."

"Uh, what?" He took the sleek apparatus in his grasping hands, then was back on the chair stuffing it somewhere in the dark near the hatch. He said, "I'll check it every day, you won't have to think about it. I'll take it up in the hills where it will live happily ever after. Okay?"

"Whatever, just do it!" she said, biting into her arm.

In addition to biting herself, another way Veblen dealt with emotional distress was to fixate on ideological concerns.

Unhappy that Paul was stuffing a trap into her attic, registering a loss of control that would come with a growing relationship and further compromise, she began to think bitterly about how phenomena in the natural world no longer inspired reverence and reflection, but translated instead into excuses for shopping sprees. Squirrels = *trap.* Winter's ragged hand = *Outdoor World.* Summer's dog days reigned = *Target.* Same with traditions—marriage was preceded by the longest shopping list of all, second only to the one after the birth of offspring.

"Paul, take this trap. You impute it with awesomeness because you acquired it and you now believe it's the crystallization of your desires."

"Can you bring me a piece of cheese or something?"

She trudged into the kitchen, to look for a snack a squirrel might *not* enjoy. She had an idea.

"Veblen?" he called.

"Coming."

"A piece of bread is fine."

"Okay, just a minute."

Shortly, she carried in a plate with her offering.

"What's that?" asked Paul, peering down.

"Sauerkraut sprinkled with mace."

"Why?"

"I hear they love it," said Veblen.

She heard him set the plate into the trap with a clap.

THEY SPENT the afternoon walking and talking about all they were about to face. It would come back to her later that Paul barely mentioned his family that day. Instead he talked a lot about his vision of their material future—the signing bonus for the trial and stock from Hutmacher Pharmaceuticals would allow them to buy a house. "You don't want to stay in mine?" she asked, surprised. She loved her house.

HER OWN VISION of the future was of happiness in the air. Something was baking. Children were playing games. There were flowers

ElizaBeth McKenzie

and substantial trees, and birds were singing in their nests. She
was living with someone who was laughing.

Paul gave a sample of laughter.

"That works," she said.

SHE WAS STILL very pleased with her little house, and how she'd
found it.

Nearly five years ago, having finally escaped from home, she'd
been sleeping in her old Volvo by the San Francisquito creek and
checking out listings by the dozens for days. She'd seen rooms in
dingy, greasy-smelling houses in Mountain View, tiny, dark rooms
in houses full of guffawing male engineering students, and a room
in the house of a high school science teacher filled with exercise
machines.

It was a warm night in September, that night. She had a soulful
bottle of beer and a slice of pizza on University Avenue, then
walked the neighborhood in the glow of dusk, down streets named
for famous poets: Lowell and Byron and Homer and Kipling
and the tormented, half-mad Italian poet Torquato Tasso. She
crunched the sycamore and magnolia and locust leaves on the
sidewalk. Just before she reached the end where the street met
the arroyo, she passed a small house so overgrown with vines that
the windows were no longer visible. The yard was neck-high with
weeds and ivy and morning glory, and in the gentle air of evening
she heard the flap of a tarp on the roof, laid over the old shingles
to protect them from rain. The chimney was missing a few bricks.
Swatches of animal hair were mixed in the litter of leaves up the
walkway, as if various creatures regularly rolled on their backs

· 32 ·

there and stretched out in the sun. The site of the abandoned house, or possibly the dwelling of an old eccentric, filled her with warmth and hope, and perhaps because she lingered there thinking how this might be a positive instance of *absentee ownership*, she fated her meeting with the person who came down the narrow driveway between the two bungalows, from a yard choked with the summer's industry of honeysuckle and jasmine.

This was Donald Chester, wearing his grubby Stanford sweatshirt stained with motor oil and paint. He was a retired engineer who'd grown up only a few blocks away in the 1930s, and attended the university as a day student before, during, and after World War II. Palo Alto wasn't always so swank, he told her. Back then, a settlement of hoboes camped around the giant sequoia by the train station, rough wooden shacks on Lytton Avenue housed kids who went without shoes, and rabbits were raised in hutches in the grassy fields behind them for supper. Before the university came in 1896, sheep, goats, horses, and mules grazed on ranch land. And before that, when the Spanish began to deed land grants, tule-gathering tribes swept through the tidal flats in bunched canoes, fleeing missionaries. If his parents, who'd struggled through the Depression eating rabbits and mending their socks until there was no more sock to mend, only the mending, could have seen what happened to dreamy old Palo Alto, they'd get a real kick out of it.

Yes, Donald Chester knew the owner of the wreckage next door. She was an elderly woman who lived in New York with her daughter, who would neither let go of the house she'd lived in as a young bride nor maintain it, and Veblen said that was good. To her it looked enchanted. To which he said, *Let's see what you think after you look inside,* and brought out some flashlights. It was one of those magical strokes of luck that a person enjoys once or twice in a lifetime, and marvels at ever after.

She followed him behind the place, where there was a modest garage built for a Model T, with the original wooden door with a sash, hollowed by termites, like cactus wood.

The back door hung loose off its hinges, and a musty odor surrounded them in the kitchen. Old cracked linoleum squeaked underfoot. A bank of dirt had formed on the windowsill, growing grass. But the huge old porcelain sink was intact. And the old tiles, under layers of silt, were beautiful. Donald Chester laughed and said she must have a great deal of imagination. In the living room, water stains covered the ceiling like the patterns in a mosque. She told him about the house in Cobb and the fixing she and her mother did to get it in shape, all by themselves. (She'd been only six when she and her mother moved in, but they'd worked side by side for weeks.) She knew how to transform a place, wait and see. Donald Chester took down her number and said he doubted anything would come of it, but he'd give her a call. And the very next day he did. The widow took a fancy to the idea of a single woman fixing it up. She priced the place nostalgically, a rent about the same as single rooms. Veblen sobbed with disbelief. She'd saved up enough money over the past few years to get the whole thing off the ground.

She loved the tiger lilies, which were out. She kissed them on their crepey cheeks, got pollen on her chin. For the next week, she started on the place at dawn, ripping vines off the windows, digging dirt from the grout, hosing the walls. One day Albertine came down to help. They pried open the windows to let in fresh air and barreled through the place with a Shop-Vac. Another day Veblen climbed onto the roof and tore off the tarp and discovered the leaks, and patched them. It wasn't rocket science. She cleaned the surface of every wall with TSP and every tile with bleach, and painted every room. Then she rented a sanding machine and took a thin layer from the oak floors, finishing them with linseed oil and turpentine. She kept a fan blowing to dry the paint and the floors all day long.

Donald Chester pitched in. He lent her tools and brought her tall tumblers of iced tea with wedges of lemon from his tree.

"You like to work hard," he remarked, when Veblen came out of the house one day covered in white dust.

In the kitchen, the old refrigerator needed a thorough scrubbing, but the motor worked, and the old Wedgewood stove better than worked. The claw-foot tub in the bathroom had rust stains, but they didn't bother her very much. The toilet needed a new float and chain, no big deal. She had the utilities changed to her name. She played her radio day and night, and by the fifth night, give or take a few creaking floorboards and windows with stubborn sashes, the house welcomed her. The transformation absorbed her for months to come, as if she'd written a symphony or a wonderful book or painted a small masterpiece. And she'd stayed on these last five years despite the hell-bent growth all around, conveniently located halfway between each parent in her outpost on one of the last untouched corners of old Palo Alto. One day the widow or her daughter would get an offer they couldn't refuse. But for now, it was hers.

The two buildings had never been remodeled or added on to, and provided the same standard of shelter as they had when built in 1920, which was plenty good. Now a week did not go by when real estate agents didn't cram business cards into the mail slots, hoping to capture the deeds and promptly have the little houses bulldozed. She and Donald liked to feel they were taking a stand.

For her first meal on Tasso Street, she boiled a large tough artichoke from Castroville and ate it with a scoop of Best Foods mayonnaise. She took the thistles out of the heart and filled it like a little cup. She listened to an opera on the radio, live from San Francisco, *La Bohème*. Surrounded by the smell of fresh paint and linseed oil, the smooth floors, the clean glass, the perception of space to grow into, she was too excited to sleep.

As she often was at night now, with Paul beside her. Sharing simple meals and discussing the day's events, waking up together with plans for the future—these things felt practically bacchanalian when you were used to being on your own.

AND SO WHAT about a wedding? Where, how soon? There was a huge catalog of decisions to make all of a sudden. If you were normal, Veblen couldn't help thinking. Part of her wanted to do all the normal bridely things and the other part wanted to embrace her disdain for everything of the sort.

That morning a lump of cinnamon twist stuck in her throat. Another gulp of coffee ushered it down. "Paul," she said. "I'm super excited about this getting married idea. But there's a lot about me you don't know."

"There'd better be," he said warmly.

"So it makes sense for the tips of icebergs to fall in love, without knowing anything about the bottom parts?"

"Well, you know, I think we're doing pretty well with the bottom parts."

She wrinkled her nose.

"But—" She went for something small. "Sometimes I sleep-walk. Did you know that?"

"You haven't done that so far."

"And if I'm around free food, I eat too much."

Paul shrugged. "Okay."

"Maybe we should go meet my mother soon," she said, biting a fold of her inner cheek.

"That sounds great," said Paul. "We definitely should."

Could he really be so accepting? Or was he just acting that way for now? And in what ways was *she* acting? Could you look at all interactions that way, as a presentation of the self, an advertisement of sorts?

Oh, cut it out, she told herself.

3

NEWS IS MARKETING

The year was starting well.

The week after Veblen said she would marry him, Paul Vreeland, MD, FAAN, FANA, FACNS (he loved the growing train following his name, all engines, no caboose) reported for the first full day of his trial at the veterans' hospital known as Greenslopes. Climbing out of his car he stood in the morning chill, tasting the fragrance of his new domain.

The hospital was the centerpiece of this government compound, assigned to the task of supporting the spent men and women of the armed forces. The range of structures told of the ongoing demands on the military, from the dowdy Truman-era offices to the flat cold war bungalows and tin-can hangars to the striking prize-commissioned buildings of recent design. Gophers and moles had the run of the lawn, which was lumpy, riddled with loose mounds of soil. (Paul had recently spotted an excellent two-pronged gopher trap while shopping to eliminate squirrels, and thought he might recommend it to the groundskeeper.) And everywhere the grounds were paced by truculent crows. Two men in worn Wind-breakers and baseball caps huddled in wheelchairs beside a Victorian-style cupola, which had been ceremoniously fenced in a pen and surrounded by rosebushes, and bore a plaque bearing the names of a select squadron of the national sacrifice.

Had he been born at another time, been drafted and required to serve, would he have mustered courage? In his lifetime, a man needed a test, and Paul thought: *This one is mine.* With a crooked smile he imagined the musical that would come of it. *Greenslopes!* The patients in their hospital gowns would come to life in their cots, and perform spirited *ronds de jambe* in the aisles.

Just then, a squirrel spiraled down the heavy trunk of the mag-nolia, nattering across the spotty lawn in fitful, myoclonic jerks. A trail of Fortuna cigarette boxes led his eye to three weary-looking women in white uniforms and blue hairnets lumped on a brick wall in smoke. Then an electric buzz drew his attention to the road, where an obese gentleman careened along in a wide, custom-ized wheelchair, waving an orange flag on a bobbing wand. Along the sidewalk came a woman in a black tank top under her denim jacket, tattoos rising like thunderheads over the mountains of her breasts, carrying a ziplock bag packed with white-bread sand-wiches. To lend some decorum to the tableau, Paul stood tall, dusted off his jacket, and turned to take the path from the lot to the main building as a limping janitor pushed a cart across the sidewalk at the drop-off circle.

A low band of cement-colored haze hung snugly over the pen-insula. He was early, did not want to stand in front like a doorman; he changed direction, taking a path freshly decked with necky red cyclamen submerged in a carpet of woodchips.

For here he was, the man who would lead Hutmacher into a new era. Under his stewardship, the clinical trials program would surpass all expectations. Here at the VA, the new wing, filling daily with volunteers, would become a model of its kind. Physicians received Nobel prizes for innovations like his. They had body parts named after them, such as Kernohan's notch and Bachmann's bundle and the sphincter of Oddi. Not to mention the fissure of Rolando and the canal of Schlemm and the zonule of Zimm! *Dr. Vreeland helped eradicate once and for all the effects of traumatic brain injury sustained in combat. Focal or diffuse, of no matter to Vreeland. Among the many types of experimental subjects, Vreeland popularized the use of the squirrel, as they tended to invade attics and make a nuisance and rile up generous-hearted women in their defense!*

Heading back into the corporation yard, he passed an earthmover stuck like a mammoth in a lake of mud, and reflected on how until recently he'd been just as mired by the failure of his nerve. That is, until he met Cloris, at the start of a run of unprecedented luck.

There he was at work one ordinary afternoon last September, slumped in the elevator, his cart much like the janitor's, thinking about how he'd run out of toilet paper that morning and how he'd have to stop to buy more on his way home, with no Veblen in his life, he had yet to meet her, when a tall, blond woman of around thirty-five tripped open the closing doors with her long striding legs and took her place at his side. It was a memory he'd committed to the permanent circuits. The way she leaned over, read his name on his lab coat, and made no foolish sentimental comments about the mixed specimens on his cart always struck him as proof of a giant leap in his sex appeal.

"Dr. Vreeland, why don't you ask a resident to take your cart?"

He grinned, tossed off something about finding it difficult to delegate.

Her eyes gleamed with the thrill of discovery. "My father says, 'If you want something done, ask a busy man.'" She had just visited a dear friend, very ill, maybe she should have a coffee before hitting the road, would he like to come tell her about his work? She was with Hutmacher Pharmaceuticals, and loved to keep abreast of the latest developments. He stood taller. At the next floor he jettisoned the cart.

"How long have you been here?" In the cafeteria they settled in plastic chairs.

"My third year. Are you a rep or something?" he asked with a mischievous poke, because industry reps were no longer allowed to do their repping at the School of Medicine, and he'd signed his share of SIIPs (Stanford Industry Interactions Policy), which covered gifts from the industry, access of sales and marketing reps to the campus, and other strategies of coercion the industry was apt to deploy.

"You could say that," she responded. "You could say I've been repping for them since the day I was born."

Moments later, when he realized over his plain black coffee that he was actually speaking to a Hutmacher, namesake of one of the largest pharmaceutical companies in the world, a modern empire, she a virtual princess, he gulped and scalded his esophagus, and worse, felt his testes shrivel to the size of garbanzo beans. To his shame, he really believed the wealthy were superior. In a Darwinian sense, they *had* to be. He could read the story of past conquests and brutal takeovers in her bone structure, her long arms and legs, her narrow shoulders, her high cheekbones and forehead, her elegant hands. The marriages that had led to her creation had been of alpha males and glorious females, and you wouldn't find the peasant's short calf or hunched trunk among them.

Meanwhile, he descended from a rough mix of Dutch farmers, Belgian carpet salesmen, Irish gamblers, and Presbyterian prigs, and he wondered what use she could possibly have for him.

"But as I said, I'm not here on business. I was visiting a sick friend."

"I'm sorry," Paul said.

"Thank you. Now more about you."

"But—" He laughed at himself. "Shouldn't you be skiing in Zermatt, or whatever heiresses are supposed to be doing?"

"That's next January. Tell me about your work!"

Who had ever asked? The subject of his study was his gold reserve, burdening his heart. "Well, I'm working on traumatic brain injury. I've been developing a tool."

"A tool? Tell me more," said Cloris, with such prosperous vitality he felt all underfunded and desperate and teenaged again.

"To make it short: I've found a way medics on the line can take a proactive role in preventing permanent brain injury."

"That's terrific," said Cloris. "How?"

"Well." Was he pitching his tool? "You want me to tell you now?"

"Please!"

He nodded, and scalded another quadrant of his taste buds. "Let's see. Where to start. The body's response, you know, to just about any stimuli, is swelling—"

"I've noticed."

His nostrils flared. "To injury. Like my burned tongue right now. The body swells."

"Yes, it does, doesn't it?"

"The blood rushes, it rushes to the—geez." He laughed, looking down. "Okay. I have no idea what we're talking about here."

"Don't stop."

He cleared his throat. "So the brain. If the brain is injured and swells, the skull, I'm sure you know"—he made his hands look like a clamp—"holds it in, and—" His neck felt hot. "There's pressure, lots of pressure."

"I understand," said Cloris.

"The pressure builds—"

"—and builds—"

"—cutting off circulation—"

"Oh, my."

He bestowed a frank, open gaze upon her, and cleared his throat. "Anyway, the cells stop getting oxygen, which sets off a chain reaction called cell suicide, technically called apoptosis, but if a craniotomy—opening up the skull—can be performed immediately, releasing the pressure, to make room for the swelling"— Paul shifted in his seat—"then no more cell suicide, and under the right circumstances recovery is achievable, up to eighty, ninety percent."

"So how could this be done?"

"Here's the problem. Say you're a medic in combat, and you need to get your injured troops to the closest field hospital, but for a thousand reasons, you can't do it fast enough. This happens all the time. You've made your determination of brain injury—"

"How is that done?"

"Nonreactive pupils. Unconsciousness."

"Sounds like me every morning."

"Ah." Paul felt a luxuriant warmth ripple down his thighs. "The point is, it's not all that high-tech—craniotomies have been practiced for thousands of years. We see burr holes in the skulls of Egyptians, Sumerians, even the Neanderthals—"

"That was for a snack," she said.

"The point being that long before there were hospital standards and antiseptics—"

"It could be done."

"Right! And so in emergency situations, medics—"

"Could do just as good a job as the Neanderthals!"

Paul slapped his palms on the table. "Right. And here's where my work comes in. I've devised an instrument that is safe, effective, essentially automatic, for the line medic to use right on the spot."

"The Swiss Army knife of brain injury?"

"Yes."

"Something every medic would carry?" she grasped, eagerly.

"That's my hope."

"Simple, easy to use?"

"Very."

"How big is it?"

Paul held up his hands to indicate a tool of about eight inches.

Cloris raised her eyebrows, then entered text in her phone. "What's it *like*? Tell me there's something like it but not as good."

He knew what she was getting at. The FDA would allow you to bypass a lot of time and red tape using the 510(k) exemption if a device was *like* something else already approved. "Between you and me, it's unique. But you could easily say it's like the Voltar pneumatic hole punch or Abata's Cranio-locum."

Her eyes sparkled and he felt wonderful. "Could it save the government money?"

"Oh my god, yes. And obviously, a lot of people's lives would be much better."

She leaned forward, to whisper. "What's your contract situation?"

"I'm up for renewal at the end of the year," whispered Paul, nervously rocking back in his chair.

"Has the Technology Transfer Office seen this yet?" she asked huskily.

"Funny you ask. I'm just finishing my report for them right now."

"I see. Can I ask you something?"

"Ask away."

"If I get back to you in a couple of days, will you let me take the first look?"

"Sure, but—"

"I think it's a no-brainer."

"Ouch."

"What?"

"You said it's a *no-brainer.*"

"I practiced that."

They walked to the hospital lobby together, Paul carrying her tote bag to the door. She gave him a European-style kiss on his left cheek, and his catecholamines soared.

She called in two days, to inform him that Development at Hutmacher was very interested in his device. It seemed that Cloris Hutmacher was a scout for her family's company, prowling med schools and biotech companies for the latest discoveries that exceeded her company's resources to discover in their own labs. She could boast of finding a new drug for arthritis at UCLA, and another that blocked harmful proteins within cell walls at UC Santa Barbara, all on her own initiative. Of course, Paul's device was a high risk Class III and would need to be tested in a clinical trial, but that was no obstacle at all. The VA center in Menlo Park was available as a testing site, and it was possible, in fact probable, that Paul could be the primary investigator in a trial there, making a niche for himself testing other patents relevant to the Department of Defense that were being licensed by Hutmacher. Hutmacher had numerous DOD contracts, she told him, and was dedicated to the men and women of the armed forces. He would be ideal.

Paul thought he would be too, but when he brought it up with his mentor, Lewis Chaudhry, Chaudhry was flatly lacking in enthusiasm.

"This project is nowhere near ready for that, Paul. You have yet to do your randomized study, you've had no peer reviews, nothing! Are they planning to piggyback it on a 510(k)?"

Paul admitted they were. "You know what an uphill battle it is to market anything. They're saying it's a major breakthrough and they can move it into practical application really fast. Isn't that worth doing?"

Chaudhry stepped back with thinly disguised contempt. "So, Paul, how big was the gift basket?"

And Paul felt sorry for the stodgy old termagant and went directly to the Technology Transfer Office to work out the details. And when he met Cloris later that week, at the office of Hutmacher's attorneys, Shrapnal and Boone, in Burlingame, and he was presented with a signing bonus in cash and stock options as well as a huge gift basket filled with bottles of champagne, fancy chocolates, aged wheels of French cheese, and even a sterling silver knife in a blue box from Tiffany & Co., Paul could see no reason not to own the moment.

Then, when Cloris invited him up to her place in Atherton, he wasn't exactly surprised. He was easing into his new incarnation pretty suavely, he thought. As he followed her white Tesla Roadster up the hill, through the gate, to the house that had been built in the manner of a French château, sandstone covered with ivy, a front door thick and iron strapped, opening like a castle, he felt overwhelmed with fate and consequence. What if she fell in love with him? What if they married? What if the elder Hutmacher took him under his wing and told the world he was a visionary? What if he became president of the company after the old man was gone, and had a private jet? What if he and Cloris became goodwill ambassadors for UNICEF, distributing medical supplies throughout Africa, stopping in dusty towns to confer with Bono and Angelina Jolie? What if everyone from his hometown, Garberville, found out? What if the psycho-bitch mother of his high school girlfriend, Millie Cuthbertson, committed hara-kiri on a bamboo mat, and coyotes paraded her entrails down every street in town?

Cloris showed off her office with its high view of the peninsula, and he lingered to admire a wall of tightly framed photo ops, including, but not limited to Cloris and her father, Boris Hutmacher, with George H. W. Bush, Cloris and her father with Bill and Hillary, Cloris with George W. Bush, Cloris and her father with President Obama, Cloris with Mick Jagger, Cloris with the Dalai Lama, Cloris with the Pope, and . . .

"Where's Cloris with god?"

She squeezed his arm.

Certificates of appreciation studded the walls, from charities and boards, medical, environmental, inner city, whippet societies. It seemed there wasn't anyone Cloris couldn't be appreciated by.

Just then, the monitor on the desk began to ring like a phone, and Cloris said, "It's Morris calling. Our weekly Skype. Do you mind?"

"Who's Morris?"

"My son."

"I didn't know you had a son."

"Yes. Divorced three years ago. He's eight."

"Oh."

"Don't worry, this will only take a minute," she said.

"Please, take as long as you want," Paul said, and he went away to wait.

He let himself out the French doors onto a sweeping sandstone piazza, appointed with various clusters of wrought iron chairs, ceramic pots embossed with fleur-de-lis, and an inverted copper fountain that funneled into the earth. Across the lawn stood a rose arbor, its few leaves yellowed and spotted with black. From there, one could see up the coastal ranges north and south, the Dumbarton Bridge crossing the bay to Fremont, and the San Mateo Bridge beyond. For some reason, all he could think about at that moment was how he was going to tell his status-conscious friend Hans Borg about this. Maybe he'd be in a position to finagle some contracts for Hans, of course he would! He'd send his parents on the big trip they'd always wanted to take, and he'd hire a full-time caretaker to manage his brother, Justin, with an iron fist.

But they would never allow that. Deflated by the inescapable specter of his disabled brother, Paul wandered past the pool and pool house, admiring the château from every angle, until he found himself before a marble goddess skirted by camellia and heard Cloris's voice through the windows. He could see her fine head before the large monitor in conversation with her son, who appeared to be slightly rotund, wearing a horizontally striped sweater that emphasized his girth. He had reddish hair and a galaxy of freckles, and his sniffles were amplified with sorrowful fidelity.

"I told you I don't have time for this," Cloris said.

The boy sobbed.

"Stop it," Cloris hissed. "Are you trying to punish me? Because I don't deserve it! I'm onto you and I won't stand for it!"

Morris cried louder, and Paul stepped back, not wanting to believe his patroness was brutalizing her child. (Maybe the kid was a horrible brat and deserved it? Maybe Cloris, unlike his parents, knew how to exert some discipline?)

"Get me your father. Now!"

The boy disappeared from the screen and Paul leaned forward again, despite himself. A hard-jawed man in a black polo shirt with a sharp cleft between his eyes took the boy's place.

"Cloris, what are you doing? He's hurt!"

"Don't expect me to fix it all from here. He wants to live with you, then be his father!"

"Cloris. Calm down. Morris, go upstairs while I talk to your mother."

"Don't let him leave. I don't want to prolong this. Sit down, both of you!"

Cloris strained toward the screen, so that her nose might have sparked with static. "I want to tell you something, Morris. When my father asks me about his grandson, what am I supposed to say? Well, you know what, I say *nothing*! I change the subject! That's because you let me down constantly. I would never tell him the things going on!"

"I didn't mean to," cried Morris.

"Stop it. Pull yourself together right now. You're such a baby. You'll have to earn my trust in the future, and it won't be nice and easy, the way everything else comes for you."

"What can I do?" sobbed the boy, whose cheeks glistened with tears.

Cloris bent, arms crossed over her chest, shouting at the screen. "Do you understand why you are in that school? You are in that school because my father went to that school and because he is on the board of directors of that school and you have every advantage in the world in that school! Do you know how bad it has to be for me to get a call from one of your teachers? You represent this family to the children of everyone who matters in Washington. And this is what happens?"

"Cloris, he's in second grade."

"And look at him. He's at least ten pounds overweight. Morris, are you listening? You are fat. And do you know what that means? *Nobody* likes little fat boys. Morris? Stop eating junk food!"

"That's more than enough," said the boy's father, and fearing that the conversation was coming to an end, Paul withdrew, in order to rush around the building to the expanse of sandstone, where he affected a casual stance until Cloris joined him again.

"There you are!"

"Nice view."

"Now, where were we?"

"Everything okay with your son?" Paul asked, innocently.

"Oh. Fine. The long-distance thing isn't easy," said Cloris, and to stay on target for the future of his device, he pushed the scene he had witnessed from his mind.

He followed her inside and she brought them drinks on the couch, and shortly, one of her hands was on the cushion near his shoulder, then on his shoulder, finding its way like a garter snake to his ear. She had a thing for the little flange at the front of the ear called the tragus, and she pinched it at least six or seven times.

"You are a gorgeous man," she said, embarrassing and thrilling him.

After a long session of making out (she tasted of vodka, and her mouth was surprisingly small, her tongue fast and flighty, putting him in mind of kissing a deer, for some reason), she threw herself back on the pillows and said, "I don't have relationships anymore. But you're hard to resist."

"Then don't," Paul said, in motion toward her, fueled by instinct.

"I was a very decadent person in my twenties. You have no idea."

He listened, with a hard tug in his groin.

"I had problems. And then, about five years ago, something shifted."

"And what was that?"

"It coincided with my work for the company. I suddenly transferred all of that excitation into my professional life."

"That's a tragedy," Paul said, grasping her fingers.

"So now, if I'm spending time with a man, which I'm not, I'm a nun these days, I'm impatient, I think about work, I double-task. I'll be smiling and thinking about my toes and separating them to aerate them. And I'll be thinking, there, that's something I can accomplish until this is over."

Paul cleared his throat. "Hmm."

"Is that fair to the man?" she pressed.

"Depends on the man." He laughed, as he only thought right, though he would never have taken her for a person with tinea pedis.

"Come here," she said, pulling on his collar.

"I think you're struggling," Paul said, with renewed interest in kissing her.

"I am."

"Maybe someone should help you with your struggle."

He reached for her skirt, and under it, just long enough to feel that her inner thighs were cold, but with that she jumped up and laughed in an agitated and sophisticated manner, and said, "Come upstairs!" And he followed like a pup.

Her bedroom was vast, with a huge bed that she rolled over in order to rummage in a bedside drawer and retrieve a bronze pipe, tamping it expertly with pungent weed. She took a few long tokes and passed it to Paul, who was so surprised in a bad way that he shriveled. The scent of marijuana was his least favorite odor in the world. Even feces on a shoe smelled better than cannabis resin.

"No, really," he said, when she pushed the smoking bowl toward him.

She indulged several more times, then flung herself back into the playpen of pillows, kicked off her shoes, sent them flying, and patted for Paul to lie next to her.

"He's coming out next year," she gasped.

"Who?"

"Morris," said Cloris, exhaling loudly. "I have to figure out something fun to do with him. I *never* get it right. What did you like to do when you were eight?"

"I don't know, the usual."

"What's the usual!" she said, hammering him with a pillow.

"Hey!"

He grabbed one from the multitude of bolsters and puffs at the head of the bed and socked her back.

"Paul!"

He drew himself up on his knees, and moved toward her, as she began to sniffle.

"How can I know the usual, I don't live with my son, there is no usual." She sniffed.

"Cloris? You okay?"

After a while she sat up, cross-legged, to dab her face with the sheet. "I get very emotional about him."

"Why isn't he with you?"

"That's old school, Paul," said Cloris. "We let Morris make his own decisions."

"Mmm. Best."

"Anyway, his father can't have him in the spring and he'll be here for a while."

"That's nice," Paul said, worried he'd failed to keep things on track. The moment seemed to have passed. He gazed at her bare feet on the bed, wondering what grew between her toes, bound up by his desire to do the right thing in the presence of an heiress, whatever that might be.

"Were you a Boy Scout?" she asked.

"Definitely not."

"A camp counselor somewhere? A coach?"

"No, no. Not me."

"You seem like the kind of person boys would admire and imitate. Like my father."

He tossed it off as if the compliment meant nothing to him, but he wanted to bury it, entomb it, make a shrine of it to worship at for the rest of his life.

"Come here," she said, and then something happened—it was kind of like having sex with someone but not quite. It was a scratching, raging, rolling catfight of flesh and bone and disclaimer—*we both know this doesn't mean anything*—until it was inexplicably over and he was almost heaved off the side of the bed. Then Cloris disappeared for about twenty minutes. Finally he wandered downstairs and bumped into her in the kitchen, dishing up bowls of spaghetti *alle vongole,* which they soon ate at a long table, discussing business as if nothing had happened. Driving back to his depressing condo just off El Camino in Mountain View later that night, he wondered if he'd just torched his whole career.

(And then he would meet Veblen a few weeks later, and would be so immediately bowled over by his feelings for the smart but spacey, undervalued woman with the handmade clothes and self-cut hair, who typed in the air and loved squirrels, that it would strike him as the closest call in his life.)

When he learned he was off to Washington, D.C., for an interview, his father said, "Terrific, Paul! You can go visit the Wall and see your uncle Richard's name, can't you?"

"Dad, I don't think I'll have time—"

"Wait a minute, wait a minute. It's right in the middle of everything, outside, and you don't have to pay admission or wait in line."

"Dad, I'm going for an interview. They're flying me out. If I have time I'll go, of course. But—"

"Are you saying, Paul, that you'd go all the way to Washington and not visit Richard's name?"

"I've visited it before, with you. I've seen it."

"Oh, I see. You only need to see it once. Paul! Get your priorities straight!"

"Dad, I'll go to the Wall if I can!" Paul barked back.

"It hurts me to think that we've only been there once. You could maybe take some flowers."

"Do they do that there?"

"I don't bloody hell care what they do there, you can take him some flowers. You can set them down under his regiment."

"I'll try."

Soon enough he flew to Dulles, riding a cab past the gentle deciduous arms of eastern woodland fringing the highway. Rising into the powder-blue skies like holy temples were the strongholds of such corporations as Northrop Grummon, BCF, Camber, Deltek, Juniper, Scitor, Vovici, Sybase, and Booz Allen Hamilton, while the gentle green grass and low trees waved around them, sprinkled with rusting conifers sick with disease. He heard the overture to a rock opera forming in his head, a rousing confluence of *Carmina Burana* and *Tommy,* and had a fleeting fantasy of supporting two careers with his boundless force.

He was taken to a building in Arlington, Virginia, a stone's throw from the Pentagon, and those on the committee, some with their uniforms and Minotaur heads, jabbing their swollen thumbs through his documents, gave him the once over.

Present were Grandy Moy, Louise Gladtrip, and Stan Silverbutton, all from the National Institutes of Health (NIH); Vance Odenkirk, Willard Liu, and Horton DeWitt, all from the Department of Defense (DOD); John Williams, MD, National Naval Medical Center, Bethesda (NNMC); Lt. Col. Wade Dent, Walter Reed National Military Medical Center (WRNMMC); Brig. Gen. Nancy Bottomly; Reginald Kornfink, committee manager, DOD; Alfred Pesthorn and Cordelia Fleiss, FDA; Col. Bradley Richter, U.S. Army Medical Materiel Agency (USAMMA); and Ms. Cloris Hutmacher.

"Traumatic brain injury in combat has become the number one killer of our troops," Paul began, gazing down the table. "It was the signature injury of the Iraqi and Afghani campaigns. Warfighter brain injury studies to date include a lot of hopeful breakthroughs on tissue regeneration, but none addresses the need for intervention on the spot, before the cascade of damage begins."

A few of them actually yawned. He responded passionately:

"Let me get to the point. For the past year and a half I have performed a rigorous study of decompressive craniectomies on lab animals with a tool of my own invention, and I'm ready to translate my results to a Phase III trial—"

"We've got a few 'animals' for you," one seasoned bureaucrat broke in, with a bitter snort.

"We're getting an extended Doberman," Kornfink said, drumming his pencil on the table.

"What's that?"

"That's what I wanted to know, but we're getting one."

"How extended is it?"

"I've heard of those."

"I'll let you know," said Kornfink. "I'm breeding them. Shelley's idea for my retirement."

Suddenly the inert committee appeared to remember why they were there, and returned to Paul, as if nothing had happened.

"Dr. Vreeland, the Department of Defense will consider cooperating with the VA and the licensor to fund this study. How do you propose testing in field conditions?"

Paul said, "The VA in Menlo Park has several vacant buildings which we've submitted petitions to use to create field conditions with all relevant noise, light deprivation, smoke, and so on."

He added, "We'll also want to invite trained medics to test the procedure in simulated conditions, rather than MDs." He cleared his throat, and pulled on his collar.

"This is something like a field trach, is that what you're thinking?" asked Bradley Richter, a sinewy man with dark eyes and a pronounced underbite, reminding Paul of a sea angler with skills adapted to life in the dark deep.

"Yes, sir. Medics easily master tracheotomies in emergency situations. For testing we'd move from cadavers to live volunteers in these aforementioned conditions."

"By volunteers, are we talking scores less than eight on the Glasgow Scale?"

"We're looking at a number like that," Paul said, having been warned by Cloris to keep this vague.

Cloris Hutmacher spoke up. "I've already met with Planning at the VA in Menlo Park and they're ready to lease us Building 301, which is a fifteen-thousand-square-foot structure currently in disuse. Any of the WOO simulator systems would fit there."

Richter took notes.

Paul cleared his throat. "If we succeed, which I believe we will—"

"People, this is huge," said Cloris.

"Cloris has an eye for the huge," pronounced Richter.

Cloris said, "It's a cusp moment for all of us."

Paul gazed around the oblong slab, at men and women who'd served the military and had undoubtedly been the trendsetters and thugs of their grade schools.

"This is clearly an opportunity of the highest order," he heard himself declare. "To serve. My country." He made methodical eye contact with each person present. "My father's brother, PFC Richard Vreeland, Company C, Second Battalion Fifth Cavalry, First Cavalry Division, died of blast wounds to his head, chest, both legs, abdomen, and right hand in the ambush at Phu Ninh." He had never mentioned his uncle's annihilation to anyone before, and the expediency of doing it now shocked him, yet made him feel like maybe he could be a player after all. The room fell silent. "As soon as this meeting is over, I'm going to visit his name on the Wall. I want this as much for our country as I want it for him."

A round of backslapping ensued. Cloris told him he was spectacular, and invited him to join some of the committee members for drinks. "Well, I'd like to, but I need to go by the Wall. My uncle," he added.

"You really meant that?" An admiring glint flashed in her eyes. She was as thin as a whip.

"Of course I did."

"Come with us now," Cloris said. "Visit the Wall later."

"But my flight leaves at nine."

She whispered, "I won't tell anyone you didn't go to the Wall. Come on!"

They went to a noisy bar in Georgetown. Cloris spent her energy speaking closely into the large, open ear of Bradley Richter. Paul perspired heavily and drank too much. He didn't end up visiting the Wall, but planned to tell his father he had. Or maybe not—maybe he'd tell his father he *couldn't*, as he'd said all along. Well, it would make his father happy to think he'd tried. Throw the old man a bone. A cab returned him to Dulles within the hour, and he received the offer the next day by noon.

PAUL RETURNED from his tour of the VA grounds by nine A.M. In the lobby, an elfin woman in a yellow checkered skirt and a white blouse with a pin of a Scottish terrier on the collar stepped out and waved at him like a crossing guard.

"Dr. Vreeland!"

Susan Hinks had soft blond hair and cornflower blue eyes, a fine fuzz of blond on her cheeks, and an expression not of an embryo but of something quite fresh. A voyeur would know how to describe it. "Welcome. It's great to meet you, Dr. Vreeland!" Her voice was charmingly nasal, with a mild midwestern twang, and her teeth were notably large and clean. "I'm your clinical coordinator and I'll be providing support in all responsibilities related to the NIH and the DOD and Hutmacher. I'll conduct follow-up evaluations, watch compliance with protocol, take care of the case reports. I'll be your liaison with the Investigational Review Board, the IRB. We've been completely overwhelmed with volunteer applications—we've still got people calling and going around the usual channels to get in."

Paul felt a surge of pride. "Seriously? Is this trial especially attractive for some reason?"

"Any trial is attractive," Susan Hinks said. "They have to wait so long for treatment in the system. If they get into a trial, they get a lot of attention."

He gave her a skeptical look.

"Are you trying to tell me these veterans are willing to get a hole punched in their skulls just to get a checkup?"

Unruffled, she said, "That's the way it is, Dr. Vreeland. Let me show you what we've organized so far. I think you'll be pleased."

He'd recently reviewed the latest iteration of the World Medical Association's policy statement, the Declaration of Helsinki, concerning the ethical principles for medical research involving human studies. Now he wanted to know: Had they followed the declaration to a T? Yes, Hinks told him. Had they filed all the paperwork disclosing his financial interest with Hutmacher?

"Form 3455, done."

"Well! Great." He followed her to the elevator, up a floor, down a corridor through some security doors that she opened with a code. A stooped man in a thin flannel shirt and jeans caked with cement pushed the blue button on a water cooler in the hallway; a woman in a butterscotch-colored sweater stood behind him. They eyed him timidly, and retreated to a room with a TV screen. "That's the family room," Hinks explained. "Since the volunteers began to arrive, we have some of the families spending all day here, thrilled to take part. Patriots to the bone."

He winced at her word choice, while she opened a cabinet stocked with sterile aprons, masks, and gloves. "Here you go," she said, and together they suited up.

The swinging doors let them through.

A gritty light touched on the ward, beds lined up military style. The cold echo of machinery bounced off the walls, along with the rhythmic hiss of chest cavities rising and falling on ventilators. A sharp whiff of ammonia penetrated his mask. Across the room, a nurse changed an IV bag, while an attendant mopped around a bed, gathering a pile of sheets bundled at the foot.

Paul grabbed the chart off the first footboard he came to. *Flores, Daniel R. Injured by landmine, north of Kabul.* He saw before him a twenty-four-year-old with a youthful hairline and an unblemished brow, missing the eyes, nose, and mouth beneath it. The roots of teeth poked from a band of purple tissue, and a breathing tube disappeared through a hole the size of a Life Saver, secured by a gasket. Where the boy's arms had once been sprouted two fleshy buds, stippled with splinters of bone.

Paul looked at the chart attached to the next bed. *Baker, Jeremiah J. Wounds suffered near Kandahar when his vehicle encountered an improvised explosive device.* The young man's eyes were open, and Paul bent over to make contact. The pupils were nonreactive. The eyes didn't see.

"And we have wonderful volunteers who work with the families, a lot of attention, a lot of hope. It's very uplifting."

"There's very little chance of—" He groped for ground.

"Dr. Vreeland, are you all right?"

Men missing parts of themselves forever, here to bolster his reputation and gain. Paul's throat closed with shame.

"Who volunteered these volunteers?"

"Hartman is the CRO who recruits for us."

"Could you tell me, what is a CRO?"

"Everything here has an acronym, you'll get used to it. The CRO is the Contract Research Organization. They get volunteers and help us package our information for the FDA. Hartman is a little corporate but we've been very happy with them in clinic."

He worried briefly about the hollow and ominous description of this corporate entity, and wanted to sputter *Seropurulent!*, which had been an ironic superlative they used in med school for terrible things that had to be overlooked. (By definition: a mixture of blood and pus.)

"Right. Okay. Have the cadavers arrived?"

"Yes, we have sixty-seven in the locker, and thirty-three arrive later this week. Would you like to see them?"

"No, that's okay. I've seen plenty of cadavers."

"Then let me show you our new MRI room."

They went out through the ward on the other side, to a corridor, where Hinks took him into another room to see the sleek and massive multislice Somatom Definition Flash scanner.

"Excellent." He reached out to pat it.

"Oh, Dr. Vreeland? Is this okay, we only have one technician authorized to operate this machine. So we'll schedule together on that, okay?"

"Fine. Can we take a look at my office?" he asked.

"Of course, come this way."

ARMORY SQUARE, 1865.

As they removed their gowns he peered back through the small window into the ward. The wounded forms in the cots looked no different from those he'd seen in photos of Civil War hospitals; he might as well have been peering through the window at Armory Square or Satterlee. The flag jutted from the wall. History repeats, repeats, repeats. By no means a rabid nationalist, as a schoolkid he'd nevertheless revered the custom of setting his hand on his heart and repeating the Pledge every morning, the ritualized blur of sounds. *Antootherepublicforwitchitstands* . . . These guys who really did stand for the country would never again stand for themselves.

Indivisible. As a kid he thought it was a stuttered *invisible.* And that it referred to the flag itself. Kids making pledges on misunderstandings. He'd thought it meant the flag flew invisibly over all.

THAT AFTERNOON Paul sat in his new office, fighting an unwelcome chill. The room was sensibly furnished with a teak desk and credenza, glass-fronted bookshelves that were empty except for the manuals for the computer and printer still packed in boxes on the floor, and a comfortable black leather chair that swiveled and reclined. Well, he'd reached a new high. He had brought his model schooner that he carried with him from desk to desk, and a picture of Veblen taken in San Francisco, which he removed from his briefcase and set on his bare desk. Her face was so trusting. He hoped he hadn't upset some invisible balance by getting the squirrel trap, for he feared invisible balances lay like booby traps all around him. He loved to fall back into a warm evening in October when they'd pulled off Page Mill Road after a concert at the Almaden Winery and made love in the weeds, and her hair was full of burrs and she didn't care. He thought at one point he'd been bitten by a snake, and he'd jumped up and she'd laughed. She was braver than he was!

All the more this past weekend, when he'd taken her up to the ski lodge at Tahoe to join Hans and the gang he used to hang with in the city—doctors, architects, financiers. He'd introduced her with satisfaction, and there were toasts to the engagement and plenty of lip service to what a hottie she was, but when they found out she wasn't on a notable career path, they seemed unable to synthesize her into their social tableau, as if Paul had chosen a mail-order bride. Having Veblen along changed how he saw them; through the loud meals at a big table in which the conversation seemed all status and swag, Paul found himself hyperconscious of their crass concerns. There was Hans bragging about noteworthy CEOs he'd tweaked houses for, Tim the stockbroker gossiping about his favorite start-ups and upcoming IPOs, Daniel the city planner waxing about a welcome wave of demolition and gentrification south of Market, Lola and Jesse droning about furnishing their new place with everything high-end, until he thought if he heard the word *high-end* one more time he would retch. Hans's wife, Uma, asked Veblen where she invested, and he heard her mumbling something about a checking account, to which Uma replied, "I'd be happy to review your portfolio and see if there's anything I could suggest," whereupon Veblen nodded and backed away, as if being cornered by a wolf.

By the time they said good-bye to everyone, he wondered if he'd ever want to see his old friends again, though Veblen remained cheerful all the way down from the mountains. To prove his loyalty to her, he made fun of Hans and Uma for buying their beautiful three-story Edwardian on Jackson Street in Pacific Heights, then duly gutting the place before moving in so that they had to stay nine months in an apartment, providing them with what could be considered a newlyweds' adventure and many things to complain about, such as their unreliable contractor and the noisy tenants of the building they were renting in. Veblen appreciated that story, or his attitude about it anyway.

He also told her he saw his friends' psychic wounds playing out in all this need for validation, and she seemed to like his analysis too.

True, there were things about Veblen that mystified him—her low-hanging job as a secretary, for one. (It wouldn't seem right, after they married, for her to be a temp. He could support her then, she could look for real jobs, anything she wanted.) And her faith in people! She really believed they'd do their best.

Three large windows looked west to the coastal range, his new horizon. He sat back in his chair and closed his eyes and tried not to start rocking, his default when he was tense. He looked for that flat horizontal line he'd discovered whenever he was in a bad way as a child. With his eyes closed he contemplated the horizontal line as if it were a brilliant sunrise that would light up a terrific new day for him. His muscles relaxed. He brought air down to the bottom of his sternum. He visualized himself not as a weakling but as a dense little torpedo penetrating the bullshit of the world, and that always made him smile.

Good-bye to all he'd escaped. He'd never have fucking duck eggs again, with those bright yellow yolks, he'd have the regular, white, chicken kind, clean on the outside, not caked with green guano. He'd never have smelly beanbag chairs, or any kind of lumpy free-form thing splayed on the ground like a carcass. He'd have heat in his bathroom. He'd never run out of toilet paper, by god, and have to use fucking *leaves*. He'd have toilet paper stacked to the ceiling. He'd keep his place clean, without smoke or the creeping reek of bong juice. Unlike his parents, he'd never throw open-house parties in which guests could arrive any time of the day or night and stay for the rest of their lives. He wouldn't have a guest room, period! He'd make barbed jokes about guests smelling like fish, so any potential guest would get paranoid. He'd never wear anything ethnic as long as he lived, he'd shop strictly at

Brooks Brothers, down to his shorts. He'd invest in stocks and bonds and have a portfolio statement, not some sticky tie-dyed bag full of limp, resinous cash!

LATER IN THE DAY, there was a knock on his office door.

"Come in!"

Through the door came a short young guy with a goatee and heavily framed glasses. He wore baggy shorts revealing thick, shapeless legs.

"James Shalev," he said, shaking Paul's hand. He had a nickel slot between his incisors, which gave him the uncanny appearance of vulnerability and viciousness combined. "Welcome to Greenslopes. I do the VA newsletter and PR, and when you've had a chance to settle in, I'd like to do a profile. Mind if I take a quick shot now?"

Paul blinked in the flash.

Shalev took the extra chair and opened his satchel, to present Paul with a short stack of past newsletters. "Here's what I do. It's actually considered one of the best hospital newsletters in the country."

"Yes, it's impressive," Paul said.

"We've won the Aster four times in the last seven years, honoring excellence in medical marketing. Look, each issue has a theme and variations, but it takes a careful reading to detect it."

"News is marketing?"

Shalev blinked, as if Paul had just emerged from an ancient pod. "Yes, it is."

The cover story was about the art exhibition in the lobby, and went on to list the names of the local artists who had contributed.

On the inside page was an article on the free shuttle bus that operated continuously between Greenslopes and the Palo Alto Caltrain station. There was a picture of the little shuttle bus. The next page had a continuing feature called "Meet Our Specialists." This month's specialist was Dr. Burt Wallman, a psychiatrist who specialized in suicide prevention. Paul restlessly flipped through the pages, not able to detect a theme.

He noted the headline WIDOWS, WIDOWERS HONORED WITH DAFFODILS. It seemed the Daffodil Society of Greenslopes gave symbolic daffodils to the families of vets.

"Did you see it?" asked Shalev.

"See what?"

"You're picking something up. Try to say what it is."

"Man's inhumanity to man?"

"Close. This month's theme is regeneration, starting over, springtime."

Paul said, "Why did you write this? *As one of the leading clinical trials hospitals for veterans, Greenslopes is proud of the wonderful relationship it has forged with widows . . . ?*"

"Nothing wrong with it, is there? Here's your dependent clause headed by your subordinating conjunction—"

"It implies that the clinical trials *create* widows."

Shalev said, "The people in your trial, they're either brain damaged or brain dead, aren't they? But nobody stops hoping."

"Nobody ever said this was about a *cure.*"

"Have you talked to any of the families?" Shalev prodded. "What do they think?"

Shalev gathered the pile into his case. "Someone they love is laid out before them, trapped in an endless sleep. You ever loved someone in a coma?"

Paul shook his head.

"From what I've seen, when someone you love is in a coma, you simply want to believe. As long as they're alive, there's hope." He snapped the latches on his satchel, and adjusted his glasses. "We had a trial in here last year with big funding, they extracted the essence of a tumor, gave it a whirl in a centrifuge, then injected a concentrated dose back into the patient."

"Immune therapy, very cutting edge," Paul said.

"The volunteers went extinct in a matter of weeks. But research-wise, hey, it was a big success. Doctors high-fiving each other all over the place."

To extract more of Paul's essence, they made plans to meet again. And after Shalev left him, Paul gauged he'd been spending too much time in the lab. Bedside manners had never been his strong suit. Maybe he could delegate them.

But the greats knew how to handle their patients. Look at the superstar neurologist Oliver Sacks. Patients adored him, stayed in touch for the rest of their lives. Paul recalled an interview in which Sacks said he loved to find the potential in people who "weren't thought to have any." That noble sentiment had haunted him since. Surely his commitment to medicine showed that he cared in his own way. Was it his job to deal with magical thinking too?

AND THEN TO TASSO STREET. Veblen had that tendency to try to coax some desired outcome from anything he told her, her face as bright as a daffodil, overpowering him with good cheer. She met him at the door and gave him a kiss. "So, how'd it go?"

"We'll see," he said.

"How's your assistant? What's she like?"

"Seems efficient." He went to wash his hands in the sink. His lifelong habit, on the hour. Wash hands. Wash off the world.

"Everything all right?"

Paul grabbed a dish towel and twisted it. "It's probably not fair to hate her for saying 'in clinic,' is it? 'I'll see you in clinic.'"

"She dropped the article? What a bitch."

"Yeah. It sounds clammy and invasive, like she's breathing on my genitals."

Veblen backed off, took two beers from the refrigerator, popped the caps. "She'd better not."

"Thanks." Bottoms up. The beer tasted bitter, and landed heavily in his gut. "It's a lot to absorb. They've had a big response to our call for volunteers."

"That's great, Paul. See? You deserve it."

"The question remains, what 'it' is I deserve." He sighed. "All these caring families are hanging around. It feels like a lot of pressure. I hope I know what I'm doing."

"That must be unnerving. Take one day at a time," Veblen said. "No one expects you to undo the damage of the military industrial complex overnight."

"Ha!" He snorted. "Are you sure?" He finished his bottle. The foam bubbled on his lips, tickling like root beer and first kisses.

4

NOTHING ABOUT YOU
IS BAD

And so, within a few weeks, the visit to Cobb was upon them. *Meet the parents*. A classic rite of passage, inevitable, except that the irregularities of her mother's personality held a certain terror for Veblen. (She reminded herself that all humans were flawed, no family faultless, and whatever happened that day, it was part of *the rich tapestry of life*.) Her mother would surely rise to the occasion this time, wouldn't she? And Paul, who routinely dissected brains, could surely endure her mother too.

The couple set off early on a bright Saturday, skirting the traffic-ensnarled Bay Area heading north, past the minaret-like towers of the oil refineries at Martinez, past the ghost fleet of warships mothballed away in the Carquinez Strait, discussing the myriad future. There were so many things to talk about when one decided to get married, and Paul had waited to share some exciting news.

"Looks as if Cloris Hutmacher has offered us her house for the wedding," he said, his voice crackling mostly with pride, but with an undertone of something else.

He told her he'd seen Cloris that week and announced their engagement. And Cloris had leaped right in. She said, why not her place in May? Small pink Cecile Brunners covered the arbor in May. Every guest could pluck one. The light in May was perfect, the days were long. Her caterer was amazing. Sadly, she wouldn't be there, she'd be away. But wouldn't it be wonderful? And Paul quickly understood that if she weren't there, he wouldn't have to worry about whatever it was that he worried about with his family around. As such, the Hutmacher venue was a feather in his cap, a long pheasant feather, such as those found on the felted hats of Tyrolean yodelers, and as the plucker of it, he wished to be acknowledged as a plucker extraordinaire.

(Which reminded Veblen, as her mind was quick to fly, of her childhood confusion between *peasants* and *pheasants*; it seemed brutal, insane aristocrats brought along "beaters" to sweep through the woods clubbing hedgerows and trees to scare them out and gun them down, which was shocking either way, really, but proved the madness of too much privilege.)

"She sure seems to like you," Veblen said, jealously.

"Purely professional," Paul said, clearing his throat.

"But you know, I was imagining somewhere outside, maybe in the redwoods."

Paul said, "Wouldn't that be kind of funky and messy? Paper plates crumpling in people's laps, nowhere for the older people to sit—we should think of their comfort too. This would be so easy, and it's beautiful there."

"I've never seen it."

"We'll go soon. And it's a real connection for us. It's not some rented gazebo."

Veblen felt strangely unmoved. She didn't know Cloris Hutmacher and didn't want the Hutmacher trademark on their wedding day.

"It's nice she offered," she said at last. "But is May too soon?"

"Not for me," said Paul, and this made Veblen smile with pleasure on the outside, and churn from within. Yet there was something bracing about moving forward fast. One could even believe in fate and unfaltering happiness. "Please acknowledge she's been great to me."

"She knew a good thing when she saw it," Veblen said.

"I guess. But without her connections—"

"You would have made them yourself," she said, stubbornly.

"You are dangerously optimistic." Then added, quickly, "I like that, most of the time."

"When *don't* you like it?"

"Let's see. Did I get phone calls from the Pentagon before I met Cloris? Did I take trips to Washington before I met her? I was puttering around in a lab. I used to wonder what it would have been like if my parents had been part of some inner circle in Washington or New York—what I could have been doing instead."

"But what you're doing is great!"

"Yeah, but I would've gone to an Ivy League school, I'd have connections, I'd have that feeling of entitlement those people have. Instead, I've had to claw every step of the way. Look how hard you've had to work, Veb, you're a temp!"

"Is that bad?"

"Nothing about you is bad. But if we have children, which I hope we will"—he squeezed her hand—"I want them to feel good about themselves from the start."

Veblen wanted a scrappy kid with grit, and said so.

"Come on," Paul said, "haven't you ever felt grateful to someone for helping you?"

Very much so. There was Wickery Krooth, her high school journalism teacher, who covered her contributions with exclamation points, and wrote things like, *Yes! I never thought of it this way! Original! You have a knack for finding just the right word.* She'd kept in touch with him until he retired. And there was Mr. Bix Dahlstrom, a very sweet Norwegian man in a nursing home in Napa who'd been her language buddy; she'd visited him three times a week for two years, holding his cool hands while they talked, until she showed up one day with her notebook and was told some very sad news.

THE MORNING DRIVE abounded with vistas of rolling hills, green only briefly before they'd go golden, ranch land and half-peopled developments spotting the terrain like outbreaks of in-flamed skin. Veblen espoused the Veblenian opinion that wanting a big house full of cheaply produced versions of so-called luxury items was the greatest soul-sucking trap of modern civilization, and that these copycat mansions away from the heart and soul of a city had ensnared their overmortgaged owners—yes, trapped and relocated them like pests.

Discussing the wedding created a perplexing hollow in Veblen. She had picked up a copy of *Brides* magazine since the whole idea came into play; it wanted to fill her mind with wedding souvenirs and makeovers and cake toppers and what she would wear on her head, but none of that stuff captivated her the way she knew it was supposed to, and she wondered if she should make it an actual *goal* to start relating to all the bridal fanfare in a more happy-go-lucky way so she wouldn't miss out on something important. How do you know if you're stubbornly missing out, or if it's just not for you and that's perfectly okay?

It was important for Paul and Albertine to know each other, wasn't it? Yet getting them together the other night had been a failure. They met at the House of Nanking in San Francisco; Albertine arrived in yam-colored clogs and argyle knee socks, her signature look.

"So you two have known each other since high school?" Paul asked, sounding strangely uncharismatic as he peeled the label off his Tsingtao, making a pile of wet paper pills.

Albertine, dipping a plump pot sticker into chili oil, said, "Sixth grade. If I hadn't met Veblen I would've committed suicide," and then chomped the pot sticker in a peculiarly mooselike way.

"Whoa," said Veblen.

"Be prepared, she's a nut," said Albertine.

Paul didn't like having his betrothed described so knowingly, Veblen could tell. Then Albertine led Paul into telling about his school days and the pot growers and narcs surrounding him. It seemed to be going well enough. It was a funny world up there where people lived off the grid and paid for everything in cash. Was it criminal or simply the pioneer spirit? They segued into malfeasance in the medical field, and Paul proceeded to describe the difference between idiocy and evil. Idiocy was the family doctor in Placer County who double-dipped a syringe into a large bottle of Propofol and contaminated it with hepatitis C, only to go on and infect dozens of people from this bottle. Evil was the internist in Palm Springs who stole organs during laparoscopic surgeries on elderly patients and sold them on the black market. It was estimated that he had made off with hundreds of kidneys, lobes of livers, sections of intestine, and even entire lungs before anyone caught on.

"Know thyself. Don't take up space in a medical program if you haven't dealt with your issues," said Albertine, and Paul sat up straighter.

Then Paul said, "Am I right in thinking that in Jungian analysis, most of the training is spent on the *self*?"

"It's too bad doctors don't have that kind of training," Albertine said, pointedly.

Then on the way home that evening, Paul shocked Veblen by imitating Albertine in a pinched, nasal voice. *"We went to school together. We are two wild and crazy girls. We love to wear our big heavy clogs and act crazy in the moonlight."*

"Stop it!" Veblen cried out.

"I'm kidding," Paul said. "How could I say anything after exposing you to Hans?"

Which led Veblen to realize these friendships were based on a phenotype exchange that occurred only with childhood friends, in which they were simply part of you forever, for better or worse. Veblen had been assigned to the tall, gawky new girl in sixth grade as her Welcome Buddy. In the first few days of their mandated buddy-hood, a boy on the playground was stung by a bee and his foot swelled up like a gangplank. Veblen made an observation about elephantiasis, to which Albertine said, "What's that?"

"Haven't you heard of elephantiasis?"

"Why would I? I can't read your mind."

"Well, it's a horrible disease from parasites that makes your body parts look thick and stumpy, like elephant legs," Veblen pronounced.

"Ha ha ha."

"It's not funny, it's very painful."

"You're trying to humiliate me so you can have the power."

Veblen was intrigued by the girl's reasoning, as comfortably skewed as her mother's. "What do you mean?"

"You're testing to see if I can be manipulated," Albertine declared, pushing her wire frames up her nose.

"I swear, there's such a thing," young Veblen declared, all at once appreciating how elephantiasis could sound as made up as *tigerrhea* or *hippopotomania*. They went to the school library and found the disease in the encyclopedia; the new girl shrugged her broom of blond hair and walked off. Veblen refused to believe in the girl's indifference.

The next day she brought one of her mother's medical journals to school, an issue chronicling a recent outbreak of elephantiasis in Indonesia. As Veblen calculated, the new girl seemed touched by Veblen's passion to lift her up on the subject of tropical illness. Not only that, but they discovered their shared inclination to laugh in the face of bizarre and horrible realities they were spared by a twentieth-century California childhood, and they'd been best friends ever since. Almost eighteen years!

STILL, broad-spectrum uneasiness led to a long lunchtime conversation outside the hospital with Albertine only yesterday.

"Why didn't you like him?" Veblen wanted to know.

"So you're having doubts."

"No, but even if I were, it's normal, right?"

Albertine, who specialized in doubts, who pointed out the shadow side of human nature at every turn, who swore allegiance to ambivalence and ambiguity, whose favorite color was gray, sounded concerned. "What kind of doubts?"

"No, you're supposed to say '*Of course! Everyone feels that way!*'"

"I don't have enough information. Maybe you should listen to your doubts this time."

"Listen to my doubts?"

Albertine described a vitamin salesman from San Bruno she'd doubted a few times before finding out he was a meth freak. Another recent doubt was over a gambling landscaper from Marin. Veblen sensed a note of triumph in Albertine when she described her apperception of the man's flaws.

"Is it possible you wouldn't like anybody I liked, just because?"

"I could see the possibilities. He's really nice looking, and he's not as alpha as he wants you to think."

Veblen tried to explain her mild feeling of doom, how it was like there was some kind of terrible alchemy under way, how it was like she was rushing toward a disaster, and how it didn't make sense because she was also excited and happy.

"Just be sure it's not a growing awareness that Paul's all wrong for you and will ruin your life," Albertine said, and then asked: "Have you read *Marriage: Dead or Alive?*"

Veblen said no.

"It's the magnum opus of Adolf Guggenbühl-Craig. He says marriage is a continuous inevitable confrontation that can be resolved only through death."

"How great! Does it have to be that way?" pleaded Veblen, feeling worse than ever. "I've already had a continuous confrontation that can be resolved only through death, with my mother."

"Exactly. All the more reason you're projecting impossible romantic fantasies onto Paul."

"Who the heck is Adolf Guggenbühl-Craig?" Veblen snarled.

As her friend told her more about the brilliant Jungian and the ponderous message of *Marriage: Dead or Alive* ("That a decent, responsible society not only allows, but actually encourages, young people in their complete ignorance to bind themselves permanently to the psychological problems which their vows entail, seems incomprehensible. The more life expectancy increases, the more grotesque this situation becomes. . . ."), Veblen began to see how ill-equipped she was to hack out a life with someone. Anyone! She'd end up bossing him around like her mother or grinding up his stuff in a wood chipper like her grandmother. Not for her. No way!

She'd been with Paul for about four months, without much of a misunderstanding. Her unvoiced needs were in remission, and Paul was impressively constant. Sure, there had been minor disagreements, moments pinched by disappointment over how to treat squirrels or value material possessions, but overall, she felt that Paul fit her romantic ideal as a man and avatar in the world. She found new things to love about him all the time: the way he always, always dropped his wallet when he pulled it from his pocket; the way he made fires in her tiny fireplace, blowing on scraps of wood and pinecones he gathered on walks; the warm smell of his head; the way he was generous and he'd bring beer or wine or cookies to her house whenever he came; how he'd help her with any chore that needed doing; the way he read the paper every morning, completely absorbed; the way he pored through military histories, biographies of generals, and epics about the sea—hearty, manly tales of bravery and adventure. He agreed it was good to avoid grocery carts with wadded tissues in them. He loved tacos as much as she did. If she sneezed, he'd laugh and say she sneezed like a cat. He took her to classical music concerts and knew all about the composers and the works. When she said she couldn't go out to a movie or a concert because she had to meet a deadline for the Diaspora Project, he didn't make a word of complaint.

Look at how tiny their troubles were! One recent evening the winds came barreling through the Golden Gate, down the peninsula from the north, unusually frigid and fierce, tearing flowers from their stems, clearing dead wood from the treetops, and then it hailed. Ice pellets scarred fresh young leaves and made drifts under the rain gutters, and children ran outside to gather them, and screamed in surprise when they discovered how they froze their hands. It was a night for comfort food, and Veblen prepared turkey meatballs for dinner, well seasoned with rosemary and sage, under a tangy homemade *ragù*, along with artichoke risotto and a salad, but when she mentioned she'd used turkey he blanched, as if she'd revealed she'd made them with grasshoppers or grubs. During the meal, he appeared to devour what was on his plate so fast he had to go to the kitchen several times to get more.

"Mmm, delicious," he kept saying. "Turkey balls rule."

"Not bad," Veblen said.

"But let's not have them too often, though, or else they'll lose their impact."

"Okay," said Veblen.

Later that evening, as she was cleaning up, she opened the trash container, and sitting on top, almost in rows as if arranged for viewing, were the turkey balls Paul pretended to have consumed. She started to laugh and asked why he didn't say something. "Alternately, you could have hidden them better, and I never would have known."

He said he was sorry, that he hadn't wanted to spoil dinner.

"But you wanted me to find them later?"

"Mmm. I meant to come back and cover them. I spaced out. Sorry."

The passive-aggressive lapse seemed duplicitously boyish and charming, but Albertine had been quick to tell her it was a missed opportunity for *individuation*.

After all, it was unrealistic to expect Paul to be her twin, to think they would react the same way in every situation, always be in the same mood, though there was no denying she craved that. She must withstand all differences, no matter how wrenching and painful. For instance, Paul didn't like corn on the cob. Of all things! How could a person not like fresh, delicious corn on the cob? And how could she not care?

"I don't like biting the cob and the kernels taste pasty to me," Paul had told her.

"*Pasty?* Then you've had really bad corn. Good corn isn't pasty."

"Don't get mad. It's not like corn is your personal invention."

"But it's impossible. Everyone likes it."

"People with dentures don't like it."

"What are you trying to say? Do you have dentures?"

"No! I'm just saying they are a sizable slice of the population."

"Not anymore. These days most people get implants."

"Not in rural areas."

"Okay, fine, whatever! But eating corn together, we'll never be able to do that?"

"I like other vegetables!" Paul practically yelled.

"Corn is more than a vegetable, it's practically a national icon."

"I'm unpatriotic now?"

"If you don't like corn, it means I'll probably stop making it. We won't go on hunts for the best corn stands in summer, driving all over until we find them. You won't be motivated to shuck it for me. The sound of me gnawing on it will annoy you, so I'll stop having it. It'll gradually become a thing of my past, phased out for good." Veblen was almost ready to cry, and she had reason. Anything and everything her mother disliked had been phased out of her life for good.

"So it's me or the corn?"

Then she snapped out of it, and they laughed about it, and she came to understand that this recognition of otherness would occur over and over until death they did part, that she couldn't despair every time it occurred, and that anyway, Paul wasn't a dictator like her mother . . . yet it was clear that your choice of mate would shape the rest of your life in ways you couldn't begin to know. One by one, things he didn't like would be jettisoned. First squirrels, then turkey meatballs, then corn, then—what next? Marriage could be a continuing exercise in disappearances.

No time to think about this now, for they had reached the long driveway of Veblen's childhood home, the handle of the hammer, flanked by elephant-sized hummocks of blackberry vines, where Veblen used to pick berries by the gallon to make pies and cobblers and jam. She'd sell them at a table by the road, and help her mother make ends meet. In the fall she put on leather gloves to her elbows to hack the vines back off the driveway, uncovering snakes and lizards and voles. In the spring the vines would start to come back, the green canes growing noticeably by the day, rising straight like spindles before gravity caused them to arc. They grew on the surface the way roots grow underground, in all directions, overlapping, intertwined. The blackberries defined her life in those days—their encroaching threat, their abundant yield. All her old chores came to mind as they rolled up the drive to the familiar crunching of the tires on gravel.

"I never would've imagined you growing up somewhere like this," Paul announced.

"Really?"

"Really."

No time to think about this either, for Veblen saw her mother advancing out of the house in her best pantsuit, an aqua-colored Thai silk number beneath which new (as in twenty-five years old but saved in the original box for special occasions) Dr. Scholl's white sandals flashed. She wore them with wool socks. Linus too came out coiffed and ironed, in a blue oxford shirt. They appeared normal, attractive, almost vigorous.

Yet how stiff and formal Veblen's mother's posture was, and how tall she stood! She had nearly six inches on her daughter.

Maybe everything would be fine!

"You must be Dr. Paul Vreeland," her mother said, in a formal style of elocution heard mostly on stage. "Melanie Duffy."

"Linus Duffy," said Linus, joining in the hand-grasping ritual.

"We have prepared a nice light lunch to eat outside. Paul, if you would be so kind as to help Linus move the table into the sunshine, we'll sit right away."

The men took off behind the house, as the women went inside. Veblen smiled. "Mom, you look pretty."

"I'm absolutely miserable," her mother said, with the men out of earshot. "My shoulders are buckling under the straps of this bra, and my neck is already ruined. I never wear a bra anymore. I despise my breasts. They're boulders. The nerve of god to do this to women! I'm going to be flat on my back with ice as soon as you leave."

"You don't have to wear a bra for our benefit. Take it off. Be yourself."

"No man wants to see a woman with her breasts hanging down to her navel."

"Take the straps off your shoulders, then."

"I'll try that."

"I love your suit."

"Paul's very good-looking," her mother said. "But I haven't sensed the chemistry yet."

"We've been here for five minutes."

"I hope he's not in love with himself," Melanie said. "Oh, good lord."

Melanie was looking at the ring. They both started to laugh.

"Don't hold it against me," Veblen said.

"What was he thinking?" Melanie said. "It's not you at all."

"Yeah, I'm trying to get used to it."

"It's the ring of a kept woman. Come in the kitchen, I need your help."

The oatmeal-colored tiles, the chicken-headed canisters, the wall-mounted hand-crank can opener over the sink, gears and magnet always mysteriously greasy, all were in place as they had been for years, and Veblen was proud of her mother's artwork on the walls around the table—the abstracts in oil and pastels, of landforms and waterways and rocks, sure-handed and dreamy. She sniffed the scent of linseed oil, and from the cupboards a trace of molasses.

Her mother removed a casserole dish from the oven, her hot mitts clenched around it. "This is a delicious recipe I discovered recently using artichoke hearts and bread crusts and just a little Asiago cheese and butter," her mother said. "Very special."

"Nice." Veblen cracked open a head of red leaf lettuce. Her favorite part was the center of baby leaves, and she removed it quickly before her mother could see and ate it.

"Before I forget, I have a strange lump on the back of my neck. Will you look at it, please? Linus doesn't have an eye for this sort of thing."

"How about later after we're out of the kitchen?"

"Now!" her mother said.

Veblen placed the lettuce on the counter, and parted her mother's hair with her wet hands. She saw a dime-sized swelling. "Yes, you have a little bump here, does it itch?"

"No. Is it red?"

"Pinkish."

"Is it indurated?"

"What's that?"

"Is it hard, with clearly defined margins?" asked her mother.

Veblen squinted at the bump. "You tell me."

"Is the texture *peau d'orange*?"

"What's that!" Veblen asked, exasperated.

"The texture of orange peel."

Veblen squinted again. "I'd say it's more like the skin of an apple, or maybe a pear. Maybe Paul can look at it," she said, sighing.

"As long as he doesn't talk down to me, that's all I ask," her mother said.

Veblen finished making the salad and brought it out like a victim. Linus had furnished Paul with a beer.

"Local brew, one of those designer jobs," said Linus.

"I taste some lemon," Paul said, nodding.

"We make our own blackberry wine on good years."

"How is it?"

"Sweet, nice for a dessert wine. We end up with thirty bottles or so, give them to friends. I'll send one home with you."

"Great," Paul said. "Love dessert wine, especially with some nice Gruyère."

"I like it with pie."

"Luncheon is served," called Melanie, bringing out the casserole and placing it on a woven Samoan mat on the table. "Paul, I want you here. Veblen, at the head. Linus, would you open that special bottle of champagne?"

"Right," said Linus, returning to the kitchen.

"No, out here!" Melanie yelled. "Watching the cork fly is festive."

Linus shuffled back with the bottle, untwisting the wires around the cork.

"Don't aim it at us!" Melanie cried.

"It's not ready yet."

"You're aiming it at us!"

Linus turned toward the house.

"Not at the wall! We want to watch the cork fly! Turn around."

Linus turned and began to wiggle the cork.

"Wait, you need a cloth."

Veblen handed him a napkin to put under the neck of the bottle. Paul tapped his fork on the table. The cork popped, and shot all of about three feet.

"Bravo!" Melanie cried. "Now, let's make a toast to your visit. May there be many more!"

Glasses clinked and Paul and Veblen smiled at each other across the table. If Paul were gracious about this day, she'd love him forever.

"Paul, we're certainly impressed by your research project," Melanie said. "I imagine you're already heavily involved, preparing to dig in?"

"Absolutely," Paul said. "I'm getting a lot of support from Hutmacher, basically anything I want. We're going to get off to a good start."

"There's got to be a bucket load of red tape for those babies," said Linus.

"More than I realized," Paul said.

"Several of my medications are made by Hutmacher," Melanie added.

"Hurrah!" Paul said gamely, raising his glass.

"And Veblen tells us you've been looking at houses?"

"Oh. That's kind of a hobby. Looking. I was pretty much raised on a commune, by the way."

"Are you planning to have a commune?"

"No, the opposite, I want to live behind a gate that no one can get through."

"You've got to escape the way you were raised," Linus said. "Boy, do I know it."

"I just want you to know that Veblen is going to be living in comfortable surroundings," Paul said.

Melanie said, "Well, Veblen, you'll really have surpassed me. I don't know if Veblen has mentioned it, but I'm very interested in medical matters, having a complicated history myself. You can never be too prepared when dealing with the health care system, wouldn't you agree?"

"That's right. Patients really need to advocate for themselves these days," Paul said.

"That's a refreshing attitude."

"I know you'll find it difficult to believe, but most doctors feel that way."

Veblen's mother dished out steaming mounds of her creation. "I've received atrociously condescending treatment over my recent migraine business," she said. "It's a wonder cads like these stay in practice."

"What seems to be the nature of the condition?" Paul asked, and Veblen's dread distributed itself through her limbs.

"Well, starting four years ago, just after my yearly flu shot, I experienced an array of symptoms ascribed to migraine equivalence or transient ischemia. Obviously, and as you know, many known foods and chemicals precipitate the condition."

"Absolutely," Paul said. "Sodium benzoate, cyclamates, chocolate, corn—"

"Peas, pork, lamb, citrus, onion, wheat, pears, the list goes on. Symptoms of mine have included imagery, hypothermia, aphasia, a feeling of rotating. Further, I've had facial paralysis, paralysis of the upper limbs, and narcolepsy. I don't believe this fits in the typical migraine profile."

"Well, I wouldn't call it typical," Paul said, hesitantly.

"Now, I have learned in time that a middle-aged woman with unusual symptoms can easily be labeled a crackpot, a psychosomatic case, a malingerer. Further, my general physician recently told me I'm 'too observant.' How can I agree with that? If not me, who, then?"

Veblen was breathing rapidly.

Paul looked at Veblen and said, "Yes, patients need to be proactive."

"I can't tell you how pleased I am to hear a doctor say that!"

"Now, the cause could be nonorganic—" Paul began.

Veblen winced.

"Nonorganic? Psychosomatic, is that what you're saying?"

"No, not in that sense—"

"What do you mean? If a migraine falls outside their specialty, many physicians don't realize that it is no longer considered psychosomatic."

Veblen said, woodenly, "Mom, let's eat."

"I can't speak for 'many physicians,'" Paul said, "but I'm a neurologist and—" He stopped abruptly to sip his champagne, temples pulsating. His jaw was seizing like a tractor, and Veblen's stomach ached. "You sound like you know more about it than I do," he said, mildly.

Perfect answer!

"That's very likely true, which is a sad story in itself. I have this central stationary scotoma when in hot or warm showers, and with exercise. I see a blur, followed by an irregular opaque gray area. Rest restores normal sight. But if I walk on a cold day, the central scotoma is lighted and nonmoving."

"Interesting," Paul said.

"Oh, another piece of the puzzle!" Melanie exclaimed, almost gaily. "Two years ago, I found an area on my chest that was *dead*—numb without feeling. Located right here—" She pointed to an area at the top of her left breast. "It was about five by five centimeters. That large! It remained dead until about six months ago, when suddenly . . . Remember, Linus, I realized that my dead spot had feeling again. Is that related?"

"Mmm. Could be," Paul said.

With that, Melanie swiveled in her chair and reached for a few typed sheets of paper that had been stapled together, hidden behind a ceramic bowl full of miniature pinecones.

"This is a complete list of my medical history," she announced.

Paul looked surprised. "My, arranged almost like a CV!" he said.

"You don't need to ridicule me," Melanie said, making Veblen jump up and retreat into the kitchen, breathing short and fast. She bit her forearm so hard she left teeth marks in it.

The risks had been known. She returned outside.

"No, not at all, I think everyone should have one." Paul was scanning the first page. "Measles, scarlet fever, tick fever, tonsillectomy, appendectomy, and histoplasmosis, all before you were fifteen?"

"That's right."

"Mmmm." He continued. "Possible exposure to gamma radiation from a Nevada test site?"

"Yes, it's well documented. I was part of a class action suit."

"Mmmm. Thyroidectomy for papillary and follicular carcinoma, I-131 ablation—neck injury, acute degenerative arthritis of neck resultant . . . pancreatic insufficiency—how did you become aware of that?"

"I had tests! How else would someone become aware of it, through a crystal ball?"

"Ciguatera poisoning, with permanent irreversible anticholinesterase?"

"Yes. I assume you know what that is?"

"I do, though in all my years in medicine I have yet to hear of anyone with this condition."

"What do you mean by that?"

"Nothing, just that it's rare. Let's see, then atrial fib, tetany, transient Cushing, psoriasis, double vision, empty sella, secondary hyperparathyroidism, primary aldosteronism—" Paul stopped reading. "Well. Very complicated. Very—impressive."

Linus sat entirely still, clasping his hands together, as if praying.

"I'm thinking there's an eye test you could have, but it must be performed when the scotoma is present," Paul offered.

"But it *is* present," Melanie cried. "I told you, it's right here, right now."

Paul's voice was pinched. "Yes, you've had a complicated history of vasomotor instability with severe neurological manifestations, including paralysis and ocular difficulties, haven't you?"

"Exactly."

"Well, then, I will write down the name of this test, and I suggest you ask your doctor about it."

"I see. I see exactly." Melanie smacked her lips and rose from the table, with the imperious and sullen bearing Veblen ascribed to Napoleon departing for Elba.

Veblen and Paul and Linus remained, in punishing silence. An intonation, an insufficiency of deference, or the way Paul's lips looked slightly pursed as he read—something had inevitably gone wrong. Linus twisted his napkin and tossed it onto his plate. "Excuse me a moment, folks," he said, getting up and following his wife.

"Oh, man," Veblen said.

Paul glared at her. "What the hell?"

Veblen looked sidelong into the house. No wonder translation came naturally to her. In the past, when her mother yelled at someone in a public place and ran away, Veblen would swallow her shame and go up to the person who had been yelled at and say, "I'm sorry. What she was really saying was that she's not feeling well and that when you took her parking place, she felt like you didn't care." When her mother yelled at someone in a restaurant and stomped out, Veblen would remain behind a moment and tell the waiter, "What my mother meant was that being corrected on what type of salad dressing to order reminded her of being scolded all the time by her mother, who was really mean."

"What she's really saying—" Veblen stopped. What was she really saying? "She reaches this point of certainty that new people won't like her and then she kind of freaks, but it's temporary."

"Oh. Wow."

"You're doing great," whispered Veblen. "Really great. It's going to be fine."

She reached across the table for his hand, squeezed it. She'd brought a boyfriend home only once before, resulting in the flash incineration of his male pride and a near immediate breakup.

Linus appeared. "Veblen?" With unnatural cheer and strained, clasped hands he said, "Would you go in and talk to your mother? You are so good with her."

She excused herself from the table and went inside, scared that Paul might be wearing thin with less than an hour of exposure. This pattern, of going into her mother's room and sitting on the edge of her bed in the middle of the day, had been going on since Veblen was a young girl. She thought back to all the times she sat starboard of her mother after bringing in a heating pad or an ice pack or little bouquets of dandelions and alyssum.

"Mom?" she said, at her mother's door.

"Come in here," her mother said, from beneath the covers. "Sit down."

"You okay?"

"No, I'm not."

"What happened?"

"That man is a complete narcissist."

Veblen counted to ten, her usual restraint. "Why are you saying that?"

"He wouldn't look me in the eye. He barely noticed you at all. He only hears the sound of his own voice." Her mother thrashed as if trying to annihilate a small creature in the bed.

Veblen swallowed, having none of it. She caressed her mother's arm through the blanket and spoke gently. "Mom, you know what? He's been nervous about meeting you, and you know why?

Because he knows how important you are to me. He wants to make a good impression."

"He didn't." Her mother coughed, slowing down.

"He's really sweet, actually. You'll see when you get to know him better."

"I want you to tell me how that man's sweet."

"He fell in love with me the first time we met."

"That's not a feat, Veblen. You're very lovable."

"People often don't get me, and Paul does."

"How dare you say that! You are a beautiful, sweet, smart girl." She began to sniffle. "How have I failed? Where have I gone wrong?"

"Mom! Stop it. Please!" She continued to pat her mother's whale-like hip.

"My beautiful girl is going to marry a narcissistic prig?"

"I beg you to stop talking about him that way, and be patient and just get to know him."

Her mother sniffled awhile. "Life is more than big houses and garish diamonds."

"Of course. Did you really want him to prescribe the test himself? Is that what upset you?"

"No. That wouldn't be appropriate. But he might have offered at least."

"That would be stepping over the line for him, wouldn't it?"

"No one ever steps over the line for me, and that's how it's been all my life. Will you help me up, Veblen? My back is in a spasm."

Veblen pulled. Her mother rose to her feet and stalked into the bathroom. When she came out she'd put on some fresh lipstick and styled her hair.

"I'm only doing this for you," she said. "Nothing else would impel me to spend another second with that man."

"Come on, it's okay." No use getting mad, making things worse. Veblen's words were cloaked in her gentlest voice, her hardy optimism, her subtle sorcery. All her mother was trying to say was that she was afraid of change.

VEBLEN HAD BROUGHT so few people here. In the living room she beheld the walls covered in bookshelves, crammed with more volumes than they could properly hold, for both her mother and Linus had many interests and were voracious readers, as well as collectors of rare and lugubrious artifacts such as masks from New Guinea and ceremonial headdresses from Fiji and Aboriginal weapons from Australia and so on. Further, Melanie was unduly influenced by the Pre-Raphaelite William Morris, and scorned store-bought furniture. She and Linus had made the sofa themselves, out of long walnut planks and foam cushions cut to the right shape and covered with an orange burlap fabric, without caring how uncomfortable it was and that no one liked to sit on it. The only factory-produced thing in the room was the old upright piano, on which Linus could play anything by ear in the unlikely key of F-sharp major, and which was flanked by an enormous collection of LPs on a heavy mahogany shelf, stacked with scores of great choral works that he liked to sing, basso profundo.

The Veblen collection sat on the top shelf, still radiating "redemptive truth and moral splendor." That's how Richard Rorty described the special books on his own parents' shelves, and Veblen couldn't have said it better about the power these books had on her in her youth. The collection consisted of at least sixty volumes, made up of anything by or to do with Veblen. Melanie's incomplete PhD dissertation, not officially bound but in a regular notebook, was the end piece. All of that energy for Mr. Veblen in due course siphoning into her daughter, Veblen.

Linus was now showing Paul his collection of fossils and arrowheads. Paul was nodding politely. "This one I found in Utah, just outside Moab, sticking out of the red soil like a thumb."

"Nice," Paul said.

"I had a beauty, seven-tiered, about eight inches long, red jasper, and I made the mistake of turning it over to the Natural History Museum in Los Angeles. Well, they have a warehouse, and they cataloged it, and it disappeared, never to be seen again. Never displayed the thing. I wish I'd kept it."

"Well, don't blame the institution. It's a repository of artifacts, and, even so, it adds to the body of knowledge. It was a good contribution," Paul said.

"I don't suppose I could entice you to help us with a chore, Paul," Melanie interrupted, "with some Key lime pie as a reward?"

"What chore?" Veblen asked, suspiciously.

"Well, last winter, a full year ago, we had that massive storm that ripped the roof off our chicken house, which I want to use as a studio, and the roof flew down into the ravine. I can't go down there because of my ankles. But Linus could easily bring it up if he had the help of a strong fellow like Paul."

"Don't say that around my dad," Paul said. "He'll give you a list of chores I'd mess up owing to my supposed laziness. Where is it?"

Linus said, "Come on, Melanie, that's a terrible job. We don't want to subject Paul to that."

"It's in the ravine?" Paul asked.

"At the very bottom. Past the still."

This was a mysterious rusted hulk they had discovered down there years before, deciding it had to be an old moonshiner's still.

"Let's take a look," Paul said.

They moved outside. Lake County was coming up in the world, and to the north one could see newly planted vineyards ringing the hills across the valley. On site the land dropped off sharply around the hammerhead, giving way to the gnarled thicket of blackberry brambles, twelve feet deep in some places, harsh and naked in winter, like a farm of cat-o'-nine-tails. Somewhere below lay the tin roof.

"We've got overalls," said Linus. "It's not that heavy, but the shape's awkward."

"Gloves?" Paul requested, as if asking for a scalpel.

"Good leather gloves."

"Hmm. What about boots?"

"I'm a size thirteen," said Linus.

"Better big than small."

"Are you sure?" Veblen faltered. Her mother's gall affronted, and yet she was deeply gratified that Paul was rising to the occasion, and strangely, his affability made her feel loved.

"I'll get the gear," Linus said.

Paul followed him inside and emerged shortly in mechanic's overalls, the big paint-stained boots, the heavy gloves. Linus came next, in his version of the same outfit. "The path starts over here,"

Linus said. He held two machetes and some clippers and handed one of each to Paul. "Just hack away."

"All right, let's do it," Paul said.

"Thataway!" said Linus.

The men began to fight and hack through the brambles. Veblen watched Paul trying to free his sleeve from a rack of thorns.

Her mother murmured, "This is a very good sign."

They went back inside, and Veblen's mother lay down on the couch.

"That job's about the worst you could have cooked up," Veblen complained.

"Paul is an able-bodied man. He should be able to help his future father-in-law with this. So what are you going to wear for the wedding?"

"Wait here." Veblen retrieved her purse and removed a picture of a dress she'd printed. Talking about clothes, they always got along. "Something like this."

"Beautiful!" said her mother, examining the picture. "Very simple and elegant."

"I'm going to make it myself, I think," Veblen said, deciding right then.

"Yes, you could copy the pattern easily. It's cut on the bias and it's very flattering." With a sudden burst of energy Melanie jumped up, taking Veblen back into the bedroom to her closet. "I might wear this." She showed her a midnight blue silk dress.

"Very nice! Where did you get it?"

"That estate sale I told you about. And over here are the things I found for you. I want a fashion show."

A heap of discarded garments, which Melanie believed to be diamonds in the rough, and therefore evidence of her superior skills in the gem fields of garage sales and the Rescue Squad Thrift Store, sat on the chair in the corner. "Wow," said Veblen. She began to sort through the items, which appeared to have belonged to an aging society woman in the 1970s. Lots of prints and polyester. "Funky."

"That's Coco Chanel. See how the pockets are sewn closed?"

"Yep."

"Finely tailored items arrive with the pockets sewn closed. I'm sorry our budget didn't allow you to experience that. You can open them gently with the seam ripper I gave you."

"Okay."

"You still have the seam ripper I gave you?"

"It's in my sewing stuff."

"That's a very expensive Swiss seam ripper. Be careful, it's sharp."

"I know, Mom." Veblen paused the appropriate number of seconds necessary for Melanie to feel appreciated.

Melanie pointed to a pantsuit with a waist sash, a bright green Marimekko cotton print. "Try that. With your shoulders, it'll look smashing on you."

Veblen sat on the edge of the bed, removed her shoes and socks, and dutifully unzipped her jeans. This seemed to be one of her mother's only joys, so how could she refuse? Her mother said, "Veblen, haven't I told you to shave the hairs off your toes? Toe hairs are very unattractive."

Veblen looked down at her feet. "Where?"

"On the first joint of your big toes. There."

Veblen doubled over and detected a few blondish hairs she'd never noticed before. "So?"

"I'm remembering one of the last things my grandmother told me before she died, oddly," Melanie said.

"What do you mean?" Veblen slipped on the pants part of the Marimekko pantsuit, but the cut was very matronly, the way the top of the pants went over her hips. She continued with the masquerade, familiar with the routine of thanking her mother profusely, then stuffing the clothes in the back of her closet when she got home or tamping them into a plastic bag and kicking the bag like a football into a Goodwill bin.

"She had opinions."

"What other great advice did she have?"

"She's the one who taught me how to cook, the right way to cut each vegetable, and she was interested in civic matters. Very practical, after her first husband died so young. Thought a woman should accept an imperfect marriage."

"What's perfect anyway," Veblen said.

"No!" Melanie cried. "You're too young to think that. If you don't think Paul's perfect, don't marry him. You don't have to marry at all, for that matter."

"That's not what I mean. Nothing's perfect. Is your marriage to Linus perfect?"

"I'm very lucky to have him."

"But *perfect*?"

"Her point was that you make a choice and stick with it. That you make a silk purse from a sow's ear. She gave me a lot of grief when I left Rudgear. She had no idea that any meeting of the minds was impossible. You see, in her day, matches that bad didn't happen unless youths were foolish and unsupervised. You will never hear that kind of advice from me. When is this event happening?"

"We haven't decided yet."

"What does Albertine think of him?"

"Um, still getting to know him."

"What are his friends like? Do you like them?"

"They're fine," Veblen said curtly.

"What about your ideals? Do you share the same ideals? That's crucial!"

"I think so."

"You'd better be sure. There's nothing worse. I've never changed my values or principles for any man."

"That's really cool, Mom. I admire you for that. I've always said that."

"In the end, that's all you have."

"I get it."

"That ring really doesn't seem like you," her mother observed.

Veblen sighed. "It's a little big," she said, though she'd been happy to have someone err on the side of surplus for her.

"I hope it doesn't represent Paul's values," her mother said. "And what about your career? Are you happy with it?"

"It's fine for now," Veblen said.

"Are you ever going to be paid for your translation work?"

"That's not the point, at least not now. I feel lucky I get to do it," Veblen asserted.

"Maybe you could translate for someone else too, someone who treats you like a professional."

"The only thing I wish is that I'd gone and lived in Norway for a while. Then I'd be fluent."

Possibly feeling guilty over standing in Veblen's way years back, Melanie changed the subject. "Well, what about that other idea, about starting your own magazine?"

"Yeah, I still think about that."

"I would love to advise with the design."

"You would?"

"I think helping you would be thrilling. We'd have so much fun collaborating."

They chatted amiably then, Veblen in her ill-fitting pantsuit bouncing a few ideas off her mother and nestling into the curve at her hip, just as she had a thousand times, viewing the glass of water at the ready for pills, the corroding gooseneck lamp, the large oak chest of drawers filled with her mother's mysterious things. For some reason the chest always reminded Veblen of a long ago moment when she glimpsed her mother's underarm as she set about applying some kind of cream from a jar. The armpit was a hitherto unknown landscape of fleshiness and stubble, and it struck Veblen as an armpit so vast and cavernous it could smuggle a pup. She'd been relieved when the arm came down and the armpit receded from sight, though, alas, not from memory.

The afternoon sun streamed past the chest in motey beams, unbroken except for a dark silhouette in the unexpected shape of a squirrel.

"Oh my god, Mom, look!"

Her mother lifted her head. "Scram!" She clapped her hands together.

"Why should it scram?"

"Why is it staring in the window?"

Veblen rose and felt a spike of adrenaline, a jab, as the squirrel leaped off the sill.

"It's checking in."

Her mother sat up. "Veblen, come here. Right now."

But Veblen moved to the window.

"Mom, I'll be right back." And she took off after the squirrel, despite her mother's calls.

Out the door, she searched for her ally, arms to the sun.

The cottonwoods shivered up an arm of the ravine, the grasses whispered. A hawk circled in the upper reaches of the sky. And all else was quiet, even the sound of Paul and Linus hacking with their machetes was faint. She scanned the trees around the house, starting with the gnarled, arthritic crab apple. There was a lot of dead wood covered in pale olive lichen. Then the old plums, the cedar, and the handsome, muscular madrone. Hours of her young life had been spent out here, busy mixing up potions or else very still, watching sunlight filter through the trees, or storms coming in across the hills, and graying everywhere, and the clip of birds dipping from tree to tree. Beetles and dark jelly newts had lived under the rotting logs by the chicken house. On some days a thousand robins would alight in the treetops for an hour, then leave in a great upward rush. Toadstools popped up in moist corners in the rainy months, and somewhere in the ravines was a plant with cotton-winged seeds that took flight through the air in unexpected spirals. A fox used to peek up at her, ears spry and soft, and wild boars came rumbling through in packs, and lone bobcats, and, once in a while, a wild mule.

At the madrone she heard a noise, and spun around.

"Come out! Are you here?"

The land was flanked on the western side by short hills. Wind liked to race over the crest of those hills, gaining speed as it swept over them, and it was not surprising that the roof of the chicken house flew the coop. She used to watch the heavy sunflower heads banging in the wind. Try whistling when it's windy. The grass waving, the burrs flying, the foxtail so affectionate to your socks. You could spin until you lost your compass. You could pull together thinking: *This is only the beginning. One day it'll come around.* She believed it, that she would one day find her way. Her ears would prick to the sound of it coming on the wind.

Was it arrogant to think a squirrel was following you around? Or to think your parents cared about you?

And yet—with those well-marked whiskers, and that topcoat, and the notable scruff, a squirrel who cared and followed you everywhere—wouldn't that be nice?

"Don't get lost!" she called into the wind.

She came back inside and had a slow drink of water, before returning to her mother's room.

"Sit here right now," her mother said.

Veblen sat next to her mother, the room darker than before.

"Don't start this now. You have everything to look forward to."

"I know I do."

Her mother stared at her, and stroked her hair. "Sweetie. What's wrong? Aren't you happy?"

"Yes! I'm very happy."

"You're having one of your attacks," her mother said.

"No, I'm not." She held her mother's hand, as entrenched as the tides. From the men outside came a few echoic yelps.

"You make me feel guilty," Melanie continued. "Like I did something wrong."

"You didn't do anything wrong."

"And I get frightened," said her mother. "That you might have some of Rudge's genes."

Veblen felt she was now required to reassure her mother how few genes of Rudge's she possessed. "I *do* have some of his genes," she said today, trying something different. "You mated with him, how can I help it?"

"Don't blame me!" cried her mother.

"Okay, well, what's done is done."

"Veblen, he is certifiably insane. It's something to look out for."

"I'll try to keep on top of it."

"As you know, all kinds of treatments are out there nowadays, the world is different, you have nothing to be ashamed of—unless untreated."

"You don't think I'm insane, do you?"

Her mother sat up. "Only when you talk about squirrels following you all over California. You're the bravest, strongest girl in the world," said her mother, squeezing her hand.

"No, I'm not." She wanted to say: *Maybe compared to you. Not compared to anyone else.*

"I won't argue about this," said her mother. "Now pull yourself together. You're about to have a grand adventure. If you can't enjoy it for yourself, enjoy it for me!"

"Wait a second. I'm insane but I'm brave and strong, I shouldn't marry but it's a grand adventure. . . . Do you even know what you're saying?" Veblen asked, irritably.

"Stop being so literal!" said her mother, who always had to have the last word.

Shortly they stood at the edge of the ravine, calling down to the men.

Linus called up:

"The *Eagle* has landed!"

Veblen and her mother hooted back.

"Paul?" Veblen called.

"Yes?"

"How you doing?"

"I've been better," he called back.

"Oh, you'll be tired tonight!" cackled Melanie, an obvious sadist.

"Moving the roof should be easier, now that we've cut the trail," called Linus.

They could hear the sound of the buckling sheet and the grunts and instructions going back and forth between the men for almost ten minutes before they could see any sign of the roof wiggling up the bank.

"This is a bitch of a job," yelled Linus, with earned ferocity.

"I second that," yelled Paul. They seemed to be getting their strength through yelling.

"What seems to be the problem?" called Melanie.

"We're being shredded alive," Paul called. "Get out the rubbing alcohol!"

"Honey, it's just very heavy and we have to hold it over our heads, and the weight shifts and our legs catch on the canes. You have no idea!" Linus called up. "We should've hired someone with a winch."

. . .

It was cooler, the sunlight weak and broken, near dusk, when the men mounted the crest of the ravine, the roof flashing triumphantly. Paul's clothes clung to him, his hair full of leaves and brambles, scratches seeping blood across his cheeks and neck.

Melanie said, "Let me get a picture!"

When her mother handled a camera, she acted like some kind of hip photojournalist following a rock band. She took a few shots of the men standing lacerated by the corrugated sheet.

"We'll get it up on top another day," piped Linus.

"Paul, you're going down in our hall of fame," said Melanie.

"Shower," Veblen said. "Come with me."

She herded Paul into her childhood bedroom, with its sea green walls and old corkboard, retaining some of the flavor of that era, such as a faded quote from somewhere she'd once typed and stuck in with a now-rusted thumbtack:

The greatest luxury in life is loneliness. All you have to do is furnish it with the inner life.

These days the room was used to store her mother's art supplies and fabrics, but the way the sun came through the windows was exactly the same, creating nostalgia and melancholy in equal measure.

He collapsed onto the twin bed, clutching a towel. "I can barely speak. Oh my god."

"They ambushed you."

"Oooooh. Yes. They did."

"I'll have to think of a good reward."

"Yes, you will."

He tried to kiss her. She whipped a pitiful thin pillow at him. He jetted it back. They mounted repeated attacks, displacing air that made her territorial map ruffle on the wall. "What's that?" Paul asked.

So she told him. The map represented a place called Wobb, with all the topography and various special places sketched in. No, it wasn't quite like Cobb. It was a place where animals had been gathering to reinstate their rights, and where a runaway girl lived by herself in a tree house and was somehow an important part of their world. Humans simply could no longer see the intrinsic value of anything. Squirrels, for instance, had thought that after fifty million years on the North American continent, it was safe to let down their guard. They had made a bad contract with people in innocence and trust, and had paid the price.

And yes, the girl had been shocked to learn that squirrels were under contract. But of course they were. They didn't get to coexist in cities and towns for nothing. *Everything* was under contract, they told her. Every inch of soil, every animal, every plant. Frustration was rife. The Nutkinistas had been gaining stature among the downtrodden. The teachings of Nutkin had become widely accepted.

Wobb even had its own language. *"Hibere wibe spibeak Wibobbean."*

"Whoa," Paul said. "Like the Brontë sisters, out on the moors with your little world."

"Who says it was little?" she replied.

His head flopped to the side, where he caught sight of something else. "Is that your old typewriter?"

"Yeah."

"I want to see it! That was one of the first things I knew about you."

Veblen could see the scruffy case under the desk. She was superstitious about the typewriter.

"It's really old and musty."

But she pulled it out, and Paul rolled over to get a look at it. Fading stickers still held to its sides.

"Bring it back with you. I think you need that typewriter."

"Why?"

"It belongs with you. Not sitting here in the dark."

She pushed him toward the shower.

MELANIE WAS ARRANGING the plates on the table by herself, a sign that she was on a first-class flight of fancy. Her eyes were bright and excited. Veblen remembered the hopes that look had inspired in her when she was a young girl wholly dependent on her mother, when Melanie wore her hair in a long braid, and was thin and impulsive, and they would set out on the spur of the moment with some aim, like finding a warehouse where they were selling pinto beans in bulk, or locating a printing press that was filling its Dumpster with old broadsides printed on fine cotton rag, or driving down to Berkeley, where one of Melanie's former professors was giving a lecture on Thorstein Veblen.

"He's great!" she said. "What a surprise to find a man like that, someone who'll roll up his sleeves like that. . . . I wasn't sure, Veblen, but he's real."

Despite herself, Veblen felt joy rise in her gullet, and her cheeks levitated, not for the benefit of her mother but for her own victory over the odds. "I told you."

"He's real. He's solid," said her mother, and Veblen watched as she opened the bottom drawer of the chest and pulled out the real silver, the Gorham Chantilly Veblen's grandparents had bestowed on their only child when they sent her to Vassar and dreamed of pairing her with a future captain of industry. (Sure enough, there had been a Dartmouth boy named Dave Dandridge, a fine captain of industry in the making, but when he proposed after two years of dating, her mother broke up with him because his expectations were way too integrated into the systems Melanie was suspicious of.)

"Very nice guy," noted Linus, with a glass of wine. "We had a great talk down there about all kinds of medical advancements and so on. He's got a good head on his shoulders."

Veblen looked at Linus, with his square shoulders and worn belt, a solid man himself, someone who didn't manipulate, who didn't think of himself every two seconds, who had always been reliable and kind to her, year after year. He took care of her mother like a nurse, chauffeur, secretary, bodyguard, accountant, and loving friend, all in one.

In short order Paul presented himself, refreshed, smelling of Dove soap, his face full of color, his skin shiny, his hair groomed and slick. He was beautiful!

And they sat for Key lime pie, with a buttery graham cracker crust, in wedges on the Limoges china plates.

"We survived," said Linus.

"Conquerors," Paul said.

"I didn't think we'd make it at one point."

"When my leg went into that snake hole, I thought that was it."

"When I took the vine in the eye, that was my low point."

They liked him, and he liked them! Tears of joy made her blink.

"Delicious pie," Paul said.

"My grandmother's recipe," said Melanie.

"Veblen's a great cook too," Paul remarked. "She must have learned from you."

Some people liked her mother and Linus. For instance, the Yamamotos, a visiting couple from Japan, the wife an artist, interested in textiles and art paper, whom her mother had pursued and won over. And the librarian couple from Sacramento, the Gilberts, interested in Native American artifacts and books. But one year the Gilberts house-sat for them and evidently snooped around, and Melanie felt violated and terminated the friendship. The Yamamotos remained friends, likely because they had crossed the Pacific Ocean for good. They still sent handmade *Akemashite omedetou!* cards. If Paul liked her mother and Linus, maybe there was a change coming on the wind.

"Well," said Melanie. "A wedding."

Paul looked at Veblen expectantly, so Veblen found herself saying, "Actually, we're thinking maybe as early as May."

"May. That's very soon!" Melanie regarded Paul with respect. "Your folks, are they excited?"

"God, yes. They think Veblen is the greatest thing that's ever happened to our family."

"They do?" Veblen said. Unfortunately, this fed into her disproportionate need to take responsibility, causing her to start worrying about all the ways she'd have to behave to continue to be the greatest thing that had ever happened to the Vreeland family.

"Well, she is," said Melanie.

"Mom!"

"This girl is very special," said Linus. "I couldn't be prouder of her."

"If you're not good to her, we'll have you for dinner!" said her mother.

"Yikes," Paul said, but Veblen was touched by the display.

Then at last, the long, milling good-bye by the car. Veblen drove, and they pulled away, down the driveway rutted and full of deceptive puddles. Paul reclined in the passenger seat. He said, once they had traveled about a mile, "Jesus god."

"That was so heroic of you!"

"I had no choice," Paul said, groaning. "She was totally pissed at first, wasn't she? Wasn't she about to explode?"

"That was normal. She liked you a lot."

"Really?"

"She did! Did you like her okay?"

He made a noise that could be interpreted as a yes.

"Really, you did?" she ventured to ask. It was like losing your balance to pick a daisy. She began to hiccup deeply, needing to keep hearing that *yes,* to pin it down for all time.

MEANWHILE, ON A hammer-shaped parcel outside of Cobb:

"Oh, my. My goodness." Melanie sat and took up a tissue from her command center, which consisted of her chair, a bear-sized fabric- and foam-covered stump with a back, next to a hand-fashioned multitiered table stuffed with magazines about art, travel, and cooking, volumes about Georgia O'Keeffe and William

Morris, and a regularly grabbed *Merck Manual* from 1998. A magnifying glass, tweezers, a mirror, and several tubes of antifungal ointment lay scattered like gear in a miner's camp. The telephone also sat there, its handle worn dull in the center where Melanie gripped it daily when she called her daughter. "Linus, come!" she cried out, without enough breath behind it, a kind of sucking gasp. When Linus didn't materialize instantly, she screamed, *"Linus!"*

"Yes?" He appeared in the doorway, a damp dish towel thrown over his shoulder.

"I just don't know what to do. I can't rest."

"Honey, there's nothing you can do. She needs to work this out on her own."

"But we know something that she doesn't. Isn't it our duty to protect her?"

"Dear, is it possible he meant nothing by it? Maybe he was trying to hurry up."

"Damn it! Do we have to go through this again? I've made my case."

"Sorry, honey, I'm not convinced."

"Listen to me. When a man wants to make a good impression on a woman's family, he bends over backward to do it. He thinks ahead. He leaves nothing to chance. This is not something he overlooks. Never in a million years."

"It is hard to believe it happened, I agree."

"You look around the bathroom, you clean up the hairs you left in the sink, you make sure you didn't leave your underwear on the floor, do you know what I'm saying?"

"I do."

"You do not leave your wet towel wadded up on the floor for your future mother-in-law to find. No, you do not. Not unless you're a psychopath trying to drive a dagger into her heart!"

"Hmm. Yes and no."

"What do you mean?"

"You might make a mistake, is all I'm saying. Maybe he's just a clumsy oaf?"

"If Veblen knew this, it would change everything. She's a very refined person. She would not stand for it."

"Let me ask you this," said Linus. "Let's say you thought he was perfect for Veblen. And then this happened. Would you have felt the same way?"

"It wouldn't have happened. A man perfect for Veblen would not do this."

Linus sighed.

"And the squirrel thing—that's a sure sign she's feeling stress. We worked so hard to help her through that. For nothing! I don't know what to do," said Melanie, and commenced again to cry.

"Come now, things will work out. If he's really an awful person, she'll learn it herself."

"What if it's too late?" cried Melanie. "She's rushing into this. That's what happened to me and Rudgear. I didn't know how bad *bad* could be!"

"But then everything turned out, didn't it?" soothed Linus. "You ended up with an adorable baby girl, and then I bumbled into your life. Let me make you some tea."

"Thank you," said Melanie, holding a blanket against the side of her face.

. . .

But in the car driving home, Veblen continued to rhapsodize over the day's success.

"You were so nice about all her medical stuff!" she said.

"Yeah, I tried."

"You understood her? You saw her good side?"

The pause was so long she might have panicked. But with a sudden snap of his neck he said convincingly, "She's a character. Smart definitely. Really fascinating."

"Paul! That makes me so happy! Did I ever tell you, I actually talked to squirrels when I was little?"

"That doesn't seem incongruous."

She reached down and pulled a foxtail from her sock. "I did. I really thought they were listening. I'd squint at them really intensely and will it to be true."

"Huh. What about it?"

"It came up today. My mother thought I was insane. Also because of how my real father is in an institution. Do you think wishful thinking is a psychiatric condition?"

Paul was notably quiet. "I don't know, Veb. I'm totally exhausted."

"I know, I'm sorry. I bet you'll be sore and stiff later."

"I am already."

She lowered her visor to the setting sun, with warm hopes for times yet to come.

5

PLIGHT OF
THE BOOKWORM

One could opine that this bewitched outlook, this confounded optimism that was Veblen's most notable feature, this *will to believe*, as William James called it, took hold early in Veblen's childhood, perhaps most urgently in the thorny days leading up to her brief childhood visits with her mentally unbalanced father. To give herself the special powers to deal with it, Veblen concocted a potion out beside the ravine, of nettles (for the muckraker), a pinch of jimson weed (for the carouser), ripe blackberries (for the sweet-toothed), and dandelions (for the lion-hearted). It hurt to swallow, but that's how she knew it would work.

In the days prior to the yearly, court-appointed visit, Melanie began to fester notably. On the morning of Veblen's departure, she simply wouldn't get up. Veblen would dress from a pile left out the night before, meant to look especially sharp when she first arrived to show off Melanie's superior taste and mothering skills. Back then Melanie made her clothes, insisting that homemade clothes were more attractive and unique, but the clothes represented to

Veblen everything that was difficult for her—how her last name didn't match up with her mother and Linus, the very short haircut her mother gave her in the bathroom every month with her sharp snapping shears whose tips poked into her neck and cheeks, how it wasn't fun to have friends over because her mother always criticized their manners or hygiene after they'd left. ("I want you to take note. Jody didn't look me in the eye *once*. Nor did she say thank you when I offered cookies. She grabbed them off the plate and didn't say a word." Or, "I don't think Terri is well cared for at home. Her neck was filthy, as if she hasn't bathed in days.")

(Veblen washed her neck often and vigorously. Also, she looked people in the eye and said thank you. She believed in an ideal human identity, and that to fall short of it would lead to exile.)

One year, Veblen's mistake was to ask if it was okay if she *didn't* take her mineral collection to show Rudgear—Melanie had packaged it up in a box the day before, made sure all the labels were in place, wrapped the samples in tissue, but Veblen knew Rudgear would despise the collection and know that it was being foisted on him by Melanie, who fostered the interest and was the one most partial to rocks.

"You're not interested in sharing something from your life? Are you going to cut us off, forget we exist?"

"No, Mom, no!"

Nothing could have been less true. Veblen dreaded the visits to Rudgear. His behavior was bizarre, erratic—only later was he diagnosed with severe PTSD and offered treatment. It was always a very stressful two weeks of being a child trying to figure out how to act to escape scathing criticism and anger (and of course there was no way to escape it, but she was too young to know that), and yet she couldn't tell Melanie the details partly because she would try to forget them and partly because Melanie couldn't handle hearing anything bad that happened to Veblen, and the visit was court decreed, and that was that. Ultimately, all her mother was trying to say, clumsily, opaquely, was that she'd miss her. And she loved her mother so much that injustices of this sort, rather than turning Veblen against her mother, made Veblen all the more resolute in wanting to be a strong person and a fair one. In some way, she wished to be a good example to her own mother and, in a dream of greatly delayed gratification, believed she'd someday witness the desired results.

Linus had been an academic librarian at UC Berkeley, and a rare-book dealer. He had a beard and glasses and a friendly word for everyone, such as the people in banks and grocery stores, all the people Melanie regularly picked fights with. He made Veblen breakfast every morning before school. He helped her with homework and looked up pertinent information in the encyclopedia when she needed it, and had lots of information under his own belt, such as a complete mastery of modern history and baseball. He regularly brought home books about explorers and artists and philosophers for her, which complemented the library at home and was how Veblen came to know the writings of William James and John Dewey and Richard Rorty and many others over the years. He liked to ski at Squaw Valley and took Veblen every winter to see the Cal Bears at the old Harmon gym in Berkeley, where he taught her how to keep track of free throws and field goals the official way in the program, with Xs and Os.

Melanie met Linus in the Bancroft Library. She checked out a stack of books and he helped carry them to her car. They married soon after at the city hall in Berkeley, when Veblen was seven. She wished for a brother or sister, even a pet, but Melanie said Veblen was more than enough.

FINALLY, IT WOULD be time to leave. She'd choke down her potion at the last minute, just outside the back door. One year Linus emerged from the kitchen, holding his glasses and rubbing his eyes. He appeared disarmed without glasses, his eyes small and blind looking. "All right, go in and say good-bye to your mother," he murmured.

Veblen would get her audience after all. Red and weepy, like a timeworn tomato, Melanie sat wrapped in her old robe. She wanted to look horrible, Veblen thought, to encourage pity. "I'm supposed to pull myself together for your sake," Melanie said. "So I suppose you'll have a wonderful time down there. But try to refrain from coming home with all that crap he loads you up with."

"I'll try." This magnified Veblen's gloom—her only consolation on her last trip was this so-called *crap*, such as the electric-pink dress with the big gold hoop on the front zipper, the supertight pants, the big inflatable pillow with all the astrological signs on it, all purchased during an impromptu shopping spree at Sears. It was hard for Veblen to understand the revulsion Melanie had exhibited when she'd unpacked and shown off her trophies. "I put the rocks in my carry-on," she offered.

"Well, good. I think it's good to show him you spend your time constructively. Do you have your books?"

"Yeah, all of them." Linus had brought home a complete set of Sherlock Holmes mysteries, as well as *White Fang* and *Call of the Wild* and a few other novels about ill-treated beasts.

"I have a very funny feeling about this trip," Melanie said quietly. "I had a dream—that you were in trouble and you were calling for me."

This made Veblen feel uneasy, but taking it as a test of strength she said, "I'll be fine, don't worry about me." Melanie often bragged of her sixth sense, of how she could predict earthquakes, and how she had known the exact moment Robert Kennedy was killed because she felt like a bullet had entered her own body, causing her to leap up and turn on the television, which was showing the pandemonium inside the Ambassador Hotel.

"I like to pretend you're Linus's daughter," Melanie went on. "If only you were."

"Sorry," Veblen said, helplessly.

"Hurry up, you'll miss the flight and then he'll call and chew my head off."

"Bye." She went forward for a kiss, but Melanie pulled her cheek away.

"I can't stand this. I hope you appreciate how lucky you are. My parents were so horrible to me, I got myself in a hideous mess."

Veblen squirmed uncomfortably. "I wish I didn't have to go."

"You won't go off on your own, you won't talk to strangers, you won't get in cars with strange men?" Melanie croaked.

"Why would I? I don't do that here."

"His values are so different from ours. For all I know"—her nostrils flared and her brow bunched—"he'll try to sell you into slavery!"

It was a joke but Veblen could picture it, being toted away over the shoulder of a pirate with a gag in her mouth, Rudgear counting his take.

"Bye, Mom."

They hugged each other at last. Melanie's big warm body comforted her, no matter what she said. Suddenly Veblen felt terrified and didn't want to leave her.

"Go on now."

Veblen held on, digging her fingers into her mother's fat.

"You're hurting me, let go. For Christ's sake! Don't do this to me! Linus, come get her! Go on! Go!"

The potion was kicking in. She let go, of course. And stood it. She had a lot of practice standing things because she had to stand them, which was a hard habit to break.

At the airport Linus bought her a chocolate bar, and told her he couldn't wait to talk about *White Fang* when she got back, and that someday soon they'd drive over to Sonoma to see the remains of Wolf House, which burned to the ground before London ever had a chance to live in it. And soon a stewardess took two unaccompanied minors on board, Veblen and a boy who looked to be about the same age. They ignored each other, but they were seated in exactly the same row.

Dear Melanie,

During this visit with Veblen, I noticed a definite trend for the worse in her personality. Probably since you are around her all the time, some of these traits don't stand out clearly. She appears to be a very unhappy child, unable to let go and almost devoid of emotion. She lacks enthusiasm for most any project and has very poor manners. If you don't do something for her now, it will only get worse.

Rudgear

Dear Rudge,

I appreciate your concern but the problems you describe do not exist here. Veblen is a happy girl with her own personality, and she can't understand why you can't accept her for herself. She is a mature young girl, interested in many, many things, has many friends and is happy. She doesn't want to change herself when she visits you and wouldn't even know how. And now she is beginning to dread her otherwise good visits for fear of your reaction to her and the pressure you put on her. I will continue to encourage her to feel at ease there, and I hope you will try to make her feel at ease as well.

Melanie

(Linus composed all correspondence to Rudgear, as Melanie couldn't quite manage to strike the right tone.)

Dear Melanie,

I believe medical help should be sought. This girl has problems, too many to list. She can't relate to any adult, only to little kids and animals. I'm sure this whole thing can be rationalized but don't do it—this kid is headed for trouble later on. You may not wish to do anything about it, but Veblen is the loser, believe me. You must know Veblen has problems and to bury your head in the sand only works against her.

Rudgear

Dear Rudge,

I am prepared to make reservations for Veblen's visit with you this summer, but until we reach an agreement I will not purchase the ticket. I appreciate your previous letter and we have discussed her difficulties with her physician in several conferences. The doctor has urged me to write you before this upcoming visit. Veblen feels pressure when she's there to behave in some other way than she is, and has become increasingly withdrawn and unhappy, not sure of her footing while there.

Yes, she reads a great deal and enjoys make-believe. Yes, she throws herself into the world of her books, and imagines great adventures. But this is normal for a child her age and it's hurtful for you to ridicule her. She found it terrifying when you grabbed her book last summer and shredded it to pieces, calling her a bookworm and telling her to go outside. (This was a library book, by the way, and we had to pay for it.)

Another thing contributing to the problem is that you find it natural to kiss her on the mouth, but Veblen is not used to that. She gives and receives affection here at home, but we don't kiss children on the mouth here. She finds it unpleasant and feels pressure when you insist on it.

Further, the doctor and I both feel that having her sleep outside in your camper to foster independence is not the answer. She feels isolated and punished and she is a young girl. This must never happen again.

We also feel it is not proper for her to go with you when you collect money, as she has heard you yelling at people and finds it frightening. It is also against my wishes that you ask Veblen to work while she's staying with you, selling those cards door-to-door. She informed me of this only recently and reluctantly, and I was quite shocked. It is not safe for a child to go door-to-door selling things, even prayer cards. It is also hypocritical because she knows as well as I do that you are not religious.

Further, Veblen told us that you frequently ask a man in a brown suit whose name she does not even know to watch her on days you work, and she feels uncomfortable with him. He has given her a wallet and a few other gifts and I don't think this is appropriate, whoever this man in the brown suit is. Who is this man?

Last but not least, Veblen loves to swim and dive. But please do not take her to the high dive at the Plunge anymore and throw her from the diving board.

Please be more relaxed with her and try to avoid judging her. She's interested in her family history and Norwegian customs— why don't you tell her more about that? As you know, she is a lovely, intelligent, and affectionate girl. If you can't curb your temper around a ten-year-old girl, then you shouldn't see her until you can.

Sincerely,
Melanie

Rudgear got so mad when he received this letter that he called up and shouted at Melanie and that was it. Veblen was never sent to see him again. For the time being Veblen was hugely relieved, but also couldn't help wondering why he didn't try to make up somehow. Well, he just wasn't strong enough, is what she figured out in time. It wasn't until Veblen moved to Palo Alto years later that she wrote to him and reestablished contact, without her mother in the middle of it.

IN THOSE CHILDHOOD DAYS, Veblen had several methods for calming her nerves, such as riding her bike as fast as possible, holding her breath under water as long as possible, climbing trees as high as possible, and typing as fast as possible. One thing she typed a lot was this:

```
MAYBE YES
MAYBE NO
MAYBE YES
MAYBE NO
```

Really, really fast. As if weighing all options.

She began typing the lyrics to songs, to remembered conversations, whatever sprang to her fingertips. She typed with the satisfaction of a pianist on a grand in Carnegie Hall. She knew her fingers by the words they commanded. Her hands had lives of their own, her servants, her ten-horse team pulling her dray.

When she typed she felt great freedom, like a wild mustang galloping across the plains.

Later, learning Norwegian with Mr. Bix Dahlstrom in the care facility, the whole world would magically disappear, leaving them alone in an enormous cavern that they could wander through nearly forever, always finding new chambers to explore. When you entered the cavern of another language, you could leave certain people behind, for they had no interest in following you in. You could, by way of translation, emerge from the cavern and share your adventures with them. You didn't have to be an intellectual in a black beret smoking clove cigarettes to be a translator, not at all. You could become one in your blue flannel pajamas, your face smeared with Clearasil.

You did.

6

ART IS DESPAIR
WITH DIGNITY

After Paul left for work on Monday, Veblen rolled her bike from the garage and heard the rubbery leaves of the magnolia shiver. Leaping from bough to bough went the squirrel, as if it could fly. Curious how the squirrel stuck around, even with a mean-looking trap in the attic.

Curkcuuuuurikieeeeecururururucuriii! The squirrel flew from the branches onto the garage roof, every spiky guard hair on its tail gathering sunlight.

"Hey, what's up?"

Seeforyourselfforyourselfforself, it seemed to chatter.

"Up in Cobb, was that you?"

His reply formed a rhyme in her head:

Whiskery day, whiskery do
No one knows me and no one knows you!

"Did you stow away in the car? Did you flatten yourself like a pancake?" she asked him. He must have laughed merrily at the pinch he'd been in, as it kept a fellow from going soft, to find himself in a pinch now and then.

The squirrel twitched and ran.

"See you later!"

Spring had come. Bright-headed daffodils elbowed through the soil, yellow acacia fanned the rooftops, humming with trains of bees. Tender young buds could be chewed on everywhere, as could those easily damaged new leaves that had the feel of baby skin. Out on the bike path, snaking around the bends in the creek, the breeze tousled her hair, morning cool and redolent of the bark of tall trees. At the railroad tracks she detoured south to University, under the sandstone archway, to enjoy the passage down stately Palm Drive, lined with parallel columns of the majestic Canary Island species. From eucalyptus to redwood to oak, sparrows, to-whees, juncos, thrashers, and jays all whistled and dipped. Ground squirrels raced back and forth over the path, barely escaping her wheels. She avoided the basking earthworms on the shores of rain puddles. Her tires crunched the russet husks that had fallen from the palms in the rain. Nature was irrepressible, and should be. If a squirrel took note of her, as if to say she was a human worth know-ing, as if to say (and you couldn't help but take it this way when singled out by an animal) that she was a human worth marrying and loving, then let him have his say!

HER MOTHER CALLED, during her morning round of transcrip-tion; Veblen called back when her break came, under an oak in the sun.

"Hi, Mom," said Veblen, swatting at a mosquito near her face.

"Veblen, did you take the typewriter from your room?"

"Yes," Veblen said.

"What made you think you could do that? Why didn't you ask me?"

"It was just sitting there. You don't need it, do you?"

"You know that typewriter is special to me! You know that!"

Veblen took a deep breath. "Okay, so I took it. Now what? Do you want me to ship it back?"

She could hear her mother swallowing some kind of liquid.

"No, Veblen. Keep the damned thing. I wonder why you did it, that's all. It seems as if you did it to hurt me."

"Hardly. Why are you so touchy about the typewriter?" Veblen wanted to know.

Her mother spoke in a near whisper. "Because it was given to me by a brilliant man who saw my potential. That was a special time for me. You know that."

"What was so special about it?"

Her mother's voice shrank further. "I don't need to justify my attachment to that machine. I'm merely asking that you're careful with it."

"What am I going to do, throw it off a building?" Veblen looked up at the roof of the hospital.

"I suppose not."

"Watch out, maybe I will," Veblen said, with actual malice.

"All right. Tease me all you wish. It's your typewriter now."

"I know it's mine. I used to take it all over."

"But you never took it away before," said Melanie.

"I took it away now."

"Yes, you did." Her mother sniffed, and adjusted her tone to sound upbeat and agreeable. "Anyway. Linus and I were talking about your desire to further your Norwegian, and we wondered what you'd say if we offered to help you take that time in Norway you've always wanted."

Veblen was a fool sometimes, but she was no fool the rest of the time, and she crushed an old acorn beneath her shoe.

"Why are you saying that?"

"What, dear?"

"Why are you saying that right when I'm about to get married?"

"Oh! Don't you remember, you said it yourself—right here in the bedroom next to me—that you wished you'd had the chance to spend time in Norway." Melanie was a bad actress.

"So what you're really trying to say is that you don't want me to marry Paul!" Veblen cried.

"No, I'm not," said Melanie.

"I wanted to go on that study abroad program ten years ago! You said you needed me at home. And then I managed to raise the money later, and you went into the hospital a week before I was supposed to leave so I didn't go."

"Oh, I'm sorry I inconvenienced you!" her mother jeered, and Veblen scanned the skies.

By now she recognized the patterns in her mother's behavior that were triggered by any forward progress in her life. When Veblen finally made her move to Palo Alto, her mother fell into a horrible snit as Veblen finished packing that last day, throwing something at her while she zipped up one of her bags.

It was a patchwork cover for her computer, perfectly fitted, finely finished, made of scraps of Veblen's childhood dresses, just like the one her mother made for her typewriter once upon a time, an otherwise loving gesture except that her mother pitched it at her head and ran from the room in tears.

"Mom?" she called.

"What?" yelled her mother.

"I love it!" Veblen said.

Melanie screeched, "Go on, get out of here! *Go, go, go, go, go!*"

"Why is she yelling at me?" she asked Linus.

"Because she loves you so much. She's going to miss you."

Veblen began to cry too. "I wish she could just give me a hug."

"Give her a call as soon as you get there, okay?" Linus said, patting her on the back. "That'll make her feel much better. Good luck, babe."

This was her send-off, and as she drove away, eyes still red, she vowed that the only way to break free from the grief her mother caused her was to make something out of it—but what?

Art is despair with dignity, she thought, and scribbled it on a scrap of paper in her car. If only she were an artist!

Now Melanie said, "Why not do your thing in Norway *before* you get married. There's no hurry, is there? Paul can keep on with his work, then you can come back and get married anytime you want. You'll never get a chance to do this again, believe me."

Everything had gone so well. Paul had brought up the roof of the chicken house and almost got scratched to death. Her mother had seemed so happy.

What went wrong?

What always went wrong?

She was supposed to thank her mother for the offer, play along without subtext. "Did I tell you what a great time Paul had?" she tried instead. "He loved you and Linus. He loved our house."

"Is that so? We'll see how long that lasts."

"Yeah, especially if I tell him you want me to go to Norway right now."

"I don't know if I'd mention that, unless you decide to go."

"I'm not going to go," Veblen said.

THERE WERE FAR more important things to do than get married, of course there were. There were exploration, discovery, all kinds of challenges to be had.

Girls who dreamed only of marriage were doomed, mentioned her mother at regular intervals throughout Veblen's life.

BETWEEN UPDATING Dr. Chaudhry's calendar and making some copies, she fell into a reverie about married life involving her cottage on Tasso, but the daydream rejected her attempt to have it because Paul had his eye on bigger, "better" houses, so she switched channels to an old daydream in which she had a job as a foreign correspondent in Jakarta, based on seeing *The Year of Living Dangerously* at an impressionable age.

There she was in sweaty khakis, there was her Linda Hunt–like friend taking her into the seamy underground, where they supported a sickly child with bags of stolen rice. There they were, ranging through the smoke of riots, bold and unstoppable, sending back reports on the hour. She used to imagine meeting a male reporter, maybe an Australian, with manly arms who grew up on a sheep station, who'd take her home to meet his family, a short hop across the Torres Strait, where she'd jump in with the chores, un-afraid of the work, and they'd soon see she was no stuck-up Amer-ican. They'd marry and take over the sheep station and her sweet old in-laws would live out their days on the veranda, watching them canter up in the evening after a long day mending fences, the shepherd dogs right behind, waiting to be fed.

Wait a second, that wasn't going to happen—she'd chosen Paul, a doctor who experimented on brains at a veterans' hospital in California, who probably didn't like sheep, and definitely would never have his parents living with them.

Probably not a good idea to fantasize about that anymore.

IT WAS REFRESHING to continue on with Paul as if she existed independently of her parents, but wasn't she misleading him?

He had no idea.

After she'd completed some filing and mailing, made a trip to the drinking fountain, and performed a stretching session behind her desk, she received a call from Bebe Kaufman, the head nurse at her father's mental health facility in Paso Robles.

"Veblen, your dad needs some new pants and all the rest of his usual supplies. When can you make it down?"

"How's he doing?"

"No change. No problems. That's the kind of news you want, right?"

"Thanks for everything you do for him," Veblen said. "I'll come soon, I promise."

"Good girl," said Bebe Kaufman.

VEBLEN HAD RISEN UP the ranks of the temp agency, and nowadays made eighteen dollars an hour, just enough for rent and food and a few small items of need. Keeping a low overhead was part of her mind-set. It made for an existence that was lean and challenging, like life on the frontier. She believed it was important to be fairly compensated for your time and work, but that it was also important not to earn a bunch of money just to play a predetermined role in the marketplace. When unforeseen expenses came up, such as when her 1982 Volvo 244 blew its head gasket, she discovered how vulnerable she was—and had to take a second job for a while, packing candles into boxes in a factory in Milpitas on the night shift. But for the most part, her life worked. She was getting better at Norwegian, and her translations came more easily. She'd accomplished things, hadn't she? All kinds of things you couldn't put on a résumé, such as deciphering the cryptic actions of family members, and taking care of them until the day they died.

COMING HOME TO the old typewriter these days was inspiring. She'd go to it to record new ideas and make lists and take in that ancient smell.

The smell was the London of Dickens, the catacombs on the Appia Antica, the Gobi Desert in winter, a dark monastery in Tibet. It was Nevada City in the gold rush. It was a telegraph office near the Mexican border. It was a captain's trunk coming around the Horn. It was a dressing room on the Great White Way in New York. Sometimes, it was a breezy little tree house in Wobb.

I love Thorstein Veblen because even after an
exhaustive survey of his life, he has never let
me down; because he bucked the establishment
not only when he was youthful and idealistic,
but all his life; because he was so free, he
lost jobs that others would have made every
compromise to keep; because he was a thorn in
the side of the powers that be; because he
posted office hours on his door, 12:30-12:35;
because although he was defeated in academia,
he never stopped contributing to the
intellectual life of the nation; because he
lived true to his beliefs, and committed not a
hypocritical act in his life; because he cobbled
together his clothes and furniture with dignity;
because he had to brew his own coffee the exact
same way every morning and would not let anyone
else do it for him; because he had a horse
named Beauty and allowed animals to wander
around his yard free, even skunks; because he
was proud of his Norwegian heritage but deeply
curious about the lives of everyone else;
because he never kissed an ass except those of
the women he loved; because he built Viking
ships for his stepdaughters out of logs and
taught them the names of the constellations
and every flower and tree and mushroom in the
forest; because he traveled all over the
continent and knew and feared its natural

resources would soon be commodified and
pillaged; because he coined wonderful phrases
to describe the follies of the postindustrial
world, including conspicuous consumption,
pecuniary canons of taste, and decadent
aestheticism; because he had his stepdaughters
dress like boys so they could run free in
summer and so that their talents and habits
would not be formed by convention; because
he spoke at least fourteen languages and
astonished haughty intellectuals without even
trying; because even now his reputation is
skewed by misinformation he did not bother to
correct; because in photos he appears foreboding
but in a hundred recorded instances he was
gentle and kind to those he loved. Thorstein
Veblen was a large gangly man with a soft voice
who mumbled, and he didn't have to prove
anything to anybody, and he doesn't still.

7

RELEASING THE TOOL

Paul's day started badly, and only got worse.

After a pretty much sleepless night thanks to squirrels, after taking a second shower to rinse out the dust, husks, and rodent shit that had rained on him when he benevolently went to check the goddamned *humane* and ineffective trap, Paul arrived at work and found a package on his desk, a white box with a label depicting a tea bag the size of a purse.

Corpsaire™ Sachet—Helps Eliminate Unpleasant Corpse Odors
Labs, morgues, autopsy rooms and funeral homes
are vulnerable to highly unpleasant odors
from decaying corpses and fluids
used for embalming.
Putrid decomposition vapors
can result in loss of morale
and create negative publicity
if they escape the building.

Veblen's scorn for medical marketing had poisoned him. He called in Susan Hinks.

"What is this thing?"

"There they are! These have great reviews on Allegro. I thought we could give them a try."

"On what?"

"The medical supply site. Lots of great stuff there."

"A little bleach usually works fine."

Hinks said, "Also thought you should know we're a little behind in our cadaver count. I'm waiting for a call from the Anatomical Board and we should be able to scrape up a few more, but I took it upon myself to apply for MUPs."

Susan Hinks was tone-deaf, missing some piece of humanity. He couldn't quite put his finger on it. He conjured a childhood for her in which a martinet dad lined up the kids and inspected the shine on their shoes and the parts in their hair. As a sex partner, she'd probably play roles without any self-consciousness, which was kind of hot. But who needed it.

"And MUPs are—?"

"Multiple use privileges."

"Oh. That's quite a privilege."

"We have thirty-four cadavers in stock. So if we get MUPs and use both sides of the skull, that will put us at sixty-eight procedures, and hopefully by that time we should have full inventory."

Paul said, "Anything else I should know?"

"It's a busy day but the families usually expect face time with the lead physician—maybe you could poke your head in and give them a pep talk?"

"A pep talk about what?"

"You can remind them how patriotic they are, thank them for their sacrifices. You could lead an informal prayer if you'd like. That type of thing goes over well."

"I don't want to sugarcoat anything about this trial."

She sighed. "Dr. Vreeland. Morale is so important. Positive spin makes the world go round. Can I tell them you'll stop in at ten?"

"All right," Paul said sullenly.

"Wonderful. Let's see, Jonathan Finger called to say the control panel has been installed, so the simulator should be up and running soon. And the simulator operator has been in touch, Robbie Frazier. Did you know he's a sound technician from THX? And the medics are here today, Chen, Sadiq, and Vasquez. I've given them a general orientation. Can you meet with them at noon?"

He nodded, handed her the Corpsaire sachets, and watched her go.

Coffee came from the cart in front, prepared by a large woman in a white uniform with a large mole on her cheek, who behaved shyly with him. He beheld bright light at the edge of a headache. Back in his office, ibuprofen, three tabs. Heal thyself.

Paul was unexpectedly slammed by a traumatic memory from science class in middle school, where Mr. Poplick, a bearded young gun from the Bronx, began to scatter the word *orgasm* through his first lecture in the sex-ed division. Paul thought he was a douche for mispronouncing *organism*, and after determining that no one else was brave enough to correct him, he raised his hand. "It's *organism*, not *orgasm*," he said, his voice huffy with ridicule.

The room was a carbuncle ready to burst. Poplick sneered. "Um, class? What's an organism?"

Hans Borg raised his hand, while others snickered. "Any kind of living thing."

"Okay. Just curious, were we talking about organisms?"

"No!" everybody shouted.

"How many of you know what an orgasm is? Spare the details, please."

Hoots and howls accompanied the raising of all hands, to Paul's distress.

"Okay, Paul. Stay after class and we'll have a man-to-man," said Poplick, and the memory still had the power to make him burn with shame.

How he'd love to rub Poplick's face in his career now, *douche bag*! Poplick the middle school teacher, the hick, the bumpkin!

He left a message for Jonathan Finger, the bright spot so far in his time at the VA. Shortly after being awarded the trial, during the planning stages in the fall, Paul had received a call from Finger, his project support representative from WOO. WOO was one of those things you've never heard of until you hear about it all the time—the Warfighter Outreach Office (a branch of the Program Executive Office for Simulation, Training, and Instrumentation [PEO STRI], a division of the United States Army, a division of the DOD). WOO was an organization that reached out across the army, the Department of Defense, and other U.S. departments and agencies to provide modeling and simulation, training and testing support. WOO provided interagency acquisitions support. WOO provided access to the full spectrum of instruments available. WOO was a really big deal.

Finger was someone Paul liked immediately. Short, balding, slightly paunchy, Finger nevertheless exuded the kind of charm that couldn't be learned. Maybe because he seemed to struggle with his current incarnation as a company man against the back-drop of a wild and crazy past. A man who'd lived the extremes, who'd dodged bullets and lived to dish the dirt.

At their first meeting in the fall, at a steak house in Burlin-game, they discussed the parameters of Paul's trial over one of the most decadent meals of Paul's life, during which he imbibed four vodka tonics, followed by a massive cross-section of prime rib, dol-lops of horseradish, a pie-sized Yorkshire pudding, and a mound of creamed spinach. Finger told him stories about his former job as an undercover courier in countries such as Venezuela, Estonia, and Thailand. After whetting Paul's appetite with his stories, Finger dropped in the business at hand.

"First, Paul, I recommend you do a little PR training with, let's see, is Hartman your CRO?"

Paul confirmed.

"You need it. You need to *own* this. They'll bring you up to speed on your public persona, how to talk the talk."

"A corporate makeover."

"Then I'm going to recommend a state-of-the-art simulation system," Jon said, three hours into the meal. "These are the ones we like." He gave Paul the list, with its string of endorsements from decorated veterans such as Clarence Obadiah Thompson, who exhibited bravery in the Dinh Tuong Province of the Repub-lic of Vietnam in 1968, saving the lives of five men in his battalion despite rocket fragments in the shoulder and wounds that immo-bilized his legs, causing him to drag himself with two men on his back through the mud, keeping them alive, once out of range, with tourniquets and jokes until they were evacuated seven hours later.

Said Thompson: *Simulation systems are the only way for the men and women of the armed forces to prepare for the difficult and dangerous work ahead.*

Paul still couldn't believe that he was now involved with the U.S. military and the Department of Defense. The affiliation made him feel heroic and serious, after growing up cosseted by peaceniks.

"Clarence Obadiah Thompson talks the talk," Paul said.

"That's no accident," Jon said.

Paul was plastered, and found the WOO products list dizzying:

- Additional Black Hawk Flight Simulator (ABHFS)
- Advanced Gunnery Training System (AGTS)
- Aerial Weapons Scoring System Integration with Longbow Apache Tactical Engagement Simulation System (AWSS-LBA TESS)
- Air Defense Artillery (ADA) Targets
- Armored Security Vehicle Multiple Integrated Laser Engagement System (ASV MILES)
- Aviation Combined Arms Tactical Trainer—Aviation Reconfigurable Manned Simulator (AVCATT)
- Ballistic Aerial Target System (BATS)
- Battle Command Training Capability—Equipment Support (BCTC-ES)
- Battlefield Effects Simulator (BES)
- Camouflage, Concealment, Deception, and Obscurants (CCD&O)

. . . and so on, all the way through the alphabet.

"What the hell is this stuff?" Paul belched, reaching capacity.

"Here's the fun part," said Finger, jiggling the ice in his glass. "Take your pick."

"But all I need are some bangs and smoke," Paul protested.

"You don't finesse this kind of study with homemade campfires and popguns, Paul. This ain't Boy Scouts! No, Paul, I'm outfitting bases and training sites all over the globe, I'm managing over two hundred contracts in twenty-eight countries," said Finger, who twirled his Patek Philippe watch in a widening swath in his arm hair. Congealed with fat, their plates disappeared with the waitress, while Finger ordered them both Brandy Alexanders, and removed two cigars from the inner pocket of his jacket and offered one to Paul. "Close your eyes and take a poke anywhere on the page. You can't go wrong."

"You serious? This is crazy."

But he did it. He closed his eyes and started laughing. He played government-sanctioned pin the tail on the donkey. Finger said, "Congratulations! You're the proud new operator of a CURS!"

"What the hell is it?" Paul said.

"Confined Urban Rescue Simulator. Perfect."

Finger looked at the part number and opened his satchel and removed his tablet, bringing up photos and blueprints of the CURS from every angle. The CURS was a set of prefabricated buildings simulating the urban landscape of modern warfare, complete with an elaborate sound and lighting system, real doors and locks, and mazelike passageways decked with sniper windows, smoke, explosions. The whole thing could be staged within the warehouse at the VA, the control panels mounted on a platform with a viewing window above. "Listen to this, Paul, customer choice of color!"

"I want orange!"

"With black stripes. Like a tiger. I'll ask! Jesus, have I told you about my adventures in the tiger trade?"

Paul was about to burst with boyish respect. "No."

"Let's just say it ended in an airport, and involved a tiger pecker and a balloon."

Since that epic meal, Finger had remembered Paul's birthday, taken him to see a few welterweight championships and a tennis benefit featuring Roger Federer in San Francisco, sent Paul bottles of Ardbeg Corryvreckan Islay single malt Scotch whisky, 4 Copas Tequila Reposado, and Parker's twenty-seven-year-old whiskey ("Jesus, Jon, this stuff is two hundred bucks a bottle!"), and even offered Paul some kind of vacation package to Cancun should he and Veblen wish to honeymoon there.

"Yuck!" Veblen said when he shared the bounty. "Are you allowed to accept this stuff?"

"We're friends," Paul said. "We genuinely like and respect each other. You can't fake something like that."

(His father would've attacked him for saying that. He loved that Veblen nodded respectfully and believed.)

At a recent meeting, Jon asked him: "So was it Cloris herself who brought you in?"

Paul delved, with unabashed pleasure, into his professional courtship by Cloris. Finger listened, a deplorable smirk growing on his face, which made Paul slow down like he'd entered a sand trap.

Finger said, "Yeah, she's pretty good at that," and Paul frowned.

AT TEN Paul dragged himself to the FDR (family day room), with its daytime television and rough plaid couches, stuffy with exhalations of abscessed teeth and old coffee, where at least twenty people had convened. Susan Hinks brightened at his arrival, and began making a herding gesture with her arms. "Everybody, Dr. Vreeland is here now. Please take a seat and we'll get started."

The faces in the room were neither padded in comfort nor forbidding. He saw chipped nail polish and worn vinyl bags, stubble and heavy cheekbones, thin hair, broad thighs.

"Good morning." He stood stiffly just inside the doorway, telegraphing, he hoped, warmth and authority. "I'm Dr. Paul Vreeland, director of clinical trials at Greenslopes." He cleared his throat, and noticed that James Shalev sat against the wall, clipboard in hand, jotting notes. "It's—always a trial in itself to calibrate our personal expectations with the expected outcome of a medical procedure. Or trial. I'm sure this has been one of the most difficult times in your lives." Murmurs of assent spread through the room, as he sought the proper notes to sound. "It's come to my attention that some clarification on the nature of the trial might be helpful at this point."

One man in the corner said, "Can't hear you."

"Sure. I'm here to answer your questions."

A wide-hipped woman raised a small hand, like a schoolgirl. "Doctor, is it okay to bring our son's pajamas and slippers and regular clothes so he can get out of that hospital gown?"

"Of course. That's fine."

"We tried to bring his pajamas but the nurses told us he had to stay in the gown."

Paul said, "Then we'll have a talk with the nurses."

"He could wear his own pajamas and slippers at the VA in Bremerton," said the woman.

Paul nodded. "There are always some loose ends at the start of a trial. Now, I'd like to explain that—"

A man with a thick, bristly neck raised his hand. "Doctor, can we wheel our son outside on nice days? It's good for him to get some sunshine and fresh air."

"Yes, by all means."

A round-faced woman with long, shining black hair said, "Our daughter is the only woman in her row and we think women should have a room of their own."

Paul cleared his throat again. "Let's look into that."

"It's only right for women to have their own room, she's sleeping in a room full of men," said the woman.

"I take your point and we'll look into it today," Paul said, with pessimistic thoughts about the ability of anybody enrolled in the trial to know the difference between themselves and the opposite sex ever again.

"I'd like to know when you'll get started, and how soon we'll be made aware of the results," said a man in a beige raincoat.

"That's right," agreed a few others.

"My husband's getting bed sores. You need more physical therapists here."

"I have a medicine skin for my husband. Do you know about those?"

"No, I don't."

"It's sheepskin, and it helps keep the weight off."

"I had a sheepskin for my son at our VA in Cleveland, and it was stolen right from under him," said a woman.

Paul held up his hands. "How many of you understand what this trial is about?"

The room went silent.

"Would someone tell me what you were told?"

"We weren't told anything!" called a man in the back. "We found out our son was coming here, that's all. We're from Oklahoma City. His doctor at the VA decided."

"I was told my husband would be treated for his TBI," said a redheaded woman holding the dense prospectus. "This is a clinical trial to help people with TBI, isn't it?"

The people in the room began to talk, trading what they'd heard. As the volume rose, Paul shrank, his stomach bunched into a knot.

"People," he said. "This is how it is. People!"

Two young women with pale skin and knitted brows were whispering to each other, and one raised her hand.

"Our dad's here and we've read the papers," she said. "And we know this trial is to test a device to be used within hours of brain injury. It's not designed to help people who have already suffered TBI such as our dad and other members of this trial. Isn't that true?"

Paul said, "That was well put. Did everybody hear that?"

The room fell quiet, mown down.

"We're here because we know our dad wants to help any way he can, even if it doesn't help him, because that's the way he is," she went on.

A woman in a heavy, rust-colored parka patched with duct tape raised her hand.

"We read the papers too. We understand all that. But for us it's better to try something than nothing. It's possible my husband could get some benefit from this procedure, isn't it?"

More murmurs from the others. He heard someone say, "We thought so too."

He was bulging with anger at their willful ignorance, stretching himself to hide it. He said, "I hope you'll all take the time to read the prospectus again and understand that in this trial we do not expect—" The faces, from every side of the room, were tense, wrung out. "We don't expect—" He felt the room closing in on him, every face trained on his. Hinks stared as if trying to cast a spell over his larynx. James Shalev scratched notes loudly onto his pad. Expectations were killing him! He couldn't breathe.

"We don't know what to expect until we've tried it," he blurted out suddenly, and the room lightened many degrees.

"My husband was in a trial last year in Bethesda, for anticonvulsants, and another for tissue regeneration using progesterone," said a young woman in a tight black sweater. "He woke up during the anticonvulsant therapy for about three hours and recognized me and asked about home and our dog, then he slipped back. It only happened once, but when everybody's told you he's never going to wake up, and something like that happens, it really gives you hope."

"My daughter has a strong will, and we think she'll pull through this," said the woman who wanted her daughter in a different room.

"My husband too," said another.

"Our son was told he might never walk after his injuries in '05. He recovered and went back. He'll make it through this if anyone can."

"That's right," said someone.

Paul looked at his watch and nodded to Hinks. "Well, then, thanks, everyone, thank you again for your support."

Someone clapped, and thanks came in murmurs. The woman with the son whose sheepskin was stolen came forward and shook his hand. Paul said, "Where was your son stationed?"

"Kirkuk."

"Tough."

"He was a runner, a bicyclist, a basketball player, an all-star Little League pitcher, and he loved to hike with his buddies in the Poconos. Summers, he was a camp counselor up at a place for disadvantaged kids. They loved him."

To Paul's surprise, his eyes misted over. Usually he hated hearing about beloved people, fearing no one ever talked that way about him. "You must be very proud of him."

He turned to escape down the hall but the two young women came doggedly after him, surrounding him by the elevator.

"I'm Sarah Smith," said one.

"I'm Alexa Smith," said the other.

"That prospectus isn't easy reading," Paul said.

"We've been reading a lot of stuff like that since our dad was injured."

"That's not always a good idea," Paul said, as the elevator doors parted. They followed him in.

Sarah Smith said, "But we're the ones who care about him the most."

He searched her face for signs of rancor, but there were none.

"We wanted to talk to you," said Alexa Smith. "We're worried he might be too aware of his surroundings to be in this trial."

"What seems to be the problem?"

Sarah Smith said, "He seems really agitated and emotional, worse than before we brought him here."

"You're free to take him out," Paul said.

The other sister spoke. "We told him that, but then he gets mad like he thinks we're underestimating him. We wondered your opinion if he's suitable."

The elevator opened, and they followed Paul down the corridor like ducklings.

"All right," Paul said, opening the door to his office. "I'll look into it."

"Thank you, Dr. Vreeland. We really appreciate it. He's been through a lot and we don't want him to be stressed out."

"Sergeant Major Warren Smith is his name," said Sarah.

They were sweet-looking girls, and when they thanked him it was with a measure of grief, and after they left he felt appalled by the whole painful masquerade.

He was sweating all over. Just then came a knock on his door, and James Shalev stuck in his large, onion-shaped head.

"Hi, Dr. Vreeland—nice job. A reality check but with a magical Frisbee thrown in at the end."

"Yeah. Thanks."

Shalev extracted his head and shut the door.

Paul did some kicks and karate chops around the room, venting generalized unease. And then his cell rang, and it appeared to be the fourth time his father had called in the past hour.

"Hey, Dad. Everything okay?"

"Fine, son. You bearing up? How was the trip to Cobb?"

"Okay. I'm at work, by the way."

"Want me to call later?"

"I can talk a minute. Her mother's a nut job, that's all."

"What's wrong with her?"

"She's a narcissist, a hypochondriac, a borderline personality, probably schizoid," Paul said, sending his chair across the room with a violent punt.

"Whoa. So do we get some points now?"

"She calls Veblen every day, which is a drag."

"Well, Marion's mother called every day too. I didn't like it, but it was important to her."

"I have to live with it, huh?" Paul sank into his chair, expelling a stale gust of trapped gases from the cushioned seat.

"Oh, yes. Don't try to tear a girl from her mother, she'll hate you for it."

"So what's up, Dad? Anything else?"

There followed an awkward silence before Bill said, "We want to come down for your birthday. And, well, I hate to ask something like this right now, as I know how it really bugs the crap out of you. But your brother needs to hear something from you. We're having a rough patch, and I know you can help."

Paul slammed his coffee cup into the trash basket, sending angry streaks of latte up the wall.

"Dad, forget it. I have to go."

"I'll get him on the phone, and I want you to tell him that you're marrying Veblen."

"What, he's worried it's not going to happen?"

Bill cleared his throat. "It's a little more complicated."

"What, then?"

Bill said, "He claims *he's* marrying Veblen."

"Tell him yourself!" Paul yelled.

Bill began to speak in the drawl that historically made Paul's chest constrict. "Son, we've tried. We've been talking about the wedding a lot because we're so damned happy for you. He's taking it all in, and this was just his way of joining into the spirit. We should have nipped it in the bud, but at first it seemed like a healthy dose of pretend. Take it from me, that night we met in the city, he saw right away what a terrific gal Veblen is."

"Tell him the truth!"

"We've been trying."

"Try harder!"

"We've backed ourselves into a corner. We don't want anything going wrong at the wedding, you understand?"

"Couldn't you assert my right to exist? For once?"

"Calm down, boy."

"Can't you see how lame and cowed you are?"

"The world is full of the cowed." Bill's voice trailed away. "He's coming in right now with your mother," he whispered. "He listens to you. Prevail where we've failed."

All at once he heard Justin's clammy breath smothering the phone, much as it had smothered his face when they were boys and Justin would lie on top of him to wake him up. "Pauly-wauly."

"Hello, Justin."

"Hello."

"Looking forward to my wedding?"

After a pause, Justin said, "Yes."

"It'll be nice to have Veblen in the family."

"Yes." In a quiet voice he added, "I'm getting married too."

"Ah, really. And who are you marrying?"

"Veblen," said Justin.

"What a coincidence! Not my Veblen?"

Justin whispered, "A different one."

"A different Veblen," said Paul. "What's your Veblen like?"

He could hear Justin fidget, the phone too close to his mouth. "She's really little."

"Ah. A really little Veblen. Good for you. Now I'm going to tell you something and you'd better listen. Stop fucking around with Mom and Dad and give them a chance to enjoy *my* wedding, which is *my* right, which is the only thing I've insisted on my whole life *not be screwed up*, do you get that?"

"Maybe. Maybe."

"Then *maybe, maybe* it's time to tell everyone about your special little connection with Caddie Fladeboe."

"No, it's not time for that, Paul, no."

"I think it is!"

Justin said, "I won't say it again, Paul. I won't."

"Let me speak to Dad."

Bill came back on the line.

"What happened?"

"I told him if he said it again I'd thrash him."

"Jesus. Was that necessary?"

"It was," Paul said. "Now that I'm done putting out your fires, I have to go perform surgery on cadavers, if you really want to know."

"You do that," said Bill. "I'm sorry we lean on you sometimes."

"If he makes any trouble at the wedding I'll take him outside and beat—"

"Enough!"

"He's a thirty-eight-year-old man."

"This is your family. Get your priorities straight."

"You too, Dad, you too."

"You've managed to piss me off, son."

"Like usual. Like since the day I was born. This isn't about Justin, Dad. Don't you get it? It's about you and me and some grudge you have against me and everything I do."

"Jesus Christ. How can you say that?"

"You make it easy," Paul said, shaking.

"This won't stand. We're coming down and we're going to hash this out. This is a new phase of your life and I don't want these attitudes getting in the way. You're going to screw things up with Veblen if you don't have things squared away with your family first."

"It's about time you noticed," Paul said, secretly touched.

And then the rest of the day—Paul met the first group of participating medics, Pvt. Donald Chen, Sgt. Nadir Sadiq, and SP5 Alex Vasquez. They had their notebooks and were up to date on the trial, eager to start. The medics scrubbed down and suited up and Paul led them to the small operating room. An orderly wheeled in a cadaver, and they peeled open the bag to reveal the body of a woman who could not have been very old when she died.

"This lady's seen better days," said Vasquez, allowing the bright light to expose unbleeding gashes on her torso, and the lack of one arm.

"Sure has," said Chen.

Sadiq picked up the notes and read off the various studies the woman's body had been used for to date, while Paul brought out his device and set about to demonstrate. To build their confidence, he told them that craniotomy, even performed on a living, breathing person, was a surprisingly safe procedure with no mortality or morbidity reported in reviews of thousands of patients. Then he showed them how his device was equipped with a light and a razor for removing hair from the area, and had an extendable nipple for applying a swath of iodine. He held the prototype to the woman's skull, had them look closely at his hand while he lifted the safety latch, and then deployed the trigger, allowing the device to punch out a three-inch-diameter circle from the woman's skull like a ballistic cookie cutter. The action was remarkably quiet, due to the pneumatic tool-muffler built into the small CO_2 cylinder. The blade was extremely sharp and the device lifted out the skull fragment in one precise motion, exactly as Paul intended.

"This thing's gonna work," Sadiq said.

"Don't act so surprised," Paul said. "Let's do it again."

Next Sadiq tried, holding the cadaver's head for leverage. He pressed the device to the shaved skull and activated. The cut was clean, and with a quick flip of the switch on the handle, the blade contracted around the fresh plug of bone and lifted it out. "The average skull is 6.5 millimeters thick. The blade is 6.3 millimeters, so it stops just short of the dura," Paul said.

"Like shooting a gun," Sadiq said, impressed.

Paul said, "That blade's coming at 42.7 meters a second."

"This thing's your baby?" asked Vasquez.

"It is."

It was Chen's turn. He swabbed the skull on the other side, held it in position, and deployed. But this time something went wrong, the cut was incomplete. A 2-centimeter tag of skin and bone held the plug in place. Chen asked, "What should I do?"

Paul said, "Don't worry. There's a removable blade on the side, for trims."

"Should I release the tool?"

"Release the tool."

Chen released the tool from its faulty grip and the skull flap fell open and hung over the cadaver's ear. Paul showed them where the removable blade was located and slipped it out, then grasped the skull flap with his gloved hand, but as he did, the short uncut section of skull broke off and the skin began to tear down the side of the cadaver's head like a strip of paint.

"Now what?" Chen fretted.

"Give it a little cut, fast."

When Chen applied pressure to the peeling skin, it peeled further, and Paul saw the flaw in his design, and that removable scissors would be better than a blade for their built-in leverage, and he told Chen to let go, and as Chen tried to let go, more skin peeled with the weight of the skull flap, all the way down the neck to the shoulder.

"My bad," said Chen. "I didn't make full contact. I want to try it again."

Paul clipped the hanging flap of skin, and Chen tried again, this time successfully.

"Packs a punch, doesn't it?" Paul said, and took some notes.

"My dad could use this in his business," said Vasquez. "It would save a lot of time."

"Huh?" Paul looked up and saw Vasquez holding the device to the wall.

"He's an electrician. You need to make openings for wires and switches all the time, and we use saws—"

"Don't," Paul said, seeing Vasquez's fingers touch the trigger, but too late.

The device sprang with a bang.

"Oh shit!" said Vasquez, coughing. "Man, that's powerful!"

Paul grabbed his valuable prototype, covered in plaster dust. A circle had been punched in the drywall, not all the way through but almost, and Vasquez gave it a small poke, which caused the circle to detach and disappear down the inside of the wall, revealing a nest of wires.

"Oh crap!" Paul started to cough with surprise.

"Sorry, Doctor. It was an accident, seriously," said Vasquez. "Look at that! I'm telling you, every electrician in the world would want one of these."

"They'd probably like having a tank too, but they're not going to get one."

Vasquez laughed.

It was a three-hour session with the medics, who made a few intriguing suggestions (a glow-in-the-dark rubber grip on the handle, for instance). They completed thirteen procedures, counting the one in which skin ripped all the way to the clavicle.

Ouch. Definitely refine that before starting on the volunteers. He knew what had to be added: sensors that would create the circuit for the trigger only when contact was equally dispersed on the full circumference of the blade.

8

EIGHT KNOTS

To some, the in-law family is a burden and a curse. But to others, it's a close-knit group with a new opening just for you, and that's definitely how Veblen looked at the Vreelands, who were in her eyes the kindest, most admirable family she could hope to become part of. She formed this estimation in faith that it would be so, because that was what she wanted, a family at ease, a family free from the heat of a central beast, traveling through vents to cook you in every room.

Back in December, before they were engaged, she met Paul's parents and brother in San Francisco. The family had made the trip for a business deal, which involved the dropping off of a brown unmarked package during a brisk stroll through Aquatic Park. She learned that Bill and Marion and Justin called themselves "the tripod," and any tasks they shared their "tripodial duties," and Veblen felt the bud of love open for them right off.

Paul, it seemed, would have preferred having his toenails pulled off, though he refused to explain why his spirits sagged so notably before the innocuous get-together, nor his reproachfully sluglike posture and defensive outbursts during it, nor the round of maniacal cackling he gave way to coming home in the car.

Justin Vreeland stood slightly shorter than Paul, weighed around 250 pounds, and had some kind of disorder that rendered him challenged in more ways than Paul could adequately describe. Paul couldn't even tell her what his brother's condition was called. He'd said: *I don't care what it's called, it's just my nightmare.*

Over the course of that evening, Veblen learned Bill had once been an oarsman in the Grand Canyon, a river guide with a love for the cliffs of Tapeats Sandstone, Bright Angel Shale, Redwall Limestone, and Vishnu Schist. A place you could still find tender spots on the earth, untouched. He had been subjected to a strict upbringing in the sprawling, postwar tracts of Orange County— his Marine Corps dad had served in the First Marine Regiment at Guadalcanal, and took no shine to fanciful daydreams, and Bill had not been his father's favorite (*Imagine*, Veblen thought, *having to deal with that, on top of everything*); his brother Richard had been the favorite, an athlete and marine himself, so Bill went his own way and saved his earnings and married his college sweetheart and bought a place on ten acres in Humboldt County, where they could have a small farm and build an adobe oven for bread, throw pots in a kiln, operate a forge, and cultivate their own vegetables as well as a fruitful marijuana patch. Paul's childhood, not something he liked to talk about.

Marion grew up outside St. Paul, Minnesota. Her father was a loyal 3M salesman with a two-inch wedge in his left shoe to boost his shorter leg. He favored plaid jackets of polyester, and carried a small silver flask of whisky in the breast pocket, along with a comb full of Brylcreem. Marion's mother had been a beautician, and spent most of her off-hours huddled in the kitchen with her two sisters, who lived nearby, smoking and gossiping about unhappy marriages and wayward kids in the neighborhood. Marion took off to discover her true self in the West and became a nurse, her natural calling. Now in semiretirement, she still substituted and did case management for the county, and was, of the three, the one Paul seemed closest to. Veblen had been quick to decide they were all good and kind, and the fact that they'd kept Justin at home and cared for him all his life was great proof of it.

It was the Ides of March. They were here to celebrate Paul's thirty-fifth birthday.

"Brace yourself," murmured Paul, as they pulled into the Wagon Wheel Motel parking lot on El Camino.

"Hellooo!" Marion ran waving across the lot.

"Couldn't they have stayed at your place?" Veblen suddenly wondered.

Justin pounded on Paul's hood. His shirt was rolled all the way up to his mouth, where he was chewing on it, revealing his white and doughy abdomen.

"No," Paul said, with surgical precision.

In the cool air Marion hugged Paul, while Justin pressed Veblen against the moist quadrant of his shirt.

"Let go," Paul barked, pulling Justin roughly.

Marion said, "You look wonderful, Veblen!" She was a solid woman in her sixties, with a blondish-gray pageboy haircut and steady blue eyes that gave the impression she had never seen a catastrophe that could unglue her.

Veblen liked their eccentric car, thick with dust and activism. *Love Your Enemies: It really messes with their minds. Don't Just Hug Trees: Kiss them too. Ran out of Sick Days So I'm Calling in Dead.* She had yet to visit the family homestead, but one night, loosened up with the help of a bottle of .wine, Paul embroidered for her the hellish landscape of his youth, replete with prowling DEA agents and infrared photo sweeps from the altitude of gnattish copters, the sweet smell of jasmine and bark and paranoia in equal measure. To Veblen, it sounded wonderfully complicated and alive.

Paul's father charged out of the room, hair wet and spiky, a child again at the sight of them. He was a robust man in a red bird-of-paradise Hawaiian shirt, with a close-clipped gray beard and silver caps on his canines, and he doted on his family as if they were his favorite characters in a story he'd written himself.

"Hey, son," he said, kickboxing at Paul with his Tevas, while his arm swung out like a gate to pull him in, then, with the other arm, Veblen, as she worked to understand the niche a father could take in a family. "Hey, you. Let's see the new machine." He circled Paul's car as if NASA had engineered it. "Never set foot in one of these in my life. How's it run?"

"Oh my god, Dad, it purrs. Wait and see. You can't even tell it's on."

"What's the hp?"

"451 at 6800 rpm."

"Wow. What you got for music?"

"Twelve speakers, Dad. Twelve! Get in, sit in front."

"Let your mother."

"No, you. And, Mom, you sit in the middle in back."

"I should sit on the hump," said Veblen.

"There is no hump in this car," Paul declared. "I've made a reservation at Aubergine."

"Hope it's good food, not just fancy," Bill said, with a grunt.

"Maybe you'll find out it's delicious," Paul said.

Bill fell in front, Marion wiggled to the middle between Veblen and Justin.

"By the way, I got a fleet discount from the hospital," Paul said, with a momentary quiver in his voice. Was he shy about its luxury, vulnerable to criticism? Something to ask about later.

Paul had previously been the owner of a trusty forest green Subaru, dusted with scrapes and scars of what she assumed were youthful adventures. Veblen thought the status car diminished him somehow, as if constipation and gout and general decay of the flesh requiring extra comforts were just around the corner.

"Old Betsy's still kicking. She's got three hundred thousand miles on her," Bill pronounced.

"You and Mom need a new car." Paul looked over the seat to Veblen. "They have an old Dodge truck with holes in the floorboards, a death trap. When I did my time in the ER, I don't want to tell you how many people I saw all chewed up because they were in lousy old junkers."

"Honey, we only drive her locally," Marion said. "We always take the Toyota on trips."

"We'll drive her until she drives no more," said Bill.

At the fancy, expensive Stanford mall, built over a vineyard in the 1950s and only a matter of yards from where Thorstein

Veblen's town shack had stood off Sand Hill Road, Bill sprang out nimbly and opened the doors for the backseaters. Marion walked with Justin, whose feet were so large they occasionally crossed and tripped him. Bill offered his arm to Veblen. Paul bounded forth into the restaurant as scout, and the hostess gathered the menus and brought them to a table by the windows, which looked out at an enclosed courtyard built around a fountain, under the cancan skirts of fuchsias that swished from pots.

"Justy, you know that flattened chicken you like, scaloppine? They have it," said Marion.

"Pork chops," said Justin.

"Let's see," said Marion, with the help of her glasses. "Yes, they have pork chops."

"I want pork chops," said Justin.

"You always want pork chops," Paul said.

"Who doesn't?" said Veblen gaily.

"Veblen, you have to get used to the rhythm of this family, we're a little slower than most, but we get there," said Bill.

"Bill, did you finish that order?" Veblen remembered.

Bill nodded. "The five hundred peace sign belt buckles. I did. Whew, was that a marathon. Justy helped a lot on that big order, didn't you, buddy?"

"I helped a lot."

"Dad, please order a full dinner tonight," Paul said. "He holds back, then he leeches."

"Evidently I'm a leech," Bill said.

"It's nice to know the world still wants peace signs," Paul said.

"It's a start."

"Dad, if you got an order for five hundred swastikas, would you make them?"

Veblen wondered what he was getting at.

"Um, no. I would not."

Paul made a show of choosing an appropriate wine from the list, an Edna Valley Chardonnay, and the waiter made a show of presenting him the bottle and decanting him a taste, and Paul made a show of tasting and approving, and the waiter made a show of pouring for everyone, even Justin.

"No, no, no," Paul said.

"Just this once?" Marion pleaded. "For a toast?"

"Come on, you guys. It doesn't mix with his medications."

"Just let him live," said Bill.

Paul wasn't happy. She could see it in the set of his face, the way he was squeezing his glass.

Marion adjusted her sweater with an air of eternal pluck. Bill leaned forward, his lips turned up.

He raised his glass and said, "Everyone, listen, please. I have something to say. Justin, listen." He cleared his throat. "In the words of the great writer and environmentalist Edward Abbey, 'A great thirst is a great joy when quenched in time.' I speak not only of our chance to be together tonight and lift our glasses, but of Paul finding peace within himself and the right woman to spend his life with." Paul's expression was one of great suffering. "I believe, son, that you have found a wonderful woman in Veblen and that your heart will open and be filled with the joy that I have known with your mother. Sorry to be so mushy, but that's how I feel. We love you, boy. We love you, Veblen. Here's to Paul and Veblen!"

They lifted their wineglasses. Veblen smiled so hard her cheeks cramped. She held up her ring.

Justin collapsed, to stare at the tabletop point-blank. "You're shaped like a worm," he mumbled.

Bill said, "First I'm a leech, now I'm a worm?"

"I love you, Veblen," Justin said. "I love you."

"Did you want a ring like that, Veblen?" asked Marion.

"It's really fancy, isn't it?"

"My goodness," said Marion. "Look at my old rings." She held up her hand to display a set of silver bands on plump knobby fingers. "I can't get 'em off. They're part of me now. Someone's going to have to cut 'em off with a saw when I die."

Bill showed his modest band too. "Will we have the wedding up on the land?"

"Thanks, Dad, but we'll have it here. Our friends are here."

Bill said, "We could throw you a great wedding at the house, don't rule it out. If you add up the costs and discover it's all too much, consider it. We've got the space, full of flowers in the summer, a meadow, beautiful. You could stand under the gingko."

"And all get arrested when the feds raid the property. Thanks, Dad, but our life is here," Paul said.

"We have a lot of close friends who will want to be there," said Marion.

"The *real* friends," Paul declared, with feeling. "I don't want every derelict who's ever camped in the backyard."

"Of course just the close friends," said Marion. "We don't want a circus."

"And I don't want Cool Breeze, no matter what you say. He

freeloaded in a tree house on our property for eight years, terroriz-
ing us with bags of excrement."

She noticed real tension in Paul's jaw, his mandibles pulled back
like catapult slings.

"It's your wedding," persisted Bill. "You know, I was thinking
Caddie and Rich could sing."

"You want a Jefferson Airplane cover band?" Paul said.

"They're terrific," Marion said. "Caddie sounds *exactly* like
Grace Slick."

"And looks exactly like Miss Piggy," Paul said.

"Your wedding," said Bill. "We don't want to butt in."

"No, you don't," Paul said.

Justin's head hung low. He huffed on his silverware, and watched
the moisture of his breath contract.

"You okay?" Veblen reached for his shoulder.

He nodded his head but wouldn't lift it.

Paul whispered: "Don't. He's pissed I'm getting some attention."

Was it true? The salads arrived and Justin began to bite at the
lettuce.

As they ate, Bill and Marion rained affectionate questions on
Veblen—she described Cobb and the scruffy little hammer-shaped
parcel her mother bought years back because it was so rocky and so
oddly sliced, no one else wanted it.

"Wait—hammer or hamster?" asked Marion.

"Hammer. The driveway is the handle, and then we have this
area bordered by ravines where the house is, shaped pretty much
like a hammerhead."

"Hamster might have been better. In terms of space," Marion
commented practically.

"I guess hamster-shaped parcels weren't available that year," Paul said.

"It's so weird how people like hamsters so much better than squirrels," Veblen added, knowing that hamsters were hindgut fermenters and coprophagists, whereas squirrels were nothing of the sort.

Maybe to veer away from the further comparison of rodents, Paul coaxed Veblen into telling them about her translation work, and her interest in Thorstein Veblen. She described the article she was translating now for the project: a history of Thorstein Veblen's Norwegian family in Minnesota.

"Sounds interesting!" Marion said. "There were many Norwegians where I grew up."

They talked about Norwegians for a while.

Paul said, "I think he helps you justify your Spartan upbringing."

She nodded. "Maybe." Something had flashed past the window. "There's a lot about him to like."

"He endures," Bill said. "He's still widely read."

"Is it okay if I say this? Veblen has a very dysfunctional family, possibly more than ours," Paul blurted out.

"What the heck!" Veblen yelped. Was this necessary?

"Dysfunctional my ass!" cried Bill. "You've got parents who love you and your brother more than anything. What do you want?"

"Don't get worked up. I'm just saying, Veblen has a real handful."

"Yes, Paul's told us a little bit," said Marion, sympathetically. "I hope you don't mind."

"What has he said?" she asked, her cheeks ablaze.

"Well—" Marion collected her thoughts. "Your mom has a lot of health issues, I guess? And your dad's in a mental hospital? And your stepdad is kind of, I don't know, a eunuch or some such? And you had a grandma who wouldn't talk to your mom, with a little megalomania? And I think there was someone else. Let me think. Oh, yes, the pilot, your grandfather, who was nice but had a second wife with a wicked temper who dressed inappropriately? And they all depended on you over the years?"

"You thought Linus was a eunuch?"

"No!" Paul blushed. "I liked him. I never said that."

Veblen found herself hiccuping and giggling. It was all rather confusing, being held accountable like this. "Well. Sounds like he's been very comprehensive."

"You know, my folks were alcoholics," said Marion.

Bill said, "We've seen it all. You stay open to your friends and you've seen everything."

Just then a squirrel crossed the flagstones, leaving a wet trail. The trail had a natural flow and, with only the slightest pooling of the vitreous fluids, looked like a secret message.

"Look," Veblen blurted, "it's spelling. I think it says muumuu." As if the creature were aware that women on the cusp of marriage were subliminally frightened by the word, carrying its associations of matronly bloat and housewifery, such that repeated exposure during the engagement period led to a great increase in cold feet. Was it the squirrel from Tasso Street?

"Where?" asked Marion, putting on a different pair of glasses. "How can you tell?"

"Even the squirrels around here are brainy," said Bill. "Here's to Veblen, Thorstein Veblen, and MuuMuu!"

Justin began to laugh and pound his thighs, expanding and contracting like a man-sized accordion. He bumped the table, causing glasses and goblets to rock. He was in a convulsion. Bill jumped behind his son and jerked the solar plexus.

"Come on, boy! Cough it out! You can do it! Cough it out!" Bill yelled.

A woman in a lavender blouse rushed from her crab cakes. "I'm an MD."

"So is he!" Bill yelled, as Paul fished into his brother's throat.

They barreled around Justin and squeezed. Paul drew away and pounded on his back, as a tarp of romaine flew from Justin's mouth like a parasail, making landfall a meter away.

"Thataboy," cried Bill.

"There's something else," Paul said.

Justin's wet eyes gazed blankly at the ceiling.

"Put him on his side!" yelled Marion. "Pat him on the back!"

Justin gurgled. Paul fished in his throat. Bill pounded Justin's back. A mouse-sized chunk of bread came up and landed on the floor.

The rattle was gone. Justin swallowed air. Color returned to his skin.

Marion said, "Honey, should we take you back to the room and let you rest?"

"I'm okay," said Justin, hoarsely.

"You take it easy, son," said Bill, massaging his boy's shoulders. "We're fine, everyone, thanks."

Justin sat up, runny-nosed. Marion dabbed him with her napkin. More towels went whipping around. Linens flashed, cutlery chinked, they returned to their seats. Someone picked up the mouse.

"You never know," said Bill, finishing his wine. "You gotta keep on your toes."

Paul remained silent, and in another minute the crisis dissipated over his plate of baby back ribs in a sesame ginger sauce with garlic kale and frissoned yams.

"Gotta stay on top of things," Bill said.

"That's right," said Marion.

"He's okay," said Bill.

"You okay, Justy?" asked his mother.

"I'm okay," Justin said.

They got around to the subject of Paul's new job, and Cloris, and how she had recruited him. For reasons that were about to become clear, Paul hadn't told them about his personal relationship with her yet. *A Hutmacher.*

"What's a Hutmacher?" asked Marion.

"From the Hutmacher family, she's incredibly wealthy," Paul replied.

Bill said, "I don't care how much money her family has, is she an accomplished and ethical human being?"

"She's amazing, Dad. She gives money to everything you believe in, you'd approve. Actually—"

Bill said, "Hutmacher of Hutmacher Pharmaceuticals."

Paul nodded. "Actually, she wants us to have our wedding at her house."

"Great connections, boy."

"Stop it," said Marion. "He's telling us he's being appreciated for his hard work, that's all."

"Thanks, Mom."

"It's not for sure," Veblen said quickly, but when Paul glared at her, she said, "but probably."

"Profiteers!"

"Dad, this is something entirely different, I'm not testing drugs, they're licensing my craniotomy device, and that's a good thing for everybody."

"Don't let them steal your integrity," Bill said.

"I won't."

"Then stick to your guns," said Bill.

"That, Dad, I will."

"I have a hard time trusting big pharmaceutical companies, you understand? It's my nature."

"I know, Dad. But give it a break. She's a very smart and discerning person. Hutmacher puts billions into life-saving research every year."

"Those people are sharks."

"Dad? Cool it."

Bill placed his hand on his heart and winked at Veblen.

"I pledge allegiance, to the marketplace,
of the United States of America. TM.
And to the conglomerates, for which we shill,
one nation under Exxon-Mobil/Halliburton/Boeing/Walmart,
nonrefundable,
with litter and junk mail for all!"

"Bill? Let's not spoil the evening," said Marion.

"Oh, no problem. I'm not the one selling my soul to Hutmacher Pharmaceuticals. Did you know in the paper today, they've just paid three billion dollars to settle a civil and criminal investigation?"

"Tell me something new!" Paul said. "You're such a hick."

"Dad's a hick," Justin said.

"Okay, Mr. Bigshot: three years ago, an executive at your sponsor, Hutmacher Pharmaceuticals, by the name of Leonard Byrd, filed a qui tam suit against the company—have you heard any of this?"

"Somehow I've missed it."

"And I take it you know what that is?"

"A whistle-blower suit. Duh."

"Yes. He revealed that the FDA was rubber-stamping Hutmacher's toilet paper because of personal relationships between top management and high-level FDA and other government officials, and this is the part I want you to listen to, Paul. Paul, are you listening?"

Paul was draining his second glass of wine, and he brought his empty glass down on the table hard. He wiped his mouth with the back of his hand. "I have no choice."

"Here's the part you need to know, Paul. Do you know what happened to Leonard Byrd?"

"Let's guess. Veblen?"

"Um," she said awkwardly. "He was found dead in a ditch?"

"Nobody knows. He's *missing*. Vanished off the face of the earth."

"Where did you hear this?" Paul asked.

"I found it. It's been hushed up, you can only find snippets about it on the net."

Thankfully at that moment the waitstaff surrounded them, and began to sing. They were offering up a piece of cheesecake hastily stabbed with a generic white candle, along with a blustery rendition of "Happy Birthday," and other diners joined in, perhaps with real emotion because of Justin's near-death experience. Applause followed the puff of Paul's breath, which extinguished the teardrop flame.

Justin groped beneath the table and pulled up a gray cardboard tube.

"Paul. Happy birthday. You're thirty-five."

"Thanks." Paul dismantled the tube, which yielded a knobby twig with bright-colored yarn tied on at various intervals. Bill and Marion watched expectantly, to add gravity to the gesture. *Justin worked a long time on this—react accordingly!* Paul smiled and looked at the stick, and Veblen hoped that he sincerely liked it. "This is great."

"He looked for days for the right piece of wood."

"It's from the Japanese cherry," said Bill. "Big limb came down in a storm."

"We planted it when Paul was born," Marion added.

"Cool," Paul said. "So it comes with a lot of feeling."

"Tell him what the knots signify," Marion said.

"The knots are for your birthdays," said Justin.

Paul looked. "Eight knots. Must be dog years."

Justin laughed. Paul returned the stick to the tube.

"Here's something for you." Marion handed over an envelope.

"We thought you might like this better than some crapola you don't need," Bill said.

Paul opened the card. Veblen glimpsed a small wad of cash inside. Paul looked at it quickly then tamped it back.

"Thanks, Mom, Dad."

"This is for Veblen." Justin pulled up a small box, and she took it from him and opened it carefully.

"Oh, wow, thanks!" Inside was a small ingot, like an artifact from the Iron Age.

"I melted it and I made it," said Justin. "And you know what it is?"

She gazed at its little curves and flourishes. "Is it a duck?"

"Yes!" cried Justin, with some drool.

For once, everyone at the table seemed happy.

"I love this," she declared.

Bill and Marion looked on with evident gratitude.

"And here's mine," said Veblen, handing Paul her gift.

It was a picture of the two of them on the beach in Pescadero, framed. In essence, a picture of them beaming at a passing stranger.

"Were we smiling at her, or at us looking at ourselves in the future?" Veblen asked philosophically.

"At the great open maw of eternity," Paul said.

"Let me see!" Justin cried, and grasped it with his greasy hands, and Paul left the table.

Back at the motel Justin stood by the rough gray trunk of the old oak in the parking lot, holding a golden acorn in his palm.

Just then a squirrel spiraled up the tree, leaping out to the end of a tapering limb. (Veblen wondered if squirrels were stirred when humans slowed to admire the nubby cupules, the voluptuous cotyledons, and the lustrous seed coat covering the pericarp, which indicated a peppery flavor. She had tried it.)

"That's it," said Justin.

"The one from the restaurant?" She peered closer, surprised to discern a certain sly wrinkle in its brow.

"MuuMuu," Justin said, laughing.

Indeed, with the orderly rows of whiskers on its cheeks, the darkened follicles at the roots, the cascade of lashes on its brow, the cleanliness of its ears, the squirrel was unmistakable. "I think you're right! How did it get over here?"

"Veblen, come in. Now!" Paul gestured from the door. What difference did it make if they stayed outside a moment more to watch a squirrel on this winter evening with their breath escaping in plumes?

"Look, you can see the squirrel's breath," she said, and Justin said, "I see the squirrel's breath. I see it too!"

"Veblen?" called Paul.

"Want to see the squirrel's breath?" called Veblen.

"NO, I DON'T WANT TO SEE THE SQUIRREL'S BREATH."

"All right!" she said.

"PAUL? ARE YOU OKAY?"

It should be known that Veblen hated sharing events with people who didn't enjoy them as much as she did. Nothing could bring her down faster, or make her feel more acutely that an hour of her life had been forlorn. Maybe it was because anytime she and her mother attended a gathering in her youth, no matter how wonderful and festive it seemed, Melanie would scorch it afterward.

One time they attended a rockhounding fair in Santa Rosa. Veblen was jubilant. She had won a raffle at the door and picked a grab bag full of polished agates, seen glorious specimens of pyrite and amethyst, and met kids whose parents obviously had something in common with her mother, people her mother could not possibly object to, people they might form bonds with and see again. But in the car going home, Melanie said bitterly, "What a circus. Those nitwits have no concept of the environment. Did you hear that idiot talking about the way they stripped that hill of every last particle? What a horror show. Nobody there had our values."

"They *do* like collecting rocks," Veblen said, her voice rising. "That's why we went there!"

"It's not what I was expecting. Never again!"

Veblen let out a blood-curdling scream, enabling her mother to feel like the normal one.

They never found a soul with the same values. The moral fiber of others was always weak and frayed as far as her mother was concerned. Other people were insensitive and crass. Other people crashed through the world like barbarians, lacking manners, lacking taste, lacking sensitivity, lacking any regard for Melanie C. Duffy.

So when Paul's mood did not match hers in the car driving home, she felt a painful flutter in her chest.

"What's wrong?" she asked again.

His eyes darted in the dark. "How can I explain?"

"Well, try," she coaxed, though she was having trouble hiding her distress.

"It's just *them*," he whispered.

"What did they do?"

"You didn't notice?"

And she bit into her forearm so hard she almost cried out. Strife in the family she wanted to love wholly and fast was a catastrophe for Veblen.

"It's just that Justin's been trying to sabotage me since the day I was born," Paul finally managed.

"How?"

"You don't get it," he growled. "See? I knew you wouldn't."

"But he's disabled—how can he help it?" She bit her arm harder, steadying her jaw.

"Helen Keller was a spoiled brat until Anne Sullivan came along. My brother needs an Anne Sullivan, see what I'm saying? They've let him terrorize me all my life and never stopped him! You know what I realized tonight? He'll probably sabotage the wedding. He won't plan it, but he'll erupt, he'll act out, and why not, no one blames him for anything, there are no consequences, he's free to do anything he wants."

"But, Paul, don't count on the worst. He couldn't sabotage the wedding, it's not possible!"

"You want to bet?"

Paul drove catatonically, a deeply wounded look in his eyes. "Veb, this thing against me, it's all he's got. So believe me, it'll happen, one way or another. It's hard for me to feel like it doesn't matter." As if aware of Veblen's resistance, he added, "I've been to counselors far and wide over this. He's got my parents catering to his every whim, he doesn't have to work or face the world, he gets their undivided attention and benefit of the doubt, and no matter what he does to me, I'm always the one in the wrong. I know it sounds paranoid, but it's real. I'm sorry to drag you into my personal hell, but there it is."

This is the price you have to pay. To be connected.

"You've never mentioned this before," she said, feeling betrayed.

"Look where he gets it," Paul went on. "You heard my father. His digs about Hutmacher? It's insane. He's this close to being one of those guys who drive around in a van with a megaphone."

"No, he's not!"

"He did say I was a doctor. That was something. Remember in the restaurant?"

"Well you *are*."

"To be healthy, I have to get rid of this baggage," he admitted.

"It's like a scar," she offered, to cocoon the matter.

"It's worse than a scar. I'm practically crippled."

"Everybody has sore spots," she whispered.

"Yep. Thank you for allowing me to have scars and sore spots."

"Mmm," she said, biting her arm higher up, where there was more flesh.

It would have been very helpful if Veblen could have been honest with herself at this point, if she had been able to admit that scars and sore spots terrified her, that she'd been helplessly driven by someone's scars and sore spots all her life, bleating like a lamb as the scars and sore spots nipped at her heels, sending her willy-nilly in directions she didn't need to go, and that she'd wasted so much precious time that in the future she really, really didn't want to be chased by any more scars and sore spots. But this she had yet to grasp.

Later she found herself catching her breath in the hallway, gazing at a mustachioed Norseman.

"Why are you always looking at him?" Paul said, irritably.

It was here, before Thorstein Veblen's portrait, that she came when she needed to find her best self, to remind herself there were many ways to achieve one's ideals, not just the conventional ones.

"He makes me feel good," Veblen said.

This appeared to further unsettle him, which she rather enjoyed, a cool slap on the buttock of assumption.

He plunked down on the edge of the bed, kicked off his shoes and socks. His shoulders sagged and his hair stuck out in spikes. Wait a minute, she loved him. She didn't want to be mad about his attitude about his brother, or make him jealous of Thorstein Veblen.

"You make me feel better," she added quickly.

Now Paul pulled the covers up under his chin. "You know they used to be nudists, don't you?" he said.

"Who?"

"My family."

"No! You never mentioned that." She had noticed an endearing pattern: whenever Paul felt guilty or in need of affection, he'd tell a painful story about his past.

"Oh, yes. When I was in about fifth grade, for about a year or so. I'm telling you, I'm lucky I still have normal sexual feelings for women. Or anybody, for that matter."

"Gee."

"You're in fifth grade and suddenly you start seeing your mother naked all the time? And your dad too? And your older brother?

Sitting cross-legged on the floor? Walking around, leaning over, reaching for things in cupboards? Grotesque."

She nodded with earnest sympathy. How many times had she borne witness to her naked mother, running to the bedroom after a shower with a towel pressed to her front? But repeated viewings of her mother's unclad emotions had been way worse, and had led Veblen to fear depressives. Back then she'd run for cover outside, where she would help frightened grasshoppers escape into the ravine, in danger of her mother's shears. (When she was in a bad mood, and even when she was in a good mood, Melanie liked to hunt them down and cut them cleanly in half, which made Veblen scream.) She'd pretend she was part of the resistance during World War II, helping grasshopper comrades escape across the border.

"So—that's why you think squirrels are horrible?" she asked suddenly.

"Why?"

"Because they're nude?"

He chuckled. "That's it. Exactly."

She kissed him and loved him intensely then, as she always did when they laughed about something together.

DRIFTING TO SLEEP, Veblen reflected on how she was sensitive to jealousy and hypervigilant over situations that created it, though in recent years she'd taken to exploring how much jealousy a normal person could stand in comparison to her mother. The rigor of her training had sharpened a fine etiquette scarcely necessary with others.

Take a classic example of her emotional training. Veblen had once slept over at her friend Joanie's house. Veblen's mother didn't like Joanie for a number of reasons, including her manners, her dress, her religion (practiced in a group setting on Sundays), and her family. Joanie's mother had been a sorority girl at Chico State, had married a contractor, and, though not wealthy, they had built a phony castle of a house. Joanie's mother curled her hair every day before Joanie's father came home. At this sleepover, she had the girls make a salad for dinner, and showed them how to peel a cucumber, then run a fat-tined fork down the sides of it so that when it was sliced it looked scalloped, and when Veblen came home from this sleepover and was next helping her mother make a salad, she excitedly displayed the new trick. To her dismay, her mother began to cry and ran out of the kitchen, saying how this was a special thing she'd wanted to teach Veblen herself, and if Joanie's mother was such a domestic superstar, then maybe Veblen would rather live there?

Linus was drinking a martini and eating peanuts at the kitchen table. Veblen said, "I don't understand why she's mad."

Linus rattled the ice in his martini glass, and took a sufficient swallow. "Your mother cares about you very much, and probably feels she's lost an opportunity to teach you something. Why don't you go into the bedroom and give her a pat and make her feel better?"

Veblen dried her hands on a dish towel. Heading for the bedroom she tightened her core muscles, assessing what would be needed for peace. "Mom?" she whispered.

It was dark in the bedroom. "What is it?"

She forayed into the dark, leaned over the bed. "Mom, sorry you couldn't show me how to decorate cucumbers."

Her mother grunted from under the covers.

"You showed me how to make radishes look like roses, remember?"

"Yes, I did," said her mother, and she opened the covers to allow Veblen in for a cuddle.

Her mother hugged her to her chest. "Does that woman still wear those curlers around the house?"

"Yes," Veblen said, seeing a way out. "Big pink ones that look like shrimp."

"And talk about her glory days at Chico State?"

"Yeah!" Veblen howled. "She's a hollow shell living in the past!"

Her mother laughed. "That's what I always thought. A very superficial woman. No interests outside the home."

"No interests at all!" Veblen exclaimed, and her mother tickled her, and they rejoined Linus in the kitchen, and when her mother turned her back for a second, Linus gave her a grateful nod, and tossed down a funnel of peanuts from his palm.

WHAT A LOT of work it had all been, she thought. Still was. Paul wasn't going to make her work that hard. He'd better not, she thought.

THE STOIC
GLACIER METHOD

In 1920, fearing that his ridge cabin up on the Old La Honda Road had been sold through a mishap with the deed, Thorstein Veblen smashed the windows of the cabin with an ax. His second wife, Babe, was dying, and he'd planned to bring her there to mend, and his grief knew no end.

For the rest of the country, recovering from the Great War, it was a year of optimism. Spirits were so high in the financial sectors, anarchists had no choice but to set off bombs on Wall Street. Veblen lived for a while in a boardinghouse in New York with Mr. James Rorty, author of *Our Master's Voice*, who regaled him with petrifying stories about the reach of the advertising industry. A massive storm cloud of excess would build during the decade, and Veblen had been fully aware of the collapse that it would bring.

Maybe it was then, Veblen thought now, that he developed his reputation for melancholy, inspiring people to describe him so pathetically, even on highway road signs:

VALDERS MEMORIAL PARK
Hwy. J, Valders, Manitowoc County, Wisconsin

One of Wisconsin's most controversial figures, Thorstein Bunde Veblen, was born near here July 30, 1857. He was not a popular teacher but attracted dedicated followers. During much of his life, Veblen remained estranged from society. His pale, sick face; beard; loose-fitting clothes; shambling gait; weak voice; and desperate shyness enhanced this estrangement and deepened his loneliness. Yet the society which did not accept Veblen the man did come to value the products of his penetrating mind. His books and articles have been described as perhaps "the most considerable and creative body of social thought that America has produced."

What nitwit wrote this? Veblen wondered, home alone with her work Sunday morning, Paul having gone out with his family. The indignity, the failure to understand anything about him! The nod to his work, but the most superficial, cowardly appraisal of his person! Sometimes she felt like *nobody* got it when it came to Veblen. All he wanted was less waste, less junk, less vested interests, less counterfeit life. Was that so hard to understand, people?

HER SPACIOUS MORNING was interrupted by a call from her mother, who expected a detailed account of the latest developments without delay. There was some sun in front on the walkway, and Veblen went outside to ventilate.

"Well?" said her mother. "Did Paul's family come?"

"Yes, they did. We went out to dinner last night, and they're coming over here tonight."

"So? How was it? Did they reveal anything about themselves this time that put you on guard?"

And though she was still feeling resentful about her mother's attempt to send her to Norway, Veblen made sure not to say the Vreelands were too great, even hinting at the problems Paul had with Justin, because nothing made Melanie feel better than knowing other people had problems.

"Lots of problems."

"Be more specific."

"I guess Justin's problems kind of eclipsed Paul's childhood."

"Is that what he said?"

"Not exactly," said Veblen, hearing in the rise of her mother's voice a forming judgment.

"Hmm," said her mother.

"Last night Paul's brother almost choked to death in the restaurant," Veblen threw in, to distract her.

"It's not uncommon. Many people sit down for a nice meal and keel over dead, with no condition at all."

"Right. Anyway, I think you'll like them, within reason. They can't wait to meet you."

"Well, good," said her mother, as if people looked forward to meeting her every day. "They're not snobby?"

"No! Not snobby at all."

"They're not—shallow?"

"No." Veblen leaned over and pulled up the taproot of a sow thistle.

"I had a very unpleasant dream last night," her mother said, changing course as a result of hearing too much good news.

"What was it?"

"That you and Paul couldn't marry. That something went wrong."

"Is that wishful thinking?"

"No, Veblen. Don't pursue that. It's beneath you. Anyway, the dream made me worry."

"It's normal for you to worry, so don't worry." She found another thistle to pull, allowing the pleasant smell of the ground to waft up with the root.

"How does Paul's father treat his wife? That's very telling."

"He's very nice to her."

"How do they treat their disabled son?"

"They're nice to him too," Veblen said. "But it's tricky."

"Oh?" Her mother's voice brightened considerably.

"I haven't figured it out yet. I need to watch them a little more."

"Well, watch, then. It's important you know what you're getting into. Are you having any doubts?"

"No, no doubts."

"Veblen, that's not normal."

"My whole life you've told me *normal* is *bad*."

"Veblen, why can't we just talk like two friends? I'd like to know what you're feeling!"

"I'm telling you how I feel. I feel happy."

Her mother let out a dissatisfied sigh. "I sit here waiting for any scrap of news from you. It's pathetic."

She definitely would not tell her mother about the squirrel following them to the restaurant and spelling *muumuu,* then hitching a ride over to the motel. "Mom, did you ever have a wedding ring?"

"Yes, I had a hideous little gewgaw from Rudgear but I got rid of it a long time ago. You know what I did with it? I hurled it out the window while driving down the highway."

"Good for you, Mom. That's your style."

"And, dear, need I ask—are you taking your medications?"

"Yes. I'm fine. I'm really good."

"No twenty-four-hour crying jags?"

"None."

"Paul's parents certainly get to see more of you than I do," her mother complained.

"I'm planning to make your pork tenders recipe for dinner," Veblen offered, shaking out her welcome mat.

"You have to use fresh parsley, not dried," her mother said. "Will you have fresh parsley?"

"Yes."

"And tenderloin? You can't use chops."

"*Two* tenderloins," Veblen said.

"In the vacuum-sealed package?"

"Yep."

"Let me know how it turns out. Will I hear from you tomorrow?"

"Yes, Mom."

"Wonderful. Live!"

"I'm trying!" she said, kicking a sodden magnolia pod into the street.

. . .

VEBLEN THOUGHT about her mother's imperative to *live!* later that day, while cleaning the place and cooking. How, exactly, was that supposed to happen? Was making pork tenderloin her mother's idea of living? Or simply that Veblen was forming new relationships with new people? She wondered if her mother would ever move beyond her current phase, hiding out in Cobb, venturing out only to go to the Rescue Squad Thrift Store. She'd been to the Rescue Squad with her mother many times, wondering why her mother felt so alive there. The shop was filled with racks of old garments and linens, shelves of broken toys and worn shoes. One whole room held telephones and lamps and outdated appliances. The older women who ran the shop knew her mother by name. "Hello, Melanie!" they'd hail her when she came in to determine the quality of the latest haul. In her bearing at the Rescue Squad was the hint of a scout from Sotheby's. What happened to her mother, why was that her life?

Veblen had once read an illustration of her mother's syndrome in the William James essay "The Energies of Men." It described the "habit of inferiority to our full self. . . . The human individual . . . possesses powers of various sorts which he habitually fails to use."

Come to think of it, she could surely be accused of the same.

THAT AFTERNOON a sudden wind shook the trees and swept off paths and walkways, only to litter them again with debris from the trees. A bird's nest came down on the sidewalk, luckily without eggs in it. A heavy branch broke on a magnolia tree down the street, and remained attached by a thick band of bark, folded beside the old trunk like a broken wing. The power went out for a while. Veblen didn't mind; she had her good old typewriter.

Young Veblen would hide in the attic to read old newsprint. A thrifty family does not make single use of anything, and papers went upstairs maybe for reading or maybe for insulation or maybe for both. The language in the newspapers was elegant, and he compared all the words he knew in his mother tongue to the words he read in the new. Many came from Old Norse, such as *anger* and *awkward*, and *geyser* and *gosling*, and *husband* and *hell*, and *outlaw* and *ransack*, and *thrift* and *want* and *wrong*.

In the newspapers he came upon countless advertisements for all sorts of strange, newfangled things:

*Steel Collars Enameled White! Having the appearance and comfort of linen, readily cleaned with a sponge!

*Non-Explosive Lamps, from the Non-Explosive Lamp Company! Satisfy yourself on the truth of this assertion!

*Electric Belts by the Pulvermacher Galvanic Co! Bands and appliances for the cure of Nervous,

Chronic, Special Diseases! Avoid vendors of
Bogus Belts and Appliances, especially the tricky
concerns who pretend to send belts on trial!

He believed less in god than the struggle of
a thinker in his nightshirt.
He cried at the death of a caterpillar.
He took apart a dead squirrel bone by bone.
He kept acorns in a can until they popped
forth with maggots.
He ran zigzag from the system and saw wages
as hour counting.
You see, the work of maintaining your life
with your own skills was never counted in
hours. The days were long and arduous, but
there was no wishing them to go by.
The very word "weekend" was a monstrous little
propaganda of modernity. Of gladness that time
had passed, your very life!

From the attic he laid his plans:
To infuriate corporate schemers!
To annoy government wasters!
To drive developers completely insane.
To teach gluttonous consumers lessons they
wouldn't soon forget!
To create havoc for the rude and the nasty,
to waylay specious marriages, partnerships, and
other misconceived unions!

```
To madden captains of industry!
To screw academic toadies!
To make "pest" his middle name!
```

PAUL ARRIVED with his family at dusk. They had spent the afternoon cruising open houses. They called out, "Invasion of the Vreelands!" as they came in with damp bags jiggling with wine and beer bottles and Hansen's pomegranate sodas, a bouquet of yellow jonquil, and a loaf of Francese bread sprinkling flour in a white paper sleeve.

He kissed her in the kitchen. "Dad and I had a talk this afternoon," he muttered. "It's the first time he's ever said he might be part of the problem. Ever!"

Veblen, who believed in slow, incremental changes, glowed with satisfaction. "See? You're using the stoic glacier method."

"Remind me, what is the stoic glacier method?"

"It's the slow process of shaping someone's behavior by force of one's own personal stoicism." ("If you wish to be loved, love," said Seneca, a Stoic of note.)

"Wow. Maybe so."

To have family and friends to make dinner for! (Though she wondered what Paul would find fault with after they left.) Cocktails (vodka and lemonade), little appetizers (mushroom turnovers), the voices, the combustion. Justin was going around examining everything in her house, even in her bedroom.

"Justy, come on, give Veblen her privacy," Bill called.

She glanced in and saw Justin leaning over and touching her pillow. Some drool spilled from his lips.

"Open houses sure have changed," remarked Marion. "They stage the place with all that furniture and fake artwork. It used to be you just went inside and saw how somebody lived, and you bought a house."

"They put in a lot of fancy bells and whistles and jack the price through the roof," Bill proclaimed. "You know what they wanted for the last one? Two point three! For fifteen hundred square feet! That's bullcrap!"

"Dad, admit it, living in Garberville you're not in the main-stream."

"It's not his values," said Marion.

"A beautiful, clean house with all the things you need aren't your values, Dad?"

"All bells and whistles."

"Your father made you a very fine life," Marion ventured. "Someday I believe you'll see that."

"It could've been better," said Bill. "I'm not saying it was the best."

THE CHEESE.

"Dad, it was okay. But things are expensive here."

In her small kitchen, with its old green tiles and Wedgewood stove, Veblen made a special drink for Justin, with fresh lemons, sugar, mint, and ice. Then she blended the rest with vodka and poured it into her best glasses.

Paul checked the squirrel trap in the attic, still empty. He'd replaced the sauerkraut and mace with a slice of cheese a while back, and now Veblen heard him gasp.

"Very funny," he said, bringing down the plate. "Fess up."

Veblen said, "It's a Rorschach of your projections, Paul. An id intrusion. Your repressed desire to believe!" And she took a picture of the mysterious cheese before Paul heaved it into the trash.

"Hmmm," Paul said, eyeing her.

"Mr. Science Man can't explain everything," Bill said.

"Dad, we had squirrels in the house, remember? How did you deal with them?"

"We lived peaceably with the wildlife."

"No, Dad, you got rid of them. We had a blackout once. We had solar anyway, but they chewed the wires."

"They *dislodged* the wires."

"Did you use steel wool?"

"I plugged a few holes. They went away."

Justin asked her, "Do you love Paul?"

"I do," she said, still thinking about the cheese.

"I do too."

Paul smirked over the edge of his cocktail. "I'm so lovable."

"Do you love me?" asked Justin.

"Of course," said Veblen, giving him a hug, wondering if he really hated Paul and wanted to ruin the wedding. He moved his body as if to press himself against her breasts. She gently backed away.

With some urgency, Justin ran to the bathroom.

"If I were you, I'd stay here," Bill said. "This is a sweet place."

"Thank you," Veblen said, grateful that Bill saw the charm in her simple cottage, with its limited market orientation and many outdated fixtures. But then it seemed something was wrong, Paul was pacing by the bathroom door, Marion was murmuring to him. Paul was angry. Marion was angry at Paul for being angry. Veblen retreated to the kitchen.

She heard Marion at the bathroom door, knocking gently. "Justy? Come on now."

"Don't just stand there, do something!" Paul yelled.

Veblen chewed fiercely on her inner cheeks, wishing she were outside with a cool breeze on her skin. What kind of crisis was it, that Justin was in the bathroom? Couldn't Paul surmount his regressive tendencies? Through the window of the place next door she saw her neighbor Donald Chester remove a flat of macaroni and cheese from his microwave, with no one to eat or regress with at all.

She sliced lemons and chopped parsley, heard the unfastening of the lock.

Then Paul's voice: *"You little shit."*

And Justin calling out: "Don't bother me, Paul!"

Veblen came out and saw Paul clamp his arms around Justin's neck, bringing his own head down where he could lean over Justin's and put his face close. "I'll bother you, you fucking asshole!"

Bill was there, pulling on Paul. Paul wedged a leg around Justin's legs. Justin butted Paul with his head and Paul screamed and Bill yelled, "Let go," and pulled Paul's legs out from under him. The cottage shook like it had been hit by a falling tree. Acid burned in Veblen's throat.

Marion took Justin to the couch. "You didn't understand," she was whispering. "You didn't, did you?" Her cheeks were reddened by a pattern of broken vessels Veblen had never noticed. "You're a good boy. A very, very, very good boy."

Bill said, "I'm sorry, Veblen. Everything is fine and now we'll move on and forget about this."

She doubted everything was fine with Paul.

"What just happened?" she whispered to him, in the kitchen.

"Later," he said apologetically, and shortly, as with plucky volunteers at a hospital, it became the job of the Vreeland family to levitate the mood above the threshold of the damned. When Veblen served dinner, Paul and Marion were overly impressed with the pork tenders, and Justin shoveled them in, and Bill made no cutting remarks about pharmaceutical companies. All joviality; no brutality. A conspiracy of sorts.

After dinner, as Paul, Bill, and Justin caught the last quarter of a college basketball game on Veblen's little TV, Marion settled on the couch and opened up a box she'd brought full of Paul's baby pictures. "Here he is at about six months," she said, offering Veblen a snapshot of a doughy slab on a blanket. "And this is his first birthday."

"Come on, man, *play ball!*" yelled Bill. He stomped his feet. The cottage rattled.

Veblen, to her dismay, was laboring to perceive the baby form of Paul as cute. She found him blockish and sour in appearance, and a jolt of alarm coursed through her while she went through the photos with Marion. Things improved when Paul reached twelve—now she could see the man in him, the shoulders filled out, the glint of humor in his eyes. But then— what was this? This Paul-boy had a pot belly and wore bizarre striped velvet pants—

"He went through a phase," remarked Marion. "We used to call him Mr. Fancy Pants."

Wasn't it vital to think your betrothed had been an adorable child? What if they had a baby like him, sour and grim? When she couldn't stand one more image of the little blob, she jumped up and offered to make tea, then grabbed the barely full garbage bag and went out with it, what Linus always did when he needed a break.

In the cool air of evening by the bins, she drew some deep breaths and watched a lappet moth bat against the window, and saw Marion, Bill, Justin, and Paul congregating in her small house. Through the glass she saw gestures of familiarity as they huddled over the pictures. Marion placed a hand on Paul's shoulder. Justin leaned on Bill. Bill talked to his boys, and for that moment, listening to their father, they sat as brothers absorbed in the family lore. What did she know about families, and how they ran? About siblings, and how they pounded each other, but loved? The normal give-and-take of family life hadn't been hers to witness. Next to the organ pipe cactus near the window, she could faintly hear the sound of the beetle burrowing into the cactus flesh, while a shower of dried needles and leaves came down from the rain gutter. Over her head stood the outlandishly upright squirrel, three young ones abreast. Their heads seemed to glow in the darkness.

"Oh my gosh," she whispered. "Are those your children?"

The squirrel quipped and chattered, and if you didn't know better you might think you were in range of a Perfect Squirrel Call, registered trademark no. 348205, a black tubular device of about four inches in length, which Veblen had been sent as a girl by her pilot grandfather, Woodrow, nothing to do with hunting, but for the magic of summoning squirrels. (Of course, she'd wondered why it was called "perfect" and what it was actually saying in the language of squirrels, and looked up the patent once to find out who thought they knew all this.) But she'd cherished it along with a few other odd gadgets he'd handed down to her, such as his old pilot's plotter and his flight calculator. "That's been high-grade, classic humor, bothering Paul the way you have," she said to the squirrel. "Chaplinesque. But really, enough is enough."

The sky was deeply black that night, scratched with silver. An attack of happiness came over her, that she'd assembled this crew, however imperfect, in her domain. Ragged scraps had always proved under her auspices to sprout new things fresh and worthy. She saw Paul look expectantly at the screen door, depending on her return.

"This is your last chance. Stop making so much noise if you want Paul to stay."

She returned inside, heart bucking. She was superstitious about making ultimatums. If he made noise again, she'd have to take it as a sign.

She served the Vreelands strawberry shortcake, with tender buttery biscuits, tart berries, and hand-whipped cream. Plates were scraped and licked. And then good-byes and good-nights were set in motion, with every permutation of hug and talk of plans bandied about before the car rolled away and vanished from sight.

Paul turned and kissed her. "I owe you," he muttered. "My neck is so tight I think I'm going to puke."

"I don't understand, what happened?"

Paul swallowed. "Don't you know?"

"What?"

He groaned softly. "I thought you knew."

She shook her head.

She followed him back to her bedroom, a paper bag in the corner, with a pink pair of panties wadded up inside.

"That's my underwear."

Paul looked sick. "I know it! This is what he does. At people's houses. Didn't you understand?"

"Oh!" she said, suddenly seeing.

"Sorry!" Paul was anguished.

Veblen started to groan.

"It's incredibly humiliating."

"Ew."

"I don't know what to say."

"It's not your fault."

"I know. But I'm bringing it into your life."

"No, it's okay," she said, starting to laugh helplessly.

"Stop laughing," he said, shaking his head. "Now do you get it? Do you understand why I get so uptight?"

"A guy has needs." To weigh the sincerity of her reassurances, she reflected on a future with a brother-in-law who stole off with women's underwear and masturbated in back rooms. It felt—not the greatest, but not a deal killer. It could be viewed as utterly human, privacy turned inside out, a common urge, no shame attached.

"It's a complete lack of impulse control, a common feature of his condition."

"Hmm. Has this happened before?"

"Fuck yes. Imagine this. At my piano teacher's house during a recital."

Veblen squeezed his arm. "Sorry."

"It's the distorted sibling rivalry he feels with me. It's *more* than his condition."

"Maybe you remind him—of what he's missing?"

"No, it's an unconscious desire to kill me," Paul said. "And I have to go along with it or else I'm a jerk!" He was shaking.

"No, you're not."

"You know what I think, Veb? We should move to another continent."

"I could get into that."

"Forget having the wedding at Cloris's house. Not with him around."

"Mmmm," she said, not wanting to sound too happy about it.

"I'll drug him the day of the wedding," Paul said.

She thought of telling Paul the squirrel had a family, but didn't want to trigger any further controversies for the night.

He took her hands.

"Are you going to throw me away?"

"No!" she said.

He waltzed her through the room until they collided with a bookcase, which released, like a fortune-telling booth at an arcade, a single volume onto the floor. *The Tale of Squirrel Nutkin.*

"Help!" Paul said.

Veblen laughed and shoved it back onto the shelf.

Then they cleaned up the remains of the dinner, the ravaged lemon wedges, the strawberry calyxes strewn on the tiles, the parsley stalks wilted by the sink, a dry mushroom cap upended on the floor. Hard grains of rice had spilled and Veblen swept them, absorbed with thoughts of deep, lasting relationships to come. She wouldn't run from Paul and his brother's kinks. She would have squirrel friends on the side! She would become like Bill and Marion's daughter, and she would take care of them until the day they died.

(But why was she thinking about taking care of them until the day they died? Would that keep her out of thrift stores and mental institutions? Why wasn't she thinking about all the fun things she'd do with Paul? Was she merely attracted to *burdens*?)

10

WAR CASH

At the VA the next week, in the ward at bedside, Paul read through the records of Sergeant Major Warren Smith. His daughters had called again for news.

SGM Smith had suffered burns over 30 percent of his body after he rushed into a burning building hit by a missile to rescue Afghan children screaming in terror from the roof. He had succeeded in reaching the children and dropping them into a safety net held by troops on the ground, but just before he could jump, a bullet grazed the back of his head. The building was fully engulfed in flames but a helicopter plucked him up and carried him to safety. He was transported to the Landstuhl Regional Medical Center (LRMC) in Germany, a top organ donation site for troops who did not survive there, where he remained in a coma for one week. Smith, however, survived, and no organs were bequeathed. He was found to have slight neurological weakness on his left side, slight memory loss and mood lability, but appeared to be on the road to recovery.

Eventually he came home into the care of his family. His burns healed, he regained full use of his limbs, but before long the family insisted he was no longer the man they once knew. It seemed a likely case of PTSD. A notation suggested the family seek counseling to adjust to Smith's trauma and personality changes.

He'd had an MRI, an EEG, blood panels, occupational and physical therapy, and counseling. An ophthalmologist corrected his lenses. In the fall, Smith had apparently attempted suicide by opening a car door in a moving vehicle. The family thought participation in a trial would be good for his morale. There was a new notation showing that Smith had been assigned to psychiatric treatment with Dr. Burt Wallman.

A tug on his coat brought Paul's attention to the man's troubled face. "Hey, buddy," Paul said. "You have two really nice daughters. You're a lucky guy."

"There's a war machine," Smith said, in his gravelly voice. "And you wanna put me in it."

It took Paul a moment to respond.

"Oh, you mean the CURS, the simulator?"

"You're gonna put me in the war machine!"

—said Smith, who was apt to slow down in the middle of a thought with his tongue too dry to say it. There were many days he'd forgotten, wigs of days, hairpieces sitting on time, and there were secret warm joys hidden somewhere he could no longer find them. He was aware of his service and his injury and the recovery plan, but there was something else they weren't saying. There was a decal over everything.

He itched in his bed, and called it a trough. He craved sun on his skin, or the fresh air tickling the hairs on his arms, or the warm glow of a real lightbulb by his bed. He missed the grease on his fingers after a taco and tuning the radio to get rid of the buzz. He heard water pouring from a spigot in the earth, washing the streets, bubbling up the best of life from the mantle and spewed away at a train stop, the witchery of men and stopwatches. The windows of mayhem had opened unto him. What could be counted on was nothing. He had been too proud of his bricks in the pile by the house. And who ever knew! All those wicked wishes. WAR CASH was how he saw the sign at the car wash, it was imbedded everywhere—

A scream came unbidden from his neck.

"ALL RIGHT, THEN. Let go now," Paul said, because Smith had gripped his wrist and it burned as it had when Justin had no mercy and pinned him down. He heard the indifferent rotation of the ceiling fans, the hum of monitors, and his own shallow breath. Across the ward a male nurse changed an IV bag on a stand, oblivious to the assault. His blood was not pumping to his hand, his hand was dead. "That's . . . *enough*."

"You all right over there?" called the male nurse.

Paul's heart was racing because a window had opened through Smith to all of the unexpressed ruin in the room, and he'd have to close the window soon or else be overwhelmed by it. His arm was slick with the sweat of the man's hand, and now Smith's nails were digging in.

"Let go!"

A call would be made to the Smiths that afternoon, laying out their choices.

"Getting your strength back, are you?" It was the male nurse, prying Smith away, wrapping him in an embrace like a straitjacket. "There we go. There we go. Look at that strength you're gaining."

Paul had a welt with puncture wounds, like an animal bite. The skin was broken in dark crescents. He fled to the sink to douse it with antiseptic, and rinsed his arm in cold water until it had no feeling in it at all.

11

THE SPEECHLESS OTHERS

I n April the days warmed fully, demanding new exploits. A thin-
ning scrim of wildlife rustled in the coastal mountains' hidden
gullies and groves. Bobcats, coyotes, raccoons, skunks, and pos-
sums still foraged the damp forests above the peninsula, between
the ocean and the bay.

By contrast, Palo Alto was now a community of unimaginable
material wealth and prestige, and traces of old, humble Palo Alto
were growing scarce. What others wished to raze, Veblen cherished. What others saw as *rundown*, Veblen saw as *real*.

Such as the spot eight miles from town, up on the ridge where
Thorstein Veblen had dragged the chicken coop to build his get-
away, and where she and Paul now stood. Paul was filming her
with his phone. Veblen's contact at the Norwegian Diaspora Project, Aksel Odegaard, had expressed interest in some video content
in a general announcement to all contributors.

*"Vi står på toppen av den gamle La Honda Road, nær Skyline
Drive, i San Mateo County, California,"* Veblen said, speaking to

the camera, and though the presentation had to be in Norwegian, she would provide an English transcript as well. *"Under oss er Silicon Valley"*—Paul panned the peninsula—"where fortunes are being made every day in the technology sector. But I wonder how many people here stop to remember that Thorstein Veblen, best known for his searing critique of society in *The Theory of the Leisure Class,* came to the small town of Palo Alto in 1906 to teach at the young campus named for the beloved son of the railroad baron Leland Stanford, who'd contracted typhoid and died on a conspicuously unnecessary but status-prescribed grand tour of Italy. Not many, I bet.

"Mr. Veblen was a true renegade, and had seen enough of the jockeying for power and money that goes on in the institutions of our higher learning. To get away from it all, he spent as much time as he could in a cabin just up here—" Veblen indicated the ridge, feeling stirred by their proximity to this history. "The cabin was built from a chicken coop he carried up the mountain in a cart pulled by his horse Beauty, where it sat for years suspended between two giant redwood stumps." Now she had Paul zoom in on a photo of the cabin she'd found in the Stanford library after work one day.

"Han ble urettmessig oppsagt from the University of Chicago and would soon be unfairly dismissed from Stanford as well. So he skewered academia in his book *The Higher Learning,* initially subtitled *A Study in Depravity.* He loved to think about how conventions solidified and spread. He was passionately curious. He loved the out of doors and wrote nearly every day on the seasonal progress of trees and flowers. He wrote about everything from anthropology and economics to the squandering of the American frontier,

FORMER CHICKEN COOP/CABIN OF THORSTEIN VEBLEN.

even about the mass scalping of the fur-bearing mammals, which was pretty farsighted in those days. He honored animals and plants by calling them *the speechless others.* He showed his stepdaughters how they could walk through a cornfield and *hear* corn grow. He was misunderstood when it came to his personal life, which was sticky and complex, and he was too stubborn and gallant to try to set the record straight. *En fascinerende og mystisk person."* And she held up her hands to stop the camera. Paul looked depressed for some reason.

"Was that okay?" she asked, secretly hoping he was impressed with her language skills.

"Sounded Norwegian enough," Paul said. "It just makes me wonder."

"Wonder what?"

"I don't know. Just makes me wonder."

They walked along the grassy ridge, quiet except for the occasional car or bicyclist passing by on the narrow road below. She was staring at the back of his strong, pumping calves, which suddenly seemed to have a different personality from the rest of Paul. At last, over his shoulder, he said, "Are you committed to having a really strange life?"

She laughed. "Probably. What do you mean?"

"You seem to admire strange and difficult lives more than upright, successful ones."

She felt good after making the video, ready to take him on. But there was another reason she'd brought him here: it was the perfect place for the wedding. After all, it was time to decide.

"Maybe," she admitted. "Isn't this place pretty?"

"Remember that comment your mother made, about how you'd really surpassed her, something like that?" Paul pressed on.

"When?"

Left, right, left, right. The calves were angry calves.

"During lunch? It was bizarre. It was when we talked about house hunting."

She remembered vaguely. "What about it?"

"Just wondering what it meant."

"I don't know, what do you think it meant?"

Paul stopped and turned, clearly distressed. "Somehow I got the sense she's jealous of you, and that you try to avoid having her feel that way because it ruptures the equilibrium you're desperate to maintain for some reason. And that maybe you feel like you have to have a strange life so that you don't surpass her."

She cringed further, wondering if it could be true. But it wasn't. She truly admired the underdogs and outsiders who felt free to be themselves. "I don't think so," she replied, begrudging her willingness to discuss it.

Paul began to walk backward, facing her, as if lit up by a pressing concern. "When you were a kid, how often would you see your father?"

"Once a year, for two weeks."

"Did you look forward to your visits with him?"

"Not at all."

"Don't kids from divorced families pine for the parent they see least?" he asked, pulling his collar away from his neck.

"I think I've told you, I used to be scared to visit Rudgear," she said.

"How come? Too normal?"

"Hey! What's that supposed to mean?"

"I met your mother and stepfather for the first time last week. It makes sense that we'd talk about things a little."

True enough, every visit was a rich cube of bouillon, so full of compressed flavors, it could be enough to make a soup to feed on for days.

"As long as it's in the right spirit."

"Doesn't that go without saying?"

They continued along the ridge. Cattle stood on nearby hillocks, grazing with their baseball glove lips in the new carpet of clover. "So why were you afraid to visit him?"

She cleared her throat, trying to gather an explanation. It was all a heaving mess in her memory banks. "Well, he was super scary."

"Really? He didn't think you were adorable and lovable?"

"No," Veblen said, matter-of-factly. She wondered what that would have been like. "I was repugnant and snivelly."

"No way!"

"Way. I cried all the time. And have you ever cried so hard you start doing this hiccuping thing? But it's not really hiccuping, it's sort of like this—" She imitated the little gasps that had been such a big part of her life then.

"So you didn't want them to get back together?"

"Who?"

"Your mother and father."

"Oh my god, no!" Her face crinkled up over such nonsense. "Never crossed my mind. *Ever*. Couldn't imagine them together."

"Interesting," Paul said.

"Why are you asking about my father, right after meeting my mother?"

Paul took his time answering. At last, he said, "Just wondered what your alternatives were."

"Alternatives? What are you trying to say?"

"What do other people say when they meet your mother? Have you introduced other people to her?"

She couldn't quite find a reply.

"You must know, you must have noticed—I mean, with all due respect—she's a classic hypochondriac. Right?"

"You think that?" Veblen's voice cracked, as did her peaceable domestic fantasies, which suddenly seemed cracked to begin with. No one would ever embrace her mother. *No one will ever love me because of her.* She was impaled on the truth of it.

From the ridge where they stood, she could see the roads and arteries lined with greening trees. Across the valley the Diablo mountains ran grassy and fault wrinkled, like brain matter. All the defining features of the world she'd been inhabiting just fine before Paul showed up. It was so much work, getting along! She felt deflated, a balloon skin on the ground.

"It's the way she *actualizes* her identity through her health problems I'm talking about."

"So she's not the average suburban housewife—" This was her standby, frayed with overuse. Her voice continued to crack.

"She's unique, yes, but—it's hard to watch Linus squirming under her thumb. Don't you think?"

Veblen felt like attacking him, tearing the sinew from his bones. "That's not squirming. They *love* each other."

"Um, you know, I'm scared if that's your idea of love. He doesn't know if he's coming or going."

Her throat went dry. Something was happening, in which she felt herself abandoning her body, traveling away. "What a horrible thing to say."

"It's scary, as a male, to see something like that," he added. "I mean, I just want to know what you think is normal. Remember when we were all sitting around the table? You hardly said a word, like you were terrified."

The more he said, the worse it became.

"I've been thinking about this a lot the past few days. I want to be open and free to talk about our feelings. I've had to bottle up a lot of stuff in my life."

"I see," said Veblen, far, far away. On a steamer bound for a penal colony, waving a long farewell, with a small white hankie wet with snot and tears.

She glanced at him briefly, striding ahead, trying to leave him behind. How could they have the wedding here now? Here was a special place ruined by this vile conversation, burnished into all she saw.

"Veb, to see it as a positive, your mother's a fascinating case, and together we can face her."

They returned to Paul's car, speechless and other, and drove back to Tasso Street in silence. He followed her up the path to the demure little building, as spare as a human could construct.

She fumbled with her keys.

"Let's say it's all biological, that her amygdala is huge and swollen. Her cingulate system is probably in tatters. The prefrontal cortex inflamed, the basal ganglia shriveled—"

Inside, the air was stale. She threw her purse onto the sofa and watched the down feather of a dead goose spiral up, then float languidly in the air for a moment, as if the goose could still fly.

"And look, that's not *you*. You're nothing like that," he offered, peaceably.

"Ha. I'm just waiting until we're married." She said it bitterly, wondering what would happen if her beastly streak ever emerged, for surely that would send him running and she could stop worrying about all this connection crap and be a self-ensnared spinster for the rest of her days. It was only a matter of time— she'd lose her temper, she'd bare her teeth, she'd bite him like a jackal—

"Actually, I like her! And I'll have a good relationship with her," Paul said speedily. "You'll see."

She was opening windows, no longer listening.

"Come on."

She shrugged, exposed down to the synapses. All blackness. Nothing left to see.

"Veb, did I ever tell you how I became interested in neurology?"

"Can't say that you did," she said stiffly.

"Kind of painful," Paul continued. "I was spending all my time in the library to get away from the freaks at home, and the librarian took me under her wing. Mrs. Brown. She was a stern old bag who pitied me, I think. I was all over the place. So one day she handed me the *Life* picture book called *The Mind*—up to that point I'd mostly been reading science fiction, but *The Mind* was even weirder. I remember seeing this one page, 'Isolated Human.' A Princeton student in a lightless chamber with no sound, his hands in gloves. I think the guy went totally crazy after thirty or forty hours. Then there were the chapters on perception and memory, but the part I was really interested in was the part on madness! All these nineteenth-century sketches of mental patients and exorcisms from the Middle Ages. And a list of phobias! Ophthalmophobia, fear of being watched. Catagelophobia, fear of being ridiculed. Nyctophobia, fear of the dark; ergophobia, fear of work; even phobophobia, fear of phobias! It was scarier than science fiction."

"So? That doesn't sound painful."

"But it was painful to be young and pitied, to need solace like that, you know?"

"Mmm. How come you didn't become a psychiatrist?"

Paul nodded. "Right, that's the thing. I did a psychiatric residency. In my review I was told I was 'too reactive' to the patients. Which maybe was true. Their pathologies had little hooks that got into me and set me off—"

"Like with my mother?"

"Basically," Paul said. "It's true, I overreact when something feels off."

More was expected of her, her usual engagement replete with queries and analysis and a kind of domestication of the topic so that it became like a furry pet with a life of its own, all of which he had come to depend on. The way a cat depends on your petting it when it purrs. The purring forces you to keep petting. Even after you're tired. Even after you want to move on. Veblen had been detained countless hours on neighborhood walks, not sure when to break away, by purring cats.

"You sure do."

(Maybe she had to embrace someone who did not embrace her mother. Maybe that was a bigger challenge than finding someone who *liked* her mother.)

"I'm sorry I upset you," Paul said. "I really am."

Or maybe it was time to pull away. She prepared a fast dinner for them, peeling garlic, chopping very ripe tomatoes that trailed seeds over her hands. They barely spoke, having little fuel for niceties. The furnace banged and she couldn't wait to crawl under her covers and close her eyes.

"Smells good," Paul ventured, finishing up a beer. "What are we having?"

"*Arrabbiata.*"

"Perfect. The food of anger," he joked.

"And bread from the bakery."

"Good touch."

"And lima beans."

They ate over her small table in silence. When the back of the forearm picked up crumbs, it was time to bring out the sponge. She stared at a crease in Paul's neck.

"Veb?"

She shook her head. "So my mother is *off*."

"Veb, I'm sorry."

She indicated indifference with a toss of her head, but she could not remember a time anyone had apologized to her, ever. "Want some more?"

"Yes, it's delicious. You're an awesome cook and a totally sexy, gorgeous woman."

He was so transparent. She was about to dish up a mean, sauce-less clump, but checked herself and threw in a moist part.

Later, clearing the plates, she said, "Paul, have you ever felt sorry for the last lima bean on the plate?"

"No," he said.

"The one that doesn't get eaten, and gets scraped into the trash?" For she really did feel sorry for it, sitting there, having grown plump, been picked and cooked, for nothing.

"Why should I feel sorry for it?"

"Little did it know, all that, just to end up in the garbage."

"I don't believe it can think."

"I guess I'm projecting onto it."

"We all end up in the garbage, sooner or later."

Veblen plucked up the lone lima bean and swallowed it whole.

"The gulf I feel between us, right now, is huge," she uttered.

"That happens to all couples," Paul said quickly.

"And do they recover, and get close again?"

"Of course they do."

"They don't break up because of it?"

Paul came over and hugged her warmly. "Veb." When she didn't reply he said, "This, what we have, means everything to me. I don't want anything to happen to us."

"Like what?"

"Well, I've seen what can happen."

She pulled away, feeling an honest stab of jealousy. "I hope this has something to do with our chemistry, not your learning curve."

"You are so quick to pounce on any reference to women in my past. It's amusing."

"I'll work on that," she replied, though there hadn't been all that many.

"You do that."

"I will. But what was her name again—Millicent Cuthbertson or something?"

"Millie."

"Millie. Cute."

He shrugged.

"If we have a daughter, we'll have to name her Millie, then," said Veblen, perversely.

"You're weird."

"Where is she anyway?"

"I don't know!"

"You haven't Googled her?"

"She's not a high-profile type."

"Why, does she work temp?"

"No. I don't want to talk about her, okay?"

"Because it was such true love, it's too painful?"

"No! What a freak."

She started to laugh, the way she liked to laugh at mysterious jokes that not even she understood. Strangely, Veblen had never thought of her mother as a hypochondriac before. But could you be a hypochondriac if you genuinely had health problems? And what if it were true, what would it mean? Wouldn't it mean that all the stuff she and Linus had done for her mother was for nothing?

"You're going to give me hell, aren't you? For the rest of my life," Paul said, hopefully.

She liked that idea. Maybe she could get away with acts of insolence once in a while.

THEN IT WAS a noisy, squirrelous night. The trap was nothing to the squirrel. He would not be trapped!

Fists hit walls, shoes hit ceiling. Veblen told Paul to put cotton in his ears.

And for the record, she took devious pleasure in the squirrel's mayhem. She could not say why.

"Veb? You okay?" he asked at one point, after the lights went out.

"Yeah. I'm tired."

"You're shaking."

"Just a chill."

"Want me to warm you up a little?"

"Sure."

He reached over and rubbed her shoulders. "How come you're not wearing your ring?"

For it was back in its velveteen shell.

"I'm getting used to it, don't worry."

"You hate it, don't you?"

"It's okay, Paul."

"I want you to *want* to wear it, that's all."

"I'll get used to it," she said, sighing.

"Let's get another one," Paul said.

After a pause, she said, "Let's just sleep."

"Okay," Paul said. "Sleep well. Love you."

Her throat blocked. "Love you too."

She shuddered and coughed. She had said the dreaded "Love you" instead of "I love you," and feared it marked a terrible turning point. To drop the pronoun was surely more than a time saver. She had a hunch that when couples stopped saying "I love you" and said the more neutered, quippy "Love you" instead, something had gone awry, leading to a quick succession of deterioration scenarios and other horrors of intimacy that need not be part of every union—she would not let them be.

She walked in her sleep that night, and found herself damp with sweat at her dresser, trying to shake open a drawer.

12

THE PASSENGER YEARS

I t is one kind of trouble to kiss your fiancé good-bye in the morning and immediately turn your thoughts to another man. But it's another kind altogether if the other man has been dead for nine decades, or is of the genus *Sciurus*.

Until this engagement, Veblen thought she knew what she was about. By thirty, she had managed to put away the simmering loneliness of childhood, finding relief in things outside herself, such as in skillfully tending family members who were scattered and needy, and becoming a secret expert on the life of Thorstein Veblen. To ward off uneasy feelings that crept in at unguarded moments, she'd drawn upon a wide array of materials and activities, keeping up with all major periodicals of the day, typing along to Norwegian films, clipping interesting pictures from magazines for some future project, taking brisk bike rides. And then came Paul, and the whole enterprise of their future. Escapist feelings at this point showed a serious breakdown in self-discipline. And strangest of all, right at the moment she should be happiest.

An analyst might ask her to start with her earliest memory. Her mother would insist she go to the doctor for a thorough workup, a philosopher might take a prod to her *facticity*, an anarchist would suggest the trouble lay with the state, and a social critic such as Thorstein Veblen would be sure to mention the many ways her instincts had been thwarted as a citizen of her age.

A few quiet sobs made her feel moist and self-pitying. When the squirrel was around, she felt grounded, real, at ease. Did it matter if relief came in the form of an animal who stuck around and seemed to care?

No DOUBT, her idiosyncrasies abounded. Needing to accommodate her mother to such an extent was clearly one of them.

In the old days, after Linus moved in and began to do the shopping because her mother came unglued in the aisles, she started to receive an apple in her lunch every day, old and grainy and tasteless. Every day she'd take a bite hoping for a nice crisp juicy apple, but to no avail. Then she'd feel guilty about wasting a whole piece of fruit that had grown to maturity for nothing, only to be buried in the tomb of her desk. One day, trying to retrieve her pencil case, Veblen disturbed the order of things and apples began to pour onto the floor, as if she'd hit the jackpot in an apple slot machine. All told, twenty-six of the bruised and moldering fruits rolled through the class, and everyone, even Mrs. Ahrendt, was laughing. The kids gathered them and had a special time out, walking down the road to a horse farm, to throw them into the feed.

The next day, Mrs. Ahrendt came in with a story she'd printed out for the class:

I was sitting in my class one day, minding my own business. I saw something out of the corner of my eye just as I was about to write. I thought at first it was Mrs. Ahrendt. I glanced up and as I did I noticed it was a shiny, red object. It was alive and moving toward me! I looked more closely at it as it advanced. I thought to myself, "It's a colorful creature from another planet." It inched closer and closer. Could it be an apple the size of a human? I blinked my eyes wildly. Holy applesauce. It was a giant walking apple with a human head. I knew that head. I realized with a shiver what had happened. Veblen, the apple-eating, apple-saving, apple-happy girl, had been transformed into an absurd, abnormal, but appetizing apple!

The class laughed and Veblen felt what it must be like to be a star. To be notorious for hoarding apples was not wholly unglamorous, and surely better than the last stunt she had been known for, covering her eyes during the class picture because the flashbulbs scared her.

"You should have told me you don't like Red Delicious," Linus said that evening. "You're right, they've been hybridized beyond recognition. I can start buying McIntosh or some nice tart Pippins."

"Okay. What about a generic banana?"

"I hope people don't get the wrong idea," said her mother.

"Like what?"

"Is she going to write something about every child in the class?"

"Melanie, this is cute. Let's not overreact."

"Why should my daughter be called *absurd* and *abnormal*?"

"Appetizing too, Mom! I'm appetizing!"

"And apple-happy," said Linus. "That's praise in my book."

Indeed, this was one of the first public compliments Veblen ever received, and thereafter, kind words that came her way put her in mind of herself as a giant, walking apple—a sure way to keep one's pride in check.

Oh, there were plenty of ways to do that.

After work on Monday, wrestling her bike into the garage, Veblen received a call from her mother, who was so excited about something, Veblen had to ask her to slow down.

"Linus and I had just gotten back from a very bleak shopping trip to the Costco in Santa Rosa when our phone rang. It was a woman named Susan Hinks."

"That's Paul's assistant," Veblen said, shocked.

"Yes, exactly. She said that Dr. Paul Vreeland had asked her to look into a referral for me, and that he wished to speak with me. Next thing I knew, he was on the phone! Well, I was quite surprised. You must know all this, don't you?"

She slammed shut the garage door. "He didn't tell me anything."

"You didn't make him do this?"

"Definitely not."

"Well, he had actually taken the time to think about my

symptoms and he's leaning strongly to the adrenal glands as the source of the problem. He said there were two possible places I could go for a study, UCSF and Stanford. Naturally I said Stanford would be my preference, so he said he'd have his assistant find out which would be more suitable and let me know. Now, I'm not joking, ten minutes later this Susan Hinks called, and said Stanford might have a place for me in the next few months. Can you believe it?"

"No, I can't," Veblen said, wondering how Paul could have done this to her. He clearly didn't understand the delicate balance they'd achieved. Her house had never felt so vulnerable.

"So I'll be able to spend some time with you, and I am thrilled. He feels I may have primary aldosteronism. If I take part in the study, I'll be hospitalized for two weeks, my diet will be controlled, my urine will be collected, I'll have a saline infusion, and I'll be given something called spironolactone. Then the study continues for one to two months as an outpatient. The only known risks are rashes, decreased libido, and tender nipples."

"Ho!" chimed Linus, somewhere in the room.

"I am really touched by this, dear," said her mother, passionately. "Please tell Paul how touched I am."

"So, you're coming—when?" Standing outside her house in the late afternoon, Veblen had almost lost her voice. It was clear that her mother was now more excited about the trial than about the wedding.

"I don't know yet. Is this a problem?"

"No," Veblen said, kicking the trunk of the Aleppo pine.

"You sound uncertain."

"No, I'm just tired."

"Have you eaten well today?"

"Pretty well."

"Are you taking your iron tablets?"

"Yeah," she lied.

"Will you ignore me when I come?"

"No."

"Will you make me feel like a hanger-on?"

"Not on purpose."

"We also received an invitation today from Paul's parents to a rehearsal dinner before the wedding, which was nice."

"Oh, good. Nothing fancy, probably just a barbecue."

"But I'm worried that if we come down the night before and I have a bad night, it will ruin the wedding day for me. I'm considering the possibility of forgoing the rehearsal dinner and getting up bright and early to drive down."

"But how bad could it be?"

"I don't sleep well in motels. I don't sleep well anywhere. Will I be able to spend any time with you or will you be busy with everyone else?"

"You're sitting with me when we eat, how does that sound?" Veblen said, groaning.

"All right. But you know how much I hate being ignored in crowds."

"I think this is enough reassurance for now," Veblen said, remembering the American midcentury philosopher John Dewey, who said in *Art as Experience* that there was a definite problem when wholehearted action became a grudging concession to the demands of duty.

"You're very good to me, dear," said her mother, taking Veblen by surprise.

SHE CAME INSIDE, threw down her bag, and was greeted by the unmistakable sound of life pent up, of plans derailed, and of a creature biting mad.

"Oh, no."

And she thought the squirrel knew better!

Veblen found her flashlight, wrestled the chubby ottoman into the shower stall, balanced her desk chair on it, and pressed aside the hatch.

A blast of warm air smacked her face, laced with an odd trace of Turkish coffee and musk. She blinked and peered through the darkness marked by a few slats of light from the vents. Cobwebs brushed her skin, clumped in her eyelashes, across her lips. In trying to clear them, she noted they were softer than cashmere. (But imagine the label, "pure virgin cobweb," which really wouldn't do. Yet silk originated in the glands of worms, and no one seemed to mind.) Her nose began to tickle. She wielded her beam.

There was the trap and the squirrel, *her* squirrel, holding on to the wiry bars like a little jailbird. The fine scruff, the tufted ears, the crisp white chest and gray mantle, and the high-flying plume of a tail.

"Oh! I'm so sorry!" She deflected the beam from its eyes. "I never thought you'd get caught!"

The squirrel rattled the bars.

"You're too smart to be trapped. Did you *want* to be trapped?"

The squirrel provided no clue.

"I'm sorry, you fine squirrel." And she made a quick decision. She pulled the trap closer and carefully lifted it down. The squirrel sat still and exuded great dignity and courage in its present circumstances. "I'll make sure you get to a good place. I can't promise what Paul might do if he found you."

She transported the squirrel outside, her face close enough to his body to smell him, a warm, lovable smell, like the top of a baby's head. She placed the cage on the front seat of her mustard-colored Volvo. A plan was rapidly forming, and after a quick look at her watch she began to pack an overnight bag, along with the assortment of supplies she'd been stockpiling to deliver to her father.

"I know a place full of squirrels for you to meet," she said, throwing her things into the car.

Did he appear to listen? She was so sentimental!

And in no time she hit the road, feeling encouraged by the squirrel's appraisal of her actions.

IT WAS A GOOD HOUR before she called Paul, past Salinas.

"Now?" he said, sounding almost shocked. "Where are you?"

"Near Soledad."

"It's weird you just went. Why didn't you warn me?"

"I'm telling you now. Don't you have a conference tonight?"

"Yeah, but I thought we'd go *together* to see your father!"

She said calmly that maybe his opinions on her mother were enough for the time being.

To which he replied, "So you *are* punishing me!"

She mumbled something about plenty of time for that. And

then asked him about the plans for her mother, the trial, what was the big idea with that?

The squirrel let out a few clucks, as three CH-47 Chinook helicopters ripped through the sky on their way to training exercises at Camp Roberts.

"She loves me now, doesn't she?" Paul said.

"Well, she's assuming it was a caring gesture. But do you really think she belongs in that program?"

"Sure, why not? The adrenals came to me in the middle of the night, like an inspiration." He laughed in a sinister way.

She shuddered. All she wanted was to walk down the sidewalk holding hands, looking at gardens, mentioning whatever she felt like mentioning, feeling happy, maybe whistling. *They had done that!*

"No, really, I've been doing a lot of—thinking," Paul said. "Your mother and I could end up best friends. I think she has some wounds I can relate to on some level."

Her eyes widened. "Really? That's not necessary."

Paul said, "By the way, the Hutmacher caterer called me, wants to discuss the menu. I didn't know what to say."

"Yeah, I guess we need to decide what we're doing," Veblen said flatly.

"If we go for it, the choices are some kind of beef *en croûte* or chicken Veronica."

"Gee, I'm not sure I'd want either. What *is* chicken Veronica?"

"Chicken with some kind of sauce—maybe with grapes."

"Now you're punishing *me*. How about neither?"

"You know, other couples spend hours poring over these details. Aren't you excited about our wedding?"

"Of course I am," she replied, changing ears.

"What about a gift registry?" Paul said next. "People have been asking me what we want."

"Ugh, those seem so greedy."

"People *like* them, Veblen. It helps them choose."

"William James liked to say, 'Materialism's sun sets in a sea of disappointment'!" She was in the mood to be annoying.

"What a killjoy!" Paul said.

"Do you know the Easterlin paradox? It's that your happiness shrinks in proportion to how much stuff you have."

"Now you're against gifts of any kind?" Paul asked, sounding slightly enraged.

She told him not to worry, they'd have their gift registry, and to wait until she got back. "In the meantime, you should read Tim Kasser's *The High Price of Materialism* and Gregg Easterbrook's *The Progress Paradox,* and David Brooks's *Bobos in Paradise,*" she continued, willfully.

Paul said, "I guess I'd better not tell you there's a boat I'm interested in."

"A boat?"

"It's a thirty-two-foot Weekender made by Sea Ray. Do you know anything about boats?"

"Nothing," she said.

"Well, the Sea Ray is a very nice brand of boat, and it would be pretty amazing to have it."

"I don't know why, but all I can think of is *commodity fetishism.*"

"This one—I went out today to see it—is incredible. And guess how much?"

"Now we're getting into *affluenza*."

"This boat's in mint condition. It's a 2004, but the family only used it a few times before the father was called to duty in Afghanistan from the National Guard. His wife wants eight thousand dollars."

"Isn't that taking advantage of someone when they're down?"

"Her husband almost tore my arm off today, by the way," Paul said.

"Sorry," Veblen said. The extraneous status symbol brought to mind a vast trove of writings Veblen had familiarized herself with about the *extended self.* "I never knew you wanted a boat."

"I've always wanted one," Paul said. "But I still have to find out about berths and insurance. It might be a little out of reach."

"A boat. Okay, I didn't know."

They said their good-byes, that they'd talk later, the skin on her face stiff with the effort of civility.

The gray highway rolled beneath her. The Salinas Valley was busy with vegetables. She passed vans filled with field workers coming home, shining RVs, dusty trucks. In a short while she turned on the headlights and began to let down her guard.

"Am I genetically doomed?" This thought always bothered her, and it was her stated goal not to be taken advantage of by her genes. "Can you tell?

"When Paul criticizes my mother it feels worse than it should. Because she's not me, right? But it ruins my wish that I've met someone who fully accepts her, and therefore fully accepts me. She's like a secret third breast! And I'd been hoping for a person who wouldn't scream and run away when he sees it. Figuratively, of course." (She and Albertine had once theorized that Hillary

Clinton had a third breast, based on a suggestive shadow in a photo.)

"Meanwhile, Paul's family is really nice, and he acts like they're *his* third breast and *I* should run away screaming. But I don't want to run away screaming!"

It seemed the squirrel sensed the gravity of the matter. She began to type *Easy Courtship Disrupted by Angst* on her steering wheel.

Shortened it to *ECDBA. ECDBA. ECDBA* . . .

"Do you criticize your family to everybody you meet? You probably all get along and love each other. I want to belong to a family like that. My next question is: should I look for someone who belongs to that kind of family? My hunch is no, because then it would be like I'm marrying the person's family, not the man. This is all so exhausting!" With that, a few tears rolled down her cheeks.

As the drive wore on, other thoughts occurred.

"Do squirrels marry? Doves and wombats do. Though I doubt any species likes to be generalized about, and there are probably plenty of single doves and wombats who are quite happy with their lives. You're male, aren't you? I've always thought so."

Rather clinical to try for a glimpse of a penis, but she did, she got just the right angle between his legs.

"Sorry. You know, when I was young, I called you *squills*."

The squirrel jumped to the fore at this point, and made a sound not unlike a set of castanets. Its plume of a tail flickered rapidly back and forth. She felt the air displaced on her arm, which reminded her of adventuring in the night. She decided to listen to Ravel's *Bolero*, slipping the CD into the portable player plugged into the cigarette lighter. She'd always loved the hypnotic piece, which starts with a lone flute and builds into a raucous throng of instruments.

"Squills, yes," she said. "My grandmother used a fake British accent when she was out in public and called them squills. My mother hated that."

All at once it felt wonderful to be out on the road, part of a convoy of trucks. She phoned in sick for work the next day, felt released. She remembered how excited Linus would get on car trips, pointing out the difference between a fuel tanker that was full and one that was empty. The empty ones bounced. There was another kind of truck she'd always liked, with a quilted rear door. Linus said those were refrigerated trucks. Her mother would get worked up about some kind of explosive hubcap on trucks that could blast off and penetrate passing cars, something she'd learned on an exposé on *60 Minutes*. She'd always yell at Linus to pass trucks in a hurry. Veblen still passed them quickly, wondering if one of the hubcaps would suddenly rocket into her car. Mostly she remembered a kind of wonderful, drowsy feeling, being little in the backseat, allowed to sleep while they drove through the night. Everyone in the right place, strapped in, looking forward. No one acting out. The passenger years.

At last she came to the old Mission San Miguel, where she had seen many ground squirrels and intended to release this one. But no sooner had she pulled off the highway in the twilight and driven around to the area outside the mission and parked than she felt full of grief and tension. In her headlights she saw the rough, rutted ground where the squirrels burrowed, and realized at once that this squirrel was not a ground squirrel at all, but a tree squirrel, a whole different sort of squirrel entirely. "I can't let you go here!" she gasped. "I've made a mistake. There might be a few tree squirrels around, but what if there aren't?" Renewed by this logic, she backed up and drove away as quickly as she could.

She remembered her spot in the old crab apple where she retreated to sit and think, lining up her spine along the trunk, eyeing the horizon. She'd let her eyes water so the view was blurry, which gave certain qualities of the world neglected by clear eyesight the chance to come forth, such as the shocking beauty of color, and she remembered this with compassion for that silly young self, which had deserved to have her hand held.

"My mother would get out the binoculars and see me talking and thought it was a sign of childhood schizophrenia, so I had to start positioning myself at a certain angle to have some privacy. Or not move my lips. So I'm a good ventriloquist."

She laughed, recalling the range of problems her mother thought she might have. "Like trichotillomania!" She wrinkled her nose remembering the trichotillomania period, when her mother watched vigilantly to see if Veblen so much as touched her hair for an instant, ready to pounce and pronounce it a pathological crutch.

"Do you know what that is? It's some kind of urge to pull out your hair. I never had that urge at all," she added. "I bet you haven't either. Your fur is your pride and joy. And it pads you and keeps you warm. So does hair."

The squirrel shook, and fluffed up.

13

THE ANIMAL RULE

While Veblen was on her way to Paso Robles with the squirrel, Paul and James Shalev were on their way to San Jose to attend the opening night of DeviceCON, the leading North American medical and pharmaceutical drug sector trade show. Hutmacher was a major sponsor, and Paul was booked to meet and greet for an hour as a "Key Innovator."

"Heard about the attack," Shalev mentioned.

The traffic was thick even in the carpool lane. "What attack?"

"You had a situation with some aggression down in the ward. Bruce Johnson had to intervene."

Not wanting to lionize the male nurse Bruce Johnson or sound like a helpless wimp, Paul said, "No big deal. Things like that happen all the time."

"Oh, sure," said Shalev. "I'm sure Oliver Sacks has been attacked by a patient or two."

"What are you trying to say?" Paul asked.

"Just that it can happen to the best," Shalev said. Paul had to slam on his brakes to avoid a Prius that had abruptly changed lanes. He suddenly flashed on what Veblen told him that Thorstein Veblen once said: *"No one traveling on a business trip would be missed if he failed to arrive."*

The two men fell into another silence. Paul was feeling uneasy about Veblen's attitude toward the chicken Veronica, the beef *en croûte,* and the gift registry. And annoyed by her attitude toward the Sea Ray and any kind of material gain. Could it signify a deeper dissatisfaction? She even sounded pissed about the trial he'd arranged for her freaky mother. He couldn't win! And why was she reading that hideously titled book, *Marriage: Dead or Alive?* Was that what a happy, excited woman read before her wedding?

"You going to the Pre-Wounded summit?" Shalev asked, interrupting his thoughts.

"Pre-Wounded?" Paul asked, absently.

"Here's what I got about it," Shalev said, reading from his phone:

While post-wound management is a well-established field, coordination of the pre-wounded is an emerging market with strong potential.

Spouses of the pre-wounded often need to know just what to expect. The summit will explore ways for these spouses to be successful after wounding. "We aim to help pre-wounded service members and their families understand the large number of unfamiliar programs and benefits that will be available to them upon wounding. We don't want them to be overwhelmed when the time comes."

"The Pre-Wounding workshops helped us be creative and the support networks were all in place once we were in the post-wounding phase," said Mary Parrot, wife of Staff Sergeant John Parrot, who transitioned from pre- to post-wounded in Afghanistan in July.

"Says Hutmacher's a major sponsor, so I figured you'd be going," Shalev said.

"Is there any limit to the marketing of warfare?" Paul blurted out. "I mean, that's over the top. Am I alone in thinking that?"

"Well, we all take part in the parasitic continuum," Shalev remarked. "You've got to admit, it's nature's way."

"Is man's way nature's way?" Paul asked, wondering if that pithy question lay at the crux of some notable philosophical debate, and made a mental note to ask Veblen.

"I can't make it to this one. I'm going to Arkansas to see my folks for their thirty-fifth. Can you picture thirty-five years with someone?"

"My parents have been married forty. But sometimes I get the feeling they don't know anything about each other."

"That's probably what makes it work," Shalev said.

Paul agreed.

DEVICECON FILLED the San Jose Convention Center, spilling out into the vast lobby, where three to four thousand rowdy, pent-up medical product developers, service providers, inspectors, contractors, and salespeople, all desperate for a few days away from home, were jostling to grab their DeviceCON tote bags and ID cards and lanyards to string around their necks in order to get on with the wine-tasting event inside. A disproportionate thrill, Paul felt, was in the air. Yet he was among the elite here, he was a *Key Innovator*! He wondered if anybody had circled his name on the program to remind themselves of his time slot, and imagined a band of executives, scientists, and headhunters surrounding him like groupies, trying to determine if he could be lured away from Hutmacher.

Paul and Shalev crawled through the crowd. Vendors, row after row of them, hawked their wares with the gusto of the cheese mongers and oyster brokers of medieval bazaars. Each booth was done up with a dramatic backdrop and various three-dimensional installations, with endless pamphlets and brochures available to hoard. Shalev took off to find the wine.

In the "Product Theater" another "Key Expert" was giving a talk on "Speed to Market for Medical Devices." Paul gazed around at the banners and booths: Abbott and Pfizer and Pharma Logistics and Cephalon and Rees and Lilly USA and Zogenix and Baxter and, there it was, Hutmacher. He made his way over. A large monitor displayed continuous feed of the senior Boris Hutmacher at a dais before a high-minded crowd, while vistas of Gothic buildings were spliced in, maybe of Yale or Duke or the University of Chicago:

". . . our most remarkable year in our distinguished history because we have launched eleven new products, each with benefits that raise the bar dramatically in virtually every field of medicine.

"We have launched Merthaspore, a combination antifungal broad-spectrum antipathogen for use in tropical hospitals. We have introduced Diablostolic, the first beta-blocker that not only reduces blood pressure with selective vasodilating but cleans plaque from the arteries. We have launched Vivacity, the only SSRI on the market that simultaneously lowers depression in adults and brings no risk of sexual dysfunction.

"I tell you, all of this did not happen overnight! Far from it! Hutmacher has dedicated itself, since my father founded the company in 1952, to rigorous research and partnerships with the top scientists in the world."

Now came an aerial view of the Hutmacher campus in Delaware, lush and green and sparkling like a self-contained biosphere. Beautiful women in white lab coats smiled seductively at handsome men in white lab coats as they passed one another on paths glinting like diamonds.

"At our state-of-the-art research campus, we work with the best from MIT, Harvard, Stanford, the University of California, keeping ourselves on the cutting edge. Our product and device lines have established us at the forefront, and our scientific and marketing divisions are second to none. Our nose for acquisitions is second to none!"

Paul listened in thrall, vibrating with the man's power and self-possession, imagining himself walking those glimmering paths. His already inflated stock in Cloris soared. You were made of platinum if you had genes from a man like that. You could slay dragons and command armies. The destiny of the world could be shaped in your hands like putty. Music swelled and applause brought the loop back to the start, and he realized he'd been hold-ing a hand to his heart.

An exec in gray sharkskin approached, arm outstretched with golden company cuff links. "Dr. Vreeland? I'm Carter Locke, VP Sales with Hutmacher. We want some photos with you by the prod-uct, and we've got a reporter here from Channel Eight, then we hope you'll join us for our red carpet after-party in the Bonfire Room."

"Bring it on," Paul said.

"Here's a list of your talking points. Focus on the breakout success of your product overseas and how favorable your dealings have been with Hutmacher." He slapped a sheet of paper into Paul's hands.

"Wait, um, there's been a mistake. The device isn't on the mar-ket yet."

"Hello?" said Locke, indicating a pyramid of toaster-sized boxes. "Wake up and smell the roses, Dr. Vreeland."

** Pneumatic TURBO Skull Punch **

Versatile Pneumatic TURBO Skull Punch well suited
to a range of hole-punching operations.

Features: * Automatically adjusted depth control *
Automatic plug ejection * Two-hand pneumatic activation *
Quick-change base * Centering plate with shield *
Quick-shaving razor * Hypodermic syringe

Pneumatic TURBO Skull Punch is a safe and versatile
solution to field craniectomy and TBI prevention!

Paul approached the heap, grabbed a box, tore it down the middle.

If they had finished the trial and gotten FDA approval, this would have been a moment to celebrate, a moment to jump and shout. But there was no FDA approval. He had not finished the trial. Obtaining FDA approval was the goal he had been working toward, approval in general something he yearned for because, well, because it would finally be based on all the hard work approval is *supposed* to be based on. Not on hurried, coaxed, prettified, or accidental results that stood in for the real thing because the real thing had not come in a timely fashion, like other results Paul had turned in. What had Hutmacher done?

The Channel 8 reporter was on him all at once, the cameraman's light blinding him.

[Never-seen clip from Channel 8 news archives]:

REPORTER: Dr. Vreeland is currently directing clinical trials at Greenslopes, the VA in Menlo Park, and is the mind behind what Hutmacher and other industry insiders are calling the greatest contribution to warfighter injuries in years. Tell us about the Pneumatic Turbo Skull Punch, Dr. Vreeland.

PAUL: (Paul is holding his hands up, blocking the camera.) I'm not doing this.

REPORTER: We know this is huge in the military arena. Are there any nonmilitary uses planned for the PTSP? Will paramedics be carrying the Pneumatic Turbo Skull Punch in every ambulance in the future?

Paul: I'm going to walk away now.
Reporter: What's wrong with this guy?

When Paul found Carter Locke, *"Are you kidding me?"* was all Carter Locke could say. *"Jesus, get a grip!"* He was trying to tell Carter Locke the truth, but Carter Locke put his hands down on the device, Carter Locke told him to shut the fuck up, Carter Locke was treating him like a heckler, Carter Locke asked some other Hutmacher flunky to take him outside, Paul was telling the flunky to get his hands off of him, Paul was then surrounded by two flunkies, one on each arm, escorting him past the entry point, stripping him of his lanyard, telling the door people he was not to be allowed back in, shoving him into the lobby, making him spin.

At that moment he heard his name. Stepping off the top of the escalator was Cloris Hutmacher. The boy he'd seen months before on Cloris's monitor, with his round, freckly face, appeared behind her.

"Cloris."

"Paul! What luck finding you right away. This is my son, Morris, Paul. He's been so eager to meet you."

"I know all about your experiment and the simulator room," Morris said. "Ask me what I know!"

The boy's face radiated so much admiration, Paul was forced to speak with a civil tongue. "What do you know?" he managed.

"It's so awesome! It's like a city, with buildings and windows for snipers, and there's a road going by with IEDs all over. There's a box in the control booth to set off sniper fire or explode the IEDs and let out smoke, and there's a switch to change the lighting to make it night, or make shadows like it's sunset, and the sound system can make traffic noises or helicopter noises, and Robbie's going to let me try it."

"Who's Robbie?" Paul asked, confused.

"Robbie's a sound technician from THX. THX is part of Lucasfilm. It's awesome!"

"He's going to let you play with a multimillion-dollar simulator belonging to the military. That's great. Cloris? We need to talk."

Morris promptly sat on the floor, battling cyborgs on his phone. They stood aside.

"It's about my device," Paul whispered.

"For men it always is." She smiled.

Oh, he could strangle her. "My device is packaged, Cloris. I've just been told it's out there, that it's already being shipped. Tell me this is a mistake. Please."

"I have some very exciting news, Paul." She placed a finger on his lips. "Shhh. Shhh." And she whispered that a purchase order from the Department of Defense was obviously the biggest prize in the business. In addition to licensing in the developing countries, Hutmacher had successfully placed the Pneumatic Turbo Skull Punch on every current DOD purchase order in the system.

"I haven't finished the trial," Paul said hoarsely.

"Paul. Listen to me." She glanced across the space at Morris, who was now standing by the entrance. He yelled, "I'm tired of waiting," and ran into the conference hall. "Bradley Richter. You met Bradley in Washington. Do you remember Bradley Richter?"

"What about him?"

Cloris spoke quietly, but her eyes sparkled. "Bradley is retiring next month, after thirty years of service to the Department of Defense and the USAMMA."

"So?"

"Paul. You're not thinking straight. We're not talking about the difference of a few hundred units. Do you understand?"

"No, I don't. We have not performed the final step in the trial on live subjects. It's crucial."

"Paul, it's all taken care of. You have nothing to worry about. We were able to use the Animal Rule."

Paul's head began to throb. The Animal Rule was a post-9/11 countermeasure for getting FDA approval fast, forgoing trials on humans, as with the snap approval of antidotes for anthrax poisoning. Using it this way was beyond a stretch.

"No way. It's not necessary."

"But it was, Paul."

"We're all set up to test! There's no emergency, there's no justification—"

"I dare you to tell the troops who are receiving brain injuries every day that there's no emergency."

He asked, "When did you submit it? Did you use my research from Stanford?"

"What else? Of course we did. It's brilliant research. You presented it to us, everything we needed was there."

"What about the simulator, what about the volunteers?"

"Paul, the volunteers can go home now. Nobody's going to complain."

"We have to make sure it works!"

"We've ended up exactly where we want to end up. Now let's

go inside and show it off and make everybody crazy with envy that it's ours!"

"I can't go along with this. We have to test the blade on live subjects. I've added a new sensor that needs to be integrated into the design. Cloris!"

At that moment, Morris ran out of the cavernous hall, wielding a unit of Paul's device, aiming it at them like a pistol.

"Put that down!" Paul yelled. "Take that away from him, it's very dangerous."

"Paul," she said, looking back at him. "The world keeps spinning. Hold on, or you might fall off."

She took Morris by the shoulder, and proceeded into the marketplace.

14

THE NUTKINISTAS

Veblen noted, pulling into her father's town, that Paso Robles, like Palo Alto, Oakland, Encino, Willows, Walnut Creek, Aspen, Cedar Falls, and thousands of other cities and towns the world over, was named for its notable trees, and marked by sprawling, convulsive oaks that were undoubtedly good homes for squirrels. She could release the squirrel on just about any sidewalk near any number of the massive oldies. But as she rolled down Spring Street, passing the town square, which was home to some mighty oaks, she couldn't bring herself to stop. "I don't want to let you go," she said. "Which is very selfish of me." Now she felt sad again, aware of her greedy feelings for the squirrel, catching herself in the act of trying to hoard him. This motivated her to pull over at once, clamber from the car, stretch her legs, and gather up a handful of acorns scattered beneath a heavy trunk. These she brought back and pushed through the gaps in the cage; the squirrel accepted one and, after turning it around and around in his hands, began to chew it to shreds. "Mr. Squirrel, nice job!" she cried, and was happy again.

It was too late to visit Rudgear tonight, his meds made him conk out right after the evening meal. She stopped at a Mexican restaurant downtown and had cheese enchiladas, rice and beans, and a Corona with a slice of lime shoved down its neck, so that the beer picked up the flavor with every sip. Delicious. She relaxed and watched a family at a table nearby, the parents feeding the children, wiping their mouths, cleaning their hands, a father and mother and two children, the unit of them unsettling to her, though she couldn't say why. She looked away, at an older man eating by himself, and that unsettled her too. She wasn't sure how to live.

Then she bought a six-pack of Corona at a liquor store and checked into The Sandman, a cheap, scruffy old motel she stayed in whenever she visited her father, only forty-nine dollars a night, real, not rundown. It offered low weekly rates as well, so many of the rooms had been taken over by families who lived there, stringing up their laundry in the windows. A developer would soon knock the place down and build dentists' offices and tanning salons, but for now The Sandman stood its ground with free coffee and doughnuts in the morning, reminding her of disappearing times. She brought the cage containing the squirrel inside.

"There you go." She set him on the bureau beside the television. But maybe the television was emitting sonic shrieks, because the squirrel began to turn in all directions. "Sorry! Here." She set him on the other double bed. There the squirrel calmed.

She picked up a few earlier texts from Paul. *WEIRD PLACE WYWH, ILY, TALK SOON,* he'd written. She texted back: *GREAT! U2.*

Sooner than she realized. Without knowing it, she had "butt-connected" with an incoming call from Paul, who had just caught his breath in the lobby at DeviceCON.

From the convention center lobby, Paul was crying out, pacing, chewing on his nails. "Veblen? Veb, are you there?"

Through the phone, he heard the voice of Alex Trebek on the television, and he felt warmly for her, that she liked to watch *Jeopardy!* in motel rooms.

"Veb? I need to talk to you."

In her room at The Sandman, Veblen heard nothing from the phone, maybe because she had set it down on the flowered bedspread, or because the TV was on, or because she was focused on the squirrel, or because she didn't expect to hear anything and so she didn't. "You okay there? You hungry still?" Veblen asked the squirrel.

"Veb, I can't hear you very well," Paul said, forcing his voice into the phone. She sounded as sweet as a distant brook, like water over stones. "Listen, this is bad. They've manufactured the device, they went ahead, they used a bogus loophole to take advantage of one of their contacts. It's totally corrupt!"

"I feel like you're really listening, isn't that weird?" Veblen said warmly to the squirrel.

"I am, but can you talk a little louder?" Paul said huskily.

"It's funny how excited I was at first, but now getting married just feels artificial, like a big unnecessary problem people create for themselves," Veblen mused.

Paul swallowed, pressing the phone to his ear so hard it hurt. "Why?"

"So, are you married?" Veblen said.

All at once he realized she was talking to somebody else, and her tone was undeniably flirtatious. Paul's mouth opened, emitting an arid croak.

"Veblen?" Paul said, weakly.

"You seem really—smart. And you're not petty at all. I can tell. But I don't want to idealize you either."

Her voice was girlish, almost sultry.

"What are you doing?" Paul murmured.

"If you idealize someone, you have nowhere to go but down."

He began to squeeze his phone like a rat.

"He already thinks my mother's weird. Wait till he meets my father. I'll never hear the end of it."

Paul, on his end, began to gasp.

"You're so handsome, did you know that?"

He cried out in anguish and must have thrown his phone hard, because it bounced up in the air like a ball, ending the connection when the battery flew out.

VEBLEN HAD NOTHING to worry about. She was relaxing on the bed at The Sandman, enjoying a beer with lime. It was heavenly.

"All right. This might sound like a dumb question, but—what stage of life are you in? Are you young, middle-aged? I know you're not old."

She checked him out, standing at the back of the cage, spinning an acorn. He was inarguably solid.

She said, "I know already. You're in your prime."

. . . .

PRIMES CAME in all sizes, and despite popular belief, could come around and around, like trees through the seasons. She remembered Rudgear's intake at Sunny Hill three years before, when it had been her responsibility as his next of kin to determine he was not, currently, in his prime.

She knew only a little about her father's youth, spent in Waukegan, Illinois, the son of a Socialist Labor Party milkman with political ambitions who committed suicide when Rudgear was ten. Rudgear joined the army at the age of seventeen, went straight to Vietnam. He lost some of his hearing. He married Melanie later but it seemed like a big mistake to both of them right away. They separated. One night, well after the separation, according to Melanie, he stopped by and they fell into old habits, and thus nine months later, Veblen was born. He sent checks for a while, but stopped. He married and divorced again. He took odd jobs. For a while he worked at a state prison. Then he had a breakdown and retired on disability and began to see hallucinations in his small apartment near the freeway, and started calling Veblen almost every night:

"Why were you looking at me that way?"

"Hi, Dad. What do you mean?"

"You were sitting there staring at me like a dead person. I didn't do anything!"

"When, Dad? I'm up here, at home."

"When you were here a minute ago, just staring at me with your mouth open," he said, losing some steam.

"It's okay, Dad. You probably dozed off and had a bad dream."

A few days later he called again, clearly agitated. "I don't like it," he yelled.

"What, Dad?"

"I saw an elephant in here."

"At your apartment?"

"I'm scared!"

"Dad, it's okay. Let me call Lorenzo, okay? He'll come over and make sure everything's okay."

"I don't like it when everybody's staring at me."

"I don't either," said Veblen. "Lorenzo will come and make sure everything's okay."

"I don't want Lorenzo to come."

"Why not?"

"He's been acting strange lately. I'd never seen that side of him before. Just looking at you like an assassin."

"Then sit tight. I'll be down in a few hours."

She excused herself from work that day, hit the road, and made it to Paso Robles in under three hours. Though worried about his condition, she couldn't help but be aware that his new personality, frightened and desperate, came as a relief. What a bully he'd been when she was a kid!

At his building, she'd taken the stale-smelling elevator and followed the sagging walkway around to his door, where she knocked and knocked some more. Then she tried the knob and found it unlocked, so she proceeded into the darkened room.

"Veblen?" he wheezed.

A gray blanket camouflaged him in his recliner. She gave him a kiss on the top of his pink-skinned head.

"Boy, am I thirsty," he said.

She brought him a tumbler of water, and he siphoned it like a longshoreman.

"I gotta get up and use the men's room. Help me up," he said.

At standing, he had shrunk by a hand. His arms were buttoned close like corn husks, and gray crescents bagged beneath his eyes. While he was in the bathroom, she opened the dusty curtains and popped the windows and started some coffee, and when he came out and sat in his recliner again he appeared slightly more at ease. Then she went to use the bathroom herself, and discovered blood smeared all over the sink.

"Dad, what happened? Did you cut yourself shaving?"

Back in the living room, she noticed a towel wrapped around his arm.

"Let me see that."

He surrendered his arm; she knelt and unraveled the towel to find an eight-inch purple welt with patches of torn, weeping skin.

"Did you fall?"

"Nope. Got in a fight with a lamp."

He nodded over at the corner and she saw pieces of his former lamp in a heap—a broken shade, the twisted harp, the socket, a cord dangling out of a shard of pottery.

"Ow!"

"I'll say, ow. I also had a fight with an elephant."

She laughed, but he wasn't kidding.

"He was right there staring at me." He lifted his hand to point to the corner and she saw that he was shaking.

She took his arm and held it warmly between her hands. His face was pale.

"Dad, I want to take you to a doctor to look at your arm, okay?"

"What's he going to do, put me in a cage?"

"This needs a good bandage on it, it might get infected."

"All right, daughter."

He rose and walked unsteadily to the door, gathering nothing to take along. She saw his wallet on the counter and grabbed it. Cards from various doctors were taped to the wall by the phone, including one from a psychiatrist and one from a neurologist, and she plucked them off and shoved them in her purse.

He was docile and followed her to the car. She took him straight to the emergency room at the local hospital. When it came his turn to fill out the admissions forms at the desk in the inner room, and she removed his wallet from her purse, he said:

"What are you doing with that?"

"Dad, they need your Medicare and insurance cards."

"I'll take that."

She handed it over. "I think your cards are inside."

He drew in his lips. "First I gotta use the men's room. Fast."

"Out in front," said the intake nurse.

"He's not himself at all," Veblen said to the woman, though painfully aware that she was still not sure what his self really was.

"No, he doesn't look right," remarked the nurse. "You did the right thing."

They waited some minutes, until Veblen sprang up to check. The nurse followed and stuck her head into the men's room.

"Nobody here," she announced. "Anybody see an older gentleman in a stained T-shirt, bald, stooped over, come out of here?"

A public misstep was not without its indignities. A woman in a yellow jogging suit in the waiting room said, "I saw a man like that, running across the parking lot."

Veblen dashed outside, cupping her hands into a megaphone. "Dad! Dad!" What if he was hit by a car or had a heart attack?

Volunteers who came around to deadhead flower arrangements and read to patients helped in the search, and fanned through neighborhoods near the hospital. The police pitched in. Up and down she combed the streets, returning frequently to his apartment, asking his neighbors to keep watch.

That evening she was sitting in her car outside the Frosty Freeze, sucking with infantile intensity on a shake, when the hospital called. Rudgear had been found at the bus stop right there, in front of the same Frosty Freeze. He had gulped down a jumbo milkshake on the bench and passed out. Someone on the street called an ambulance. His blood glucose levels were at 610, meaning he had gone into a diabetic coma. His mismanaged diabetes, coupled with his psychiatric problems, led to the involvement of Adult Protective Services, whereupon he was sent to a home, which worked for a while until he crushed the fingers of an aide who was helping him into a car for a doctor's appointment, trying to flee. At that point he was transferred to Sunny Hill for psychiatric care, and in that facility he had stayed for nearly three years, without much incident of late. She sometimes regretted depriving him of his freedom, despite his difficulties caring for himself. But it didn't have to be forever, did it? There were different kinds of primes, he could have one again.

"DIDN'T YOU ALWAYS think Trappist monks were trappers?" Veblen asked the squirrel. She was relaxing with a Corona and musing about the mysteries of the ages. "I did. I pictured monks out in the forest setting traps for beavers and minks. But you know what, Trappists aren't trappers at all. They just like to make and sell stuff, even coffins. Ha! Thomas Merton was a Trappist. Do you know Thomas Merton? He was a wonderful poet. That's what he made, poems.

"You know, the sad thing about Thomas Merton, he was electrocuted next to his bathtub. At least my mother always said so whenever I went near a bathtub with something electric.

"Want a raspberry?"

She pushed one through the cage, where the squirrel sniffed it and left it alone.

"Sorry you're in there." She looked around the cage of the motel room—the proportions were about the same.

The Corona bottle was empty. She popped another.

"Hello in there," she said. "There's a song about how you have to say *Hello in there* to people with hollow, ancient eyes, and I've had this superstition ever since I first heard that song, that if I always say *Hello in there* to people, someday I won't be lonely when I'm old.

"There's a lot of potential for being lonely when you're old. Especially in my family. I've been working on that. Don't want it to happen to me. You don't think that's why I'm marrying Paul, do you? Just as insurance against being lonely?"

The squirrel had settled into a corner of the trap, its tail wrapped around its body like a comforter.

"By the way, you don't have hollow ancient eyes. *You know that old trees just grow stronger / and old riverrrrrrs grow wilder every day . . .*'" she sang out of key, relishing her tipsiness.

There was another part of her life, she told him. She'd had a radio show at her high school called *60 Seconds*, uncovering scandals.

She told him about "The Case of the Avenging Drill Team," when the Drill Team burned a fellow student journalist in effigy for writing that they were automatons. And "Investigation of the Senior Election Irregularities," which revealed ballot tampering. And the one called "School Is a Chamber of Guts," about sixteen scary death traps on campus.

In high school, journalism brought her a certain swagger, her hands on the keyboard, where unexpected thoughts poured forth, a way to speak up and get to know herself. To think there was this wealth of activity locked up inside her made her feel hopeful and brave. *Hooray, I might be more than I seem.*

Remembering her muckraking portfolio put her in excellent spirits, and she began to jump from bed to bed, attempting flips. It was fun. The springs in the beds squeaked like lobster baskets, inviting the guests in the next room to imagine all sorts of things going on that weren't going on at all.

"Ain't it funny how an old broken bottle / Looks just like a diamond ring . . ." she sang. "Hey, you know *The Tale of Squirrel Nutkin?*" she asked him, midair. "When I was a kid—I thought the message was—that if you act like a pesty—little jerk—you lose your tail."

The squirrel rose and stretched.

"No, but after a while—I began to look at it—differently. I realized it's—this," she huffed. "Nutkin was—a genius—a trickster—a philosopher—and probably a cad. But there he was—putting his life on the line every day. You consider him a hero, don't you? You know about the movement, don't you? The followers of

Nutkin—the Nutkinistas?" She laughed at herself, out of breath. "Old Brown the owl is *the man*."

This was all part of the story of Wobb. There, squirrels had been enslaved in munitions factories in great caverns inside the mountains, but the movement was arming itself. The revolution would not be televised! She was smiling so hard she worried she might look wolfen.

"*Tear down the waa-aalls! Tearr doown the waalls, motherrfuck-errs! Tear down the waaaaa-aaalls!*" she sang, until someone began to pound the wall, like Paul used to pound at the squirrel. She came down on her knees with a resonant thud.

"Oops." She laughed and took another gulp. She hadn't gotten this drunk since high school.

"Let it be known why he taunts that owl. It's necessary to taunt owls! They've been skinning squirrels alive for eons! So have hawks.

"The Nutkinistas believe the more they taunt, the more they break down the old paradigm.

"Which is like realizing you're not going to take it forever when your family gives you hell."

A beam of light crossed her face, a car parking in the lot. Guilt trimmed its hooves onto her lap, as she saw herself as complicit in a variety of crimes against childhood, especially her own.

"It's all very perplexing," she said, more soberly. She found her cell phone in the folds of the shiny bedspread, called Paul. But he didn't answer, and she muttered good-nights into his proxy ear.

"But in Latin," she said to the squirrel, because he still seemed to be listening, "*perplexed* means thoroughly involved. Entwined and engaged. Totally the opposite of just being confused or out of it. It's like people got too lazy to think being perplexable was a plus.

"Oh, well. It's not so bad sleeping in hay," she remarked, crawling between the sheets. She was growing drowsy, and found herself remembering the time she ran away from home to spend the expanse of a night in a horse barn. It was the same horse farm where she and her class had brought all the rotten apples from her desk, all those years ago. The sensations were indelible: the creaking beams, the sudden rush of air through the cracks, the snorts of the horses, and the rustling hay.

There she was, breathing the warm smell of horses and listening to them snort in the frosty air, and feeling like every heavy thing was off her back, a horse that had bucked its saddle. Kind of like tonight.

She felt an intimation of change. That until now she was a Christmas tree that had been decorated by someone who hated Christmas.

"Tell me more about what's up in your world," she said, sleepily. "Tell me more about everything."

15

I MELT WITH YOU

L ittle did Veblen know that Paul, in a fit of jealousy so painful
it shocked him, in realizing how little he knew about the
woman he loved and wished to marry, convinced that she was
spending the night with someone in a motel somewhere, some
monster stubborn and bulky and impassable trying to take away
the only thing that had ever mattered to him, who wanted to suf-
focate him, who wanted to break his bones and crack his neck and
leave him for dead, was about to do something he'd never considered doing to any living being, let alone Veblen. He dumped
Shalev back at the parking lot at the VA (after ranting about Hutmacher's flagrant misuse of the Animal Rule, then enduring
Shalev's lurid reprisal of the pharmaceutical murder in *The Fugitive* and how Paul had better look out), and drove to Veblen's
house, where he commenced to ransack her drawers, cabinets,
closets, even pulling all the boxes from under her bed, looking for
any scrap of betrayal.

He was panting, sweating, his heart on the gallop. In the melee he found old belts and ugly clothes stuffed in bags. He found old tangled telephones and a repulsive carving of turtles in a conga line. He found outdated samples of Paxil, Zoloft, and Prozac in the back of a drawer—what the hell? Was she on antidepressants? Why hadn't she told him? In her underwear drawer he found a bar of soap he'd given her, and a pressed flower from the side of the road where they'd made love, wrapped in a small plastic sleeve.

In her bedside drawer were nail scissors, an inhaler, a pencil sharpener with a picture of an elephant on it, a pouch full of lavender, a stash of bookmarks from Kepler's bookstore on El Camino, and a small brass bell.

Under the bed, in long flat boxes, he found folders with clips from the high school newspaper that Veblen had written. He found folders full of articles printed from the Web about Thorstein Veblen. He found folders stuffed full of random pictures clipped from old magazines—lots of animals, nature scenes, people with strange expressions on their faces. Everything he found made him love her more, but anger drove him to unearth something damning. He opened one notebook and saw "The Adventures of Hexi Pu, Chinese Girl Detective with a Shriveled Arm" typed on yellowed newsprint.

```
Hexi Pu liked to solve mysteries even though
she had a shriveled arm. She thought that maybe
the shriveled arm would attract attention, but
it didn't, so she was able to solve lots of
crimes anyway. Sometimes having a shriveled arm
allowed her to get sympathy and a way into
people's lives, better than if she had a normal
```

arm. Also, being Chinese was a plus. People
tended to think she was smart and shy, maybe
a disciplined musician. They didn't suspect she
was a detective. Also it was hard to tell her
age. She could still pass as a girl, even go
into high schools under cover.

Hexi Pu liked asparagus and broccoli so much
that she married an asparagus and broccoli
farmer. His name was Dan. Dan also farmed
other veggies but he increased production of
asparagus and broccoli after marrying Hexi Pu.
He liked her shriveled arm, it reminded him of
a little kitten.

Paul shook his head and flipped through another notebook.

There is something that makes me feel like a wishbone.

Why did he want to marry a woman who wrote about shriveled
arms and felt like a wishbone?

It was damp under the myrtle tree, and it was damp under Myrtle.

This made Paul strangely horny. She bewildered him. She put
her energies into lost causes and scraps!

He pawed for love notes and confessions. He came upon manila
envelopes stuffed with old correspondence from friends, from
grandparents, and then, in a special folder, dozens of letters pressed
in bundles tied with string. They had been written with a fountain

pen by some guy named Luke, *the pompous ass!!!!!!!!!!!!!!* And were covered with sketches of machinery and buildings, as if little Lukey fancied himself a budding Leonardo.

> *I'm writing you from the Place Concorde, looking at the Eiffel Tower.*
>
> *In Paris, one tends to be overwhelmed. The buildings are gorgeous and the boulevards wide and beautiful. Vienna was beautiful, but on a smaller scale. Vienna was only "whelming."*

What an *asshole!!!!!!*

He moved like there was cement in his joints, shoving the boxes back under the bed, closing the drawers, feeling like he'd raped her space and made himself all the more unworthy of her love.

A sampling of what was on her bookshelves: *Don Quixote*; *Leaves of Grass*; *Candide*; *The Vested Interests and the Common Man*; *Sult*; *Min kamp*; *Ut og stjæle hester*; *The Horse and His Boy*; *Absentee Ownership*; *The Tale of Benjamin Bunny*; *The Varieties of Religious Experience*; *Alice's Adventures in Wonderland*; *Achieving Our Country*; *The Story of George Washington Carver*; *Mrs. Dalloway*; *The Innocents at Cedro*; *Watership Down*; *U.S.A.*; *Contingency, Irony, and Solidarity*; *The Tale of Peter Rabbit*; *Our Master's Voice*; *The Portable Veblen*.

He paced around her cluttered little cottage, gasping for salvation. What had she been Googling lately? There was no stopping him, he was turning more despicable by the second. He flipped on her desktop. In her history he scrolled through *World Heritage Sites, France, Roman ruins, Orange*. This was good! This had to do with their honeymoon ideas, and he felt instantly cheered. Then he saw *squirrels, cute squirrels, great squirrel migrations*, and *sciuro-phobia*. Aha! She wanted to pin a phobia on him, pathologize him! Continuing down the history: *are college degrees really important, irritability, families of disabled, psychologists Palo Alto*. Goddamn it!

He'd resisted the impulse to analyze her gray matter, the way you never want to truly imagine eating human flesh or find the buttocks of a male friend sexy. You have the capacity to run any image through your mind, but some of them you pass up. Hypoxia set in, of the magnitude of the night terrors he'd experienced as a child, loathing infinity.

In the hallway he came face-to-face with the great Thorstein Veblen, Veblen's god, the man she most admired, the grand inquisitor presiding over their lives. Who needed him? Who said he was welcome here? *Fuck you, asshole!* In what could only be called a hallucination, Paul suddenly felt a stout sense of presence, as if Thorstein Veblen were standing before him, confronting him over his bourgeois materialism, his peevish personality, and, most of all, his unsuitability for Veblen Amundsen-Hovda. Paul's fist flew out and sent a spider web of cracks across the surface of the glass, and the picture fell off the wall. Droplets of blood rose on his knuckles.

Shit. What was he doing? He had to blow this joint. He slammed the front door as if a good slam could help, and then he stomped angrily into Palo Alto as if an angry stomp could help. Now what? Now what! Cursing and nearly sobbing, he forgot where he was going and why, but then found himself slumped at a bar in a bistro, full of loud talk and the smells of olive oil and garlic, where he ordered himself a vodka straight up, and then another. He ordered some bruschetta from a gorgeous woman with pale skin and a piercing on her nose, a heart-shaped face, and a jade pendant shaped like a lily pad against her chest, with her hair up and little tendrils hanging down around her neck, the skin on her chest the texture of a neonate's. Other women would have him, wouldn't they? A doctor? He could have someone new in a week. A day. Right now! Somebody smart and beautiful . . . someone who bored and annoyed him . . . selfish and vain . . . no. There was only one woman for him in the world.

He imagined telling his parents the wedding was off, and receiving their undivided scorn for the rest of his life.

He managed to crunch the bruschetta with some delicacy, so that the woman behind the bar wouldn't think he was a pig, all the while wishing he were alone so that he could crunch it like a pig, and crumbs and grease could fly. The woman looked his way, and smiled a few times. He probably looked troubled, an invitation to anyone who noticed.

It had not been a foregone conclusion that he would come as far as he had. And yet to look at him you would not know his achievements gave him much pleasure.

HONORS BIOLOGY, tenth grade. Sixteen years old, testicles hot and itching, pimples pressing up on his chest. Fascinated by the paradox of the digestive system, he wrote his first scientific inquiry, "Why the Stomach Doesn't Digest Itself," in the fall, and his teacher, old Mr. Gielow, with his funny two-tone glasses and his leprechaun-shaped head, told him it was the best damned student work he'd seen in all his years at South Humboldt High. He told Paul, who had been struggling to find his niche academically, that he was a natural scientist, and asked him what he planned to do for the science fair, where he could make a big splash.

"I'm thinking of assembling a bunch of snails to prove that they make sounds when under duress," Paul said.

Gielow frowned. "Now, is this in contention? I don't know much about this."

"I don't either," Paul said. "I really want to find out."

"What kind of duress?" Gielow wanted to know. "We need to follow the guidelines of the Animal Welfare Act."

"Invertebrates aren't covered by the Animal Welfare Act," Paul said. "Anyway, it's not like I'm going to feed them Sluggo. I'm putting them in a crowded bucket."

"All right. And then?"

"So the project will be to observe and record them until I get my results."

Because Gielow had never tried to cut him down or discourage him in any way, Paul told him the story behind it all, from when he was ten years old, peeling snails from the stumps and rocks in the garden, from the broadsides of kohlrabi leaves and rhubarb, across which they'd strewn their silvery trails. It was one of his chores to fill a pail with them and take them to the hen house. This one morning he had counted seventy-two, sliming and squirming, eyes extended on thick rubbery stems—and it had been faint at first, rising to a shrill pitch. He came charging with his bucket back to the house.

"The snails were screaming!"

"I'd scream too if you were feeding me to the chickens," said Marion, who was flipping zucchini pancakes on a blackened griddle.

"It sounded like—" He dropped his jaw to strike the right pitch.

Justin sat at the table spooning up his daily bowl of mush. He said, "Like this, Paul?" and began to imitate Paul imitating snails in a most loud and lunkish manner, yodeling so cavernously Paul could see his fleshy uvula, hanging in his throat like a slug.

Paul began to gag. "Cut it out!"

Not Justin, no way.

"Shut up!" Paul heaved a few times, but Justin's yodel only grew louder, and Paul went over and slugged him squarely in the chest.

"All right. Go to your room and calm down," said Bill. "Do you hear me?"

"He wrecks everything!"

"Wrecking what?"

"Dad, I heard snails screaming!"

"You punched your brother for that? Go to your room and take a deep breath and pull yourself together!"

Gielow grasped it all. "So you want vindication."

Paul nodded with gratitude. "Exactly."

Gielow said, "My brother was a bastard too. No better motivation. I know you'll do an excellent job."

Later at the library, Paul's friend Mrs. Brown helped him find two promising references, *Invertebrates Around Us* and *Gastropoda Today*. Zeroing in on *Helix aspersa*, the common garden variety, Paul searched for documentation. At home he set up his experimentation center, a stress-inducing bucket with a microphone affixed, and filled it with at least seventy robust snails. He took pictures of every step of the process, prepared the abstract, drew diagrams, and was well ahead of the deadline, giving himself plenty of leeway lest the circumstances that caused snails to scream be difficult to reproduce.

He learned there were more than thirty-five thousand species, making *Gastropoda* the second largest class of *organisms* on earth. He studied diagrams of the pulmonary vein, the pedal ganglia, the buccal mass, the dart sac, and dissected a number of hapless standbys in the process. A great deal was made in the literature over the fact that the internal structure of *Helix aspersa* was asymmetrical, but Paul found it much more interesting that snails were hermaphroditic, possessing the organs of both sexes.

Early on he had one unexpected result—snails seemed to enjoy escargot. Almost every night there were one or two fewer in the bucket, thin fragments of shell scattered on the bottom. Cannibals! Paul planned to make much of this repugnant discovery and found supporting text in *Gastropoda Today,* and maybe that should have been enough. Maybe he should have been satisfied with the unexpected, rather than insisting on a predetermined result. After all, many of the greatest discoveries of all time were purely accidental, falling under the heading of what scientist Max Delbruck named "The Principle of Limited Sloppiness." Look at Sir Alexander Fleming and his moldy petri dish, which led to penicillin. Look at Pasteur trying to kill some chickens but vaccinating them instead. Roentgen playing around with vacuum tubes, nothing to do with seeing people through to the bones!

So what else had factored into his discovery that distant morning? Paul recalled the old battle of the crack. He and Justin had shared a bedroom for years (until Paul seized the old laundry room as one of his first steps on the road to self-definition) and Justin's things had always taken up a lot more space than his. Justin had a wheelchair for occasional use, a sleep apnea machine that roared, and big bulky clothes and shoes, and he wore braces on his legs then. But brothers shared rooms, Bill insisted. He'd always shared a room with his brother Richard. There was no reason Paul and Justin couldn't. Paul's bed was stuck behind the door, and one day he deliberately pushed it away from the wall about a foot. And every time he came back into the room, the bed had been pushed back. Diligently, he'd pull it out again. At night, as his parents whispered between themselves and came to Justin's cries when he fell out of bed, Paul faced the wall and the crack between it and him and fostered an angry determination to hold on to the space no matter what. In the mornings, as they dressed for school, Justin always had to stub a toe on the protruding bed and, with an exaggerated bellow, try to squeeze Paul's crack out of existence.

Were the screams of the snails something he'd fabricated to assert himself? To show he had a will? One afternoon, alone with the mute gastropods, Paul began to think the screaming-snail memory was, after all, a myth of his cheerless youth. Like the myth that peace signs and slogans such as *War Is Not Healthy for Children and Other Living Things* were ever going to change a fucked-up thing.

In kindergarten, did he really chase a girl all around the school who wouldn't accept his Valentine?

1995. BY ALL ACCOUNTS, the van and the people pouring from it that day looked like they belonged in Clinton-era Humboldt. Many of them lived off the grid themselves, in parts of New Mexico, Oregon, as far as Saskatchewan. There was a man with blond dreadlocks, another man with brown dreadlocks, a Jamaican with black dreads streaming down his back, a woman wearing a sari tied around her waist, blond hair caught in it. Wiry weathered men jumped out, grabbed duffel bags and army surplus ammo cases, not for real ammo but to keep cameras and valuables dry on the river.

There were Marshall and Kip, with their cutoffs and bare feet, their Guatemalan *calzoncillos,* and their woven vests. There were Cool Breeze and Curtis and John. Cool Breeze wore a scarf around his head like a pirate. John kept aloft a Hacky Sack with the talent of his blackened feet. Curtis had straw-colored hair and a dirty mustache. There was his mother's best friend, Caddie Fladeboe, who looked like Mama Cass, laden with turquoise stones.

Paul remembered the smell of them invading the house, the decibels reached by their voices in chorus, while he retreated to his bedroom to finish his project. Tomorrow was the fair. He had everything to perfection, except for one small detail. The inevitable pungent smell of burning pot invaded his room first, followed by the happier aroma of his mother's cooking, which drew him out at last, a huge vat of lentil stew and whole-wheat flatbread and a salad full of nasturtium flowers, but the BO of the group and the way they all sat together in a pile, shirtless, raspberry nippled and muddy toed, made him return to his room as soon as he'd filled his plate, and he ate alone on the edge of his bed designing moats and drawbridges to surround the house he'd have someday to keep them all out. And after he practiced his presentation he climbed into bed, stuffed cotton balls in his ears, which made him feel all the more isolated, then drew a pillow over his head.

· · ·

IN THE MORNING, he had to wake his dad for the keys to the Dodge truck, Betsy—and had to step over the guy with the blond dreadlocks and one of the women together in a sleeping bag in order to get out the door, with his display board tucked under one arm, and the bag containing the tape recording and the report in the other. Bill followed him out to say good-bye, despite having stayed up partying all night. "We picked up some crazy friends, didn't we?"

"Yeah. They stink."

"I'll hose 'em down today, will that help?" Bill said.

"Probably not."

"So you ready to go with your report?" Bill asked, almost as an afterthought.

"I got my results."

His father nodded, but clearly couldn't remember the details of Paul's report at that hour.

"So you and Mom are coming, right?"

"Today?"

"Of course it's today. You know it's today!"

"Sorry, son. I'm feeling a little flat."

Pressing this small advantage, Paul said, "I was wondering. Don't get mad. Would it be okay, since people are here who can watch him, if you don't bring Justin?"

"Why?" Bill looked pained.

"So you can look around without worrying about him."

Bill scuffed the ground with his moccasins. "Justy loves your school events. He gets so much out of being part of your life. Come on. Think how little he has compared to you."

"Dad, please? These people are going to be here, right? Can't he stay with them?"

"We'll see."

His father said good-bye and good luck and Paul tore off. As he rammed Betsy up the dirt road, always hoping to destroy her so they could get a new car, he wished Justin had never been born. To wish someone had never been born required, per Paul's method, an elaborate journey in a microscopic submarine up the progenitor's urethra into the gonad, where missiles were deployed in all directions, mowing down sperm by the millions.

THAT DAY IN BIOLOGY, they shared their reports before setting up the displays in the gym. Paul's turn came and he stood before the class and said:

"And finally, after twenty-seven hours of recording time, the proper conditions asserted themselves and the snails began to emit sound, which I will play for you now."

He could barely look at Gielow, who beamed at him so paternally it was scary. The recorder was queued. As it began to play he could hear the sounds from last night's party—the Grateful Dead riffing on "Truckin'," pillars of laughter, loud and moronic—but looking up at his classmates, he realized these were the normal sounds of hearth and home in these parts.

It sounded cheesy, grating, the way he'd rubbed the mic along the box, and when the sound rose in pitch to a whistle from what was clearly a narrow opening, culminating in an explosive, slurpy sound, Paul cringed. Though it was very clear to him that these sounds could be produced by shoving a plastic straw through a Styrofoam block, he prayed it wasn't clear to anybody else.

"Oh, my word," said Gielow, after Paul let the tape run on. He gazed furtively around at his classmates for signs of mockery, but they were ready to believe. This alone was a startling discovery, worthy of a project someday. "Fantastic. Did you have doubts all those hours before? Was there a point at which you wanted to give up?"

Paul nodded fiercely, rationalizing that the facsimile of the noise was valid. To share what he'd heard had been his aim. To expose others to the awesome truth about snail sounds had been his purpose. To come in empty-handed would have left him nowhere, with nothing, though he vowed he'd never do anything like this again.

"Yeah. I had all the usual doubts when you have an unproven theory. I knew what I'd heard was real, though, so I was determined to wait."

"Let that be a lesson to us all," Gielow said.

People in the class asked decent questions. "Do you think they make noise only when stressed out?" "Did the other snails react to the scream?" "Do you think it's communication, or just some kind of gas like a fart?" He handled the questions deftly. He had once heard the noise loud and clear and that's what mattered most.

Later that afternoon, Paul stood beside his project in the assembly room, waiting to explain it to the roving judges. On one side of him was Millie Cuthbertson, the girl he'd liked since fourth grade, with her quiet and refined ways, her self-control, her friendly face.

Her project concerned the heart rates of dogs when taken to the vet, who happened to be her mother. Her standard-sized thirty-six- by forty-eight-inch display board was covered with pictures of various breeds, pictures of the vet/mother, and neatly colored graphs that showed the names of the dogs and their usual heart rates and their rates at the vet, glued onto orange and green construction paper for accent. Paul secretly thought this could have been a third grader's experiment, but since he liked Millie a lot, he said, "Nice. Did you use a certain protocol with the vet?"

"Like how?"

"I mean, was your mother exactly the same with every dog?"

"Sure. She's very professional."

"She doesn't favor one breed over another?"

"We have a collie, so it's possible she likes collies more than other dogs," Millie considered. "But if you look at the statistics on the collie that *wasn't* ours—" She searched endearingly on the chart, allowing him to look down the armpit of her blouse where he could see her bra, which was very plain and white. "Here, well, look, it's one of the lower ratios. Let me see. It's the second lowest, after the deaf fifteen-year-old Yorkie. That's a good point, Paul."

Paul nodded modestly. "I think of things like that."

"Have you seen my project?" interrupted Hans Borg, on the other side of Millie. Hans had made schemata of Hagia Sofia in Constantinople from various angles and had analyzed the structure for weak spots in case of a great quake.

"That's neat," said Millie. "How did you think of it?"

"My family toured Europe last summer," Hans said, rather smugly for someone so pale and pug-nosed. "Turkey was totally the most amazing." Paul had never been to Europe, and at this point hated Hans, who frequently dropped hints about a rich grandmother in Los Angeles who wanted nothing more than to finance Hans in all future whims, great and small. Paul had seen Millie carrying around a copy of *Atlas Shrugged* lately, so while Hans Borg was being questioned by a judge, he asked Millie what she thought of Ayn Rand. Then he told her to check out *Slaughterhouse-Five*, and mentioned that Vonnegut's uncle had been a brilliant scientist who invented the seeding of clouds, and that another relative of his coinvented the horizontal panic bar on public doors after nearly burning up in a theater fire. The brand name was Von Duprin and the "Von" was from Vonnegut. This *Jeopardy!*-quality trivia seemed to impress her, so the conversation continued to open up. He told her a story about how a dead, bloated cow in a field once exploded on his dad. She told him how her mother had found a two-pound brick of hashish in the stomach of a Labrador.

All the while, Paul's head turned to the door for his mother and father, arriving late, breathless, apologetic.

He played his recording for the judges when his turn came. One was a long-haired man in a yellow sweatshirt, who said, "So you took the recorder like an interviewer and sat there?"

"No," Paul said. "I had it mounted over the bucket. When I couldn't be there I just let the tape run. Then I'd go back and listen."

"And were you present when the recorder picked up these sounds?"

"Um, yes, I was," Paul said, making sure to keep his story straight.

"You were there."

"Yes."

"And what did you see at the time?"

Paul stared into the middle distance, beholding a Saturnalia of snails. "They were crawling all over each other—it was chaos—I couldn't tell which one was doing it. I mean, it's not like one was standing up with its mouth open, like an opera singer."

"I see," said the man. He narrowed his eyes at Paul like an assassin. "May I hear that recording again, please?"

What a prick.

The other judges moved on, but this arbiter of pubescent efforts lingered and listened to the recording again. "One more time?" he said when the tape ended.

Was there some fatal flaw in the recording? Maybe the guy was a certified Foley artist and knew exactly how Styrofoam could scream.

"Very interesting," said the man, and made some notes.

"I bet you're going to win."

"Me? Nah."

"Yes! You're in a league of your own."

Millie's parents came by next. Millie's mother had a square, ruddy face, with platinum curls fitting tightly on her scalp like on a Roman bust. She wore a necklace of bulbous black pods, and the gold watch on her arm had dug a canal in the pattern of chain mail on her stout wrist. She had coral-colored lips that looked ready to lecture, and other parental units stopped to talk to her about their dogs and cats. Millie's father was shorter than her mother, an affable-looking CPA with an air of inertia.

"Screaming snails!" he said. "That's wild."

Paul and Millie had been laughing and she said, "Mom? Has anyone ever taken a bug in to see you?"

Her mother ignored the question, preferring to continue her conversation about heartworm treatment with a sheltie owner.

"Mom?" Millie was laughing. "Mom!"

"What is it, Millie?"

"Has anyone every brought in a bug as a patient?"

"Don't be silly. Reptiles. I had an elderly corn snake with pneumonia last month. Put her on antibiotics and she's doing beautifully."

Her mother began talking to another parent about a recovering boxer with a broken forearm.

"A snake's not the same as a bug," Paul said, sensing an opportunity to triangulate, which was his deeply ingrained habit in the presence of overwhelming favoritism for his brother.

"She's so busy," said Millie. "She works all day and gets calls all night."

"My parents are supposed to be here," Paul said.

"You live the other side of Wilson's?"

"Yeah."

"Maybe they had a flat tire."

"Figures."

He abandoned his display at one point for the pay phone, dialed home, and left an irritable message on the crusty, seed-covered home machine.

Back inside, the awards ceremony was starting, but watching the door for his parents distracted him. Third place went to a guy in eleventh grade with "Tractor Factor," measuring the rust on farm equipment. Second place went to "Birds of a Feather" and a twelfth-grade girl who did a biodiversity study in a nearby valley. Millie looked at him expectantly and Paul cleared his throat, and then they announced the winner—Hans Borg, for "Will the Walls Come Tumbling Down?"

Millie leaned over and whispered, like a geranium in his ear, "You were robbed."

He left swiftly. Just as well his parents weren't there. His ideas about going to medical school, recently nurtured by Mr. Gielow, were fragile within him, and anything that pointed to him being inept in the sciences he tried to keep strictly under wraps. This included car trouble. A man of science ought to be able to fix a simple car, but here was Betsy inert, the ignition switch coughing like an old bag saying her tea was cold. Cough. Cough. Goddamn it!

Yet surely the mighty of the earth experienced humiliation too. Probably even more, because they were always out there pushing on the front line! The mighty ignored it or kicked it squarely in the jaw. That's what he had to learn. Not to cower like a scolded pup under a newspaper, but to bark, to back the master into a corner flashing his fangs!

From the driver's seat, he saw Millie crossing with her father. They lived just across from the school.

"Guess what, my car won't start," he yelled out the window.

"Come use the phone at our house," called Millie.

"Okay," called Paul.

He ran to them gratefully.

Millie's house confirmed everything he had believed about her—nice and pretty and neat. Containing nothing to be ashamed of. No equipment for the handicapped. No Zig-Zag packages on the end tables. No grotesque lamp stands forged in the backyard. He phoned home and still there was no answer, and he left another message, saying the fair was over and the car was dead and would they call him at Millie's.

Millie's mom had gone back to the pet hospital. Millie's dad, who worked from home, said, "We can drive you home, Paul."

"Thanks, I'll wait," Paul said. "It's a long way out there."

"I'll drive him!" said Millie, and the arrector pili in the area of his groin contracted mightily. "Please, Dad?"

Millie's father had a faraway look in his eyes, as if judging this to be a meaningful rite of passage in his daughter's life. He nodded, but then, as if remembering fatherly protocol, said, "But you know there are a lot of crazy people out there. You've got your illegals who do the picking, you've got your cartel members coming to make deals, you've got crazy nuts defending their property with AK-47s, you know the drill."

"We won't pick up anybody hitchhiking," Millie said, as if that solved the problem.

"And maybe you could call me when you get there, before you turn around? So I know where you're at?"

"Sure, Dad. Thanks!"

"Paul, how's that road? Do you see a lot of crazies out there?"

Paul said, "I've never seen any guys with guns. I avoid the hitchhikers. They usually wait at this one spot, so I just go by and it's fine."

"All right, then. Have fun, you kids." He started to root around in his pile of tapes next to his desk. "Listen to this if you want. It's really good."

Suddenly Paul saw the cosmic trade-off. Hans Borg got the science fair, but he got time with Millie. The world stayed in balance. They climbed into her parents' Jeep Wagoneer and drove off.

"Thanks," Paul said. "Your dad's nice."

"Compared to my mom."

Paul was shocked to learn there was a crack in the perfect surface of Millie's life. "She doesn't seem that bad."

"You have no idea," Millie said, emboldened. "Remember when she said 'Don't be silly' when we asked about bugs? That's her campaign against the world. *Don't be silly*. She just wants to stifle everything."

"I hate that," Paul said.

"Me too."

They drove up through the forested hills, along a creek lined with ferns. Paul rolled down his window and let the air go through his fingers. He realized the less he cared about the science fair, the less his failure tainted him. "I'm glad you see through Hans Borg," Paul said. "He's so full of himself."

"You know who likes him?" said Millie. "Christine." Christine was a chubby girl at school who drew on her hands and was the sister of younger twins who excluded her.

"Good," Paul said. "I'm sure they'll be very happy together."

"Christine used to like *you*," said Millie.

Paul pulled on his collar. "Really? What made her stop?"

"Oh, she knew someone else liked you."

His cheeks burned, and he crumpled up a dollar in his pocket.

Millie said, "I love this song!" and turned it up, *"I'll stop the world and melt with you,"* and they had all the windows down, drawing in the smells of the forests and the damp ground, and birdsong flitted in the windows as they passed. Paul felt as if he were in a film about a teenager who was about to lose his virginity.

"Want to hear a weird dream I had?" Millie said. "I was a dog. A Border collie, I think. And since I was a dog I was happy because I knew my mother was going to take care of me."

"Whoa. Really symbolic!"

"I know. It almost sounds like I made it up, but I really dreamed it."

"I dreamed once my brother was stabbing me, right in our living room, and that my parents just kept shellacking some cabinet they bought at a flea market."

"Whoa! Your brother has MS, right?"

"No, it's some kind of brain damage."

"I've seen him in town and he looks nice."

"He's not that nice."

"Once I dreamed that Gielow was showing us his formaldehyde jars and specimens and he said one of them was his nose but it actually looked like a penis. And he *had* a nose when he said it, so in the dream I knew he was lying."

Paul laughed, aroused by her willingness to say the word *penis*.

"He liked yours much better than Hans's," she said.

"You think?"

"Definitely. When Hans did his in class, he was taking roll."

"Mine could've been better," Paul said.

"It was so original and risky. It was based on something undocumented."

"True," Paul said, feeling better about himself. A willingness to risk and be caught up short, that's what he had, as nothing great was ever accomplished without mistakes and humiliation first.

"What's the worst thing you'd do if you could be invisible?" he asked.

"Probably go into a bakery and take bites out of everything."

"That's all?"

"I don't think I'd rob a bank or anything. It wouldn't be satisfying to get rich that way."

"I'd probably get on a plane and go somewhere as far from here as possible," he said, starting to laugh. But she stuck out her lower lip in a flirtatious pout.

"For what?"

"Well, to start my clinic."

"So it would be altruistic?"

"Yeah, ultimately."

"My mom pretends she's altruistic, but it's an act. She's so phony it makes me sick."

He enjoyed Millie's complaints about her mother, and felt a keen bond.

"Turn left," Paul said when they reached a fork in the road.

"Turn up there at the big tree," he said a little later.

"Is this your property now?"

"Yeah," Paul said. "Just go around that grove, and we're there."

He went on high alert as they rolled past the trees into the clearing. He didn't want her to linger and see Justin or the hippies. The van was still parked off to the side, as was his parents' other car. Had they simply forgotten? He burned.

"Well," said Millie.

"Thanks," said Paul, starting to climb out. "I gotta get going so thanks and see you and—"

"But remember what my dad said, about calling?" Millie asked as she turned off the engine. "Besides, I want to see your snails."

"Oh, yeah," Paul said, wondering if that was a euphemism. "Sure." He looked around, assessing the risks. "Okay." He paused. "Some freaky friends of my parents are visiting, so don't hold it against me."

"God, around here?" said Millie. "I don't care."

Just then he heard a sound from the forest, and Hacky Sack John ran across the meadow, naked except for a Peruvian knit cap with llama silhouettes woven into it.

"I hate these people," Paul muttered, and Millie laughed.

Walking up to the house, they encountered a circle of the guests lying on blankets, arms spread, staring up at the sky. "It's a beak," someone said.

"I see it," said another.

"Quick, inside," he whispered to Millie, but a voice harpooned him right through the neck.

"Pope Paul!" It was Cool Breeze, lifting his head and squinting.

"Yeah, hi," said Paul, and he and Millie ran up the steps. Inside, he encountered a strong mix of odors: a stinking bong must've tipped, spreading its foul water into the carpet. In the kitchen, flies had lit on a feast around the sink, bowls with cookie dough clinging to the edges, cracked eggshells on the floor, a baking sheet sitting on the open door of the oven with one melted chocolate chip left on the edge. There were carrot tops, brown lettuce leaves, and a partly chopped onion all over the counter, and the big vat of lentil soup from the night before was now encrusted on the outside as well as in, and the ladle lay across the stovetop, crustiest of all. Three large flies threw their bodies at the window over the sink, as if hoping to break through the glass. The wall clock ticked loudly.

"This is gross. It's not like this normally," he insisted.

"Can I have something to drink?"

Paul tried to find clean glasses, but had to wash them, filling them with soapsuds, nearly scalding himself to make sure hers was sanitary enough. "Water? Juice?"

"Juice."

Cider sat in a brown jug on the counter, the kind his parents made in the fall from their own apples. At least the lid had been screwed on.

"I want to see your room," said Millie, taking a gulp.

"Don't you need to call your father?"

"I'm not his flunky," Millie said, licking the juice off her lips.

The cider was sweet and flavorful, and Paul could at least feel proud of their cider-making abilities. "Stay here. I want to see if my parents are upstairs."

The farmhouse was a hundred years old, drafty and full of squeaks. He ran up the narrow wooden steps, but his parents' room was vacant. Justin's room was empty too. He stopped in the bathroom quickly, squirted some toothpaste into his mouth and spat it out, then brushed his hair and looked at himself in the mirror. Something about his eyes looked funny, kind of velvety and deep, his pupils black as trampolines. He wondered if Millie thought he was handsome, and approached the mirror with his face as if to deliver a kiss. This was a bad idea. He backed away and ran downstairs.

Millie stood at his bedroom door, peering in. Coming up behind her he was greeted by the sight of entwined naked bodies on his bed, then overpowered by the smell of sweat and the sound of slapping skin.

"Shhh," she whispered. Her eyes looked black and velvety too.

"Shit!"

He tore out the back door, where he knocked over a broom, which clattered down the back steps. The broom on the ground in the dirt looked pitiful. He sat with it, and thought about the broom's existence for the first time in his life. It was the same broom they'd had all his life. A red-handled broom, with blue and orange stitching through the broomcorn. Paint peeling all along the handle. He remembered riding the broom when he was little and pretending it was a donkey named Freedy.

How could he have taken so much for granted? Why did it stay, year after year, to sweep for them?

He looked up in time to see Millie descending the back steps with her blouse unbuttoned, the small mounds of her breasts exposed. Her nipples were small and tender in appearance, and came closer until only inches from his face. She rubbed a bud on his nose. He had planned to tell her about the broom but it was the first nipple of a girl his own age he'd ever seen. Millie kissed him. It was the first kiss he'd had on the lips with his mouth open. Her mouth tasted like root beer.

Then came a fermata, how long they sat on the ground at the bottom of the back steps wrapped up kissing and touching. She kept laughing and tossing her hair. "I'm hot," she said often, with glassy eyes. "I feel so hot."

His head felt open at the top, like a chimney that she could pour something into.

"Put your hand here," he said. She touched his hair. "Is it open?"

She nodded. "Wide open."

"I think we're on drugs," said Paul.

"I'm hot. I feel hot."

From his father's forge he heard the maddening drone of "Scarlet Begonias."

"Everybody's happy," said Millie. "I feel like going into the woods."

"Let's go into the woods," said Paul.

"Let's take a blanket."

His legs felt like wheels, and they rolled him right into the smithy, where his father's hearth stood cold. All the tools out on the table. The forge had another room where his father had his office and kept his stock. He saw the back of Justin's head rolling against the desk.

"Justy?" Paul said. But Justin didn't hear him, and then Paul saw the bobbing crown of Caddie Fladeboe, who was mouthing the head of Justin's penis, slipping her lips over a bulb the size of a beet.

"Hey!" screamed Paul.

"Hey!" cried Caddie Fladeboe, lifting her damp, rosy face.

"What the fuck! Get out of here!"

"Leave us alone! We're joyous beings!" Caddie declared.

"You little shit!" he yelled at Justin. "You can't do anything but you can do this?"

"Don't tell Mom and Dad," Justin cried.

"Ha! We'll see about that!"

No! No! No!" keened Justin. "No, no, no!"

Paul grabbed a blanket off his dad's chair and Millie followed right behind. He didn't say another word until he'd taken her back to the house and handed her the telephone.

"Call your father and go home," he said.

"What's wrong?"

"My brother's a pervert! And now you know it!"

"I didn't even see. I'm cool with it."

"He thinks he can do whatever he wants!"

Millie said, "You can do whatever you want too," and brought his hands to her hips.

"CHAINSAWS," MILLIE WAS saying to her dad on the phone, holding Paul's hand.

"Someone's using a chainsaw?"

"I saw some chainsaws," Millie said again.

"Honey, you okay? Are you heading back?"

"I could but I started to feel dizzy on the drive. I think I need to lie down."

"Sure, honey. Take forty winks."

"Okay, Dad."

"Call me later, okay?"

"Okay, Dad. Dad, I think I should stay here tonight."

"Stay there? Hmm. Can I talk to Paul's parents?"

"We'll have fun," she said, smiling at Paul.

"Honey, let me talk to the mother or father. I want to make sure it's okay."

"Daddy? There's a tree outside covered with flags."

"What kind of flags?"

"Red and white and blue flags. American flags."

"Really? That's good. They have a guest room out there for you?"

"Yes. They're cooking."

"Barbecue. All right. I'll tell your mother. It's probably better than driving that road home alone."

"Thanks, Dad."

"Give me the number out there."

She gave him the number.

"Call us before you leave in the morning, all right?"

"I will."

"Hey, great job at the fair today. I was so proud."

"Was Mom proud?"

"Mom was proud too."

Millie hung up the phone and led Paul down the steps, into the forest, where she took the blanket from him and spread it on the ground like an expert. Then she kissed him. She ran her tongue over his teeth and his lips. She sucked on his mouth and kissed him harder, and placed his hands in her blouse and then she was pushing herself against him, feeling the solid feeling in his pants right by his zipper, and something was there behind those barriers that was hard and powerful and she pushed against it all, this package she wanted to spring open and unwrap under a tree on a soft bed of duff, and she was pushing him down and trying to open his package, and that heavy belt came first, that impossible bolt and rivet, that zipper with rusted teeth that wouldn't budge, and there it was, there it was. A silky-skinned penis so much larger than a dog's, and so much more colorful! It was purple on one side, with green stripes and red stripes and small black paisleys around the base, and shiny, and shapely, like a tall ride at Tomorrowland.

"Millie?" said Paul. "Should we?"

"Yes."

"I love you," said Paul, positioning himself over her.

"I love you too," said Millie, with a hungry, yearning feeling between her legs.

He pressed but it was a bone and she moved him to a softer spot. "More," she said, when he felt a slight give.

"There?"

"More!"

Paul had been a virgin until a few seconds ago, so was not exactly sure how to manage *more*. But he tried.

"More," she cried. She began to giggle, and he felt the vestigial remains of his baby fat in her hands, and saw himself as a master Tillamook Cheddar log, Millie as a pliant grater beneath, a Cheddar who wanted to be grated, a grater who wanted to be Cheddared, and even still he managed it, until he was melting all over her as Cheddar will do, and his eyes were blurry and confused and then he saw in a flash exactly how many heartbeats he had left in this world, and it wasn't so many really, and Millie thought so too because they cried and said they wished they were one person, and for a while, they really did feel like they were one being fused in flesh.

· · ·

NIGHT FELL, and the sounds in the woods frightened them, and drove them back to the house. Bill and Marion were making a tall vat of curry in the kitchen.

"Paul!" roared Bill. "Where you been?"

Marion dropped her spoon and came over to them and began to pull dried redwood needles from Paul's hair, and Millie's too, and then she hugged them as if they were innocent children. "We're so sorry," she said to Paul. "We missed it. We took a little detour today, if you get what I mean."

Bill came over and whispered, "They laced the cider with Mr. Natural. We were on Planet X. We went all the way past Wilson's to the waterfall. Didn't remember a thing about real life until we got back."

"We are so sorry, Paul," said Marion, back to stirring the spicy yellow curry. "Tell us about the fair."

"Where's Justin?" Paul asked.

"In bed," said Marion.

Paul said, "What's with Caddie, anyway?"

"What do you mean?" said Bill, who always defended people from Paul's attacks. "She has a great way with all kinds of people."

"Yeah, she's great, all right."

Millie giggled.

"The fair, Paul, tell us what happened," asked Marion.

"His was the most creative and interesting of anything there," said Millie. "Doesn't matter he didn't win."

Paul blushed.

Bill and Marion and Millie got into a conversation about Millie's project, and everybody was getting along, because that was his parents' gift, they became a loveseat and made everybody in the world feel warm and welcome except him.

MILLIE AND PAUL enjoyed the status of being boyfriend and girlfriend for two months and four days. And for years Paul would hold the memory guarded and close, sure that no love could ever surpass it. How they got along! How he loved the fuzz on her arms and her hip bones and the root-beery taste of her lips, and how they could fester in their parents' faults for hours, and plan lives without them. They took long walks every day after school, went to movies and used bookstores in Arcata, ran on the beach, played video games at an arcade and had ice cream cones and, best of all, he kept a blanket in the back of the car for finding special spots in the redwoods, one in particular at the center of a grove of six giants, which reminded them of Stonehenge because they saw how the sunlight created shafts through the trees, which moved a few centimeters every day, and they began to record it on a piece of paper until one day Millie turned to him in the street after school and said, "I think I'm pregnant."

It stopped him short, and not because he was unhappy about it.

In a mere second he was able to see down a road that had never been open to him before, and from which he now wished to travel and never look back. On that road, all his hopes and dreams and ambitions were left behind like the piles of garbage his parents' friends had strewn in front of their house, and a new life as a young father with Millie as his wife and their simple hopes and dreams and those of their child flashed before him, infinitely more inviting. He nearly gasped at the beauty of his vision, and took Millie's hands.

"That's great!" he cried.

"No," she said. "My parents will never speak to me again."

"No, it's not true," said Paul, and he took her backpack off her shoulders, and they sat together on the curb in front of her house. "They'll be happy after they get used to it."

"Don't you want me to get rid of it?"

"I mean, it's up to you, but if you want to have a baby, I'll do it. We can get married," he said, flushed with love.

She looked puzzled by the idea, and he blushed more.

"That's so, so sweet," she said, kicking a rock into the road.

"I mean it."

"Really?"

"More than anything."

THERE THEY WERE, standing before her parents, proclaiming their innocent desire to marry and have a child.

"You've got to be kidding," said Millie's mother, who was looking at Paul with something like disgust, but worse.

"No, Mother, I'm very serious."

"You're sixteen years old. You're going to college. You're nowhere near ready to marry and raise a child, and even if you were—" Her thin upper lip retracted all the way to her gums, and she gazed at Paul with utter loathing.

"Mr. and Mrs. Cuthbertson, I'm planning to do premed in college and—"

"You think you're going to be a doctor?" said Millie's mother. "Doing projects about screaming snails? Do you know what the judges were saying about your project?"

"Jill, come on," said Ron.

"Your results were a crock, weren't they?"

"I resent that remark!" Paul said firmly.

Millie said, "Paul wouldn't cheat. You wouldn't cheat, Paul, I know you wouldn't."

"Chuck Gielow swore on his mother's grave for him," said Mrs. Cuthbertson. "It was pathetic."

"With all due respect," Paul said, his voice rising to a squeak, "I plan to become a psychiatrist or a neurologist, and I plan to go to the best schools."

"Where are the best schools, Paul?"

"Mom, Paul is totally smart and dedicated! Stop talking that way!"

"Millie, the friends you want to make are the friends you make in college. I can't wait for you to get out of this hellhole of drug dealers and potheads, and I would never approve a marriage to someone whose parents make their living illegally."

"Mrs. Cuthbertson—"

"*Dr.* Cuthbertson!"

"I beg your pardon, my mother is a county nurse and—"

"I know all about them," said Millie's mother. "If I'd been home my daughter would never have gone out there that night."

"Don't start that again, Jill," said Millie's father.

"You live in your ledgers. I actually go out and see the kind of things going on around here!"

Paul blinked and wished to push her off a cliff, at the bottom of which lay finely sharpened spikes.

"Mom, I love Paul."

"You're not having a baby, you're not marrying this cheat, over my dead body!" screamed her mother.

"He wouldn't cheat! I know he wouldn't cheat!"

Millie began to cry, and when Paul put his arms around her, her mother grabbed her, pulling her out of reach, out of the room.

"Ron, I expect him to be on his way," Millie's mother said. "He's going to pay for the procedure, and he won't come near Millie, or we'll send the police to pay a visit to his house. Out! Out! Out!"

"Mom!" cried Millie, and Paul tried to go to her, but Millie's dad put an iron grip on his arm.

Under his breath, Millie's father said, "I don't entirely agree with her, but there's nothing I can do about it."

Paul said, "Don't you have a say? What about me? Don't I?"

Ron said, "I don't think so. Not with an underage girl."

"Underage?" He was five months younger than Millie.

"Now go," said Ron Cuthbertson.

"But—"

Ron put his hand on Paul's back, and pushed him to the door. Then out the door.

The door closed behind him.

Outside he took one look at their prim mailbox with the squirrel on it and punched it with his fist. It hurt more than he expected. Fists were built for punching, weren't they? Why were his so soft? The mailbox popped open and he grabbed it like a

pumpkin and twisted it from its mount and threw it on the ground
and stomped on it. The buckling metal tore a hole in his sock at
the ankle, and he bled. He looked back at the house but no one
was bothering to watch. He bit his lips and got back into his car
and screeched away. He and Millie would work it out. They'd run
away! He went around the block in the Dodge, so fast he had to
swerve around some kids on bikes, until the car was fishtailing on
the greasy wet road, and his brain went to the fishtail file and
heard: *Go in the direction of the skid,* and then he heard, *No, go in the
opposite direction of the skid,* and they both sounded right so he
chose the wrong one and the truck spun and collided with a fire
hydrant, then flipped and rolled upside down right in front of the
house where the sheriff lived.

"The rejections I've received have been, by no means, definitive," he mumbled to himself, hanging upside down, lulled by the
rhythm of the declaration. *"The rejections I've received have been, by
no means, definitive."*

Millie was abruptly taken out of South Humboldt High and
sent to a private girls' school in Tacoma, Washington. Paul sent
many letters but received no reply. And to this day, the word *cheat*
had the power to undo him. He even tremored at any word that
sounded remotely like it, such as *cheetah* and *Chee-tos*. He never
heard a word of what happened to her, until the information was
digitized.

16

NEVER THE SAME AGAIN

Paso Robles was crisp and bright the morning Veblen and the squirrel ventured over to Sunny Hill to visit Rudgear. Up a quiet street, where the mad could free-range in pajamas. A trailer court and an underfunded animal shelter frowned from the other side of the road. Surrounded by a carpet of brittle oak leaves, the archipelago of lime green buildings for the mentally unbalanced had been built around 1965.

Skill-building groups, general activities, small therapy groups, community meetings, physical and recreational activities, were idealized ways to describe what Rudgear was offered there. Every year his psychiatrist received, from any number of pharmaceutical companies, including Hutmacher, several all-expenses-paid vacations at conferences in luxurious resorts. In between his vacations he'd come by and sign off, with a quick blink, Rudgear's list of nineteen meds, a third of them redundant and unnecessary.

"Okay," Veblen informed the squirrel. "I'll leave the window open, and I might be awhile, but you'll be all right, won't you?

And then I'll bring you back to Palo Alto where you belong. For all I know you have a family there."

The squirrel settled back comfortably into the corner, radiating consent.

She removed the bags of supplies from the trunk and applied herself to her task, entering the building with practiced calm. In no corner of the complex was it possible to escape the aroma of institutional cuisine—creamed corn, tubs of sloppy joe, acidic apple juice, canned fruit cocktail, defrosted nuggets of fried chicken or fish sticks.

"Veblen, how you doing?" asked Bebe Kaufman, who always wore a running suit and a set of keys on a long black cord around her neck.

"Fine, how about you?"

"'Bout the same. Your father fell in the hallway yesterday, didn't have his shoes on right. He bleeds and bruises; he's lucky his bones are strong."

"Any changes in the medications?"

"No, everything's the same. His diabetes is under control, and no hallucinations in a long while. But when he's scared, boy, do I feel bad for him. He's been peaceful lately. He's a real gentleman."

Veblen held up her bags. "I brought all the stuff—two new pairs of pajamas, three pairs of drawstring pants, new socks, all the toothpaste and powder. Oh, and that coccyx pillow."

"Nice girl," said Bebe, whose approval Veblen mysteriously sought. "I'll put it down on his inventory."

She marched down the hall to see her father, past custodians in their whites on chairs in a break room, mops at rest against the door. Past a woman with chattering teeth in a purple velour robe in a wheelchair. Past a small, round man peering from inside his room, wearing no more than a white undershirt and shorts and shin-high brown socks with holes at the toes. Around a corner with a lithograph of a beagle fetching a ball in a baseball diamond, past a woman who looked like an ancient contessa with sharp noble features, who always wore lipstick, to an elevator that descended to a floor of all men. An attendant paced the hall with a wad of keys on his belt.

Father. It had a much more nebulous definition than *mother.* In this case it was a name, a shadow, aiming darts at her from the darkness.

She drifted in like a stray feather. No use startling him, deep in his chair, watching the History Channel.

"Hi, Dad."

"Hi, kiddo." He had green eyes like hers, but his skin was pinker, and he was bald and had scabs on his head, some of which were protected by gauze. His polo shirt, white with blue stripes, had been laundered so much it was see-through, yet stained everywhere, even on the sleeves, and his brown sweatpants had turned a sickly yellow color, probably thrown in with bleach. A framed picture of Veblen with her arm around him sat atop his bureau (she'd given it to him), and several versions of Van Gogh's sunflowers on laminated placemats were taped to the wall by his bed.

She came over to the chair and gave him a kiss. He gave her a kiss back. Then he continued with his show, about Normandy and D-day.

"They just showed a guy talking about the blood pooling under the trees, and now those trees are huge. Blood meal. He was run over by a tank and lost his legs. Of course, those kids'll never be the same mentally, they won't be right."

Veblen nodded. It was one of his manias to end nearly every story: "He was never the same again." "She was never the same again."

"So I came down with a squirrel in the car," she told him.

"Oh, really?" He loved animals.

"Do you want to see him?"

"Okeydoke."

"Okay. We'll go look in a minute. I want to tell you something. I have some news. You ready?"

She sat next to his chair, on the edge of the bed, but he looked a bit scared.

"Yeah, what's that? You win the lottery?"

"No, but it looks like I'm getting married."

She saw his chest cave in.

"Dad? Did you hear me?"

He peered at her sidelong. "What do you want from me?"

"Nothing. I only wanted to tell you."

"Marriage is not my forte."

"Maybe it'll be mine."

"I hope so, kiddo," he said. "I didn't have much luck."

She got up and breathed deeply and walked a few times around the room. To change the mood, she retrieved the bag of treats and dangled the peanut-butter-filled pretzels and soft licorice before his eyes.

"Oh, goody," he said.

He was not supposed to eat foodstuffs from the outside, but

Veblen always snuck in the licorice and pretzels because he loved them so much.

"Don't let the warden see," he said.

"Want some juice too?"

"Yep."

She poured the juice into a coffee cup and watched TV with him awhile. More footage of D-day, GIs pouring from landing crafts onto the sand.

"There's no such thing as a good war," he said.

She nodded thoughtfully.

"You know what I did in Vietnam?" he rasped.

"What?"

"Killed women and children."

"Tell me about your friend Ybahn and the Montagnards," Veblen coaxed.

"They were the sweetest little people, but we ruined them—the whole culture. They were never the same, they lost everything."

"But those stories about the big feasts they'd make you, I like those."

"I think so."

That was all he managed. There was a time when talking about the Montagnards, the tribal hill people of Vietnam who furtively helped the U.S. military during the war, provided relief from his more troubled recollections.

"Paul, the man I'm going to marry, is a doctor, and works with vets." As soon as she said this, she felt sad. Was this marriage thing going to work or not?

"I can sure use some help," said her father.

"I'm sure."

Another stick of soft licorice went in, blackening his lips and tongue.

"Dad, do you remember your parents speaking Norwegian when you were growing up?"

"Nope," he said.

If she could only ask the right questions, to unlock him!

"Did they ever tell you anything about their childhoods?"

He reached for another licorice stick, chewed awhile. "Nope. We had some kids in the neighborhood, got mixed up with some rough guys, talked them into robbing a store. They were caught, thrown in jail. When they came out, boy, they were never the same again."

Veblen nodded. She patted her father's arm, where he had a large shiny scar, and realized she didn't know its origin. It was a puzzle to imagine him and her mother hanging around together, but according to records, they shared the same address in Sacramento for about six weeks in a newlyweds' apartment full of useless wedding gifts, like fondue kits and lazy Susans, drinking and brawling into the night, all youthful and fecund and feral faced, cherry lipped and flushed, annihilating their woes in carnal plenitude. *They were never the same again.*

"So, Dad, you've got some nice new pajamas and some new pants and socks. Anything else you need?"

"I could use one of those—those things, those long things."

"What long things?"

"I don't know what they're called. They're—very long." He motioned with his hands.

She looked around the room for clues. "What do you use them for?"

"I don't know, Veblen. I need some air!"

She stood up and paced the room. "Sorry, Dad." She fiddled about, trying to make improvements for him. She opened the window for fresh air, pulled back the heavy curtain for more light. She straightened a picture she'd given him, of tigers. He loved tigers. She wandered into his bathroom and neatened it, wiping droplets of urine off the toilet rim and some hairs out of the sink. Back in the room, she hung up a few of his sweatshirts and placed his tired old caps on hooks. He looked at her then and jutted his hand. "More, please."

"Want to go outside for a little while? It's a beautiful day."

"Not really."

"Let's go outside for five minutes, the sun will feel good."

"All right."

He rose abruptly, pretzel crumbs powdering the floor, the dandruff of food. "I'm quite a sight."

"You look good," she said, gently taking his arm.

She moved him slowly toward his door. "Straighten up," she reminded him. He pulled his chest up. "Good."

Arm in arm they took the hall, heading for the serviceable garden courtyard. Outside they sat on a concrete bench in the shade. Primrose and four-o'clocks and a small burbling fountain did what they could to lend some cheer.

"This is a pretty nice place," he said. "Did you hear we had some excitement?"

"No, what happened?"

"We had a van parked across the street for weeks, and my buddy down the hall, Bob, called the police, couldn't get a word out of 'em. And Bob has a friend whose daughter is a secretary over there and he finally calls her, tells her about the van, gives her the license number. She looks it up. California plate, by the way. Turns out it's registered to something called the ABC Key Company in Washington, D.C."

Veblen knew his way of thinking. "How strange."

"You bet it's strange. He saw a scope coming up through the roof one night."

"What did you do next?"

"What could we do? The cops were in on it. We were careful what we talked about after that."

"You know what, Dad? They like you here a lot."

He was breathing heavily. "Do I have to stay here?"

"No. Do you want me to find out about a new place, nearer to me?"

He thought for a moment. "I don't think so."

"Will you come to my wedding?"

Venturing this request, she felt a surge of anxiety.

"I don't think I'm presentable enough."

"But, Dad, you're fine. Paul's family is casual and relaxed. They even used to be nudists!"

"Holy mackerel," said her father. "They'll call me a baby killer and tell me I'm going to hell."

"Everyone will be impressed with your service."

He was quiet for a while. "Was that what it was?"

"Yes, of course it was."

He rocked a little.

"What would I wear?"

"We can shop for a new suit if you want."

"A new suit."

He was quiet again.

"I can't give you away. I have a shaking problem and I also have to wear a pad."

"That's okay, Dad. It won't be a traditional wedding."

"I don't do well in crowds. I need air."

She sighed, but her cheerful side told her that a challenge could lift a person up sometimes.

"Let me think about it," he said.

She kissed his cheek. "Really! Thanks."

"Thanks, kid. I'm feeling a little shaky now. Maybe we better go back in."

"But don't you want to see the squirrel?"

"Maybe next time."

"I won't bring him next time, Dad. Just for a second."

"I don't think so. I gotta go."

She couldn't insist. She'd never owned him, the way some girls owned their fathers, and for that matter he didn't own her. She helped him up and they shuffled inside through the glass doors, down the long hallway, into his room, where he plopped back into his chair and synced up with the History Channel. She sat on the bed and for the next hour they watched a documentary on the Mexican War of 1846–48, one of the lesser known wars on the list maintained by the Department of Veterans Affairs.

"Dad, I'll call you next week, okay?"

"Thanks," said her father, crunching a peanut-butter-filled pretzel.

"You'll keep thinking about my wedding, about coming?"

"That I will, daughter," he said.

She stood in the doorway for a few minutes, watching him dig around his molars for the mashed-up pretzels that clung to them, and soon realized he'd forgotten she was there.

She moved away, down the hall with the spongy carpet, installed to cushion falls.

ON HER WAY OUT, she found Bebe.

"So it's possible I'm getting married in May, and if I do, I'd like my father to come. You think he'd be okay?"

"*Possibly* getting married? Don't you know?"

"I mean, *am*. Yes." She became clear right then on everything, the whole thing, that it would be at Cloris Hutmacher's house, which would be good for Paul's career and make him happy. It didn't matter *where*, after all. Why had she been so stingy?

"When was the last time he traveled, do you remember? Hold on, I'll get out the chart."

"I don't think he's traveled much at all. I took him out for frozen yogurt once."

At that moment, Ted Waxman, the director of Sunny Hill, appeared, apparently on his way to a tennis match, and he shook the tips of Veblen's fingers.

"Mr. Waxman, Miss Amundsen-Hovda is getting married and wants her father there, Rudgear. I'm looking at his status for passes."

Waxman said, "Congratulations. Let me take a look."

He took the file, rifling through officiously. Then he cleared his throat a few times and read some notes that had been clipped to the front.

"It appears he hasn't been out of the facility for two years. His behavioral record is faultless, but we would still have to progress him through the pass system before releasing him for an over-nighter. I take it the wedding is not in Paso Robles?"

"The Bay Area. Atherton."

"Did you consider having your wedding here, to ease the situation with your father?"

"Um, no," said Veblen, in all honesty. Should she have?

"Well, every family has a different style," Waxman said. "Some don't include them at all."

"It's sad," said Bebe.

"Yes, it is, but by the time they come to us, they've dished out enough abuse for a lifetime, and the families have had enough," Waxman said.

Bebe said, "It's obvious he was good to you, probably a wonderful dad growing up. I can tell you're very close."

Veblen cleared her throat uncomfortably.

Waxman continued, "So let's see, we'd start him on a patio pass. If he stays on the patio, then he'll advance to a progress pass."

"Is it progress to stay on a patio?" Veblen asked.

"You bet it is. Then if he meets acceptable behavior guidelines he can get a peer pass, and we'll take it from there."

"What are acceptable behavior guidelines?" Veblen wondered.

Waxman said, "No murder and mayhem." He coughed. "Of course I'm being facetious. We have a very good reputation." He lowered his voice. "It happened before I was here."

"So we'd better start the process right away," said Bebe.

"Do you think he'll be able to have a good time?" Veblen asked, a bit doubtful.

Bebe said, "Girl, it's your wedding. Your dad should be there whether he has a good time or not."

"I don't want it to be an ordeal for him."

"*He's* the ordeal, right? Pay it back!"

They laughed with the guilty pleasure of caretakers, and Waxman said, "Ladies, I have piles of work waiting for me." And he vanished out the back door with his racket.

"I should come get my father myself, don't you think? So he feels safe?"

"Drive down here the day before your wedding? I'll arrange it with our transport service. It's settled. Don't worry about a thing," said Bebe, as she had many times, Veblen reckoned, to people whose loved ones were about to make a noose with their sheets and hoist themselves in the closet, or stick a dinner fork through their nasal passages into their brains.

"Thanks, Bebe."

"MAYBE ONCE some giant picked up my father and set him down somewhere else, like I nearly did to you," Veblen said to the squirrel, as they hit the road. "And he had no idea how to get home or be okay again. And then everyone thought he was crazy."

She bit into a yellow Delicious she'd brought along.

"Geez," she said. "You know what? If you think about it symbolically, the military was the giant, and it plucked him up in

Waukegan and set him down in Southeast Asia—and he was never the same again."

No argument from the squirrel.

"Funny how Bebe thinks we've always been close. I'm glad Paul didn't come, I'm not sure he'd get it."

The squirrel's tail flickered gently.

This prompted another call to Paul, again met with an immediate recording. Strange that his phone would be off, and that he hadn't called her last night or today.

Her thoughts wandered. "You know, I wonder if the gentlemanly title of squire could be connected to the word *squirrel*. Way back, of course. Although I've heard it comes from the old Greek *skiouros*, which means shade ass."

He jauntily lifted his tail and fanned it out over his backside!

"I know the old English was *aquerne*, like acorn. And the German word for *squirrel* is *Eichhörnchen*, which means something like oak-kitty. Nothing to do with squires or knights at all. In fact, your name is used derisively a lot of the time. To be *squirrelly* is to be crazy, nutty, weird. Outside the norm. And to *squirrel* something away is to be a hoarder, a stasher, a miser, a skinflint.

"Why has your name been so abused?

"It's not fair. Thorstein Veblen's name was abused," she said next. "They called him the nutty professor and thought he was some kind of freak. But he had two stepdaughters who adored him. He'd show them natural wonders in the woods, like how balsam sap was good for blisters, and he'd wake them up in the middle of the night to see special stars, and he'd teach them interesting words, and he'd make them pens out of feathers! He was actually really chivalrous when you look into it. One time I went to Chicago with Albertine; she was going to a Jung conference. And I went to the archives at the University of Chicago and read his correspondence. I think his first wife was kind of like my grandmother, really difficult and weird. Plus, this is kind of weird, she had *infantilized genitalia,* which means she couldn't have sex or whatever, which isn't good for a marriage, even though they stayed together for years. Sorry. TMI?" She laughed. Her mother would kill her for saying TMI. But she could say it all she wanted, she was free! TMI! TMI! Actually, come to think of it, TMI sounded stupid. "You see, I need to come to that conclusion empirically, not just avoid saying it because my mother tells me not to, you know what I mean?"

In a while, she said:

"I guess I should tell my mother what's going on. Is that what you're thinking?"

The squirrel had no doubt.

"It's going to be a difficult conversation," she assessed.

The squirrel knew this too. That he acknowledged it made her feel infinitely stronger.

"All right. I should get it over with."

So after a few more miles, she called home.

"Hi, Linus!" she said, as the squirrel bore witness. "Can I talk to Mom?"

He spoke in a hush. "She's outside right now. We put the roof back on the chicken house and we cleaned it up, so she's having some fun out there with her art supplies."

"Great," said Veblen. "Should I call back later?"

"I hear you've got all kinds of plans in place for the big day," Linus said.

"We're trying. I think it's coming together."

"Mind if I get some information?" asked Linus. "Now might be a good time."

"Go for it."

"Good. So I understand this is happening at a big fancy house in Atherton?"

"I guess it is. But just for our families and friends. The owner won't be there."

"All right, good. That was making your mother nervous. Now, we wanted to know, will there be parking, and will she have to walk a great distance from the car? Her ankles are really bothering her."

"You guys can have priority parking, right next to the house."

"Terrific. And—will there be a room she can rest in, if she needs to lie down?"

Veblen rolled her eyes. "Sure, no problem."

"Okay. And then, will I have access to the kitchen, to make sure I can get her water at any time, or ice, that sort of thing?"

"Yes," said Veblen, keeping her eyes on the road. "Whatever you need."

Linus cleared his throat. "All right, Veb. Just a few more here. Food. Have you checked that she can eat what's on the menu?"

"How about if you send me the latest list of stuff she can't have and I'll show it to the caterer."

"Okay, good plan. I knew you were thinking of her. Do you remember what happened the time we went to my colleague's wedding in Walnut Creek?"

"Remind me," said Veblen.

"The jackass caterer had the list months in advance, but all she made for your mother was a bowl of carrots and a hard-boiled egg."

"I'll have whole main dishes she can eat," Veblen asserted.

"Terrific. I'll go get her now. Take care, Veblen."

She waited, then heard the distinctive snap of the screen door, and her mother clattering into her place by the phone.

"Hello, dear. Did Linus tell you? I've had a lot of arrhythmia the past few days. I had to go to the hospital."

"Oh my god. You okay now?"

"I think my calcium was low."

"Yeah, that's bad."

"It bleeds out because of my adrenal problems. There's nothing I can do about it."

"Sorry, Mom."

"Well, that's me," said her mother. "I'm a little worried about what to wear to this very posh affair."

"It's casual. It's just a house. Don't worry about it."

"When you're me, there's always something to worry about. Everything goes wrong for me, and you know it."

She had something else to say, and it was harder. Maybe later. Maybe her mother would scream. She noticed the squirrel staring at her, gripping the bars of the trap.

—*Go on, you can do it.*

She took a deep breath.

"Mom?"

"Yes?"

—*Get it over with, now's the time.*

"I'm driving back—from Paso Robles. I had to take a little trip to bring Rudgear some supplies."

"Oh, damn that man! That's the last thing you need."

"No big deal. Anyway—" She hesitated, but the squirrel stared at her with utmost trust, waiting patiently for her to do the right thing. "Well, time has gone by, and I was thinking it would make sense to have Rudgear come to the wedding."

She could swear it, the squirrel beamed and fluffed out all around.

And she could hear her mother's nostrils flaring, her breath rifling the hairs often found therein.

"I suppose that's reasonable," said her mother, at last.

"You think so?" Veblen said, passing a truck full of spinach.

"It's reasonable if you want me to be—miserable."

The squirrel stood by.

"Mom." She took a deep breath, bolstered by the sturdy presence of the squirrel. "He's not a brute anymore. He is a shell of a person you can take pity on, okay?"

"Everybody gets old, even serial murderers. Does that mean we should take pity on them?"

Her mother would say anything to win an argument.

"Frankly, I resent the fact you have anything to do with him. Why did you find it necessary?"

"Because they needed a next-of-kin person to have power of attorney, and they got in touch with me. It's okay, really."

"How is it okay?"

"I don't mind, it doesn't bother me."

"So you're stuck taking care of a man who never cared for you one iota?"

Why did her mother always have to tell her that her other relatives didn't care about her? She'd often told Veblen her grandmother didn't love her because she didn't love Melanie, her own daughter, and if she couldn't love her own child she couldn't love anybody. And that her grandfather Woodrow only liked her because she was a young woman and wasn't fat and ugly. "Mom, if you were in my position, you'd do the same thing, wouldn't you?"

Her mother let out a strangled sigh, bordering on a groan.

"All right. So, do you think he's wonderful, and that I kept you from having a loving relationship with your father?"

"Don't twist things."

"Is he still in that home for the mentally ill?"

"That's where he is," said Veblen, her hands rigid on the wheel.

"I see," said her mother. "I told you all along. At least I can have that satisfaction."

"Yes, at least."

"I knew he was mentally ill after one week with him."

"How?"

Her mother sighed again. "We were on our honeymoon and Rudgear thought a man at a table in the restaurant was staring at him, and he got up in the middle of dinner and left."

"He still thinks people are staring at him."

"Then he wouldn't speak to me for the rest of the night or the next day. He turned into an icicle. It was terrible."

"Yeah, it must have been," said Veblen, recalling one of her adult encounters with her father.

It was a visit not long after she moved into the cottage on Tasso Street, when she was still fixing it up. And only the second time she'd seen him as an adult. He came dressed in a jacket and tie and took her to lunch at an upscale restaurant on University Avenue, acting almost like it was a date, and brought her a gift that day, an appliance purporting to save a VCR from overuse. (She still had one.) In other words, when a video ended, you were supposed to haul out this electric piece of junk and plug it in and rewind your video in it. To make it all the more horrible, Rudgear had purchased an accessory for the gadget, a red-striped vinyl cover.

"Gee," Veblen had said, "thanks." Why not have a separate refrigerator that precools your food to save the real refrigerator? Or an electric box that gets your food hot before you waste the oven? Or sheets to put over the main sheets, or towels to wrap around the main towels, what the heck. How about getting another one of these rewinders to save *this* rewinder? Commerce was based on so many miserable, hoodwinking ideas that the device depressed her, but she tried to hide what she felt.

As Rudgear knelt to plug in the unwanted rewinder, he had to fiddle with the VCR and DVD cords, which had been shoved behind the small crate on which Veblen's TV was balanced. She noticed he was sweating and told him not to worry, that she'd get one of those power strips and plug it in later.

"I can't do this," Rudgear said suddenly. He stood and brushed himself off, his face pallid and damp. "How can you live like this?"

"Like what?"

"Like—some kind of drug addict! I gotta go. I gotta go!"

He moved for the door, struggling with the handle, so agitated he could barely turn the knob. She placed a gentle hand on his back and told him not to worry, she was still fixing it up, that it was going to be nice, that he should sit down and have some coffee with her. But he grabbed the doorknob with both hands, ripping it open, kicking wide the screen door, tripping down the steps. He bolted for his car, threw himself in with a slam. She pelted the window with her palms.

"Dad!" she'd cried. "Stop!"

His body arched as he jammed his hands into his pockets.

"Please don't go!" she begged.

He pulled things up from his pockets, loose change, Life Savers, receipts, finally producing the keys, which fell to the floor of the car. He hit his head on the steering wheel as he leaned forward to fish for them.

"Please, Dad!"

Why was he leaving?

Why was she calling him *Dad*?

He really did go. He drove away from the daughter he was trying to mend with. She had a long cry on the front steps until she felt drained and empty.

Now her mother said, "I don't want you to find out Paul is mentally ill after a week," diversifying her gripes.

"No, that wouldn't be fun."

"Is there any chance of waiting a little longer?"

"I don't know. We'll see." She pressed on the gas, wanting to get home.

"Why? Is something wrong?"

"Nothing. I'm tired. I might know Paul better than you knew Rudge," Veblen added, keeping her eyes fixed on the road.

"Yes. That's because I love you and I've put my life into raising you, and therefore you are not finding it necessary to run into a man's arms like I did. I hope."

She had her own wounds, hadn't she? She had her own reasons to run, wouldn't you say? But none could compare to her mother's. "Fair enough."

"I'm an utter failure, except for raising a beautiful daughter. That's my one accomplishment in life."

"You're a great artist, Mom, and you had a good career for a while."

"Please don't patronize me. I know of what I speak."

"Okay."

Silence again.

"Veblen, you may not know it now, but marriage affects everything that happens to you. Your mate becomes the mirror in which you see yourself. If he doesn't see you as a beautiful pearl, you'll wither. Does he see you as a beautiful pearl?"

"Maybe I'm not a beautiful pearl."

"You are! Don't ever say that to me!"

"Okay, I'm a beautiful pearl."

"He is not vindictive and insane?" asked her mother.

"I thought we were talking about Rudgear," said Veblen, lowering her window a little to revive.

Her mother took a deep breath. "All right, then. So all I need to do is accept the fact that on the otherwise happiest day of my life, I have to see Rudgear Amundsen-Hovda and behave as if it's just another day in the park. The man who emotionally battered me, and contributed nothing to your upbringing except for heartbreak and suffering. Yes. Let's do it!"

"You knew he was shell-shocked in Vietnam when you married him."

"I was too attracted to him to think clearly."

"So you admit he's had a hard life."

"So have I. My mother bloodied my nose every day of my youth."

Veblen cleared her throat. "I know your life was horrible. Your father was always away and your mother was a sociopath and nobody knew it. It was a childhood unbearable by all standards, even compared to fly-covered, starving children in Africa."

"Are you ridiculing me?"

"No, I really mean it. To be isolated with a madwoman all your childhood must have been—hideous. Suffocating. Awful."

"Must have been?" cried Melanie.

"Was! *Was!*"

"All right, then," said her mother. "Have Rudgear come for your reasons."

"Thanks, Mom."

"And who will give you away? I suppose you've asked Rudgear?"

"No," said Veblen, "no, I was planning to ask someone else."

"Oh. Linus?"

She hadn't planned to mention this yet, but a rush of feeling for Paul, whom she missed now, and for her mother, propelled her onward, come what may.

"No, you."

Her mother screeched, "Me? Why *me*?"

"Because—you're the one."

"Sweetie," Melanie stammered. "That's very unorthodox."

"So what? Come on, you know we have a matriarchy going on here. Remember when we read Bachofen together?" Bachofen wrote *Mother Right*, which attempted to demonstrate that motherhood was at the center of all religions and societies and behavior from the beginning of human history.

"I get very nervous in front of people," said her mother.

"But you could do it, couldn't you?"

Her mother's voice fell to a whisper. "I am fat and ugly."

"Mom, I want you next to me. You're the one who's always been there for me, and I love you."

"Oh, dear. I'm sorry I'm such a wreck."

She was watching the traffic ahead of her. "We'll both be wrecks together," said Veblen, with small tears in her eyes.

"My pride . . . I can barely move . . . I'm as wide as a barn . . . I'll fall over right in front of everybody. I won't be able to let go of you."

Veblen said, "Practice, Mom. You can do it."

"I feel very stressed now."

"I'd better go," Veblen said. "We'll talk more later."

"I love you, sweetie."

"I love you too."

Veblen's determination with her mother usually paid off in cases where Veblen was proving her love. In cases where Veblen tried to create distance, she'd been much less able.

"She'll have a great time and later she'll know it was right," said Veblen to the squirrel. "She'll be thrilled that I wanted her so badly. She'll complain but she'll do it."

She looked at the squirrel, who, despite his misgivings about the wedding, knew a righteous act when he saw it.

Oh, to be out on the open road. Oh, to tell her what one squirrel's life added up to!

He might choose the final fight with his wife, atop the old oak in Wobb, from which she cursed his name and pushed him off the weak end of the branch. And all the vitriol thereafter, when she tried to ruin his career. But that was ugly stuff, and deep down he bore a loyalty to the woman he couldn't forsake, no matter what she did.

He could describe his picaresque education and his work, or his special studies on numerous topics including the ethnopoetics of—her. Might seem a bit like cozying up. Best not.

He could talk about each and every one of his children, for they sparkled in his crown like jewels.

Abigu, Ataturk, Nan-bon, and Cleede were his first. Abigu and Cleede, artists now. Ataturk had a temper but with the proper nuts under control. Cleede was a wonderful mother with many children of her own. And then Devonian, Dwormuth, Dragwood, and Eleide—would she really want to know?

Devonian was a master carpenter. Married, nice family. Dwormuth was an intellectual, working on a dream book. Dragwood had a daughter with knee troubles and spent much time at her side.

Egon, Wauna, Dinse, and Dwee came during a cold winter that nearly killed them. Dinse was at loose ends, and Dwee was a firefighter. Wauna sorted acorns at a plant, but was a supervisor. Egon made carpets and had a beautiful wife and was a wonderful dad.

Sato, Finkie, and Forbush came next. Finkie and Forbush lived in an imaginary world of their own, and stood apart from the rest. Sato was married to a horrible man. Gaffy, Gozo, Gander, and Gree were still learning. Rather childish but affectionate. Gaffy had some singing talent. Hattie, Horti, Heino, and Ife were politically active, and Heino was interested in philosophy. Itti-ko, Ivory, Ion, Jellyboy, Jips, and Ringie sprang from an unusually large litter. They were all small and delicate, but they'd turned into very interesting squirrels. Ivory and Jellyboy had an aptitude for speech. Calarak, Tanga, and Quipper were prone to outbursts and tears, and had very tight muscles. He loved them, of course. Zeonides, Latereen, Driver, still youths. Wollister, Viluk, Razzztak-hive, Vlee, Chupperwhupper, and Lou were single births, and perhaps that's why they were extra clingy.

Though they tried to gather for big mash-up suppers on Sunday afternoons, it wasn't always easy. Every family had its burdens. Sato lived with a sadistic blue jay, and Calarak danced at a strip-tease. That had been a tough one.

"But you love your family, what can you do," said Veblen out loud, clearly understanding everything.

And that pleased him, she could see.

MEANWHILE, THE DAY was coming to an end, and the sun had gone down behind the coastal mountains. Traffic wore its lights. Field workers were piling into open trucks that hauled their Porta Potties behind them.

Squirrels were thinking about the night ahead, and how to avoid owls.

One squirrel was inside a car, returning to Tall Tree, California.

She knew where to take him. Before turning onto Tasso Street, she parked alongside the creek bed, and toted the cage out in the dark. Down the bank she skied on dry leaves, and beside the rivu-let nestled the cage on the ground. It had been a long day.

"I'm so sorry to drag you all that way in such ignominious fashion. But here you are. And don't forget where I live! Come by again sometime. If necessary, we'll do this all over again!"

Paul could say what he wanted. This squirrel had no intention of burning down the house.

A breeze unsettled the trees, and a nightingale laughed. Crunching and gnawing could be heard in nearby shrubs. The night animals were out and about. The smell of rotting leaves drifted up from beneath her shoes, and she brushed a papery moth from her cheek. A rhyme formed in her head:

The Flying squirrel flies, and the Irksome squirrel irks.
The Spinning squirrel spins and the Smirking squirrel smirks.
The Crapulous craps and the Lurking lurks;
But when the Talking squirrel talks, none but a Listening
   Human works.

Veblen gasped. "A listening human, eh? A rare variation on the Q chromosome? About .0000000000000001 of the population, you say?"

She attempted to picture all those zeros in her head, recognizing this was about one in eight billion.

"That's the whole population of the world! Of people, of course. Are you saying I might be the only person, on earth, who listens?"

If that wasn't a nod, she hardly knew what was.

"Well."

She made no move to go; she felt like sleeping on the bank.

"Here we are, then."

The squirrel was quiet in the cage. She marveled that he wasn't rattling about in a petulant frenzy.

"We hit it off, didn't we?"

And she opened the trap door.

The squirrel appeared in the moonlight, standing before her. A beetle was crawling across her hand before she thought about time again. And the squirrel ran down to the ribbon of flowing water, and drank. She saw it scooping water into its hands, washing its face, squeezing water from its tail. It was a beautiful night, all silver on the branches and leaves of the tall trees around her, and the ground glimmering as well. "I think a person ought to go sit outside every night of their life. How can it be good for us to miss this? We stay all closed up in our houses with lightbulbs. This is so beautiful!" she said to herself. She dug her hands into the mulch around her, and kept watch on the squirrel, who continued to cool himself in the creek, flicking his tail like a magnificent plume. "Yet you wish to sleep in the attic," she teased the squirrel. "When you could be out here under the beautiful moon." She thought of hawks and owls then, coming down with their hungry talons, and said, "It's nice to sleep where owls and hawks aren't flying past, though. That's the truth." For hours you could not trust the world to take care of you, when you closed your eyes. Every creature knew it.

She saw two small figures coming down to the creek, soon nose to nose with her squirrel, three tails now twitching together, some quiet conversation between them. He had friends, family here. She had done the right thing!

"Good night," she called.

. . .

—D*AD, YOU ALL RIGHT? Did they cut open your brain and put electrodes on it and fill your skull with dyes?*
    —*Not this time. I was simply on a road trip with a friend.*

SHE WENT HOME and started to sing. *"I've just seen a face . . . / He's just the squill for me . . . / lalalalalala."* And laughed at herself. It was madness born of a surplus of feeling, that's all. As a girl, visiting a farm on a school trip, Veblen fed hardened corncobs to a crowd of gnashing hogs, and felt the terror of the tug of their mouths. She saw a calf being born, watched it licked by its mother into standing, and heard the busy cluck of chickens extruding their eggs. She survived a goose peck to the leg and combed the glorious mane of a mare. Indeed, the day seemed to portend a future so full of riches, on the school bus coming back she found herself bawling her eyes out. "I like that farm *so much*," she said, surprising her teacher, who only wanted to comfort her for something simple, like an earache, or a scraped knee.

17

OFFENSE IS MANDATORY

The clock said 1:30 A.M., and light streamed in from the hall. All at once Veblen realized Paul was there, kneeling over her, rolling her in bed like a log.

"Who did you go with!" he gasped, pungent with grape tannins. "Who were you with!"

"Paul?"

"Why didn't you call when you got home?"

"Stop it, I'm awake."

She sat up and rubbed her eyes and ran her hands through her hair, pushing it out of her face. Sipped water from the glass by the bed.

"I called you a bunch," she said. "You never answered."

His voice sank with him to the floor, as if he were going down with a heavy weight around his neck. "You're my best friend, Veb, my moral compass."

"I'm not that great."

"I love you, and everything about you, and if I can make you happy, I'll be the happiest person in the world."

"What's wrong?" She'd never seen him like this.

He rubbed his face roughly. Dried leaves drifted from the tangled mane of his hair, as if he'd been hiding in a tree. Brown redwood needles were sticking into the back of his shirt. There was a small gash over his left eye. "You were talking to someone—about our wedding," he said thickly. "You—" He could barely bring out the words. "Fuck! How could this happen! You told him—you said he was *handsome*."

"*When?*"

"Last night when I called you!"

It took her a few moments to place it, and placing it caused her to turn pink. "Oh! Paul, no. It's not what you think at all." She climbed out of bed and put her hands on his shoulders. "You mean, I answered, but didn't talk to you? You heard me talking?"

"How can you laugh?"

"I wasn't talking to a person. It was the squirrel."

Paul looked up, wrinkling his nose like a snout. "Please. God."

"No, it's true."

"Stop it."

"The one we caught in the trap, Paul. I took it along to let it go."

He drew back resentfully, and began to hack.

"*Handsome?*"

"He is."

He looked savage. "That's sick!"

"It's no big deal, I was amusing myself."

"In a motel with a squirrel?"

She told him about trying to find the right place to release the squirrel, finally bringing him back here instead. He thought her daft and desperate, it was clear. And there was much mortification in being caught unawares. Yet so much better than being caught with another man.

"Laugh, Paul, laugh."

"I'm trying." He looked rumpled and slack, an old coat on a hook. "Imagine it from my side. I really thought—you were talking to some guy in a motel. I thought it all last night. All today."

"Paul." Offense was mandatory. "Why didn't you call me back?"

"I mean, you asked if he was *married,* what's that supposed to mean?"

Veblen said, "Well, he's not. He's divorced."

She rose, put on her robe, passed the place where Thorstein Veblen was supposed to be to absorb his empathy. His own relationships had brimmed with difficulty and misunderstanding. Where had he gone? She found him wedged behind the bookcase, the glass cracked over his face. "Oh, no! How did this happen?"

"So you prefer animals to human beings!" Paul called out.

"Maybe some," she said sadly, laying the portrait down.

"Then talk to squirrels all you want, if that's your thing. Become the next Beatrix Potter."

"I don't actually want to be the next Beatrix Potter." (She had read the artist's biography and found the woman a bit too repressed to be her hero.)

"Talk to the little fucker all you want, see if I care. Maybe I'll find some cute little gopher wench to spend time with."

"You do that!"

"So where's the other man now?" he asked, clearly bluffing about gopher wenches.

"I told you, I let him go, somewhere he'd be happy."

"He's out of our lives?"

"Does he have to be?"

She warmed milk in a heavy pan, spooned in cocoa, poured it into her favorite blue mugs, trying to remember what else he might have overheard.

"Here," she offered.

"I've suffered a trauma," Paul said, slumped at the table.

"I'm sorry, Paul."

He raised his head slightly.

"Veb, I went out of my mind while you were gone. I went on a bender."

"Sorry."

"I'm recalibrating," he said, gasping. "You were hanging out with a squirrel. Great."

"That's right."

Paul made a sound like a growl. "Can I say something, without you taking it the wrong way?"

"I guess."

"Is it possible you're a little stressed out?" One of his legs began to bob with nervous spasticity.

Was she? She counted on herself to withstand everything. And yet, who said she had to? What would happen if she broke down now and then? And why had she just spent a whole day and night feeling utterly carefree, and now here was Paul, hassling her?

"I felt fine until you got here."

"Maybe there's something you want to tell me," Paul said impatiently.

"Like?"

"Like about *mood-enhancing medications?*"

"Well." This was a surprising change in tack. "Okay, what about it?"

"I don't care, but why didn't you tell me? Don't you trust me?"

"What, have you been going through my stuff?"

"Of course not," Paul said. "I saw you take some once, but I didn't say anything."

She looked around, wondering what else he'd seen. "Did you come over and punch Thorstein Veblen?"

Paul squinted at her. "Are you insane?"

She hated that he said that, hated it.

"You're supposed to be happy right now, that I wasn't talking to a guy in a motel. Not interrogating me or implying I'm insane."

"I'm happy," Paul said sullenly.

"Really happy, maybe ecstatic, like jumping up and down." His whole bearing looked distorted, as if he'd spent the day folded up in a box.

He drank the rest of the cocoa, setting the empty mug on the table with a clap. "There's something else," he said.

And that was when he told her about DeviceCON, and about the premature release of his device, and the unorthodox use of the Animal Rule.

"Oh, Paul!" Veblen said. "Oh, I'm sorry, that's horrible."

"I know it's horrible. Would you stop shrieking?"

"I'm not shrieking!" she shrieked. "Maybe you should call *60 Minutes!*"

"What are you . . . Stab Cloris in the back after everything she's done for me? Don't you understand how hard I've worked for this?"

"So you're just going to go along with it?" How he felt about this was everything—it was dire.

"Why do you make everything so black-and-white?"

"You know, Cloris might be nice to you, but you know what she's like? I'm just going to say it. She's like an ichneumon fly. Thorstein Veblen said captains of industry are like ichneumon flies. They jump on fuzzy, friendly caterpillars and lay eggs in them, and then the eggs hatch and the larvae eat the caterpillars from the inside out."

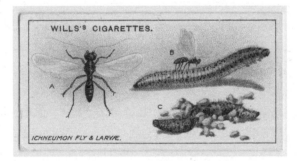

ICHNEUMON FLY.

"I'm really glad I'm getting to see this side of you," Paul said.

"Well, I hope you've been able to see the ruthless side of Cloris Hutmacher."

"Oh, so ruthless she's letting us have our wedding at her house, that's really ruthless!"

"Who needs her big fat stupid house?" Veblen yelled.

"Oh, really? You have someplace better?"

"Anywhere would be better!"

Paul shook his head. "You are so *limited*. I had no idea."

"Limited," Veblen said, fighting back tears. "Well, if I'm so limited, then what are you doing here?" In a gesture her mother had spent years training her to make, she said, "Leave, then! Don't be here with the limited person. Go!"

For a moment it looked like he might say something. But he didn't. He turned the knob and went out into the night.

SHE RAN OUTSIDE, saw his car turn the corner at the creek.

End the attachment.

"No!"

She heard it in the trees. *End the attachment.*

She stood still as the moon poured silver over the rooftops, and had the sensation of tasting air. The air was supposed to matter. There was so much you could gorge on in a nanosecond.

She feared him, she feared everyone, she feared herself the most.

"I can't get married," she said out loud. The world accommodated her voice. "What was I thinking?"

18

THE CURS

The bed of a tortured soul is always in shambles by morning. Blankets thrown to the floor, sheets twisted like ropes. Paul's phone buzzed, waking him from a painful dream about returning to high school to graduate and being given a plastic garbage bag to wear as his gown. His eyes had crusted over, and his pillow was drenched with drool.

"Yeah?" he managed, unhinging his jaw.

"Paul? It's Susan Hinks."

Paul sat up in his bedroom in Mountain View, disoriented, rubbing his eyes with his fists. He'd spent very little time at his own place in the past few months; it was as if his life before Veblen filled him with shame, as if in those days he'd been a clown with a naked backside, having darts thrown at his ass cheeks by laughing chimps and frat boys.

Now he remembered. He'd called Hinks late last night, said to call him back, no matter what time. So he jumped up to get his blood pumping and asked what she knew about the release of his device.

Nothing. But she'd received a message from senior management at Hutmacher yesterday afternoon announcing some kind of adjustment in the trial. She was to take today off until she received further instructions. That's all she knew.

"Susan, you've coordinated other trials. Has this ever happened before?"

"They're all different, Dr. Vreeland."

"But is it—have we done everything—right?"

"I hope so! I really have tried to do a good job."

"It's okay, Susan. You did a great job. I wasn't saying—"

"Just last week I sent the binders to everybody on the IRB, and over to Hutmacher, and I checked all the permissions and release forms for the human study a few days ago, and all our supplies are stocked and I returned the cadavers and we just had a pizza party with the families of the volunteers, and—"

He reassured her further, told her he'd go to the VA right away and find out what was going on.

He got up, made some coffee, took eight hundred milligrams of Advil, ran his hands through his hair, started the shower, opened his mouth, lost his balance, fell against the cold tiles. He remembered how the manager proudly referred to them as "honed Italian marble" when he showed Paul the apartment, along with the other architectural details meant to appeal to what Veblen had told him Thorstein Veblen called the *emulation instincts* of the striving classes, such as heated towel racks, clubby brass plumbing fixtures, a Jacuzzi bath, and a cedar sauna. How many nights had he spent alone here with frozen pizza and a remote control? Nights trying to make plans with scattershot calls. Weekends so vast they felt like a graveyard of bones.

Yes, he was in hate with the world that morning, livid with loneliness. He'd written Veblen a ten-page letter during the night, full of remorse and regret and declarations of his love. But the gremlin of anger made him tear it up and grind it in the disposal in his sink, because he had no idea what he was dealing with. Was their current state of alienation an ethical dispute, or was the ethical dispute a front for some deeper problem she had with him, some ultimate horror she'd experienced during his family's visit, some glimpse she'd had of him when he'd least expected it, which revealed him to be a loser and a fraud?

Cheater! Cheater! Cheater!

But he wasn't. Cloris was trying to make him cheat, but he would not!

Maybe a hired sniper would fell him before the day was through. Or maybe some Hutmacher henchman would drive him off the road so it looked like an accident. They'd think of something. *They had their ways.*

Then he was shredding El Camino, wishing he could vaporize everything in his path. He honked at a wobbly cyclist, feeling great stress, which was manifesting in a body rash, itching, and the sensation that saliva was oozing between his lower teeth, necessitating the jutting of his lower jaw like a catch tray.

He'd heard it said that every man needed a friend he could turn to if he had a body to dispose of, and for Paul, Hans was the one who'd be there with the bag.

Hans knew the real him, verruca vulgari and all. In high school, after Millie was sent away, he and Hans formed a gluey allegiance; Paul realized that Hans's penchant for self-inflation rose from his neglect by a world-class set of jerks, his parents, and decided he was worth knowing. Hans was the only person alive who'd ever sided with him about his brother, Justin, without an ounce of guilt. He had a supersized capacity for hatred, as elastic as a colon, as vaulted as a cathedral, as open as a prairie sky, and so was therefore able to hate Justin with an amplitude even greater than Paul's, spending many hours coming up with twisted accidents that could befall him, making Paul laugh to the point of pain.

It was Hans he called when he first found Millie on the fledgling Internet, back in 1999. In those days, he used a primitive search engine called Alta Vista, and results were spotty. (She'd evidently married a veterinary student and by now they had three children and took up space in Portland.)

No, there was only one person he could call at a time like this, and Hans picked up on the second ring.

"Hey," Paul said heavily.

"Hey, what's happening?"

"I need to talk."

And Paul launched in. Everything, Cloris, the trial, his fight with Veblen.

"Oh, man," said Hans. "Nip this in the bud or she'll have you by the balls the rest of your life."

"But her reaction was sincere, and she's right."

"Sincere is the worst. Sincere is how they get your balls. I'd say, 'Babe, don't go all pro forma on me, this isn't about right and wrong, it's about *us* against *them*.' And remind her there's no true purity in the world."

A small detail had been worming its way through his mind since that evening he'd spent with Cloris Hutmacher, something he'd been unwilling, until now, to unsheathe. He said to Hans, "Question. If you were with a woman, and you're making out, you're already in her bedroom, and suddenly she tells you she has athlete's foot and thinks about it while she's having sex, what would that communicate to you?"

Hans snorted. "I'd wonder what else she had growing, and where. Who we talking about?"

"Someone before Veblen."

"Let it go," said Hans. "When you strike out with a woman, don't they always look better in hindsight?"

"I guess what I'm saying is, there's no way she was into me if she'd say something like that."

"Why torture yourself. It's old news."

But it was hard to let it go—his professional standing seemed to be forming a warm puddle around his feet.

"It's like the way people go to the bathroom in front of their pets," Paul concluded, bitterly.

"You've lost me, dude."

"Like they're not on the same level of consciousness."

"But sometimes you can't help it. They follow you everywhere."

"It's like taking a dump in front of your dog."

"Let it go, man."

"And I was the dog."

"Don't look back!"

"Fuck." Paul swallowed. He noticed a nick on the new dashboard and a field of greasy crumbs around the parking brake, indicating that everything in radius of him would end up ruined unless he did something to change.

All at once, despite his nausea and headache, he felt plentiful with purpose.

"Hans, I'm going to have to file a whistle-blower suit against Hutmacher Pharmaceuticals."

Hans groaned. "Why rock the boat? Uma's already telling people Cloris is one of her clients. Try a little diplomacy, turn it around!"

"It's too late for that. I want you to make sure Veblen is taken care of if anything happens to me," Paul continued, feeling courageous for the first time in his life.

"You're scaring me, brah! Cool off before you do anything, I'm serious."

"I have to move fast. I just wanted you to know."

"I've always got your back, you know that."

"Thanks, man."

THE BOAT he would rock was no skiff, it was a vessel the size of the world. It was a craft loaded with everything Veblen admired the other Veblen for drumming about, captained by extravagant greed and filled with plundered treasure. A heavy, foundering ship, gorged to the gills.

Crossing the grass at the VA, he crunched acorn husks beneath his shoes, and ducked as a jay dipped aggressively close to his head, and watched a squirrel run up an oak with less hatred for the little mammal, with eyes and ears and lungs and appetite not so different from his own. He had regularly purchased lab animals for his work, ordering from troubling laboratory lists such as this:

Lactating Female—$25.00
Pregnant—$20.00
Newborn <6 days—$6.95
Exbreeder—$15.00

without giving it a second thought.

When the squirrel reached the crook of a low branch, it turned and flicked its tail with the sass of the metronome perched on his old piano, and Paul lurched with recognition. The full tail, the white crests around the eyes, the brindled paws—could it be the squirrel from Tasso Street? The squirrel was flicking its tail at him, chortling.

Chuukksklsllslslslls!

"What do you want from me?"

Chuuuckklsldlkls!

"Is it you?"

Chkkkkkkkkkkkkkkkkcrekkkkkkkkkkkk! the squirrel clucked.

The creature seemed to be trying to tell him something, and he gave it one last regard.

"What? Spit it out. Stop beating around the bush!"

As he walked closer to the hospital he noticed a cluster of cars arriving and parking near the back exit, the double doors wide open for discharges. With a quick sweep he spotted a multiple amputee from his trial, bundled in street clothes, being loaded into a van fitted for wheelchairs. In the back of a station wagon, he saw another of his volunteers being fastened in by his wife.

Paul ran straight up to the ward.

Bruce, the male nurse, was in conversation with a woman who had gathered her father's clothes and toiletries. An orderly pushed the man in his wheelchair into the elevator.

"What's going on?"

Bruce shrugged. "Beats me. The party's over."

Paul sprinted down the corridor to his office—the desk, credenza, and swiveling leather chair had been removed. His computer was gone too. His files, his records—all gone. His model schooner lay on the floor in the corner with a snapped mast, and his picture of Veblen sat beside it.

He called Cloris, left an insinuating message. It was time to bring the whistle to his lips.

With his phone he started to compose. He pulled up the addresses of Grandy Moy; Louise Gladtrip; Stan Silverbutton; Vance Odenkirk; Willard Liu; Horton DeWitt; Reginald Kornfink; Alfred Pesthorn; Cordelia Fleiss; John Williams, MD; Lt. Col. Wade Dent; Brig. Gen. Nancy Bottomly; Col. Bradley Richter; and Cloris Hutmacher. He included everyone on the Institutional Review Board in Washington; several top officials at the FDA; and Susan Hinks, clinical coordinator. Then he opened a new screen and got the address for the editors of the *New York Times* and the tip line at *60 Minutes* and added them as well.

To All Concerned:

I'm writing about the Pneumatic Turbo Skull Punch, US Patent #8,999,863, currently being manufactured by Hutmacher Pharmaceutical Corporation, based in Wilmington, Delaware. I

am the patent holder of record, and until today was the primary
investigator for a clinical trial being conducted at Greenslopes
Veterans' Hospital in Menlo Park, California. Certain
irregularities in the completion of this trial have necessitated the
writing of this letter . . .

With the sudden violence of a riptide, the text was sucked backward, and no amount of further input could hold it in place. The words were disappearing.

Certain irregularities in the completion . . .

Certain irreg . . .

Cert . . .

Within seconds it was over. The document was blank. The screen made a noise like an old needle scraping across an LP, and shut down.

Paul snorted with a unique blend of terror and ecstasy.

He ran out to the copier in the hall and removed a piece of paper from the tray. Then he began to write the letter by hand. Simple and direct, details to come. He wrote fast but signed at the bottom slowly and carefully, so that his name was clear for all to see.

Then he made twenty-five copies, leaving one in the copier for insurance.

Spyware, huh? He anticipated his father's told-you-so's and Veblen's told-you-so's, and yet to have told-you-so's to fall back on could be looked at as the support he'd need going forward, a way to reunite with Veblen, unless it backfired because she didn't like to share grievances. To turn to the light and do the right thing, that's what mattered now. He was going rogue!

Out of the building, across the grounds. The squirrel resumed its chatter as he neared the oak, and he hesitated, arrested by its insistency. He almost spoke to it. He almost said, "You *were* trying to tell me something." His mouth was dry and his eyebrows were burning, and the squirrel screeched and snapped its tail. He began to run.

He came to Building 301, found the door propped open. Had they started on this too?

The staging ground for the Confined Urban Rescue Simulator took up more than half the interior of Building 301. The lights were on in the elevated control booth and, jumping the newly fashioned plywood steps, Paul threw open the door and discovered a chubby boy in a striped sweater lording over the controls. It was Cloris's son, Morris. A scrawny but prosperous-looking guy in an upmarket hoodie sat in a chair beside him.

"Well," Paul said, rolling the stack of letters into a tube.

"Hey, Dr. Vreeland, I'm Robbie Frazier. Too bad we never got the chance to use this honey. Thought Morris could have some fun with it before we break camp."

"Morris is not the first person I imagined using this."

"This is so awesome!" yelled Morris.

Below them, visible through the Plexiglas, lay an eerie scene: a few shadowy two-story buildings with shuttered windows, parked cars and trash cans crowded in a narrow alley between them. It was currently nighttime in the Confined Urban Rescue Simulator, and through a speaker the sound effects of a violent siege could be heard. Inside the control room, a black, yard-long panel deployed all the effects of a battlefield. The CURS was soundproofed from the rest of the warehouse and visible only through the heavy Plexiglas where Paul now stood.

"Is Cloris Hutmacher here at the VA?" Paul said loudly.

Robbie shook his head. "Can't tell you the lady's whereabouts. We've got today to get this thing broken down, that's all I know."

"Can you stop it, please?"

Red sliding switches, now grubbied by Morris's pudgy little hands, controlled light levels across the CURS. Blue switches produced explosions in a range of decibels and timbres, as well as gunfire from assorted weaponry. There was a black knob for volume control, an orange switch for sirens and helicopter noise, and a whole bank of brown switches for human effects, which Morris demonstrated. Paul shuddered when Morris produced the sound of an American screaming for his life, while another toggle generated aggressive Arabic shouts.

Paul looked through the glass at the urban landscape, now exploding and smoking, obviously fake yet primally terrifying anyway. Despite his parents' intense antiwar agenda, or probably because of it, Paul had always admired the pageantry of the great battles of the ages. When they'd read Shakespeare's histories in high school, he'd been completely swept up in Hal's personal test at the Battle of Agincourt. Until then, the young prince had been considered a major fuck-up. At Agincourt he had his chance at majesty, and earned it. *"Once more unto the breach, dear friends, once more."*

"It's even better than CoD!" Morris yelled. "Want to try it?"

A figure seemed to dart through the strobes.

"Is somebody in the simulator?" Paul asked.

"It's closed," Robbie Frazier said. "That's why those lights are so disorienting. You just *think* someone's there."

Paul ran down the steps and let himself inside.

The door disappeared in the shadows, and all around him were whispers and approaching footsteps, scuffling, shouts, and then the sudden reports of machine guns. An Apache helicopter tattered the air with such force he clapped his hands to his ears. A grenade exploded to his left and set his teeth humming. A barrage of gunfire rained across the sky and he leaped between a parked SUV and the building, dazed after ten seconds of exposure.

How the hell could you do a procedure in a shit storm like this? The phony wind screamed and drove grit into his skin. He quickened like an animal, hackles rising. The wind filled his cheeks like balloons. Grains of sand pitted his eyes and he blinked and spat. He shook at the sounds of bombs and helicopters, overwhelmed by the smells of phosphorus, sulfur, and potassium chlorate drifting past in explosive puffs.

The waste of this was insanity. Fuck Jonathan Finger! Fuck Cloris! He would have gone straight to the DA's office to spill everything, but at that moment he felt a pair of hands go around his neck. He arched his back and caught a glimpse of Sergeant Major Warren Smith falling on him, his arms like giant prongs, eyes fried with accusation, the crater on his nose turning white.

DURING THE sixty-nine seconds he was struggling for his life in the CURS, Paul managed to survey an array of his personal failings.

It was clear, as his carotid arteries were compressed with great force and he dropped the pile of his game-changing letters in order to fight back (and as the copies scattered and were sent aloft in the wind, funneled upward in the direction of a fan that sucked them into a vent), that something had gone very wrong in his life.

During the moments Paul was being garroted by Warren Smith, he saw the chain of events that linked this brutal moment to all the follies of history. Smith didn't want to go back into the war machine, and who could blame him? He thought with ardent tenderness of Veblen and the hurt he'd caused her, and then of his mother paying a morning visit to a recently defunded geriatric facility in Humboldt County, sitting on a worn canvas chair listening to an old man talk about his dry, itching skin for which no cream gave relief. He thought of his father out in his forge, waiting for the fire to get hot enough to bend some iron, anesthetizing himself for some past hurt with a moist bowl of garden-fresh sinsemilla. And he thought of Justin at his day-care facility, wondering if his brother remembered giving Paul a piggyback ride through a field of snow, a long time ago when they were boys, and Paul hugged his neck and promised to make him some Creeple Peeple with his mold, but never did, because he couldn't bear to do anything in the plus column for Justin. Did Justin remember that? During the moments Paul was being strangled, he thought of Cloris Hutmacher spread-eagle on a catamaran in some Caribbean clime, daydreaming about a new tax strategy with the tuneful name of *variable prepaid forward*, which would save her untold millions in the coming years, and would allow her to partake of another fun tax strategy, in which she'd purchase a private gallery, set up a private foundation, and donate her own art to the foundation and gallery, and still control everything.

While Paul was being strangled, he foresaw pallets of Hutmacher products being removed from Boeing C-17 Globemaster IIIs with the aid of Manitex Liftking forklifts at existing U.S. military bases in Afghanistan, Kosovo, Germany, Italy, and Iraq. Not to mention Japan, Okinawa, Kuwait, Macedonia, South Korea, and Australia. As well as Bulgaria, Bahrain, Brazil, Djibouti, Greece, and Guam. And of course Israel, Spain, the United Arab Emirates, Greenland, Oman, Qatar, Saudi Arabia, Kyrgyzstan, and the Netherlands. And furthermore, Portugal, Turkey, and the UK, and how much it all had to do with the ticklish tragus of Bradley Richter from the DOD, no one would ever know.

And his beautiful, adorable, lovable fiancée was figuring out how to break up with him. And squirrels were planning a day to migrate en masse. And a poorly chosen diamond engagement ring lay cold and despised in a drawer.

Paul had never been strangled before, but he knew that if his carotids were pinched much longer, he'd go unconscious, and then if Warren Smith kept at it his brain would die. He did not want his brain to die, despite all his flaws, and he rolled and jerked and did everything he could to stop it. The acorn-sized amygdala in his forebrain was in full panic mode, screaming to his hypothalamus to pump out corticotropin-releasing hormones, which were then triggering his pituitary gland, which was then jetting out a stream of adrenocorticotropic hormones, which were then traveling through his bloodstream to tickle his adrenal glands atop his kidneys, which then spewed cortisol with all their might. The cortisol kick increased his glucose production and therefore the fuel for his brain and his body, so he was able to claw at Smith's face and neck with renewed urgency, while his heart fibrillated wildly, and his breath became shallow and his skin poured sweat, all agents of an autonomic nervous system beyond his control.

And then Warren Smith let him go, just like that. As if he'd measured just how much Paul deserved and this was enough. Paul found himself discarded on the ground in an artificial alley with sniper fire cracking overhead. He'd survived. He breathed deeply.

Eventually he rolled on his side, pushed himself up. He felt dizzy but he managed to stand. He could walk. He moved slowly through the CURS door, pausing unsteadily at the base of the stairs to the control room. Then he took another deep breath and left the building.

Outside he smelled the earth and heard birds singing their songs. He lumbered across the grass and recognized the sound of the squirrel, chippering and signaling, urgent and shrill, over the sound of tires spreading gravel through the parking lot. Squinting in the sunlight, he saw Cloris Hutmacher throwing her Tesla in gear.

The squirrel shrieked and ran zigzag, directly into her path.

As Cloris made her trajectory for the exit, Paul clapped his hands to scare the squirrel from its course.

Squirrels, oddly, have a tendency to weave back and forth in front of cars, then freeze, unable to decide which way to best escape them. They can't be blamed for their failure to adapt to modern technology after forty million years. The zigzag escape works quite well with predators, and is sophisticated in most respects.

But laws of motion, an understanding of trigonometry, and a knack for assuming the worst all told Paul the squirrel would soon be flattened by the car. Which left him no choice but to run forward and throw himself in the way.

No, she wasn't going to stop. She wanted to run him down like an old dog. *"You want a piece of me?"* he barked, ablaze in his head, driven mad by the idiocy of all mankind.

And taking that on, he felt no fear. Only the certainty that he was looking the leviathan square in the eye.

He presented himself, fists up, teeth bared.

Thrrump, bump, thrump, thrump.

19

MAYBE YES, MAYBE NO

Veblen, miserable all night, rose at dawn trying to imagine her life without Paul, while trying to clear her mind of the prejudices that might be clouding what she needed most to see.

She cradled her broken portrait of Mr. Thorstein Veblen. "Why didn't you say something sooner?"

His face looked three-dimensional all of a sudden, as if he were about to erupt with words, and she smelled bacon in his mustache.

In Palo Alto, as all over northern California, there existed a phenomenon in which dried autumn leaves still clung to the trees in spring, even as the meristems began to bud. She could hear the old leaves rustling, being pushed aside.

She was on the brink of something, a break from the harness, with the possibility of new life at the margins.

IN LESS THAN an hour she was at the beach, after taking the narrow road over the mountains where fog huddled at the crest, winding down the other side to Pescadero. It was the same route Thorstein Veblen would take to the coast in his cart, pulled by Beauty. In 1929, his ashes had been scattered at this beach by a group of his closest friends, and for that reason, when she dug her hands into the sand, she was sure that there were still bits of him there, and that she was touching him. She wrote her name in the sand, and watched it erased by an indifferent wind.

The beach was long and sandy, broken up by coves of ancient lime and sandstone, always hollowing. Could the word *erosion* be related to *eros*? Love, doomed to cave in? (Later, when she had a chance to look it up, she found that *erosion* wasn't related to *eros* at all, but to *rodere*—to those who gnaw, to rodents!)

She remembered something Robert Reich once said: "Ordinarily, I'd never recommend you take a book by an economist to the beach. I wouldn't even recommend you take an economist to the beach. The exception is Thorstein Veblen, and his book is *The Theory of the Leisure Class*. Veblen wrote this classic in 1899, near the end of the Gilded Age when robber barons ran wild, but the book is just as fresh and relevant today. . . . We're in America's second Gilded Age. So take Veblen to the beach and learn more about it—but don't expect him to give you much social status: He's in paperback and he's cheap."

Well, she didn't need to take him. He was already here.

Gulls screamed and flew close. In the sand she found a shard of glass.

Was it possible to love the contradictions in somebody? Was it all but impossible to find somebody without them?

Had her mother made of her a ragged-edged shard without a fit?

The ocean was rolling in sheets.

Endlessly remaking the ocean bed. Endlessly full of sand.

She wanted Paul, she loved him. He'd do the right thing, given time to think. She'd overwhelmed him with negativity about Cloris, the way her mother always overwhelmed her with negativity about everything. When overwhelmed with negativity, one had to resist; it was a law of nature.

Something had been hovering in her thoughts, and she called her mother from the small furrow she'd made for herself in the sand.

"No, Linus, I need to speak to her *now*," she said.

Her mother came on the line expecting a crisis. "What is it, Veblen? What's wrong?"

The air was as salty and unfathomable as the sea.

"Why did you name me Veblen?" she asked sternly, without explanation.

"What on earth? My heart is probably going two hundred beats a minute. What is this about?"

"You always told me you put your values and ideals before any man," Veblen said, eyeing the gray horizon. "That there was nothing more important."

"What are you trying to say?" said her mother. "Have you and Paul ended it?"

She gouged the sand with the shard. She wrote *MAYBE YES, MAYBE NO* with it, then obliterated the words. "You made it seem like your values were so important that you named me after Thorstein Veblen," Veblen said, remaining focused.

"Am I under oath here?" said Melanie.

"So tell me now or never," she pressed on, as a long procession of noble pelicans winged past. "Could there have been another reason you named me Veblen?"

At this her mother declined to respond, and the silence was long and maddening.

"Mom?"

"What, Veblen?"

"Didn't you name me Veblen for another reason?" she asked, a little more gently.

"I don't know what you mean," said her mother.

"After you got upset about me taking the typewriter," Veblen said, "I remembered it was your PhD adviser who gave it to you. How often does that happen? I suddenly thought. Then I remembered other stuff, like the time we went to hear that lecture in Berkeley about Veblen's writings on the 'quasi-personal fringe,' which I thought might be a euphemism for pubic hair, by the way, and then you wanted to say something to the professor when the talk was over, but his wife and daughter ran up and all of a sudden we rushed out of there. And in the car you cried."

"How could you possibly remember that?" Melanie said.

Veblen said, "You loved him, right?"

Melanie was quiet again. But finally she said, "I suppose I did."

"Professor George Twaddle?"

"Mmm."

Professor Twaddle. A married man, unavailable, twice Melanie's age. Veblen didn't want to hear the details, except: "Rudgear's still my father, right?"

"Unfortunately, yes."

"You're sure?"

"Of course I'm sure. That's why I worry about your sanity."

"Well, I don't care about that. But I care that you didn't name me after Thorstein Veblen because of Veblen's philosophy. It was because you loved Professor Twaddle."

"It wasn't a good situation," Melanie said.

"No, how could it be?"

"Be glad I didn't name you Twaddle," Melanie said.

"You misled me!"

"Veblen, he and I shared great admiration for Thorstein Veblen. It's what drew us together. Don't act like this is a shocking discovery."

Veblen yelled, "It's like my whole life is built on a smokescreen!"

"Veblen!" cried her mother. "That's ridiculous. It was all tied together, can't you understand that?"

"Why did I believe you?" Veblen cried. "I always believed everything you said, like it was the final word."

"I really don't understand the problem," Melanie said, "and I don't know why you're trying to make me feel guilty. I think I've said enough."

"You'd better not be harboring some feeling that Twaddle would have been better than Linus," said Veblen, viciously. "If you think that, in any part of yourself, then—you're a total fool."

And having said what she had to say, she ended the call.

VEBLEN DROVE BACK over the mountains, aiming straight for the VA. She would surprise Paul at his office. She'd tell him she was emerging from a lifelong delusion about her identity and priorities. She'd tell him she might need some time, it might take awhile to unravel, but she wanted to and that's what mattered.

And when she parked under a splendid old oak with many branches, there came a call from Garberville, but she thought, *Not now.*

Climbing out of the old yellow Volvo, she received another call from Bill and Marion's number. She ignored it still.

She started to run, feeling the warmth of the sun and the rub of the grass under her soles, remembering how running used to make her pretend to be Mighty Mouse, shouting, *"Here I come to save the day!"* and later on, Maria singing, *"The hills are alive . . ."* and then thinking it very strange that she could not run across grass without pretending to be someone other than herself, for even now she found herself in search of something to think when running across grass. But now there was a beehive in her pocket—an unknown number this time, which she decided to intercept.

"Hi, is this Veblen? This is Susan Hinks, I'm Dr. Vreeland's assistant at the VA. I'm so sorry, I have some serious news."

"What?" Veblen said, standing on the grass at the VA, looking around.

"Dr. Vreeland is in the hospital. He was hit by a car."

"What?"

"We don't know all the details yet. He was taken into the VA hospital and now he's been moved to Stanford."

"Is he okay?"

"We'll know more soon. He's breathing."

"Just *breathing*?"

"I've also called his parents," said Susan Hinks. "We're all praying for him."

"Oh," mumbled Veblen. A crow cackled in the oak.

"It's all very confusing. Cloris Hutmacher was driving, you see."

"Driving? The car that hit Paul?" Veblen choked.

"Yes. It's not a happy day for us. She seems to have known about Dr. Vreeland's letter."

"What letter?"

"Well, you see, Dr. Vreeland wrote a letter about some questionable steps Hutmacher may have taken to rush the trial, and then next thing we know she's hitting him with her car, so we're all a little bit in shock."

"Oh my god!"

As she stood there absorbing the news, her mother called.

"Veblen, dear, Paul's parents just called us. Have you talked to them?"

"I know what happened."

"Veblen, he's a strong man and I think he's going to be all right."

"How do you know?" cried Veblen.

"I asked to speak to one of the doctors," said her mother. "Marion Vreeland called me because they couldn't reach you. She was very calm and it was extremely good of her to call and tell me."

"Who cares if she called you?" Veblen cried out. There was a time when abreacting to her mother was out of the question, untenable. The slightest ripple between them terrified her. She was aware that her mother had trained her to turn herself inside out, like a pocket to be inspected for pilfered change.

"Get a hold of yourself! We're coming down right away."

The oak leaves shivered around her.

20

SOMETHING BAD MUST
HAVE HAPPENED

Veblen navigated the ICU, where murmurs from the frail human chain rose softly in every room. Just having to name Paul at the nurses' station flooded her with emotion.

She found him lying thirty degrees semiupright behind a curtain, intubated, breathing on a ventilator. Mounted on the wall above his head was a screen with the running script of his functions. Wires crisscrossed to many parts of Paul. To one side of the bed was an IV stand holding up a dangling bladder of fluid, which drained through a clear tube connected to a starfish of plastic taped to his hand. A small box mounted on another stand directed more wires at Paul's head, half mummified in an inverted funnel of bandages, and an ICP monitor ran to the suboccipital burr hole in his skull. Foam cylinders expanded and contracted slowly around each leg.

She moved closer and peered at his bandaged face. The skin around his eyes was splattered with tiny red marks, as if he'd been attacked by a pin. Dark purple welts rose from under the loose neck of his gown.

She placed her hands on the skin near his elbow, and kissed his head.

His eyelids fluttered, only for a moment, to the sounds of the machines, hiss and beep, beep and pump. For a short while she watched his vital signs on the monitor, but the slightest deviation made her lurch.

She bit into her arm.

A nurse walked by and told her to drink some water. "You get dried out and tired in here," she said. Veblen went and drank from a fountain, but probably not enough. It was too cold.

THE MEDICAL BUSINESS had so many arms. In a daze, she fixated on how many product lines were in her range of vision at any given angle. Pharmaceuticals, latex gloves, sanitizers. Monitors, data retrievers, linens. Mechanized beds. She thought of the multitudes of crafty sales reps coming round and acting fun and sassy just in order to shove all this stuff down the hospital's throat. And yet, so what? What was the point of noticing this? Was a hospital supposed to be thrown together by local artisans and craftsmen? What was there to do?

SHE CALLED ALBERTINE and discovered she was in Atlanta for a conference. They talked but how could she not know her best friend was in Atlanta for a conference? What was wrong with her? Why was she so—limited?

. . .

IN THE LATE AFTERNOON, the Vreelands signaled their arrival from the parking lot. She migrated through the corridors to guide them in.

"Any change?" Bill asked.

"Not yet."

"What the hell happened?" Bill wanted to know.

As they slipped through the hospital, Veblen told them what she'd learned from Susan Hinks and the first responder's report. The last part of the trial had been abruptly called off. Paul had tried to speak to Cloris Hutmacher in the parking lot; somehow she'd hit him with her car, he'd injured his head; surgery had been performed to remove the hematoma and release pressure.

"Holy Jesus," said Bill. "Did I predict this, people? Did I?"

"I don't understand," said Marion. "How on earth?"

"What did I tell him? Did he listen?" Bill cried out, but Veblen stopped him.

"There's something I want you to see." She handed him a copy of Paul's letter, which Susan Hinks had brought her. Copies of the letter had mysteriously come spewing out of a vent in Building 301, raining down on a meeting of the Daffodil Society, which was planting bulbs. The Daffodil Society members had been of mixed minds about what to do with the letters, but had decided by a vote to send them to their intended targets.

Bill read, and began to shake. "That's my boy," he whispered. "Marion!"

As Marion read, Veblen told them that James Shalev had supplied his view of the incident, for he'd arrived at the VA just in time to see Paul waving his arms at a white Tesla in the parking lot. He reckoned Paul was signaling the driver about something. And then—and this is what he was clear on, and would be required to testify about repeatedly—he saw the Tesla *speed up*, throwing Paul into the air.

"Oh my god!" cried Marion.

"Jesus!" Bill cried out savagely. "We're going to ream them good!"

In the elevator an older man in a wheelchair was pushed by a younger man who might have been his son.

"Are you okay?" Justin said to him.

"What's that?"

"Are you okay?" Justin said again.

"He's just fine, thanks," the younger man said as the elevator doors opened, and he pushed the wheelchair out.

"He's not fine," called Justin. "Is Paul fine?"

"We hope so," Veblen said, leading them down the corridor.

"I want to give him a lizard," said Justin.

"We'll get to the bottom of this and then some," said Bill, as they pushed through the curtain.

"Be very careful of those tubes," Marion said. "Justy? Do you see?"

"I see."

"Oh, baby," Marion said, taking account of her unconscious, monitored son. She gently found a way to kiss his head.

Bill grabbed Paul's cannulated hand. "That's my boy. We're going to bring those motherfuckers down!"

Shortly the fuzzy outline of two figures loomed through the curtain:

". . . from the windshield or impact with the ground. The

patient presented with abrasions on the palms, face, knees, elbows, hypoxia, hypotension, and with CT scan a five-centimeter subdural hematoma at the occipital lobe. Incongruously, we're also detecting signs of manual strangulation—petechiae around the eyes, ecchymoses on the neck, scratches here around the chin—it doesn't quite make sense."

"Glasgow rating?" asked a woman.

"Nine. His pupils are reactive. He's received mannitol—"

"And he's on a ventricular catheter?"

Veblen stiffened.

"Yes, his ICP's steady now at fifteen mmHg."

"I assume you're aware that the major morbidity from this type of injury, post-CSF drainage, is from thromboembolism?"

"Yes, he's receiving low-molecular-weight heparin in his drip."

"And have you considered therapeutic hypothermia?"

"Since this may be multitrauma, we don't generally—"

"*May* be? Does he have multiple traumas or not?"

This voice, a woman's, was deeply known to her.

Notes were shuffled. "He has a greenstick fracture of the left humerus, a clavicle fracture, and a left proximal fracture of the tibia."

"It's safe to assume that anyone with brain injury who has lost consciousness could benefit from therapeutic hypothermia, is it not?"

"Yes, I suppose based on theoretical considerations it's reasonable."

"I wouldn't waste another moment," the woman said.

Veblen jerked back the curtain. "Mom?"

Melanie stood there, radiant and imposing, her features etched with purpose. She had on a crisp seersucker jacket and white blouse over gray pleated pants, and towered over the stooped man in the white jacket.

"Hello, Veblen. This is Dr. Munoz, who has been assigned to Paul."

Bill and Marion pressed in.

"What a terrible accident!" Melanie said with surprising warmth, embracing both of them.

"Well, I tell you one thing," Bill said. "Hutmacher's going to pay for this if I have to hunt down every high-level executive and turn their lives into a living hell!"

Dr. Munoz said, "Are you the parents?"

They acknowledged their son eagerly, Veblen noted.

"We're seeing positive signs. He's regained consciousness twice. The hematoma was relatively small and we removed it within ninety minutes of onset, so there's every reason to believe your son will come out of this with little or no debilitation."

"Do you know my son?" said Bill. His voice strained and shook. "He was a neurologist here at Stanford, and now is running trials at the VA center. He was conducting a trial to help brain-injured patients when this happened."

"What an unfortunate coincidence."

"I'll tell you what's no coincidence. My boy was alerting the authorities about some serious corruption this morning when this happened. You'll be hearing more about this case, I can tell you that!"

Within a few minutes Linus joined them, and Veblen began to feel numb. The meeting that she had anticipated for so long now seemed irrelevant, and she wished them all to leave.

"We love Veblen," said Marion. "You did a beautiful job with that girl."

"I think so," said Melanie.

THEY GATHERED in the waiting room, discussing the facts of the case as they knew them, theorizing on what Cloris might have hoped to gain by mowing down Paul, and all of them taking turns clutching and propping up Veblen, pacing with her in the hall. She finally excused herself and returned to Paul's bedside. She couldn't stand the sight of anybody. Eventually Linus came by to say he and Bill were doing a food run, would she like anything? She shook her head.

Marion came in awhile later. "Go on, go have something to eat, or at least something to drink," she said. "You'll need your strength."

"I'm not hungry."

"Go get some fresh air, then," Marion said, and Veblen complied so Marion could have her turn with Paul.

"Sure you don't want some food, Veb?" Linus was out in the hall. "We've got an extra chicken burrito here."

"No, thanks."

"Come sit with us awhile."

Reluctantly she found herself in the waiting room, listening to the banter of her mother and Bill. Justin had fallen asleep in a chair in the corner, his chin resting on his chest.

"For years, Melanie and I have worked tirelessly on conservation at the Grand Canyon," Linus was saying. "Melanie has taken several trips on her own."

"Now, were these trips dory or pontoon?" Bill asked.

"Dory," said Melanie. "Pontoons are for the birds."

"That was my outfit," said Bill. "We were the only dories operating then. Do you remember any of the oarsmen?"

"Let's see, Don Blaustein, Kirk Chung—"

"Ah!" cried Bill. "My buddies!"

"François?"

"Yes!"

"Mitchell?"

"Yes, yes!"

"He made a pass at me," Melanie said.

"Oh crap, yes, Mitchell was a hound," said Bill. "Not to say you weren't special." He cleared his throat and recited:

"'When your spirit cries for peace, come to a world of canyons deep in an old land . . .'"

"My god, we knew August Fruge!" cried Linus. "He was with the UC Press for many years and put out many fine wilderness books. Almost published Melanie's monograph, 'Backroad to Unkar.'"

"I'd like to read that," Bill said. "The canyon was my world, seven years running."

"It's a very thoughtful piece about communing with the earth," Linus said.

"How can you talk about the Grand Canyon when Paul's in a coma?" Veblen said suddenly, incensed that they were getting along so well.

"*Ahem*, we're trying to keep everyone *calm*," said Melanie. "He's not in a coma, Veblen. Come sit here." She patted the seat beside her. "It's an induced state of rest."

Veblen didn't move. She was tired of hearing about her mother's "wonderful" one thing she ever did besides sitting at her command post scratching, and she was tired of Linus making a myth out of it. "It's the only thing you've ever written, so don't make such a big deal."

"Well! That's a wonderful thing to say," said her mother.

"I'm going."

"Veblen, come back and apologize," said Linus.

"No, I don't need that right now," said Veblen, angrily.

"Veblen, now!"

And with that, Veblen did something else that was very unlike her, more unlike her than just about anything she'd ever done. She threw herself at Linus like a bull, and he staggered back. "Stop! Making! Everything! About! *Her!*" she cried.

"We're here advocating for your fiancé, and this is what we get? We're going to say good night," said Melanie, pulling Linus by the arm. "Grow up, little girl!"

She held back ten seconds, then ten more. Then she ran after them, missing the elevator, tearing down the empty stairwell. She caught sight of them exiting through the automatic doors in the lobby. "Stop. I need to talk to you!"

"You've humiliated me in front of the Vreelands," Melanie said, walking on.

"Stop and listen to me," Veblen said. "I'm serious, stop walking right now and turn around!"

Her throat was parched. She watched her mother's angry buttocks propel her mother's bulk a few more steps, but then the angry buttocks gave up. The angry buttocks pivoted around.

Linus looked grim. Very grim.

"What is it, Veblen?" said her mother.

Well, she didn't know what it was. Her mother had an IQ of 185 and could beat her in a game of chess wearing a blindfold. Couldn't she be the one who knew what it was, for once?

"Does it really matter if you're humiliated right now?" Veblen said, weakly. "Do you really have to be the number one priority right now?"

"What do you think I spend every second of every day since the day you were born thinking about, Veblen? Do you think it's me? You are very, very spoiled. We will spend the night and leave promptly in the morning."

"Do what you need to do," said Veblen, crossing her arms.

"That expression is vile," Melanie said.

VEBLEN SPENT THE NIGHT in the hospital next to Paul in a cot, not wanting to leave his side. Nurses came and went all night long, and all through the night she tracked the sounds of the monitors.

She turned over, eye to eye with the catheter bag, which was now half full of Paul's pale urine, clearly stamped with the name "Hutmacher" on the outside. Sick! Every hour or so she'd rise and look at Paul's face, and place her hand on his forehead, and say his name.

In the morning she regarded herself in the institutional bathroom mirror, under fluorescent lights. Things didn't look too good. After she splashed her face with water, dried it under the hand blower, and brushed her knotted hair, it was relatively convenient to wind through the hospital to her office in Neurology and explain to Dr. Chaudhry what had happened to Paul and why she would not be at work that day.

"He's here in the ICU?" Chaudhry asked, and when she told him why, he was stunned. "That takes the cake."

"Definitely."

"Veblen, I'm very sorry. Please take all the time you need."

"Thanks."

She returned to Paul's room, and Dr. Chaudhry came by an hour later. He'd conferred with the doctors in the ICU and been told that Paul's prognosis was good. Then Laurie Tietz came by with a large latte and a big blueberry muffin, and gave her a long, warm hug.

8 A.M.

Veblen sat beside Paul thinking of ways to cheer him up. She picked up the telephone by the bed as if a call had come in. She said, "What are you selling? Life membership in the golf and country club? *Errrghhhhhhhhhhhhhhllll—*" She gurgled and retched and hung up in burlesque fashion. When there was no response she added, "Remember you said you liked it when I did that? I hope you remember.

"I can't wait to go to Tacos Tambien as soon as you're better. *Carnitas!* Lime! Cilantro! Yeah!"

No reaction. Nothing at all.

"Let's share more grievances," she tried. "I've been way too uptight about that. What was I afraid of?" She stopped a moment to find something unpleasant Paul had tried to share with her. "You know, I hate smelly hippies with bags of excrement in tree houses too. Have I ever told you that?"

Nothing. "Paul, and you know what else I can't stand? *Nudists.* And you know why? The *ist* part. Give me an ecologist, a violinist, an artist. But if you're just a nudist, get a life, you know what I mean?"

She checked the monitor—to her disgust for nudists, his vitals showed no response.

"Turkey balls aren't as good as regular meatballs, you're absolutely right, and I'll never make them again, so help me god."

She looked at him closely.

"And what's so great about corn on the cob, compared to love?"

Saying *love,* Veblen felt something break inside herself that was brilliant and deafening, a desperate roar. It was a pinch, a crack, a tear. It was roaring, sweeping, aching, bending, a torrent carrying her away.

8:20 A.M.

"You know, I've been thinking about you and Justin and—from the outside it's easy to be judgmental but—it was *your* childhood too—" Paul twitched, and maybe she'd hit a nerve. "It's uncool when he steals people's underwear, definitely. And you know how they call themselves a tripod? Well, that's so cruel and unfair to you! It hurts just thinking about it."

She looked up and saw Bill and Marion standing behind her, confused and wounded by what they had heard.

"Oh! But I hope—don't take it the wrong way!"

They retreated quietly, and her instinct was to regain their approval, to follow and mend. But she didn't.

"Paul, I've alienated both of our families. Ha! The way you wanted it. Now it's just us."

11:00 A.M.

Paul's colleague James Shalev stopped by. He told Veblen he'd been part of the trial from the start, and now that he'd witnessed the accident, he felt like he had something to say about the whole symbiotic FDA / pharmaceutical industry / DOD triumvirate that wasn't exactly positive.

"I was with him at DeviceCON the night he found out his device was out. It was mind-blowing. We even talked about it being risky, like in *The Fugitive*. Unbelievable. He's a hero."

"Thank you," Veblen said.

11:30 A.M.

Paul's friend Hans showed up; he'd heard the news from the Vreelands.

"Hey, Veblen," he said, embracing her. "He knew this was about to happen, and he told me to take care of you if it did."

Veblen listened, a lump in her throat.

"I've already written down everything he said to me that morning and put it in a safe place. I'll be the first person up on the stand to testify. He's my man."

"Mine too," Veblen said.

. . .

12:00 NOON

Linus came in carrying a bag. "So what's the news?"

"It's wait and see," Veblen said. "He's stable. Where's Mom?"

"She's out in the car. She's a little shaky. She is upset and doesn't want to make it worse by coming inside. But she wants me to tell you she's standing by. We're going home today but she'll be waiting by the phone, of course."

"Fine," Veblen said.

"Here's a bite to eat, we picked up some items at that bakery you like," Linus said.

"Thank you."

Linus shook his head. "This is a terrible thing, babe. Is there anything I can do?"

"I'm sorry I attacked you last night," she said, and hugged him.

"There, there," Linus said. "I'd blow my top too, if you or Melanie were hurt. I'm going to take your mother home now and you call later when you can, all right?"

"All right."

THE DAY WAS LONG and dreadful. Whenever his eyelids flickered, she wondered if he was seeing the world like a newborn, "one great blooming, buzzing confusion," as William James imagined it.

She remembered a concert they had attended in San Francisco one evening in the fall, shortly after they met. The program included three concertos, and ended with Peter Ilyich Tchaikovsky's Piano Concerto no. 1 in B-flat minor, op. 23. It is the showy yet rousing concerto heard when advertising any pianist's greatest hits. And Veblen kept waiting for the theme at the beginning to return, but it never did, which was a buzzing confusion to her untrained ears.

Paul stood in ovation as the young pianist took his bows. "My god, that ending," he said, in awe. "That's probably my favorite finale in all of classical music."

She had been puzzled. "Really? In *all* of classical music?"

"The way it builds. It's just about perfect."

It was a moment in which she sensed unplumbed depths in him, and a minefield of shallows in herself. She'd have to listen to it again. To everything again.

SHE USED TO THINK falling in love was alchemy, that animals had weddings, that coal was a gemstone, that mountains were hollow, that trees had hidden eyes!

THE FOLLOWING MORNING, just as Veblen pushed up from the cot, as the new shift began to bustle, she heard a voice say, "I'd kill for a cup of coffee."

She looked up. Paul's eyes were open, and he smiled, as if there were nothing strange about being attached to an IV with a cannula in his hand, his head fully wrapped, his leg in a full cast, a profusion of tape all over his chest, cardiac monitors and brain monitors beeping and signaling on a nearby screen, a catheter lodged deep in his urethra.

"Paul!"

"I guess something bad must have happened," he said.

CAN YOU PATENT
THE SUN?

"So," Veblen said. "Not just bad, but also weird."

Paul took her hand. "Very weird."

Paul was out of the ICU, in another room resting after a battery of tests. According to Dr. Munoz, there were excellent N20 components in his evoked potentials. His corneal reflexes were first-rate. His extensor motor responses were superb. There had been no myoclonus status epilepticus whatsoever. His neuron-specific enolase levels were below thirty-three micrograms per liter. His creatine kinase brain isoenzyme was within range. Brain oxygenation and intracranial pressure were normal. He had retrograde amnesia about the immediate circumstances of the accident, but that was thoroughly anticipated by Ribot's law. He scored VIII on the Rancho Scale for postcoma recovery, the highest possible. He was "appropriate and purposeful." Yet the more he remembered and the clearer his mind became, the more ill at ease he felt.

He began to insist that he must leave the medical profession. That he must find something entirely new.

Veblen let him say such things, as if he needed to drain himself of a poison.

He remembered writing the letter about the discrepancies in the trial, but could not piece together what happened next. There was something nightmarish on the periphery, some obviously false memory of a struggle. Sure enough, Veblen reminded him he had visited the simulator just before the accident. That was where he'd dropped his letters. Paul said, "Then that simulator is something else. I have this strange impression of being in some kind of hand-to-hand combat."

"Visitors," the nurse announced.

Veblen looked to the door. Two young women came in, escorting a well-built man shuffling with the aid of a cane.

"Sorry, is this a good time?" one of the young women asked. "We don't want to bother you."

"No, come in," Veblen said, and they introduced themselves as Sarah and Alexa Smith, their father as Warren Smith, a veteran who had been a participant in Paul's trial.

Paul sat up stiffly and placed his hands over his neck.

Sarah said, "See, Dad? Dr. Vreeland is okay. See?"

Smith squinted at Paul, then turned for the door.

"Our father has something to say," Alexa said. "Dad, get out your coping cards, remember?"

Smith stopped and pulled some index cards from his jacket pocket.

"Go ahead, Dad. It's okay," Sarah said.

Smith began to read: "What happened was a mistake, and I apologize for that. I take full responsibility for my aggressive, impulsive, and insensitive behavior. I have a history of blaming others for my problems, and this needs to stop. I take responsibility for causing you pain."

Smith finished. He folded up his cards and returned them to his pocket, then turned again for the door.

"Pain?" Paul said. "You're Sergeant Major Smith, am I right?"

Smith stopped and nodded.

"I appreciate your kind words, but really, you have nothing to apologize for, do you?"

"Let's go," said Warren Smith.

"Well, that's nice of you," said Alexa. "Um, also, we feel really bad telling you this, but we're not selling the Sea Ray, right, Dad?"

"The Sea Ray!" Paul nodded. "Well, I guess that didn't prove to be the most popular idea. Good luck with everything then."

"You too, Dr. Vreeland, you take care!"

They shuffled out with their father.

"What did he do to you?" Veblen wanted to know.

"I have no idea," Paul said, still rubbing his neck. "Come here. I can't believe what I've put you through."

"Don't even think about it."

"I wish I could remember it better. Cloris really tried to kill me?"

"She hit you with her car," Veblen confirmed.

"There's something about Cloris Hutmacher I've never liked," Paul said shrewdly.

He drank some water through a straw, then said, "In Vienna in the late 1800s, there was this medical-device-maker guy, Erwin Perzy, and he tried to invent a surgical lamp that would be brighter than the bulbs they were using at the time. He knew that setting a candle behind a glass of water enhanced the light, so he started playing around encasing bulbs in globes of water, then adding tinsel and white sand for reflection. It didn't work for lamps, but you know those things called snow globes?"

"Yeah."

"That's what he ended up inventing. To this day, that's what he's known for."

"Really! That's a great thing to be known for. I love snow globes. They're way better than surgical lamps."

"Not if you're having surgery."

"But, Paul, your device works and it's still going to do all the things you hoped it would."

In statements issued through Hutmacher's attorneys, Shrapnal and Boone, Cloris claimed that Paul threw himself in her path, and that the accident had nothing to do with the allegations in Paul's letter, nor with the research materials for the trial found in the boxes in her backseat. An investigation was under way.

"Dad's all over it," Paul said. "He's got some hotshot activist lawyer on the case."

"I know. And that guy James Shalev wants to write about it."

"Oh my god." Paul rubbed his temples fiercely. "He has guts."

"Paul, you know what? A couple of nights ago, I had an outburst with my mother. I kind of attacked her." She said it almost proudly.

"Oh no!"

"And yesterday, I was talking to you before you were conscious, and I said some stuff your parents overheard, and they're upset too."

He looked surprised. "No one could blame you for being stressed out."

"You think? I don't feel myself, upsetting people."

Paul struggled to sit up more, but managed only to lift his head. "Oh, look, a squirrel!" he cried happily, pointing into the oak outside the window.

Sure enough, leaves were scattering under the rush of a squirrel's feet down the long arm of the oak, and Paul was smiling at the sight of it.

"Paul, you seem totally different. You hate squirrels."

"You think I have brain damage?"

As a matter of fact, she was starting to wonder.

"I don't think it's brain damage," Paul said soberly. "But we'll make sure. I'm having some realizations, that's all."

"Really?"

His brow wrinkled sensibly. "Do you know what Jonas Salk said when he was asked if he'd patented the polio vaccine? He said, 'Can you patent the sun?' The idea of a patent was shocking to him. What humility! I feel like—maybe I've been on the wrong track." His voice cracked, and he swallowed and pushed back into his pillow. "I can't explain it, it's like someone turned a fire hose on me. All these slimy layers of meaninglessness are coming off. Why shouldn't you talk to squirrels?" he said, with a faraway look in his eyes. "You know what happened to me a long, long time ago?"

"What?"

"Well." He rubbed his eyes. "Now I'm nervous. What if you don't believe me?"

"Try it."

"Okay." He tried to push himself up on his elbows. "Once, seriously, I'm not kidding—I heard snails *scream*."

"Really?"

Paul nodded. "When I was a kid."

"What did it sound like?" Veblen asked, with great curiosity. Snails had a lot to scream about. "Sort of like a hiss?"

"No."

"Kind of a slurp?"

He tried to re-create it, clenching his jaw, his breath squeezing past his tonsils.

"Wild." Veblen laughed.

"You believe it?" he croaked.

"Sure, screaming snails. Of course!"

"Don't break up with me right away," he said suddenly. "Give me another chance, okay?"

22

THE MAN-SQUIRREL
DEBATE

Once in her readings of William James, Veblen had come across an anecdote that greatly irritated her. Professor James had gone on a camping trip with a cohort of his brainy friends, and upon returning from a solitary hike found them all in heated conversation around the campfire. It seemed there was a squirrel clinging to the trunk of the large sheltering tree at their site, but no matter how fast one of them went around the tree to catch a glimpse, the squirrel moved too, always keeping the tree between himself and the nuisance.

"Does the man go round the squirrel or not?" was the heavy metaphysical question in dispute.

Some of the geniuses said that of course the man went around the squirrel. The tree was fixed. The man went around it. Period.

But the rest of the experts said that as long as the squirrel rotated on the trunk, keeping its belly pointed at the man, then the man never did go "round" him.

James, ever the reasonable one, the humanist supreme, settled everyone down by pointing out that the key to the dispute lay in what "go round" meant in the most practical fashion. And on this they all agreed. The agreement laid the groundwork for pragmatism and ordinary language philosophy and future camping trips, this strange accord from the "unlimited leisure of the wilderness."

Yet Thorstein Veblen, an admirer of James who would have read this essay published in 1907, might well have wondered what James meant by the unlimited leisure of the wilderness, and might have asked for no shuffling evasion about explaining it.

The Brahmins were splitting hairs about the words "go round" while a squirrel was taking care not to be roasted on a spit for dinner. Since when is this unlimited leisure?

Even James, the great empathist, had his blind spots.

William Morris, her mother's hero, had blind spots. He was seen as effete and ridiculous by Professor Veblen after he paid Morris a visit in England. Veblen came home and blasted Morris's Kelmscott Press and the whole Arts and Crafts movement for producing overly precious items for the wealthy, the only ones who could afford them—*decadent aestheticism,* he called it.

Veblen himself was flawed. By god, he could breathe only from one nostril! He must have snored terribly. And he didn't like dogs. How could he not like dogs? And he did his dishes in a bathtub with a hose!

Yes, everybody had blind spots and flaws, and she knew how to ignore others' blind spots and flaws. While she was by temperament very forgiving to others, she was not inclined to be generous to herself. Nothing offended her more than her own faults, which seemed to be revealing themselves lately with alarming frequency. She was muted and superstitious, stunted and weak, and if she spent much more time thinking about it, she'd have a list that rolled out the door on a scroll. There was no perfect being out there, accepting, intelligent, kind, creative, full of life and appetite. *Muckraker, carouser, sweet-toothed, lion-hearted.*

Or was there?

23

HELLO IN THERE

Within the week, Paul was out of the hospital and back at his apartment in Mountain View to recuperate. Bill and Justin had returned to Garberville; Marion was most suited to nursing Paul. He was gaining strength and appetite rapidly, and Marion cooked for him and picked up his prescriptions and helped him remember what had to be taken when, but he was eager to be independent again, to have the space to think.

Veblen would stop by every day and visit, but mostly she and Paul talked on the phone, like people just getting to know each other. When they talked, Veblen would stand at her front window, watching a tall slender palm down the road sway like a colossal cattail. The palm would hypnotize her, taking her away to a world where human solidarity prevailed.

Her mother was leaving her alone for a change. It was remarkable how little time she'd spent worrying about the fight they'd had when Paul was in the hospital, and how little damage control she'd indulged in since. But after a few days had gone by, Veblen longed to talk to her again, and called.

Her mother answered immediately.

"Mom?"

"Yes, Veblen."

Veblen said, "Mom, I'm sorry I yelled at you at the hospital, and I hope everything's okay."

Melanie sniffed. "I can understand you were under a lot of duress," said her mother, picking up without evident melodrama. "How are you feeling now?"

"Okay," Veblen said. "So you're not mad?"

"I was hurt and disappointed," her mother said. "But I've put it behind me. How is Paul?"

"He's good, just a little tired."

"Tired in what way? Is he keeping food down?"

"Yes. His head hurts, and so do his ribs and his leg."

"He needs to start physical therapy right away."

"He started, don't worry."

"What's happening with the attorney?"

"She says it's likely Cloris won't be charged with any criminal offense for the accident. But she's going to help Paul with the whistle-blower stuff," Veblen said. They proceeded to discuss how this would impact Paul's career, and Veblen was able to tell her mother that through the efforts of Dr. Chaudhry, Stanford wanted him back. But whether Paul would accept was another story.

"And what about the wedding?" Melanie asked.

"We'll see," Veblen simply said.

"His parents have been very civil to me. I know that's not the point, but it meant a lot to me," Melanie said. "Marion called the other day to see if I was all right and we talked about the stress you're under. I don't know when anybody's shown that kind of consideration for me in years."

"What about Linus?"

"*Besides* Linus. And you, of course."

"Well, good," Veblen said.

"I know you've been very busy, but you haven't heard anything further about my trial, have you?"

"No."

"I hope this isn't a pipe dream," Melanie said, sighing.

"Don't you have a better pipe dream than that?" Veblen accused, and her mother actually chuckled.

"I wish I did, dear. Wait till you're my age."

They talked a bit longer. Her mother wanted to hear about how Paul was coping with the everyday details of life with a broken arm and leg, and even inquired about the degree of chafing in his armpits. She also had been thinking a great deal about Veblen's health and how she might be under a lot of strain. Through the blinds Veblen could see a light coming on in Donald Chester's kitchen.

Hello in there.

THAT NIGHT, Veblen dreamed about the wedding. She dreamed that they were standing on the ridge overlooking the great expanse of the Pacific, up near Skyline Drive, and that the earth began to rumble, but it wasn't the work of the San Andreas Fault. Everywhere before her the fields and meadows were moving. All at once she saw squirrels, millions of them, running, shoulder to shoulder, forming a huge blanket, as far as the eye could see, one of those vast migrations that had been noted across the continent by settlers and pioneers. Squirrels began to pour through the clearing where they stood, around the guests, making them scream, and all the while Veblen was calling out to calm them: *"They're only moving on! It's all right! They're moving on!"*

When she awoke her muscles were sore, as if she'd been running in the stampede.

24

DOOMED TO WONDER

Year upon year in Garberville, in the spring near noon, the sun will pour through the front windows of the Vreelands' house and illuminate the bookshelf, where sits a portrait of Bill Vreeland's brother Richard. Not the portrait of the marine in his dress blues who stood at attention on the mantel at Bill and Richard's parents' house in San Diego from 1966 until their residue was boxed up in the nineties, but one of Rich skateboarding in a striped T-shirt and cut-offs down a hill near the high school. This year, Justin was studying it intently when all at once he began to wail, "He's *gone*! He's *gooooooone*!" and pound on his skull. Bill could normally talk him out of his outbursts, but this one went out of control. As Justin howled, Marion, who had only just returned from a week taking care of Paul, rushed to embrace him, but he pushed her back against the bookcase, and her wrist was not broken but deeply bruised.

Bill had to bind Justin's arms with a canvas strap that he didn't like using at all, and gave him some sedation, which he also didn't like to do, and then they had to decide if they should take him to his day group or not, and since the car ride to town usually soothed him, they thought they'd give it a try despite the tumult, and by the time they reached town he was docile, and after he went in without a hitch they sat outside on a redwood bench and Marion cried.

"I want to take care of him as long as I can," she said, rubbing her twisted wrist.

Bill watched a dragonfly land on his leg in the sun. "We need to have a plan. Someday we won't be here for him. And before that, there's going to be a day when we're not up to it anymore. It kills me to say that, you know that, don't you?"

She sniffed. "Who would fly his Banana-57 into the room every morning? Who would make his cinnamon toast the way he loves it? Who would help him get all the threads away from his toes in his socks? Who would pull up the tongue in his shoes? Who will care enough? No one will care as much as we do!"

"I think we need to decide *where.*" Bill rubbed his beard with the back of his hand, then bounced his hand on its spring action. "That's all I'm saying."

They remained on the bench in stillness, as if catching their breath for whatever came next.

Bill thought about the blood he'd noticed a few times in his urine, wondering if he should tell his doctor, and then he thought about his mother's death ten years ago, and of wrestling her rings off her cold knuckles in that eerie, silent room.

Marion thought about the day Justin was born. After all her pot smoking, trying to find herself in movement and music, the world lurched in a new direction, and she'd never looked back.

In a while the members of Justin's group came outside for their walk. Justin was paired with a woman named Alice who had Down syndrome, and he and Alice were holding hands.

They rested in the sun. Marion believed in lightness. For his part, Bill considered this a time for atonement, and never scheduled a thing but an hour on the bench.

Buried in the folds of the past was a candlelit room in the communal dome where they'd all lived, with Caddie Fladeboe and Cool Breeze and the rest of them, all young and sure, waiting as Marion withstood labor, dabbing her with sponges and proclaiming her beautiful, and she bearing up like all earth mothers had done before the modern medical system denatured the birthing process beyond recognition. They massaged and coached her to push and push and push and push and push, and Justin arrived after forty-two hours with a cord around his neck, blue.

Some said it was meant to be, that all the moments of their lives that led to the decision to have him at home were part of his legacy, and that they mustn't blame themselves, but Bill struggled. He relied on modernity in other ways. By now he had a cell phone, he had a car, he loved the Internet, he wasn't thoroughly medieval. Why had he insisted on being medieval at the birth of his child?

"Marion?" he said abruptly. "We need to tell Paul what happened. It's time he knows. We've screwed him up."

"What happened when?"

He felt a flash of anger, for there was nothing else that had *happened* compared to this.

"When Justin was born, Marion."

She opened her purse and looked into it, as if trying to locate a secret passageway to escape through.

"Why?" she cried. "What good would it do? Can't you leave it alone?"

"Marion," he said. "We feel so guilty over Justin's birth we can't even talk about it. That's what Paul grew up with, the feeling something wasn't right. We were always so busy with Justin, trying to make up for our mistakes that we hung him out to dry."

"We didn't make a mistake," Marion said. "We did everything exactly right."

"We'll never know, and that's why we're doomed to wonder."

"That's all we need is for Paul to know."

"Marion, he's more capable of forgiveness and understanding than we've given him credit for. We're not giving him the chance to grow."

"I stopped trusting myself," Marion said quietly. "I didn't want to decide anything anymore. Here's one more thing to decide."

"Let me decide," Bill said.

THE CYBORG

In her home office before her monitor, Cloris was reassuring her former husband that reporters were not bothering their son and that she was more than happy to put him on a plane to Washington tomorrow.

No, of course she hadn't hit the idiot on purpose. It was a huge pain in the ass and her father wasn't speaking to her and she didn't want to answer any more questions or she might explode.

Morris had been creeping along the wall, holding Paul's device as if it were one of the four-barreled guns in the cyborg game. *"Bam! Bam! Bam! Bam!"* He wasn't listening to the words his mother was saying, but he registered the tone—definitely cyborg.

"Don't give me that. He gets more attention than any child should."

"I think you need to take a look at yourself, Cloris," said her ex-husband.

"Morris, get over here and tell your father you're ready to go home."

Morris didn't come. Cloris was rocking violently in her ergonomic executive chair, siphoning liquid from a large tumbler.

"Morris?" called the cyborg father. "Come here, son. I'd like to see you."

Morris began to shuffle around the perimeter of the room, keeping his back on them, trying to figure out which of his special powers to use.

"I've made an appointment with Patricia's psychologist. The one her son sees."

"What about sports?" Morris's father said. "If you could just get him busy on a team of some kind, soccer, Little League, maybe swimming?"

"Do you know how stressful that would be? He doesn't want to do anything normal like that. He will not go."

"Son, you need to get yourself active, okay?"

"How soon we forget. Last year he agreed to the soccer then moved around the field like a robot."

Morris was directly behind his mother's chair now, going through his defense options: *Teleport? Shape change? Energy shield? Perplex?*

"I don't have that kind of trouble, Cloris. Morris is more than happy to play tennis when he's here. Aren't you, son?"

At that moment, Morris spun around and placed the Pneumatic Turbo Skull Punch on the top of his mother's head, and squeezed the trigger. This was the perfect weapon to use on a cyborg. There was a loud report and the device kicked back in his hands, pinching out a bone-white disk, cascading with blond hair and a strip of skin.

"Cloris?" Morris's father said. "Cloris, what is it?"

"What . . . was . . . that . . . sound?" Cloris said, in a slow, rasping voice.

Then she crumpled forward, fluid spilling from the large, vulnerable opening (LVO) on the top of her head.

"Morris? What is happening to your mother? Morris!"

"Mommy?" Morris cried. "Want to play a game?"

26

WE CAN BE TOGETHER

According to Adolf Guggenbühl-Craig, the Swiss analyst and author of *Marriage: Dead or Alive*, a wedding is more than a party or a legality. It's no less than a boxing ring, two people facing off, acknowledging their separate identities rather than their union, in the company of all the people who lay claim to them. A wedding is the time and place to recognize the full clutch of the past in the negotiation of a shared future.

Try devoting a few pages to that, *Brides* magazine!

Three days before the wedding, Linus called to say Melanie wasn't feeling well, that her blood pressure was sky-high, that her ankles were as big as hams, and that her heartbeat was as irregular as everything else about her physical being. But he assured her they'd be there. (*As if they wouldn't?* Veblen wondered.)

On Friday, Bebe Kaufman called to report difficulties getting Rudgear into the van assigned to deliver him, and Veblen had to implore him over the phone.

"Did I say I was coming?" he asked, vaguely.

"Yes, Dad, you did."

"I mess up everything, don't I?"

"No. Dad, it's a two-and-a-half-hour drive and you can watch the History channel when you get here, how about that?"

"I get a little tired of the History channel."

"Fine, you can watch whatever you want. Get in the car and I'll see you in a few hours."

"Yes, ma'am."

Veblen was meanwhile stitching her dress and pressing open the seams. The dress was a simple white A-line made of rayon that had cost her all of thirty-two dollars in materials, and seemed to fit nicely, though she hemmed one sleeve higher than the other and had to rip it out with the expensive Swiss seam ripper and do it again. She wasn't very good at sewing, but did her best.

Then Albertine, with her long legs and horn-rimmed glasses, arrived and set up in Veblen's kitchen to begin food preparations, which she had offered to do as soon as she'd heard about the date and plan.

"Two girls from Cobb, doing the job," Albertine drawled, tying up her hair.

Veblen said, "Just promise that whatever you witness today and tomorrow, that you won't hold it against me more than anything else in your arsenal."

"I'll try my best," vowed Albertine.

By midafternoon the Vreelands came to Tasso Street, and Bill stayed with Justin a long time in the car before bringing him in. Marion began to help in the kitchen without a moment's pause.

"Oh, my, you girls have done such a good job organizing everything," she said.

Paul would be back soon. He was out doing errands with his best man, Hans Borg.

The Sunny Hill van arrived at two-thirty, and a muscular man with a shaved head helped Rudgear out of the back. Rudgear wore one of the new plaid shirts Veblen had brought him, blue jeans, flip-flops, and a Panama hat. "Hey, Dad, you're looking good! Come in." She took his arm, which was covered with Band-Aids to hide bleeding spots in his thin skin.

Bill came forward and shook Rudgear's hand and told him what a great daughter he had, though Rudgear did not comment, perhaps because he'd never registered Veblen as his daughter, which made sense given how little time they'd spent together, but also, because of how much work she'd put into being a daughter, was kind of sad. He straightened up at the sight of Marion, and even more so at the sight of Albertine, but when he was introduced to Justin he stepped back and said, "What are you staring at?"

Marion said, "Rudge, Justin is a special person and when he stares it just means he's interested, right, Justy?"

Rudgear said, "Don't get too interested, buddy."

Veblen said, "Dad, how about some pretzels?"

"I'd like that, ma'am," he said, taking a spot at her table.

She pulled a heavy bowl from the cupboard and the bag of pretzels from another, pulled the plastic apart, and sent pretzels cascading across the counter and floor. She rubbed her eyes, felt a pain in her collarbone. She poured the remaining pretzels in the bowl and for a moment envied them for being senseless scraps of gluten. She noticed how uneven her fingernails were on the eve of her wedding. What a clod she was! It had never occurred to her to do anything about them.

Music came from her living room, Jefferson Airplane's "We Can Be Together," which was Justin's favorite song.

"Here you go," Veblen said, bringing Rudgear the pretzels and a cool glass of water.

"Thanks much. Nice bowl," said Rudgear.

"Thanks."

"Used to know a kid who had a voice," he said.

"Oh, really? You mean, in Waukegan?"

"Yep," said Rudgear.

"*Tear down the walls! Tear down the walls!*" Justin sang.

Rudgear winced. "Are we prisoners here?"

"No, Dad. Would you like to take a walk?"

"Yeah. I better use the facilities."

"Back there," Veblen said, fearing he would crawl out the window and run away. Well, the window didn't really open so he was trapped.

"Veblen!" called Marion. "Do you have any oven mitts?"

"Somewhere. I usually use dish towels."

"Veb? Do you have salt?" said Albertine. "The shaker's out."

"Try the cupboard over the stove. We might have to get some."

"Veblen, do you mind if we move the furniture around in the living room? If Justy can dance he'll get rid of some energy and that will be good for everybody," Bill said.

"Sure, go ahead," said Veblen, and the song started up again, twice as loud. The cottage shook under Justin's feet.

Rudge returned to the room, shrinking from the noise. "Lord, have mercy," he cried out, as if in pain.

"Rudge, don't you like music?" called Bill.

"No. Is that what you call it?"

"Bill, maybe turn it down a little?" Marion asked.

"I need some air," said Rudge, moving for the door.

"We'll turn it down, Rudge, no problem," Bill said, and Justin reached out and touched his arm.

"Get your paws off me!" Rudge shouted, even more desperately.

Justin latched on to Rudge's sleeve, whereupon Rudge took hold of Justin's arm and twisted it like a peg. Justin screamed.

"Hey, none of this!" Bill said.

"Dad, stop it!" Veblen cried.

"To hell with all of you!" Rudge yelled, and charged out the door.

"Dad!" cried Veblen. "Come back!"

Justin jumped up and down like a jackhammer. *"He hurt me! He hurt me! He hurt me! He hurt me!"*

She cleared the cottage in time to see Rudgear running to the end of Tasso Street, where he disappeared down the bank of the San Francisquito Creek.

Okay, no big deal! Probably lots of people had to chase their parents to get them to their weddings, at least metaphorically. She smiled for a second, and then she started to laugh.

A cramp seemed to be forming around her heart. *Did the cramp go round the heart—or not?* She wondered if she could get a bunch of intellectuals excited about it.

At the arroyo's edge, she could not see her father or tell which direction he'd taken, so she ran along the edge, surveying the historic gully next to which Gaspar de Portola and his men camped during their 1769 exploration of California. An acorn woodpecker worked on a tree. "Dad, I'm worried about your blood sugar levels. Where are you?" she called out.

"Dad?" she cried out. "I need you!" Maybe this was the wrong thing to say, he didn't like being needed. "Dad?" Maybe that was wrong as well. "Rudgear!" she tried, and then slid down the bank.

"Well, this is swell. Why are you doing this?" she cried. Didn't anyone care how she felt, didn't anyone care if her wedding was fun for her? She had an actual hair appointment coming up, Albertine had insisted on it, though her hair never held a style, was always lank and floppy. Now she'd probably miss it, but who cared. No one cared, that's who!

"*Stop*," she told herself, trying to tap her resources. "Stop." She sat on an uprooted log, typing on her thighs to mend.

When you're weary, feeling small

Even on a phantom keyboard, typing did so much to alleviate stress!

When tears are in your eyes . . .

Faster!

. . . I will dry them all

Through her wet lashes she saw lilies embedded in the mud shale bank, just like the ones around her cottage, and wondered how they got here. Possibly transplanted by squirrels. Creeping snowberry and a few saplings of dogwood grew along the bank too. Gazing through the fluttering leaves, she saw geese overhead in a V, at such an altitude they made no sound or ripple. Then came a rustling in an oak, a shredding of bark, and a wiry cry, much like a tin noisemaker spinning at a New Year's party. Next thing she knew the squirrel was perched on a small tuft of dry grass protruding from the sandstone embankment, staring right at her!

"Ah, it's you! Boy, am I glad to see you!"

She didn't even have to squint to make it real.

Crrrrrrrrrrrrrrrrrrrrrrrrrrk!

"What are you trying to say?" She coughed, and noted the round outline of something the size of a grapefruit, flat, rusted, jutting up through the alluvium; she dug her fingers in around it and kept wiggling it until it came loose. It was a large can, mostly rusted, with some print still visible—Hawaiian Punch. The top of the can had been punctured by a church key, in two triangles on either side.

"Oh my gosh, this is from such a long time ago. I remember gagging this stuff down at school parties. I remember someone using the church key thing and asking my mother why you had to do it on both sides, and how I felt proud that she thought it was a good question and how she explained it released the pressure to flow better." She drifted into thoughts about that time in her life, when her mother's knowledge seemed so potent, there was no need to go anywhere else for the truth. Then she detected something else, the size of a ring, caked in dirt, and she dug it out and brushed it off. It was a ring, all right, possibly made of silver, with suns and moons pressed into it, and even with the dirt caked on, it fit her ring finger perfectly. "Hey, I can't believe it. I'll have to wash it and see, but I think I like this ring!" She smiled and said, "You wanted me to find this, didn't you!"

In May the pool-riffle channel was nearly dry. But it was clear that in times of high water this was a conduit for a great volume of organic debris. She felt fortunate to live near such an active riparian corridor.

"Thank you," she said. "Thank you very much."

Why had this squirrel attached to her, taken such an interest? What did he want? What did he see?

All at once she could hear Bill's voice calling to Rudgear, just around the bend. And the squirrel leaped from the outcropping and ran past her, unearthing clumps of sediment and mulch.

"Rudge, you gave us a scare! My kid's got a condition, he's mentally disabled! He didn't mean anything. He's a five-year-old in the body of a man!"

She jumped to her feet and sprang over the rocks.

"He's not all there?" Rudgear was saying.

"No. He's not all there," said Bill.

"I didn't think so. You can tell a kid like that a mile away."

They came into view, and Veblen saw Bill attempting to help Rudgear up the rocky embankment, holding him by his bandaged arm.

"He has a hard time keeping his hands to himself, it's beyond his control. We need your help getting through this wedding. I want my wife to feel the joy of having her other son married. I don't want stress, and if you could help us with Justin we'd be grateful."

She came up behind, to lend a hand. "Well done," she said.

Rudgear said, "I'm no good at anything!"

"Come on, Dad, you're doing great."

"Veblen, maybe you could get behind him and give him a boost."

She braced herself against Rudgear's backside, as Bill pulled on his hands from above.

"I didn't go to Nam, but my brother died there," Bill said, grunting.

"Your brother," repeated Rudge.

"Died at Phu Ninh," said Bill.

"You home when they came?"

"Yep," said Bill.

"Betcha your folks were never the same," said Rudge.

"That is correct," said Bill.

"It's hard on a family when you have a handicapped," Rudgear said, as Veblen pushed.

"Wouldn't trade it for the world."

"My brother was handicapped," her father said, as they struggled upward, almost to the top.

"I never knew you had a brother!" Veblen said.

"He died when I was eight. My mother wouldn't let me say his name."

"That's hard," said Bill.

"She never got over it."

"Sorry, man," said Bill.

"She was never the same."

Rudgear wheezed as he crested the bank.

Bill put his arm around Rudgear to lead him back.

"I could see making a raft and riding it down to the salt flats, couldn't you, Rudge?" said Bill.

"Give the frog a loan," Rudgear said.

"Whatever you say," said Bill.

"Knick knack paddy whack, give the frog a loan."

"Rudge, you'd better get your ass in gear for your daughter's wedding," Bill said.

"I can't remember the joke."

"Did you hear me?" Bill said.

Rudge grunted.

"Dad?" Veblen said. "I never knew you had a brother before, that's sad. What was his name?"

Rudgear was breathing heavily, and he didn't reply.

"I just want to know, since he would've been my uncle," Veblen pushed him.

"His name was Hugh! Stop talking about it. What's the point?"

"Okay," she said. "Thanks for telling me."

Rudgear said, "My daughter wrote me a letter when she was five years old. It said, *There are no monkeys in the world.* That was the whole letter."

"I did?" Her voice cracked.

"Veblen is profound, we know that much," said Bill, giving her a nod.

RUDGEAR FRESHENED UP and got hydrated, and was in better form by the time Melanie and Linus arrived in the late afternoon. He strutted from the cottage on Tasso Street to greet them at the curb, and Veblen took out her camera because it was the first time in her life she'd seen her biological parents together, which she'd always told herself didn't mean anything to her, but now somehow it did, if only for the record. Rudgear tapped into a dormant reserve of suave, and to her amazement took Melanie's hand as she rose from the car and kissed it. Then her mother didn't wipe off her hand or call him a pompous ass, but rather smiled and embraced him, and Linus had to come around and intrude on the reunion to introduce himself, which also went well. Rudgear and Linus shook hands like men who had shared a hardship.

Both men had shiny pates. "I see we have the same barber," said Rudge, and Linus let out a convivial hoot.

Bill turned chicken brochettes on the barbecue in the back that evening, under the shaggy, sap-oozing pine. The evening was lovely. The warm light of late afternoon blued after the sun dipped behind the coastal ranges. Around them the sycamores, liquid amber, and magnolias darkened. Leaves rustled, and Veblen went in for a wrap.

As she conveyed items in and out her back door, she sampled the conversations around her:

"I want to make sure we have enough put away when we move forward with a child," said Uma Borg.

"We rarely dine out," said Melanie.

"Mostly spy novels," Donald Chester was saying.

"How much does a polar bear weigh?" Rudgear was saying to Caddie Fladeboe, who wore a voluminous grand boubou with gold embroidery, and had her hair in a stylish turban.

"How much?"

"I hope enough to break the ice."

"My dad worked for 3M, we had enough Scotch tape around the house to mummify everybody in Minneapolis," said Marion.

"The guy turned into a monster and I split. He's confused about women in general," said Caddie Fladeboe.

"Marching band," said Linus. "I had an all-star silver bugle with a leaky spit valve."

"Our name comes from Friesland, in the Netherlands," Paul was saying. "It's famous for the Friesian horse."

Hans Borg said, "You'd have to say Frank Gehry. Really, you would."

"Dear, would you bring me some water?" asked Melanie. "Room temperature?"

"I got to the point where I'd cut an apple in half, then couldn't decide which half to eat first," Rudgear was telling Albertine.

"I'm going to marry Veblen," Justin was saying quietly to a downspout.

"Everyone, I'd like to make a toast," said Bill, raising his glass. "In the words of the late great Frank Zappa: 'If you end up with a boring miserable life because you listened to your mom, your dad, or some guy on TV telling you how to do your crapola, then you deserve it.' Paul and Veblen, I think you'll understand me when I say that we'll always be here for you, but that your own crapola is where it's at. Right, everyone?"

"Yes! Here's to Veblen and Paul! Hooray!"

During the evening Veblen got stomach cramps and ran back and forth to the bathroom, because she was sure that hours of forced merriment would backfire, and that someone would soon give vent to pent-up grief or rage. Paul hobbled in on his crutches at one point, and embraced her.

"You okay?" he asked.

"Intense, isn't it?"

"It's unreal."

He hugged her warmly, and she could hear his steady heart.

Maybe she depended upon a disturbance—it was her role to assert calm. But her services weren't required at this festivity, and Veblen had the distinct impression that everyone else was having a better time than she was. Why couldn't she relax, inhabit her authentic self? It felt very strange indeed. Thoughts such as *What is it to inhabit a rich, twenty-first-century democratic society?* and *How can an inhabitant of such a society be more than the enactor of a role in a previously written script?* came to mind, but not quite. She was not the philosopher Richard Rorty. She was Veblen Amundsen-Hovda, and she didn't process her thoughts that incisively. What she envisioned, how she saw progress, was hard to put into words. If she had to point to an ideal time in history, she might call it *a time when a shoebox mattered.* But how could you have solidarity with others when you thought in terms like that?

27

SEE FOR YOURSELF

"Marry, and you will regret it; don't marry, you will also regret it; marry or don't marry, you will regret it either way." So said Søren Kierkegaard, that rumpled, bewildered Dane.

Up the old La Honda Road, near the crest of the coastal ranges, the squirrel warmed in the sun while some of his offspring chattered nearby in the trees. As in a dream, he saw a plastic bag blowing up the ridge through the green and golden meadow, full of lupine and dandelion and filaree. It bounded over old stumps and bulging roots and rocks and stones and depressions, racing and halting, flattening and rising on a draft.

He blinked drowsily in the light. The bag blew into his tree, inflating and rising, spinning and twirling, then filled out with the certainty of flesh.

—*Ah! Son!*

—*Dad, are you okay?*

—*I need spectacles! I thought you were a plastic bag.*

The boy had grown a goatee and joined the Nutkinistas. The

squirrel didn't like it, but a young man had to find his way. *"Death to the fascist insect that preys upon the life of the people"* was what the boy had tagged on the bridge across the creek—just at the spot where the couple had agreed to this union.

That was in the chill of winter. Now it was a brighter day, the sun bounding toward the solstice. Not a gust or a cloud nor even a massive horde of his kind to stop them. The kits were living and loving. Jays and warblers spoke over one another, but not loud enough. Wasps built on the lengthening days, too busy to sting. Even the wildflowers were whispering. Or was that just the sound of his life-fuse burning down?

His old dad used to say: *No matter how well wound, the workings of the clock wind down.*

—*So, meet for an early dinner, Dad?*

—*Since when do I take an early dinner?*

It seemed a considerable number of folks had found their way to this spot, not to witness a disaster, but to cheer this couple on. They parked in a line along the narrow road, and marched upward, the men in pressed Hawaiian shirts with gray hair gathered in ponytails, the women in ethnic prints and ceramic jewelry.

The parents of the man wound ribbons around the branches and trunks of the trees, and placed flowerpots all around. The woman's stepfather helped set up the chairs and tables on the ridge, and a few musicians arrived with their resonant wooden hulls to tune them. The woman's friend brought up large artichoke soufflés in big rectangular pans, baked hams stuck with cloves, yeasty rolls. She had made a cream cheese–frosted carrot cake, three tiers tall.

Miss Veblen Amundsen-Hovda stood at the bottom of the

clearing, wearing her simple dress. She held a bouquet of small white rosebuds, and had lily of the valley in her hair.

The man took his place at the heart of the grove, still on crutches. Next to him was another man holding the simple silver ring that had been found in the gully. The musicians produced a pleasing tune, and the young woman turned and whispered to her mother at her side that she loved her.

The mother whispered back: "What am I going to do without you?"

"You still have me," the woman said.

"It'll never be the same," said her mother.

"It'll be okay, you'll see," she said, squeezing her mother's hand. Then she let go, and advanced to the spot between the stumps.

THE SQUIRREL had made his rounds the night before, stopping at the Wagon Wheel Motel on El Camino, in time to hear the mother say: "Maybe Paul is better than we think."

"Maybe so," said her man, who kissed her shoulder.

"Linus. What's got into you?"

"I guess it's the motel room, it brings back memories."

She laughed. "We've had some fun, haven't we?"

"I believe so."

"She and Paul must have a terrific sex life, or none of this would be happening."

"Could be," said Linus, snapping out of his reverie.

"Rudge looks awful," Melanie said.

"Did he ever look good?"

"He used to be a very attractive person. It's shocking. It's the medications that hollow you out like that. He shook your hand?"

"He did," said the man. "A fairly firm handshake."

"Veblen doesn't look anything like him, does she? She looks much more like me."

"Very much so. She has your smile, your eyes."

"I'm sorry we didn't have much of a wedding," said the mother, reaching for her husband of many years. "I wasn't sure it was going to last, remember how provisional I thought it all was?"

The man nodded. "And have you gotten used to me yet?"

"Yes, dear."

"Have I turned out how you hoped?"

The mother's throat lumped up. She might well wonder if she'd truly reciprocated all the kindness and love he'd shown her, and if she could ever catch up.

"You didn't even want to marry me. You thought I was a dud," the man chided.

"No!"

"You thought I was a square, not your type. You liked the early Jack Nicholson type. The dangerous guys."

"Sometimes you don't know what's your type until it finds you."

That was enough. The squirrel moved to the room in which the man's elders were staying. There, before him, stood the groom in tears, embracing his mother and his father in a confessional and cathartic moment at its peak. The older brother was joining them; the groom was letting him in.

Well. He took a deep breath and moved on.

In the course of observing the goings-on at the Wagon Wheel that night, in between several mealy oak nuts, he also witnessed the man known as Rudgear trying to run away twice, requiring the groom's elders to guard his door. And later, he saw the older brother struggling with the elders, and he had to be tied to the bed and injected with alprazolam. It had not been an easy night for anyone.

The officiant began to speak. Everyone settled. The woman turned to the man between the sacred stumps, on a bed of redwood sorrel, with a long view of the cobalt sea.

He remembered an afternoon in her youth when the weather was warm and the sun fell for hours on her shoulders after she'd packed herself a lunch to spend the day in the century-old crab apple by the ravine. There was a comfortable crotch about ten feet up that held her like a travois, and sometimes she fell asleep in it. He'd watch her to make sure she didn't fall. There came a time when the sun came straight down on the part in her hair, and she'd felt her scalp burn. Later, small beetles came out along the shady sides of the limbs, colliding senselessly like tiny bumper cars. She noticed a wound on the tree where a branch had split, full of earwigs that she dug out with a twig, scattering them from their hermits' home. Then she regretted it, and wondered how hard it would be for the earwigs to start over.

Was it worse for earwigs to lose their home in a tree, or for a tree to be riddled away by earwigs? she had asked out loud, knowing full well there was no answer to it.

"And into this estate these two persons present now come to be joined. If any person can show just cause why they may not be joined together, let them speak now or forever hold their peace," spoke the officiant.

Justin chose the moment. His chair squeaked loudly as he flung out his arms and said, "I was strangled. When I was a baby! And Paul understands me now."

The guests all turned to behold him, strangled as a baby.

"Quiet down, Justin," said Bill.

"Paul understands me! Because I was strangled when I was a baby!" Justin yelled again, starting to cough.

Bill stood and pressed Justin back into his seat. "Quiet, boy. I mean it."

"Paul, do you understand me now?" Justin called out.

Veblen looked to Paul, who said, "Dad, it's okay. I do, Justin. I understand you now."

Bill hesitated, then sat again. Justin kicked his legs.

The squirrel scuttled down the redwood, and dashed around them in that zigzag pattern that made squirrels look totally insane.

Perhaps he was.

"Oh, he's lovely!" someone said, pleasing Veblen very much.

"Yes, look at it."

The squirrel was having fun, putting on a show.

"When a wild animal comes near people, it means it's sick or rabid," Melanie declared, and for the squirrel, that was the last straw.

"I was strangled, but now I'm okay!" bellowed Justin, beating his chest.

"Shhhhhh!" hissed Bill.

"Holy god, it bit me!" screamed Melanie, for it seemed the squirrel had stopped under her chair and given her calf a strategic pinch.

Linus kneeled in the duff to examine the wound.

"I'll have to be treated for rabies! God almighty, I'll have to go under those needles! Get me some ice!" sobbed Melanie, and even her former husband, Rudgear, jumped up to be of help.

There came a scratching sound and some fiber showered down from the redwood, and then came a chittering in the tree.

Seeforyourselfforyourselfforyourself.

So there was a pause in the proceedings, as the wedding party splintered to help Melanie with her new sore.

The couple held back, to help by not helping.

And from a branch in the tall tree, a small gray squirrel released a mighty roar.

APPENDICES

APPENDIX A

Dr. Raymond Bullen
Dept. of Endocrinology
Clinical Study Center
Stanford University Hospital
Stanford, CA 94305

Dear Dr. Bullen:

Thank you for your attention during my recent participation in your clinical trial at the Stanford University Hospital. As promised, I'm enclosing a list of my current problems. Though the trial failed to detect primary hyperaldosteronism, I'm hoping these random recollections will help add to the overall picture you may be forming, but I'll leave that up to you.

1. gums, very bad condition
2. left side pain, lymph nodes under jaws, around ear, parotid and mastoid area
3. psoriasis and other skin eruptions

4. *continued hand difficulty, discomfort, rigidity, poor circulation*

5. *pain in hip*

6. *distended abdomen*

7. *alternate constipation/diarrhea*

8. *atrial ectopics and other arrhythmias*

9. *hiatus hernia, periodically*

10. *discomfort in groin*

11. *neck pain*

12. *change in face shape over the last 1½ years*

13. *inside mouth, white and peeling*

14. *intermittent complete drying of eyes and mouth*

15. *spasms in larynx in middle of night while asleep. Horrible experience.*

16. *shocks down roof of mouth*

17. *lumps on face, eczema around nose*

18. *at irregular intervals, floating stools, whitish and puttylike, or yellow and chalklike*

19. *sequelae in right leg, ulceration at site of animal bite*

It means the world to me, your acknowledgment that mine is an extremely complex case. I welcome further comment.

Sincerely,
Melanie Duffy

APPENDIX B

....

TBI and Indigenous Sami
and a Man with a Mission

Tromsø, Troms County, Norway—Dr. Paul Vreeland, an American neurologist, began his career trying to make a difference for American troops injured in combat. He notes that it might seem incongruous to find him living and working now among the Sami people of Norway, one of the most peaceful people on the planet. Vreeland, who suffered injuries in a widely publicized accident with American pharmaceutical heiress Cloris Hutmacher last year, was ready for a change after leaving his post at Greenslopes Veterans' Hospital in Menlo Park, California. "I still wanted to do something that mattered."

Vreeland is now affiliated with the University of Tromsø and the Center for Sami Health Studies. "Snowmobile accidents are a common hazard in the life of the herder," Vreeland said recently, in his ATV on the way to the scene of an accident. "For much of the year the herders lead a nomadic life and suffer many unreported accidents. What we hope to do here is create awareness of these injuries and train people on how to prevent the consequences."

According to Vreeland, diagnosing a brain injury is not simple, and sometimes there's no time to lose. Some fifty to sixty thousand Sami still depend on the reindeer for their livelihood, and herders are often far from medical facilities when they sustain injury. Vreeland believes that with proper training, early TBI diagnosis and treatment may become part of basic first aid among Sami herders.

When Vreeland is not out following the migratory path of the reindeer, training, and treating injuries, he is educating others at the University of Tromsø. His wife, Veblen Amundsen-Hovda, works for Translators Without Borders and participates in the Norwegian Diaspora Project out of the University of Oslo.

Was the transition difficult, from the hotbed of California's Silicon Valley to the quiet city of Tromsø?

"Nothing could have prepared me for the natural beauty of this area, nor for the satisfaction I've gotten from taking part in the time-honored traditions of these people," Vreeland says. "You think you've got it all planned. You never know what life has in store for you."

APPENDIX C

65 Ways to Say Squirrel

Ainu—*akkamui*
Albanian—*ketri*
Apache—*na'iltso'*
Arabic—*sinjaab*
Armenian—*skyurr*
Azerbaijani—*dələ*
Basque—*urtxintxa*
Cherokee—*sa-lo-li*
Chickasaw—*funni*
Chinese—*songshu*
Croatian—*vjeverica*
Czech—*veverka*
Danish—*egern*
Dutch—*eekhoorn*
English—squirrel
Estonian—*orav*
Filipino—*ardilya*

Finnish—*orava*
French—*écureuil*
German—*Eichhörnchen*
Greek—*skiouros*
Haitian—*ekirèy*
Hausa—*beram-bisa*
Hebrew—*snaiy*
Hindi—*gilahari*
Hopi—*sakuna*
Hungarian—*mókus*
Icelandic—*íkorna*
Igbo—*osa*
Indonesian—*tupai*
Irish—*iora*
Italian—*scoiattolo*
Japanese—*risu*
Korean—*dalamjwi*
Lakota—*tasnaheca*
Lao—*ka hork*
Mandinka—*kerengo*
Maori—*ke-rera*
Mbunga—*nganu*
Miwok—*mewe*
Navajo—*hazèitsoh*
Norwegian—*ekorn*
Papago—*chehkul*
Persian/Farsi—*sanjaab*
Romanian—*veverita*
Romany—*viaveritsa*

Russian—*belka*
Sami—*oarri*
Sanskrit—*kalandaka*
Seminole—*wiyo*
Sioux—*nayhenowenab*
Swahili—*kidiri*
Swedish—*ekorre*
Tamil—*anil*
Thai—*krarxk*
Tibetan—*say mong*
Tlingit—*dasq*
Turkish—*sincap*
Uigar—*tiyin*
Vietnamese—*con sóc*
Welsh—*wiwer*
Yiddish—*Ww'ww'rq*
Yucatec—*ku-uk*
Zapotec—*bi'achez*
Zulu—*ingwejeje*

APPENDIX D

....

Cloris Hutmacher Discusses Her Work
with UNICEF

JOHN DAVIDOW, HOST: She grew up in the family that started one of the world's largest pharmaceutical companies, with annual revenues in the neighborhood of forty billion dollars, and she's faced a difficult year battling it out in the courts, but it's Cloris Hutmacher's role as UNICEF's goodwill ambassador that is now at the center of her life. Since being appointed earlier this year, Hutmacher has been all over the world—in war-torn Sudan and Somalia, in Zimbabwe, the DRC, and Libya, helping children who live in crushing poverty. But for Hutmacher, the work is far from over. Hello, Cloris.

CLORIS HUTMACHER, UNICEF GOODWILL AMBASSADOR: Good morning, John. Suffering is always a part of human existence, even mine, and, and, I'm sorry, but I forgot what you were saying.

DAVIDOW: That's fine, Cloris. Tell us a little bit about the pictures we're looking at right now.

HUTMACHER: Let's see, here I am in Somalia. I look good here, don't I? As you know, Lifeline Somalia was sabotaged several times, but there are still many, many good hotels for foreign visitors. We stayed in a very nice one. UNICEF has hotels in more than one hundred thirty countries in the world. Please speak up, I can't hear you.

DAVIDOW: Of course. Maybe you could tell us something about the medical crisis you underwent last year—some kind of brain injury, as we've heard from our sources?

HUTMACHER: No, that is a mistaken identity I would like to correct, John. I had a minor problem and I'm very lucky to live near a sophisticated medical facility. I've always been very fortunate and that's important to me.

DAVIDOW: Well. Cloris Hutmacher, some people would have retreated from the public eye after being found guilty of felony kickback schemes, false and deceptive acts, and obstruction of justice. Not to mention being named in a major whistle-blower suit against your family's company, and overseeing the worldwide recall of a recently acquired medical device, enraging stockholders and costing the company millions in settlements and legal fees. Was this public service ordered by the courts?

HUTMACHER: John, the courts have nothing to do with this. We do not abide by the law. The important thing is, I've learned a lot this year about what really counts.

DAVIDOW: And what is that, Cloris Hutmacher?

HUTMACHER: I will mention that to my board.

DAVIDOW: Cloris Hutmacher, heiress and humanitarian. We wish you all the best.

HUTMACHER: Everyone does. Would you repeat that in the form of a question?

APPENDIX E

....

Justin Richard Vreeland and Alice Caitlin Benjamin

Invite you to join them for their wedding at
their new home, The Courage Center

September 15 at 5 o'clock in the afternoon

COME READY TO BOOGIE DOWN!

APPENDIX F

Dear Veblen,

I know you are busy. Maybe you could just answer the questions and send this sheet back.

Did you read the biography of Ibsen and what did you think?
_____ *What did Paul think?*_____
_____ *Is there a theater in Tromsø?*_____

*How long does it take to drive from Tromsø to Oslo?*_____
*To Trondheim?*_____ *To Bergen?*_____ *Have you taken any trips yet?* _____

*What is the cost of gas per liter?*_____

*Do you have mildew problems in that area?*_____

*When will you send more pictures?*_____

*How is your Norwegian progressing? Do you find yourself able to
understand people in most situations?*_____
_____ *When will you meet Mr. Odegaard? Does
he know you're living in the country? Can he find you more work?*
_____

*What is your current waist size?*_____ *Hip?*_____
*Bust?*_____ *Please measure in inches.*

*Has Paul got his work better organized so he's less stressed
out?*_____

*How many days is he gone when he's following the herders? Have
you met any of them?*_____
*As I am fascinated with textiles, would it be possible for you to send
me something? I'd give my left leg for one of the Raanu weavings.*

*Are you financially in good shape?*_____

*Have you heard from anybody, such as Albertine?*_____
*Do Paul's parents keep in touch?*_____

*I will continue to buy cold weather clothes for you at the RS. Unless
you don't want them anymore. Please indicate.*_____

*How are your back and your neck?*_____
*You mentioned stress after the move. Are you feeling all
right?*_____ *Don't neglect your health because Paul
is a doctor. It's a paradox that is unfortunately a reality.*

*Did you like the long blue snowsuit in the last box I sent? Is it too
short in the crotch?*_____

*Have you met your neighbors?*_____ *Who are they?*
_____ *Please describe the demographic of your
neighborhood.*_____

*Have you been able to furnish the place without spending too
much? Do they have thrift stores there?* _____

*What is your salt consumption?*_____ *It is not healthy. What
are you eating now, anyway? Have you tried that sweet brown
cheese they're known for?*_____

*Have you seen any wildlife? Are there squirrels there, god
forbid?*_____

Fill in and return! I am waiting!

*Love,
Your Mother*

APPENDIX G

....

Kjære Mamma Og Linus,

Alt går bra. Takk for alle brev og pakker med varme klær. Du vet akkurat hva jeg trengte Mamma. Jeg skal også fortelle deg at det er mange, mange ekorn her i Norge, over alt, fra tre til tre, vakre røde norske ekorn! Dette er bare en kort hilsen for å si hei og at jeg savner deg. Jeg er veldig opptatt, og jeg skal skrive mer snart!

Have fun translating—☺
Veblen

ACKNOWLEDGMENTS

Thank you very much Rosemary Ahern, Wallace Baine, John Blades, John Chandler, Carole Conn, Donka Farkas, Peter Farkas, Karen Joy Fowler, Syed A. Haider, Deborah Hansen, Richard Huffman, Kathryn Kefauver, Richard Lange, Kat Meads, Liza Monroy, Roberta Montgomery, Micah Perks, Jory Post, Melissa Sanders-Self, Catherine Segurson, Paul Skenazy, Patricia Stacey, Peggy Townsend, Alfredo Vea, Vito Victor, Dan White, Sally Wolfe, and Jill Wolfson, for your invaluable contributions to my spirits and these pages.

To Judy Kmetko at the Lane Medical Library at Stanford, Tom Lamb III at Carleton College, and Jay Rorty, thank you for your help with my research. Thanks to S. Brian Willson and Becky Leuning of Portland for our enlightening conversation about the care of military veterans. Sarah Warner Vik and Sigmund Vik of Trondheim, Norway—*tusen takk*! I also appreciated the use of the Veblen archives at the University of Chicago and the congenial atmosphere at the McHenry Library at UC Santa Cruz.

ACKNOWLEDGMENTS

Thank you to C. Michael Curtis for publishing an excerpt of this novel in *The Atlantic* and for the duration of his encouragement. Thanks also to the Center for Cultural Innovation, Silicon Valley Creates, and the Sustainable Arts Foundation for their generosity.

Thank you to Emily Forland for embracing this novel without hesitation and for all your great ideas and camaraderie since. Ed Park, thank you for so many things, including being exactly the right editor for this book; collaborating with you has been an honor and a pleasure. Thank you very much also to Penguin Press, Ann Godoff and Scott Moyers for such wholehearted support and to Juliana Kiyan, Matt Boyd, Annie Badman, Caitlin O'Shaughnessy, Ruth Liebmann, Robert Belmont, Wendy Pearl, Justin Goodfellow, and Megan Sullivan for all your help.

And in the UK, my thanks to Anthony Goff and Fourth Estate, with special thanks to my editor Anna Kelly. Thanks also to Lottie Fyfe and Rebecca Petre, as well as Georgina, Patrick, Tara, Vanessa and Lettice who wrote me such kind notes.

Talking to Bart Cox about old Palo Alto was one of the best parts about this, and he is greatly missed. As is Isabel Cox, whose house on Tasso Street I remember so well.

Emily Cox and Christopher Wrench, thank you for your help with the images and for your love and unstinting goodwill.

Thank you to Steve for everything that made this possible. Nick, it was delightful to discuss the writings of Bakunin, Žižek and the Situationists with you, and then apply them to *The Tale of Squirrel Nutkin*. Stuart, it was you who put me on track originally, and our many talks about animals, Teslas, business and consumer issues, translation, and the fine points of storytelling inspired me especially.

PICTURE PERMISSIONS